PRAISE FOR THE SHAMAN MYSTERIES:

Beneath the Tor:

"Nina Milton has created a unique fictional world in her Shaman Mystery Series, featuring Sabbie Dare as a young shaman. They each have a cracking pace and convey the evocative landscapes of Somerset. Always, the depictions of shamanic journeying are vivid and authentic. Reading *Beneath the Tor* kept me up at night much later than I wanted, because I could not bear to miss the next bit."

—Ronald Hutton, author of *The Triumph of the Moon, Shamans,* and *Pagan Britain*

Unraveled Visions:
"[A] thrilling tale."

—*RT Book Reviews* (four stars)

"A mystical mystery … Nina Milton skillfully integrates the shamanistic elements into her mystery making this sequel to last year's *In the Moors* an absorbing tale."

—*Mystery Scene*

"This well-written story is incredible knowledgeable, suspenseful, and a truly cool adventure into the world that lies 'beyond.'"

—*Suspense Magazine*

In the Moors:
"Sabbie Dare is the most compelling protagonist I've met this year … Milton's tale is riveting."

—*Library Journal* (starred review)

"A fast-moving thriller likely to draw in readers."

—*Kirkus Reviews*

"A truly spooky story set in the Somerset Levels, which had me on the edge of my seat."

—Ali Bacon, author of *A Kettle of Fish*

"*In the Moors* has a cracking pace, evocative landscapes, and a shocking twist at the end. I've rarely read depictions of shamanic journeying that have felt so authentic."

—Ronald Hutton, author of *The Triumph of the Moon and Shamans*

BENEATH
THE
TOR

ALSO BY NINA MILTON

In the Moors (Midnight Ink 2013)
Unraveled Visions (Midnight Ink 2014)

Children's Fiction
Sweet'n'Sour (2009)
Tough Luck (2012)

NINA MILTON

BENEATH
THE
TOR

A SHAMAN MYSTERY

MIDNIGHT INK
WOODBURY, MINNESOTA

FIRST EDITION
First Printing, 2015

Book format by Teresa Pojar
Cover design by Ellen Lawson
Cover art: iStockphoto.com/20894066/©Andrew Rich
          iStockphoto.com/47914144/©da-kuk
Editing by Nicole Nugent

Midnight Ink, an imprint of Llewellyn Worldwide Ltd.

Library of Congress Cataloging-in-Publication Data
Milton, Nina.
    Beneath the Tor / Nina Milton. — First edition.
       pages ; cm. — (A Shaman mystery ; #3)
    ISBN 978-0-7387-4382-0
    1. Shamans—Fiction. I. Title.
    PS3613.I59198B46 2015
    813'.6—dc23
                                    2015021909

Midnight Ink
Llewellyn Worldwide Ltd.
2143 Wooddale Drive
Woodbury, MN 55125-2989
www.midnightinkbooks.com

Printed in the United States of America

This book is dedicated to the people who manage without me while I'm stuck in my writing: my family and my dearest friends.

ACKNOWLEDGMENTS

This book had its seeds in my visits, over the years, to the town of Glastonbury. I have deep connections with many of the people who live there or use it as a sacred and spiritual base for their work. In particular, I would like to thank the generosity of Nicholas Mann, whose wide breadth of knowledge on Glastonbury was my foundation stone, especially his books *The Isle of Avalon: Sacred Mysteries of Arthur and Glastonbury* (Green Magic, 2001) and *Glastonbury Tor: A Guide to the History and Legends* (Triskele Publications, 1993). Both of these were by my side as I wrote. Thanks too, to Mara Freeman, an authority on the mysteries surrounding the Isle of Avalon. She had just finished writing *Grail Alchemy: Initiation in the Celtic Mystery Tradition* (Destiny Books, 2014), at the time I was completing *Beneath the Tor* and, again, I found this inspirational. Thanks to my son, Joe Milton, for talking me through the basic philosophy of the story.

I would also like to thank to Ronald Hutton, who has personally been an unflinching support to me as a writer. The team at Midnight Ink should be thanked for making the Shaman Mystery series possible, for believing in me as a writer, and for being such good guys generally. Finally, I need to yet again thank my agent, Lisa Moylett, who has long been my beacon of quality for good style, strong narrative, and persuasive characters.

ONE

ALYS

ALYS WAS DANCING AS the stars reeled, dancing on Glastonbury Tor on Midsummer Eve.

She danced as if the drumbeats were bursting out of her. As if her feet were charmed to never rest.

It was a hot night, balmy as a tropical coastline, and Alys wore little more than a t-shirt and some tiny shorts which displayed her thighs, slender and toned. She'd kicked off her shoes to spin and bop. She wore her hair blond with one of those zigzag partings that take ages in front of a mirror. I thought she looked half the age she was; all night she'd had the energy of a teenager.

Ten of us—a group keen to explore shamanism—had climbed the west side of Glastonbury Tor as the sun slipped from the sky in a shock of red. I'd been taking the lead up the steep grassy slope and was finally in sight of the hill's crest, where the ground spread and flattened as if it had been sliced off, like the top of a boiled egg. I could

1

already hear the people, the drums. My own pulse quickened. The party had begun.

Alys had grinned as she'd surged past me, heading hotfoot for the summit. She'd balanced on the edge above and exploded into jumping jacks—from sheer joy, it seemed to me—her long legs gold in the last sun.

Wolfsbane had leaned on his staff, an ornately carved piece of ashwood, and pointed with his unlit cigarette. He was a chain smoker when he got the chance, but didn't have the breath to light up on the climb. "That girl is going to make a terrific shaman. I can't wait to start working with her."

"Alys is a shaman virgin." Shelley had looked at me and given a secret wink. "You go gentle with her, Wolfsie."

Alys had given the rest of us a wide wave of her arm and disappeared into the revellers. As she did so, another of our group sprinted the last leg of the path in highly unsuitable white Levis, taking the gradient as if life was at risk.

It was Brice, Alys's husband. He'd never wanted to come here. He'd tagged along because Alys had persuaded him. It was evident he wasn't used to this wild-child wife.

"Didn't you say Alys was in banking?" I asked Shell. "She's not exactly typical."

"They're both bankers, Sabbie, her and Brice."

"Banker?" Wolfsbane grinned at us. "Wanker."

Shell's lips had thinned; I thought she'd sucked them in to stop them trembling. "They're my friends, Wolfsie." She'd pecked a kiss on his lips and chased up the hill. I followed her, and all at once I was in the middle of the party to end all parties, five hundred feet up from the plains below. No invitations, no streamers, no food, and no music, just the incessant hammer of the drums, which would not stop until the sun rose. I was sure the population of Glastonbury town, in the valley below, tossed in their beds to the bongos, djembes, and Irish bodhrans.

I tried counting the people; it felt like every pagan and new-ager from miles around had come to be on this hill at this sacred time. The perfect June day had become the perfect Midsummer Eve Night.

"Come and dance, Sabbie!" Alys had screamed at me, bouncing on the grass of the Tor as if it was a trampoline. For a while I'd kept up with her crazy pace until she'd spun off into the crowds, stealing flowers and snatching at hands. She became everyone's mascot. In the subdued light of flares and torches, her skin was translucent.

After that, I didn't catch sight of Alys for hours at a time. It was after three a.m. when I spotted her disappearing into St. Michael's Tower. Drummers surrounded her, the high roofless walls of the ruined church magnifying their booming rhythms. From nowhere Brice arrived at the tower's archway. He pushed through the drummers and took Alys by the hand, easing her away, leading her to where he'd laid out their two sleeping bags at the far end of the Tor. He'd zipped them up to make one double bag and he wriggled into his side, patting the space beside him.

I was sitting with Juke and Ricky, too far away to hear what he said, but I could guess her answer, because I'd heard her affirm it earlier in the day: "*I won't stop dancing for a second. Not until I salute the rising sun. An initiation on the Tor on the Solstice night.*"

I knew she meant it because, even as Brice pleaded for her to come and lie with him, her feet did not stopped tapping. She skipped away, laughing and blowing him kisses.

The crowd had thinned. All over the summit, people were curling into bags or simply wrapping fleeces round themselves and kipping where they lay.

Juke had finally got his head down—he was an amorphous blob hidden inside his sleeping pod. I'd known Juke for around six months. He was a paradoxical mix; at twenty-five he held down a job that affected people's lives, yet tonight he'd danced like a kid straight from school. On the other hand, his mate Ricky, not much younger and still in the middle of his degree, didn't have Juke's party spirit. He'd soon given up on dancing and spent most of the night sitting cross-legged at the very edge of the Tor, a duvet slung over his shoulders, staring out over the landscape below us. His old head on young shoulders intrigued me. We sat in silence for a while, enjoying the predawn darkness.

The landscape was a black mirror. The town was asleep. Over my head, almost close enough to reach up and touch, a fattening moon of white gold was shrouded by ragged strands of cloud. Below lay the mystical Vale of Avalon and the flat Somerset Moors. A damp mist rose invisibly. I felt myself reconnect with the fine-spun layer of enchantment that surrounds Glastonbury Tor and I shivered. "Why is it always coldest before dawn?"

"The earth's surface cools all night long." I hadn't expected an answer to my question, but Ricky was giving me one. "There's a steady loss of energy that can only become greater once there is no input from the sun. Actually, that goes on for at least an hour after dawn, the length of time it takes for the sun's warmth to equal the loss from the ground."

I'd noticed earlier that Ricky's head was packed full of trivia. He seemed a smart boy, and l loved the way he jelled up his hair into a surprise to match his overdosing of white face power and black eyeliner. With his knee-high, shiny lace-up boots and the embroidered waistcoat over a billowing shirt, he resembled a Transylvanian vampire.

Shell flopped down beside us.

"Where's Wolfs?" I asked.

"No idea. Said he needed to clear his head before dawn." She checked her watch, a big yellow plastic affair. "The drummers have been going for almost five hours. They're amazing, Sabbie."

"They're empowered by their own raw energy and the thud of the beat in their bones," said Ricky.

"I think they're on something a bit stronger than raw energy!" Shelley said.

There were plenty of peddlers up there, but I'd avoided them. Too many E tablets and you wouldn't care if you were in a club or here on the Tor. Too much acid and you'd be flying off it. Too many beers and you'd be nasty to know by sunrise. Too many spliffs and you'd sleep through it.

"I love it up here," said Shell. "I'm gonna get Wolfsbane to show me how to walk the Tor labyrinth."

"That's hours of walking," said Ricky. "Inner meditation."

Her teeth glinted white as she flashed a grin. "And how. Tantric sex when y'get to the top, yeah?"

Ricky didn't reply, and to cover the silence I said, "Last time I walked the Tor labyrinth, I reached the top, and, next thing I knew— I was flat on my back."

"You fell over?"

"I'd passed out."

"You were crossing the ley lines," said Ricky. "Each line disassembled your spirit. Until you were totally discombobulated."

Shell giggled. "I love that ... discom ..."

"Bobbed," said Ricky. He put his hand on her bare arm. "You feel cold. I wish I'd invented a hot-water bottle for tonight, one that stays warm without power input." He shifted until his duvet was equally over both their shoulders.

"Thank you, kind sir." Shell lowered her voice, muffled already by the duvet cave, and eased herself closer to him. Ricky didn't look directly at her, or make any further move. Shell was Wolfsbane's girl, and Wolfs was a respected person in the shamanic community. This had to be in Ricky's mind as Shell chattered on, her voice slightly husky, her hand rested on his thigh. He looked ill at ease. Discombobulated, even.

It was none of my business. I lay on my back for a while, watching the sky. I was sure I could detect just the tiniest promise of light on the rim of the northeastern horizon. The drummers knew it too; they redoubled their efforts, holding their bodhrans high above their heads as if they were weightless.

I rolled onto my stomach. A handful of dancers were still going strong. Alys was among them, turboed up like a child who'd had too much ice cream, hollering and whooping. I could hear her from the far side of the summit.

I saw her dance.

I saw her drop.

She fell to the ground without a stumble or cry.

She fell awkwardly, one leg trapped under the other, her head thrown back.

I stared for long seconds, waiting for her to rise.

Alys didn't get up. She didn't move at all.

I stood and ran, but one person reached her before me. Ricky dropped onto one knee and touched her gently on the cheek. "Alys? Alys!"

There was no response.

"What is it?" I barked. "What's wrong?"

"Exhaustion, I'd guess."

Shell was scampering towards us. I screamed at her. "Get Brice! Quick!"

My phone was in my back pocket, switched off to save batteries. I fumbled with it, cursing the slow turn-on. I got a signal. I bloody-well should get a signal on the top of this rock.

Word began to spread, people realized something was happening. The drums trailed off. The other dancers closed around us.

"Give her air, please!" I cried into the silence.

Ricky looked up. "She won't need air."

"What?"

"I saw her spirit go."

"What? No, Ricky!"

Someone pushed forward. "I'm a hospital nurse." He nodded at my phone. "Nine-nine-nine. Now." His purposeful, healthcare-professional hands were already feeling for Alys's pulse.

I was through to emergency services. The operator asked me for the address. Panic made the phone damp in my hand. "You're going to need a helicopter. We're at the top of the Tor."

"You're on the top floor?"

"No! The Tor. Glastonbury Tor!"

The nurse was counting his compressions. I watched as he raised Alys's chin and breathed deeply into her mouth, his fingers pinching her nose. He wasn't stopping, wasn't thinking of stopping, but Alys had not responded. Someone brought a flashlight. In the yellow beam, Alys's face was pale, shocked, as if she'd seen something from another world. Eyes open wide. Lips white. Gone forever.

Her t-shirt almost covered her pink shorts. The t-shirt was white; it had stayed white all through her dancing. The nurse rested the heels of both hands at the centre of her chest, where a flaming orange sun was situated, surrounded by the words *Have a Crazy Summer Solstice*. I could see her ribs through the t-shirt, I flinched as they bounced at each compression, as if they were brittle plastic. Up on her dancing feet, Alys was lean, tanned. I'd thought she had a figure to die for. Now she looked shrivelled, as if already turning to ashes.

"Put the phone to my ear," said the nurse. "Let me speak to control."

I did as I was bade automatically.

Shell had managed to rouse Brice. He pushed through the crowd, stopping short when he reached his wife. Brice didn't touch Alys. It seemed as if the nurse's actions, so smooth, so in control, prevented interference. He held out both hands as if hoping she might rise into them. His bare feet crushed the grass so that it sprang up between his wide-spaced toes. I realized the grass was green. The sun was rising and no one was taking any notice of the dawn. The nurse talked with staccato bursts into my phone as he counted his compressions, on and on.

Brice howled.

The cry lifted like a bird, a black carrion crow, rising from the Tor, already five hundred feet above the valley floor. I was sure that the whole of Glastonbury would hear his cry—that the air ambulance would be able to navigate by it. It was the howl of a man who has never before felt this much pain. He collapsed onto the ground beside his wife. His wails subsided. He called her name, over and over, eyes stark with fear and grief, his hands fluttering over Alys's head like birds at dawn.

Most people had kept their distance and kept their voices respectfully low. They all knew who Alys was now; the girl who had danced all night. I heard a soft giggle far back in the crowd, the embarrassed reaction of someone not used to facing death. Brice heard the laugh and looked round with a face of thunder.

"It's too late."

Ricky hadn't meant me to hear his words, but in the silence I caught them clearly. "Don't," I cried. "The ambulance is on its way. There *is* hope."

His eyes were stark. He shook his head, confirming what we all knew, but longed to deny.

"I saw her spirit rise, Sabbie. It's already gone."

TWO

WOLFSBANE

As soon as the air ambulance had arrived, the paramedics took over from the hospital nurse, rolling Alys onto a stretcher that disappeared into the 'copter. Brice and Shell clambered on board and seconds later, the helicopter had done that bouncing, flopping movement to get airborne which makes them look so vulnerable.

The crowds on the Tor watched until it was a dot. We had come to celebrate the dawn. That was forgotten now.

Wolfsbane and I sat with our backs up against the stonework of St. Michael's Tower, sipping at our water bottles. The sun was up, but there was a high breeze. I could feel Wolfs's bare arm against mine—cold as a snakeskin. He had a single tattoo high on the shoulder, a pentangle surrounded by foliage, and a pewter arm torc in a Celtic design, so tight around his arm, I wondered if it made his fingers tingle.

"What do we do?" I'd asked him.

"We go and tell Stefan our workshop's over."

Officially, the shamanic workshop had started yesterday, when everyone had arrived at Stefan's house. It was supposed to go on for the rest of the week. But Wolfs was right; we'd have to cancel it now.

Wolfsbane rounded up the five remaining workshoppers. He gave Yew fifty pounds and told him to treat them all to breakfast in town. We watched them go, then set out on the three-mile walk to the workshop base. We took a slug's pace, as if not getting to Stonedown Farm would allow time for a miracle.

As we tramped along a country path, Wolfsbane mounted a fence that took him into a small enclosure where two old oaks stood proud. It took me a minute to catch him up. I found him leaning into the farther of the two oaks, his arms hugging the trunk, which was so broad it would have taken several of us to surround it completely. I rested my hand on the gnarled and weathered bark of the other tree. The day was warm, bees already buzzing in the foxgloves. A woodpecker rapped with furious persistence in the distance.

"Oh, listen," I whispered.

We stood in silence. I couldn't imagine a better way for us to recharge our spiritual batteries. Eventually, Wolfsbane turned round. He hitched his thumbs into the waistband of his shorts and looked at the ground, as if the weight of what we'd seen only an hour ago was dragging at him. "I think I might have to apologize to Brice."

I found myself gawping. Not a deliberate act, but I was startled by his words. *Apologize* seemed altogether the wrong sentiment. When someone you know has lost the love of their life, you condole. You keen and sorrow with them.

"Why ever would you need to apologize to Brice?"

Wolfsbane leaned right into the trunk of the tree and closed his eyes. "This is Magog, you know."

"Oh," I said, recognizing but not quite placing the name.

"The twin oaks. End of an avenue of ancient oaks."

"Gog and Magog. I remember." The oaks were almost leafless and white with age. "They're dying, Wolfs."

"They're dead."

I put my hands over my mouth. "That's sad."

"They're the last, Sabbie. The rest were cut down—heck, a century ago. Even then they were millennia old. It's their time."

"It wasn't Alys's time."

Wolfs looked around before he spoke, as if informants might be hidden in the branches above us. "I'm worrying about the tea..."

"Tea? What tea?"

"The flying tea."

His eyes were shadowed by the bare branches above him, but I knew he wasn't looking at me. I'd never seen Wolfsbane discomfited. I'd never even see him stick his hands flat in the pockets of his shorts, as if he wanted them out the way. Wolfsbane loved to have his hands on show, they achieved as much communication as his words.

"I watched you gather the ingredients for that tea," I said.

Garden sage to heighten senses, mugwort to induce visions. Lemon balm leaves for calm alertness plus honey and spearmint for flavour. That would hurt no one and probably didn't do much more than a cup of English Breakfast.

"Stefan came up to me," said Wolfsbane, "while we were preparing the opening to the workshop. Asked me why I didn't use something a bit stronger than garden herbs."

"Like what?"

"He had tablets in a sealed plastic bag. Some sort of high. Said it was completely safe. Said it was completely legal."

"A legal high?" My innards felt as hollowed as a dried gourd. "They're not safe. And they're not legal, Wolfs, not at all."

Wolfsbane shook his head, a slow rhythm of despair. "What I can't face … what I couldn't bear … would be if we were responsible for Alys's death."

"Wait—you let Stefan add this stuff to our flying tea? We all drank it?"

"No! Of course I didn't. I told him to keep it to himself."

"*For* himself, I suppose."

"I don't much care what he did with these pills so long as he didn't crush them into our teapot."

"Did you see him do it?"

"No. I would have chucked the brew out if I had."

"But do you think he did?"

My knees were giving way under all the implications. I was trying to remember how I felt after drinking the tea. As a kid, I had tried most forms of unnatural stimulant. I'd never take anything nowadays, but I would recognize the effects. As far as I knew, "legal highs" were like ecstasy or speed. Your heart races and your mind races with it, and suddenly you love everyone in the universe. Sage and mugwort could make you light-headed. You lose your inhibitions a bit and your tongue gets loosened. But surely I'd have spotted the difference.

"We should go to the police," I said.

"Hey—whoa, Sabbie, stop right there. We need to ask Stefan first."

"I'm not sure Stefan would tell you the truth, especially if he thought he'd end up at the police station."

Wolfsbane leapt the fence and was disappearing up the lane. "Twenty minutes to the house, if we stride it!"

I caught Wolfsbane up and jogged alongside him. "If Stefan says 'no, I didn't do it,' you'll believe him, will you? Because I might not."

"He's a mate of mine. He'll tell me straight."

"He's not a mate," I corrected. "He's a business associate who currently is pissed off with you."

I hadn't liked Stefan McKiddie when I'd first met him, four years ago. He thought himself a bit of a comedian. He had a way of not laughing at his own jokes, as if he was on stage. I've got used to him over time, but when I'd arrived for the start of the workshop, yesterday, he had already been in the middle of a spat with Wolfsbane which I was still trying to get to the bottom of.

"What if he didn't put the stuff in the tea?" I asked. "After all it's a bore, crushing pills. What if he just offered them around, instead. Did he offer you one? Did he offer Alys one?"

"Did he offer you one, Sabbie?"

I scoffed. "He'd know my response."

"You're searching up the wrong track."

"Am I? We need to report this so that the forensic toxicology report can take it into account."

Wolfsbane skidded to a halt. He snatched at me, hands tight round both my elbows. He was usually a gentle person—a hugger of trees who was now hurting me, digging nails that were slightly long for a man into the bare skin at the crook of my arms.

"You're going over, Sabbie," he said.

"What?"

"A boyfriend in the police force is never a good idea for someone with an alternative lifestyle."

"Is that any of your business?" I snapped.

If Wolfs's nails hadn't been hurting me, I might have agreed with him. Rey Buckley and me were as suited to be together as a snake and a ground squirrel. Being diametrically opposed in most things—outlook, type of job, interests—only seemed to fire up the passion between us. I tried putting Rey out of my mind. I thought back to the moments before Alys died, when Shell had been flirting with Ricky.

"Where were you, by the way? When the sun rose?"

"What?"

"Shell had been looking for you." I might have added that he should keep a better eye on his girlfriend. I shrugged off his grip and rubbed my elbows, throwing a final remark over my shoulder. "Whatever you do, don't apologize to Brice. Just extend your condolences. We don't know how she died, yet."

"You make it sound as if it was murder!" His voice was thin against the summer sounds as I marched on. "None of us had anything to do with that death. Do you hear me, Sabbie?"

I'd never met Alys or Brice before Midsummer Eve.

That previous morning, I'd snatched an early lunch and taken the thirty-minute drive from Bridgwater to Glastonbury, heading for Stonedown Farm, a rambling old building a few miles outside the town. The owner, Stefan, let out rooms for events. Wolfsbane held regular sessions there under his company brand of Spirit Flyers, and I'd agreed to help him with a shape-shifting workshop—it had seemed like a neat plan to begin it by celebrating the solstice on the Tor.

The first person to book a place was an Australian traveller called Anagarika Dharmapala, of all things. The second was Juke Webber, who studied shamanism with me, and he invited his old university roommate, Ricky—they'd just reconnected on Facebook. These three bookings made the workshop seem viable, especially when Freaky and Yew, both established shamans, signed up in their usual way. After that, things went sluggish. No one had money to throw around anymore. Just as it seemed we'd have to cancel the event, Shell had come up with a couple of friends—Brice and Alys Hollingberry. We firmed up the arrangements and booked the rooms in Stonedown Farm with Stefan.

Stefan McKiddie was a shambling bear of a man with thick brown hair just beginning to show signs of grey, and an unpredictable temperament. When I arrived at Stonedown Farm he was sitting at his kitchen table, muttering in a low voice to his long-standing partner, Esme, a woman as cold as a jar of frogspawn. She took a look at me and flounced out of the kitchen, knocking against my shoulder hard as we passed in the doorway.

"Hi," I said.

"Wolfsbane's in the workshop room, if you want him." Stefan stared into his Barleycup, not drinking, not looking up, even when Wolfsbane joined me at the door. I could feel Wolfs's tension; it seethed out of him. With only seven paying clients on this workshop, I had guessed he'd be a bit on edge, but this was something bigger.

"I've just been into the workshop space," he barked at Stefan. "It's a mess."

I'd been eyeing the piles of dirty crocks. I'd clocked three saucepans coated with old porridge, implying they hadn't washed up for several days. The kitchen often smelt of forgotten food, but it felt totally neglected this time. I could see mould growing out of a line half-empty mugs on the window sill which looked like it might take over the planet.

"Hey!" Stefan was clearly stung. "I made a start."

"So make a bloody finish, will you?"

I'd taken Wolfsbane's arm and dragged him away before the verbal turned nasty. "What is going on?"

"Stef has increased his prices by almost twenty percent."

"And he's only just told you?"

"Well, no, but it's despicable. He's a total slimebucket."

"Couldn't we have used a different venue?"

"I'd already advertised this one. Taken deposits."

At that point Freaky and Yew arrived and wreathed us in hugs, and Wolfs calmed down.

Freaky lived in a caravan in a corner of Stefan's field and he'd seen our cars in the driveway. Yew lived in Yeovil, a short drive away, where he worked at a hostel for the homeless. They mucked in on the cleaning with dishcloths and dusters and by the time Juke, then Ricky, had turned up, the place didn't look too bad.

The unknown element of the group, Anagarika, came by foot from Glastonbury town, crunching up Stefan's weed-infested drive strapped into an enormous backpack. He seemed affable enough— he took Wolfsbane's hand and pumped it up and down while slapping him between the shoulder blades. "Always wanted to meet you, cobber. Honoured. I'm goin' learn lots from this workshop, that is for definites."

Within moments of meeting Anagarika, Juke and Ricky seemed smitten by his big Aussie personality, while I was pinning a "pseudo" label on him. His unpronounceable chosen name was driving me mad and there was a smell about him—maybe he'd picked it up from the boarding house he was staying at in town—an oily aroma, as if he'd rubbed something meant for greasing an engine into his hair.

Alys and Brice had come last, arriving in a sharp yellow Smart Car which looked like it had the smallest fuel footprint in automobile history. For a moment or two, as Brice pulled their bags out of the back, he was the centre of male attention. A thought occurred to me for the first time: there were a lot of blokes. Not a very good gender balance. Shell and I weren't actual workshoppers, after all, which left Alys as the only paying female participant.

Juke had been fawning all over Brice's car. "I'm thinking of trading in for one of these," he'd said.

"It's a limited edition Cityflame." Brice smoothed its wing as if it was a massive yellow cat.

"What's wrong with the car you've got, Juke?" I often forget that other people have a surplus of cash at the end of the working month. Juke ran an office that offered help to displaced persons and asylum seekers, and he earned a good salary for someone in their mid-twenties.

"Smart Cars are cool. But I'd have black."

"Too right." Anagarika's accent was so strong it felt phony, which was nuts because by then he'd passed round his phone to show us the pictures of his Melbourne home. "To be honest with you, mate, I don't think a bloke should be seen half dead in a yeller car?"

Brice had turned his back. Luckily Shell burst out of the house at that moment, sweeping both Hollingberrys into warm, plump hugs and spiriting them into the kitchen.

They sank into the background as we'd opened our first ritual circle and Wolfsbane raised the idea of joining the dancers and drummers on the Tor for the all-night vigil.

Brice shook his head. "Sounds like purgatory to me."

"I'm going, darling."

Alys had lifted her cup of flying tea. Brice drank from his at the same time. "Okay. If you're sure…"

Shortly after, Shell and Alys had disappeared entirely, and it wasn't until I'd been getting ready to leave for the Tor that Shell had come up to me and asked if I had any painkillers. "It's not for me, it's for Alys."

"Isn't she feeling well?"

"To be honest, she's having humongous period pains. She gets them every month, poor woman, but she thinks she'll be fine for tonight if she can just get on top of the cramps." Shell was a buxom woman who dressed with style; she always wore some form of jaunty headwear, even indoors, and a selection of jazzy earrings.

"Esme has a bathroom cabinet chocked with over-the-counter stuff. I'll see what I can find."

"Don't tell her what they're for, will you? Alys is a bit sensitive."

Alys had been lying fully-clothed on the bunk she'd been allocated in the girls' bedroom when I'd shown her the blister packs: Aspro, paracetamol, and ibuprofen caplets. Her face was pale, half hidden by her mussed up hair. She'd been clutching a hot water bottle to her tum. She chose the ibuprofen, saying she didn't like the taste of aspirin and couldn't swallow big tablets.

"Don't let Anag get to you," I'd said, trying to find the heart of the problem. "I don't know him well, but he's looking like a jerk."

"Shell says the same."

"Are you sure you wouldn't rather stay here tonight?"

She'd shaken her head, raising a sports bottle half to her lips. "This will help, it's isotonic. I'll be fine in fifteen minutes, I'm sure I will. Wouldn't miss it."

Shell had clicked the bedroom door shut behind us. "Alys really wants to go up the Tor. She did from the moment I told her about Wolfsie's workshop."

"It's going to be manic up on the Tor," I'd said. "And cold, later on. She'd be best staying put."

"She's determined, Sabbie. Once Alys has made up her mind, no one can stop her."

THREE

THE GREEN KNIGHT

HE SEES HER FIRST.

He looks away, quick, hoping she hasn't spotted him in the crowd. It's pointless. Morgan le Fay is here to collect him.

Everything turns to water. Everything trembles—knees—fingers—breath.

Like lightning flashing across a dry sky, a migraine strikes at his temple.

She's been away a long time. The years apart have been like an immunity from prosecution, but they have also been a prison cell.

She hasn't changed. Not a day older. Not one grey hair in the mass of raven black, not one wrinkle on her neck. She still wears glitter on her lashes and earrings that tangle in the wild curls. Her cheekbones are just as hungry; her lips just as red. This high summer's day, her shoulders are pearl white above a tight bustier of beech green lace, blood-red leather pants spray-painted onto her legs. In her hand is the silken leash. She keeps it taut because Selkie, her cat, is an alpha male with a proclivity for trouble.

She's here—of course—because of the useless, beautiful death.

A woman died on the Tor, almost as the sun rose.

She was no more than a child, the way she lay on the grass with one thin leg curled under her like the broken proboscis of a moth. When he'd seen her he'd wanted to wail out his distress, but could not because her legitimate lover, the man she was with, had made the deepest howl of despair he'd ever heard. It filled the space of the Tor; a lamentation that moved under the skin like a parasite.

Then, in the awful, silent moment after the lover's cry, someone had laughed. The sound made him want to vomit. He'd gripped his fists and swung round to confront, but clamped his jaw and stayed still.

The guy who had laughed put his hand across his stupid mouth. This guy, shabby in combat khakis and a green padded lumberjack shirt with a line of grease around the neck. This guy, with the sense of humour of a hyena, brought dishonour to a place of mourning, disrespect to the howling man and the dancing damsel.

An evil thing to do.

Morgan le Fay is standing beside the high wall of the Chalice Well. She does not look his way, not once, but the cat stretches its flexible neck and regards him with sapphire eyes. Selkie's eyes are an extension of Morgan's.

There is a thread. She ties it on the first encounter. It never can be broken. No matter how many passing years. Not breakable. He can still feel it at his solar plexus. The thread is a leash and it pulls his feet towards her, until he's close enough to see the simple ornament round her neck: velvet tied in a knot and the bloodstone hanging in its golden clasp, fairy features carved into the tumbled crystal.

"You remember last time, acolyte?"

He swallows and swallows again. "Am I ... am I still your acolyte, then?"

She raises a hand, gestures. "Death of beauty. Death of grace. Death of love!" Her voice rings out, and he glances round.

The muted crowds stream down from the Tor. Amongst them, the guy in green shuffles towards Glastonbury town. The guy who had laughed his disrespect. He walks alone, as if shunned.

He should be shunned.

"Did you hear him?" Stupid question. Morgan hears and sees like cephalopods feel. "He sniggered at the girl lying there ... *dying there* ... as if the whole thing was some big, hilarious joke."

There is a look in her eyes. The black centers gleam. "That, acolyte, is the Green Knight."

"Yes! The Green Knight!" A fable they'd read about. Together, turning the pages of the book. Those old times.

"He has struck the dolorous blow," says Morgan.

A shaft of light moves in his head. The pain stops him from thinking. His hands are like aspens. He's plugged up with Morgan. He drags a memory through the headache. In ancient times, damsels were struck by a dolorous blow—raped or killed in a fit of lust or temper. "He ... didn't *rape* her ... did he?"

"That must be the rationale."

The acolyte can't see properly, his breath comes fast and his stomach is screwed, the way it always was when he and Morgan were together. When he tries to swallow, his throat rasps, painfully arid. He shakes his head to clear it and the migraine clangs. That is the rationale. This man, the Green Knight, is to blame. He's a trickster who offers nothing but his trickster's laugh.

Morgan is following the Green Knight now, keeping behind him, stopping a short way from him as he waits by the bus stop.

"I remember the dolorous blow," the acolyte whispers at the white of Morgan's shoulder. "When a damsel is struck by such a blow, the land becomes a wasteland."

"A desert. Barren. Shrivelled."

"And … doomsday comes upon the land …"

She nods once. "Unless the foe be struck down."

Swords and shields clash in his head. He wants to do it; beyond question, he must strike the knight down. He bites his lip, feels the taste of iron like a drug. And in his breast, a stirring, as if a trapped bird was fluttering awake and struggling to get out. "I want to come back to you, Morgan."

"Your initiation will be hard. A journey of pain."

Initiation. Hard. Painful. Like last time. "What … what should be my weapon?"

"Extemporize, acolyte. Use whatever comes to hand."

The dolorous blow. Infected with foes. Wasteland. Everything ravaged. Black dots over his vision. The sun hot on his face. Six in the morning but already the solstice sun is too bright. His eyes water. He's dazzled by the sun and the return of Morgan and the drums that still echo inside his aching head.

She can make that happen. When he's with Morgan le Fay, hours are moments. Her needlepoint heels glint in the sun; he's lost in the dazzle. They stride for leagues over the hills and moors of Somerset, never losing sight of the Green Knight.

Finally, the perfect place. Morgan le Fay rests one hand on his back, briefly. The chill of it is like an ice statue. He blinks and there is the weapon.

It's only a stone, kicked into the gutter, but it will do.

He hefts it in his hand.

The Green Knight turns into a quieter road, full of shuttered houses set back from the road. The acolyte looks at the stone. All he hears is the laugh of the Green Knight, grown loud and long in his mind. All sees is the damsel, her legs askew beneath her limp body.

"This is for her." The stone is loosed from his hand. It bowls in an arc through the air.

The stone strikes true. The knight's knees buckle. He slumps— an almost slow-motion descent onto a grassy verge.

"Life from life!" the acolyte screams. He's jumping as he screams, like a child who's bowled a stunning shot. "Death of beauty!"

Then he's running and running through dazzle and drumbeat, his heart rupturing inside his chest.

FOUR
STEFAN

BIT BY BIT, EVERYONE straggled back to Stonedown Farm.

Shell, looking washed out with what she'd been through, arrived around midday. She brought the news we all knew anyway.

"Alys was pronounced dead on arrival. Brice is in pieces. His parents are on their way, and Alys's family. I'm afraid I'm not stopping. I've come to take Brice's car to the hospital."

"Here," Ricky passed her a mug. "Lemon balm and spearmint tea."

Shell left before Anag and Juke turned up. Anag had a silvery cauldron under his arm; Juke was carrying the tripod that came with it.

"It's a Gundestrup replica." Anagarika's eyes shone with his find, as if a bit of shopping could take the sting out of anything.

Yew pushed his hair from his eyes. His usual plait had unravelled after the night on the Tor and since he'd arrived back from Glastonbury town he'd been brushing his thick hair with a paddle brush. It seemed to bring him solace. He got up from the kitchen table and his hair flowed over his shoulders, full of electricity. He took the cauldron off Anag, weighing it on his open palm. "It's made of resin, you dunce."

"So?"

"So why get the tripod? You can't put this over a fire."

"I can do what I like with it, ta very much."

"My friend"—Freaky always started his little lectures with *my friend*—"the fleshpots of the High Street are for tourists with bulging wallets."

"Yeah? Well, I live here, as it happens. I'm pally with a lot of the tradespeople in town. I got a discount on this."

Freaky raised an eyebrow. "I've been in Glastonbury since 1969. I don't recall seeing you around."

"I'm in digs. Magdalene Street? Taking a good shifty. I fancied having a cauldron and I paid hard cash. Nothing wrong with that."

"My number one recommendation: if you wanna be a shaman my friend, you'll have to do better than look to replica cauldrons for help."

"I'm already a shaman. I've done several courses."

"Okay. Recommendation number two: shamanism is not something you can pick up on a weekend course. It is years of dedication. A lifetime commitment. A calling. Not playing with cutesy High Street tat. Ours is a better street—into the awakened self. A blessing, eh friends?"

"Mostly a blessing," said Yew. "Sometimes a bane."

"I don't need your lecture, mate," said Anagarika. "And it wasn't a weekend course. It was the full, advanced, practitioner training with Francis Gialias. Right here in Glastonbury. Yup; the fees are eye-watering but like I've been saying, I got a discount."

"So, recommendation number three: you can't buy shamanism. No one should charge you for this knowledge. No one."

"You're being a whacker, Freaky. The fee for this workshop—which, excuse me, you are at—was a hundred pounds per day."

I knew for a fact Freaky had not paid quarter that amount; he couldn't have found the money. Wolfsbane liked him at the workshops because he had such a long history ... he was a Glastonbury icon. Freaky didn't miss a beat. He flicked his dreadlocks, forty years of hair that had never seen shampoo, and came straight back.

"There are certain types of transaction that are fair and reasonable. Like, we're hiring out sleeping space plus use of the kitchen, bathroom, and the big workshop area. There's petrol for the coordinators. And their time, their expertise. That's an exchange of energies, friend. A blessed way of being."

"Maybe let's leave this subject alone for a bit," said Juke. He put the tripod in a corner of the room, as if he didn't want to be associated with it any longer. "Talk about something else, huh?"

"Juke's right," said Ricky. "Someone has just died. We don't want arguments."

I had to tell them sometime, and this felt like my cue. "Actually, we're all going home. Wolfsbane is postponing the workshop. No one will lose their payment. It'll be directly transferred. We'll have a discussion, when he's ready, to find out when everyone is free."

Anag counted up the half dozen people in the kitchen. "Where *is* Wolfsbane?"

"He's ..." I paused. Wolfsbane had gone into Stefan's side of the house, and he hadn't returned. I didn't want the others to know what they were talking about. "He's journeying," I lied. "To ask his guardians for strength and comfort for us all."

"If he's walking between the worlds, then I don't see why we shouldn't."

"Wolfsbane and I have decided it would be disrespectful to Alys to continue this workshop now."

"Alys *and* Brice," said Ricky. He'd been collecting up the empty mugs, and he stood, a cluster of them in his fist. "Even so, we could do something to mark her passing. Something to allow our own grieving to take a positive shape."

"That's profound, Ricky," said Yew. He leaned back on a kitchen chair and began to replait his hair, fingers flicking rhythmically at the three locks until a tawny-shaded braid snaked down his back. He finished by transferring a rubber band from his wrist to the plait end. "I get what Ricky's saying. It doesn't seem right to leave without doing anything at all. I mean, would Alys have wanted that?"

"Yeah, I'd like to—" Anag broke off and looked away.

"Like to get your money's worth?' sneered Freaky.

"Okay!" I had to raise my voice. Freaky was usually such a mild man; Anag had managed to snip one of his nerves. I hoped they wouldn't both be at the next workshop. "Okay, let's go into the workshop space and settle ourselves. I'll guide you into a visualization."

I led them into the big room off the kitchen. I was confident it was no longer full of the spiders I'd found when I'd shifted the sixteen budget sacks of dog food and the twenty outers of canned cat food and the three boxes of cat litter into the utility room to join the horse nuts, chicken pellets, and bags of sawdust. I'd pumped each floor cushion to prevent a spray of dust emerging each time someone lay on one and had gone over the ancient carpet with Stefan's hoover, removing, it felt at the time, the last vestiges of the pile.

"Have we all got a power animal that can help us? Some sort of guardian that we can communicate with? An intent, whether or not that might be a shape-shifting experience?" They were nodding their heads so I got them to settle and unzipped my drum case.

"Love the painting," said Ricky, pointing to my bodhran.

"Freaky did it. It's my power animal, Trendle."

"An otter. Wow. Would you do one for me, Freaky?"

Freaky inclined his head. "It would be my honour, friend. We can speak later, perhaps."

"Yeah, don't forget to exchange the energies," said Anag, but he kept his voice down and Freaky chose not to respond.

Ricky leaned towards me. "I don't think I've got a power animal yet, is that okay?"

"Use this as a chance to go searching for one. Look for openings in the land, where one might emerge from a Lower Realm. And be sure to ask them. Don't take anything at face value in the otherworld."

He flashed me a grateful smile and I started taking the group into a quiet mood. I lifted the drum and began a soft but fast tapping beat. I planned to walk them through a benign and tranquil setting. I didn't want anyone going down into the roots of the World Tree or having encounters with dead souls. I wanted them to leave Stone-down able to drive their cars, at least.

"You are in your safe haven," I began. "The portal from where you always begin your journeys…"

I'd decided to wing this a little by portraying aloud the images I experienced as I made my own journey. I hardly felt my wrist move as the drum pace and volume crept up.

"Trendle?" I whispered beneath my breath, and my otter came into view.

"I am here, Sabbie." He already knew. I could tell it in his voice. He knew how I was feeling, and why. He knew more about my spiritual life than I did myself. I followed him into an avenue of oaks, ancient as gods. I described the trees which stood at the top of the avenue, Gog and Magog. I'd seen them earlier as they really were, but here they were in glorious June leaf and filled with oakish inhabitants—beetles, birds, butterflies. I found myself touching the bright green summer leaves. I snapped off a single one.

"Choose one tree in the avenue." I was beginning to mumble a bit. "Sit beneath it. Be ready to gain its wisdom."

In my mind's eye, I settled down at the base of Magog, my back against its roots. The vibration of the drum tingled in my fingers, my hand, my arm, my heart. The ground was damp under the seat of my jeans. I twirled my oak leaf between finger and thumb. I moved further and further into this place, and my voiced faded away.

They were all on their own now, in their own journeys. And so was I.

———

At the bole of the oak was a hole, big enough to push a boot into. It was fashioned from the way the surface roots bent and wound together. I leaned against the trunk and dropped into this space. I fell and fell, as if the roots went on forever.

I landed on my back on a soft surface.

Above was a cloudless sky, deep blue, the sun at its zenith. Below me was bare soil, cracked and dusty and almost entirely coated with worms. They were everywhere, moving constantly. I eyeballed a single worm. It was pale for a worm, clean, like it had just had a wash from a storm, yet the surface of the earth was dry as toast. One began to climb my leg. Another started its journey. I plucked them off and took several steps backwards, worms squidging under the sole of my foot.

I picked up my gaze, viewing the horizon. This dry earth and its seethe of worms went on as far as the eye could see. I was at the centre of a massive cropland ready-ploughed but not yet sown with seed. It would be no good sowing seed, I couldn't help but think, until the rains came.

I looked down at myself and cried out in horror. The creatures were oozing all over me. A shudder convulsed my shoulders. Earthworms had never bothered me, I loved finding them in my garden soil, but this was worms gone crazy.

"Trendle!"

My otter barked once, and an opening, as clear and amazing as the parting of the Red Sea, spread before me, worms wriggling away in both directions. I was so shaken by their numbers, I broke into a run, tripping and flailing over the ruts in the ploughed soil.

In the distance, at the end of the path, I saw a small hut, surrounded by a wattle fence. It was the only thing rising from the plain. As I drew closer, I saw it was built of rough timber with a reed roof, glassless window, and low doorway. It looked off-kilter in this place.

In front of the hut a man was sitting cross-legged, tending a fire with a stick. He was crooning to himself.

> *Under ze world a father does not know his child,*
> *Oh-oh!*
> *In this country a father cry for his child,*

Oh-oh.

In zees country, under ze dying world.

He sang the words over and over. His accent gargled in his throat. His eyes were filled with sadness, like rock pools under stars, but no tears spilled or fell. He rocked his body, occasionally laying down his poker to hug himself with his arms. When his song came to an end, he lifted his head and trained his gaze on me.

"Can you tell me what the worms signify, please?" I was sure this was the question I should ask.

He didn't intend to answer my question promptly. He took time tending his fire, which was contained in a small ring of heat-blackened stones. His skin was black as the stones. His hair was ash-grey with age. His wet eyes were reddened in the fire's glow and when he finally spoke, I saw that his teeth—where there were teeth at all—were blackened and slanted.

"Zees the dying world, *oh-oh*!"

"A Lower Realm?"

"Uh-hum. Ze void existing in darkness."

"Can I enquire, sir, for your name?"

Again, he didn't reply. On the fire was a shallow metal bowl, filled with liquid that bubbled and steamed. He gave it a slow stir using the same stick he'd tended the fire with.

"I am lucky," he said, giving me a sideways glance.

"How, sir?"

"My brew, it need one las' magic. Green leaf. We never see no more round here."

I looked, with a start of surprise, at the oak leaf in my hand. I reached out. The man took the leaf. His nails were ridged with the work of ages, the cuticles thick with dirt. He let the leaf float onto the surface of the liquid brew. For a moment, it did not move. Then, all at once, it sank as if the concoction swallowed it up. He dipped his stick into the brew again, chanting as he stirred.

Under ze world a father seeks his child,
Oh-oh!
Mon cherie bring blessings, oh!
Fortune favour ze lucky and ze dead.

The old man lifted off the bowl without protecting his hands. He placed it carefully on the ground, which hissed and cracked from the heat of the bowl. His eyes narrowed. "I see you proper now. You child of pretty lady. You have question?"

I opened my mouth and closed it again. I'd left all my questions behind.

The man chuckled in his throat. Beside me, Trendle was holding my silken braid in his mouth. This was the woven cord I used to connect to the otherworld sometimes. The man stepped clean over the fire, took the braid, and dipped it into the bowl of brew until it was saturated. He gestured and I put out my arm, mink brown compared to his black sable. He tied one end of the hot, dripping braid to his wrist, the other to mine.

"Now go in zat hut," he said.

The cord, only a metre long, should not have stretched the distance of the path, but I reached the doorless entrance without the braid tugging and stepped through.

Suddenly, I was in an English woodland. Trees grew as far and wide as I could see—oak, ash, hazel, and beech. The sun slanted through the branches. A smell of summer came into my nostrils and I stared, bewitched, by the sudden change.

Deep in the trees, a shape moved. I shifted position to get a better look and felt the silken braid tighten on my wrist. I was not allowed to wander. A creature turned tail and fled—a flash of pale rump. A red deer. A female—a hind.

Outside, the old man and my otter waited by the fire. The man tugged at my braid and it slid from both our wrists. He handed it to Trendle for safekeeping.

"Now," said the man, "quickly; be gone."

In the same instant I was heading up the earthy tunnel into sunlight. I was at the bole of Magog, where my journey had begun.

Trendle looked up at me, the braid still dangling from his jaws like a fish. "Call-back," he said.

"What?"

On that instant, I felt the chair pressing on my spine and the drum heavy in my left hand. All through my journey I had continued to pound out a regular rhythm. I changed the beat to signal the call-back, took a sharp, deep breath, and opened my eyes to the room.

———

After a communal journeying, there is always silence for a time. For ten minutes or so no one spoke while we scratched away in journals and took sips of water. I made a careful record of my journey. As the drummer for the group, I hadn't expected to drop into a trance so easily, or have such a vivid experience. I wondered if it could have been connected to the fact that my whole body worked the drumbeat.

"Okay," I said at last. "I'll pass my rattle round so that those who wish to share their journey have the chance."

Juke was on my left; I passed him the rattle and he read out what he had written. A simple journey, but as his shamanic teacher, it pleased me. I'd first met Juke at a party he was throwing. I'd thought he'd been trying to chat me up, but he sincerely wanted to learn about shamanism. He'd been my student since. Back then, he'd held the world's burdens on his back, and it thrilled me to see how he'd been able to discard these, along with the suit jackets and neatly trimmed hair. Today he was wearing a sleeveless leather jerkin over a t-shirt showing a grinning face surrounded by branches and leaves, with vines growing out of its mouth and nostrils—a Green Man. A leather thong around his neck held a pentagram imbedded with a crystal. He passed the rattle to Freaky, who declined to talk about his journey.

Yew went next. Yew had a cultured Kentish accent, which I always enjoyed listening to, long pulls at the vowel sounds as he described the complex conversation he'd had with the oak tree he'd sat under in his journey. "I have an affinity with oak trees," he said, looking around at us. "I've spent a lot of time living in them."

"You've lived in trees," said Ricky, with a tinge of awe.

"Yew was once a road protester, weren't you?" I said. "A first-wave eco-warrior."

"We'd protest about anything, to be honest. Bypasses, quarries, nuclear power stations, the full McCoy."

"That's so cool," said Ricky. "Is that a philosophy you've got, to prevent that sort of destruction of the environment?"

"This was the nineties. A lot of new road plans were threatening rare species. Butterflies, toads, you name it. And the trees—they wanted to take down so many ancient oaks, ashes, yews even. It was criminal. We built platforms up there so that they'd have to fell us, as well as the trees." He grinned. "Called them 'twigloos'."

"It's sort of sad, that all this was before our time." Juke had a wistful tone to his voice. "We don't protest anymore, do we?"

"There's plenty to challenge." Yew was still holding my rattle, which meant the others shouldn't really interrupt him, but I let the conversation continue. "Big business never stopped wrecking our environment. GM crops, toxic industry, fracking. Plenty to demonstrate against."

"I don't know if we've got the bottle, nowadays," Ricky said.

"You can do a lot online. I miss the protests, but I confess I'm getting a bit old to face a line of coppers in riot gear."

"You're hardly over the hill, Yew," I said.

"Come your forties, you start longing for a comfortable bed. And I love my job. Okay, sometimes I get the urge to load my teepee into the van and set off, but ..." He gave the rattle a deliberate shake to suggest he'd finished and passed it to Ricky, who looked down at what he'd written for several long moments, before giving a slightly embarrassed laugh.

"I can't equal Yew ..."

"You don't have to." Yew clamped his hand over his Ricky's shoulder. "Tell us."

"Well ... first time I've managed to shape shift successfully." He bent his knees up and encircled them with his arms, like a girl. "I was a sea eagle."

"Wow." Juke passed him his water bottle. "Nice one."

Ricky wrapped his fingers around the damp plastic and gulped. "I hardly knew such a bird existed. Don't think they live in Britain."

"Highlands of Scotland, they do," said Freaky.

"Tell us about it," I said.

"Well, I was outside this ancient barrow. You know, where Neolithic people used to bury their dead. Sitting on the top was this massive bird with a bright white edge to his tail and a beak shaped like a bowie knife. I put out my hand and the bird flapped wildly. Scared me, actually. It landed on my wrist. Its talons really hurt. It started calling. God! What a sound. Like a screechy laugh, getting more and more manic. I said, 'Are you my power animal?' As I spoke, I entered its body. I sort of *was* ... the bird."

"You shape shifted," said Anagarika. "What a corker. I've always wanted to do that."

"Anag, Anag," Freaky's voice was despairing. "Recommendation number four: if you want great journeys, you have to practice. Then practice harder. Everything you need to know is right inside you."

"You can stop knocking at me, you bloody bastard," said Anag.

I jumped from my chair and it clattered backwards, falling with a thud onto the carpet. That took the fight out of both of them. "You should all know better than to interrupt someone when they're holding the rattle."

"It's okay." Ricky put up his hand. "I'm not saying more." He tried to pass the rattle to Anag, but the Australian dropped it onto the carpet.

"I'm off to pack my havvie."

"We need to centre ourselves before we leave this room." I fumbled for Anag's hand. He took it; I felt him calm. I badly needed Wolfsbane's clear leadership. I couldn't believe he was still in Stefan's half of the house. Maybe they'd made up their differences and were trying out some of the homemade mead Esme brewed from their own hives.

"You never told us about your journey," Juke said to me.

"It's okay. Like Freaky, I intended to leave it recorded in my journal."

One by one, the workshoppers stood and joined hands. I led them into taking some deep breaths and thanking the spirits. We began a round of goodbye hugs. I went into the kitchen, put the kettle on, and got the biscuits out.

Where was Wolfsbane?

I slipped into Stefan's side of Stonedown Farm. The house was rambling, with two staircases—one originally, I assumed, for the servants. This made it ideal for letting out; Stefan and Esme were able to hide in their half of the house when the rooms were in use. I moved into the living room.

Summer sun streaked through roughly pulled curtains. Dust motes danced in the shaft of light where the three of them were standing, Esme between Wolfsbane and Stefan, the two men facing each other like warriors.

"I will never forgive that," Stefan was saying.

"You've got it wrong." Wolfsbane's voice was hushed, as if anger had made him breathless.

"Yes," said Esme. She put her hands to her mouth, biting on the knuckles. "Wrong end of the stick." She was in a skin-tight pair of black leather trousers which showed off her flat stomach. Her black top was equally tight over muscular shoulders, sequined around the low neckline to enhance her bulging breasts. Her short hair, a shock of royal purple, was half hidden by the silky tangerine scarf wrapped round her head. Her height rivalled both Stefan's and Wolfsbane's.

There was shuffling at the doorway. I turned. The workshoppers had followed me, even Anag.

Stefan stared dramatically at the six of us, then turned to Wolfsbane. "Get your hangers-on out of my house. Now."

Wolfs didn't budge. If anything he seemed to be squaring up for a fight. "You're not listening. I said you were mistaken. I want an apology."

"Fuck off."

They'd reached that moment of anger when all you see is redness and hate. Stefan side-stepped Esme and grasped Wolfsbane by the shoulders and shoved hard, off-balancing him and following through with further shoves to his chest, pushing him towards where we stood, gaping, in the doorway. "Get—out—of —my—house!"

All at once things went up a gear. Wolfsbane grabbed Stefan roughly by the arm. Stefan shook him free, tightened both his fists and raised them to his face. Neither of these men were natural pugilists, but Wolfsbane ate sparingly and exercised regularly, while Stefan was getting portly; he was puffing already, suggesting his heart would not bear sudden exertion.

"Cut it out, you dipsticks," said Anag. He pushed between them. "You are both way outta fucking order."

He fisted his right hand into Stefan's jaw, then stepped back, gripping and re-gripping his fist, like it needed a cooling-down exercise.

Ricky shot me a pleading glance, as if I was the only person there who could stop this thing, but I was too busy disbelieving my eyes.

Stefan staggered round in a circle and fell heavily onto his back. His head hit the carpet, so sticky with long-standing grime that he seemed to bounce.

Esme let out a tremulous cry—it hardly felt as if it had come from her; Esme wasn't the sort to show emotion—and ran to him, cradling his head with her hands.

Stefan groaned. "What the fuck?" He put his hand to his injured jaw.

Esme turned to us all. "Get OUT!" she yelled. "GET OUT!"

Anag supported Wolfsbane from the room, although he hadn't been hurt at all. The other men followed, like an armed guard. I stood my ground.

"What was that about?" I asked at last. My voice was breathy, but I had it under control.

"Piss off, Sabbie," said Stefan, struggling to sit up.

"I'm going, don't worry. I just want to know; why row on this dreadful day?"

"No need to bring Alys into it. She's got nothing to do with this."

"She's dead, Stefan!"

"I could've been dead, if I'd landed on that thing." He nodded at the ancient stone hearth.

I glared at Esme. "What was it about?"

"Don't ask me."

"But I am. Because you were here."

"Nothing. Really. Loss of control, that's what it was. Bloody men, if you ask me. They have no idea how to cope with stress."

"Who was under the stress, Stefan or Wolfs?"

"It was ..." Her eyes were burning. She was having trouble managing her own anger. "None of your business."

I hunkered down and looked Stefan in the face. The redness from Anag's punch glowed under his chin stubble. "Are you okay?"

"Yeah." He nodded once.

"Is this about that pack of white tablets you showed Wolfs?"

"What?"

"Was it about the tablets? The ones you wanted us to all take. Did you give one to Alys?"

Esme pushed between us, closing her arms round Stefan. He buried his face close to the foam of her bosoms, so that his voice was muffled. "Go away, Sabbie. Please."

FIVE
RICKY

WE GOT OUR BAGS out of Stonedown Farm as fast as we could. There'd been no powwow over rescheduling the cancelled workshop. Never was too soon for my liking, especially when Wolfs began thanking Anag for what he seemed to think was a rescue, rather than a violent attack on the host.

We said our goodbyes on the gravel area near the garages. Freaky disappeared back to his caravan, which had stood for years at the edge of Stonedown's land. Anag strode along the drive towards his digs in town, flourishing his hand as each of the cars passed him.

Soon, it was just Ricky and me on the driveway. "Can I drop you anywhere?" I asked him.

"Er ..." He passed his bag from one hand to the other.

"Where're you headed?"

"North Bristol."

"That's where I was brought up. I'll give you a lift, if you like."

"You can't do that!"

"'Course I can. Hop in."

"It's out your way."

"I'll drop in on my family. They can't live too far from you."

He slung his bag in the back and climbed into the front. "Thanks."

A sort of gloom settled between us in the car that wasn't easy to shift. I fell to wondering if Alys's death had to be the most shocking event to ever happen on the Tor. The hill was millions of years old and had seen lifetimes of things. Once it had been surrounded by inland sea, creating myths of gods and kings and saints. Perhaps for the spirit of the Tor, Alys's death was trifling; one moment's breath over millions of years.

I realized how silent we had both become. Ricky was staring out of the window, but, I fancied, not seeing anything.

"You okay?"

"Yeah." He stretched, as if he'd only realized how tense he'd been. "Processing."

"Mmm. And if it's like this for us, how must it be for Brice and Alys's family?"

"Don't think I'll ever forget." He paused, went to speak again, but didn't quite make it, sinking back into silence.

I waited until I'd taken the slip-road onto the motorway then said, "It's not just Alys, is it? Something's playing on your mind."

Ricky looked at me sharply, but didn't respond straight away. His eyes were thick with eyeliner and mascara and there was a fine layer of talcum powder over his cheeks, which made him seem even more vulnerable—as if the makeup helped him face the world.

"I ... I heard a lot about you, before I came to the workshop. Juke told me how you spot things about people. He said you can locate things, like the shaman of old."

I wasn't keen to confirm this. Any success I'd had in the past might never be repeated. I hated raising people's hopes. I tried half-changing the subject. "I'm sorry the workshop didn't go to plan. Especially as you had such a great shape-shifting experience."

His face was open and as puzzled as a child's. "How does that work? I don't understand ... like ... being the eagle was partly my imagination ... but ..." His voice dropped. "It was so *real*. I didn't even know about sea eagles, but all at once, I was one. I could feel this tiny heart beating and it was inside me—my skeleton felt light as balsa wood." He stretched his legs into the well of the car. "My brothers and I used to make these model aircraft when we were kids, out of balsa wood."

"You can find out more about your sea eagle," I said. "You can just lie down, close your eyes, and let yourself go to meet him."

"I will. I like the quietude of journeying. It's healing. I got sick, first time I went to university. I had to leave my business studies course and go home." He grinned to himself. "Couldn't cope with all the partying. I learnt to meditate while I was getting my health back."

"You look pretty fit to me. And you're back at uni?"

"Yeah, I've started another degree from scratch. Philosophy. Very cerebral, but working with shamanism balances that out. 'We're so engaged in doing things to achieve purposes of outer value that we forget the inner value, the rapture that is associated with being alive.'"

"Wow, that's profound, Ricky."

"It wasn't me. It's a quote from Joseph Campbell, *The Power of Myth*. We don't connect to nature anymore. It's the constant frenzy of the twenty-first century. I find that hard, sometimes; that's why I got ill." He gave a short laugh and pinked under his white makeup. "Sorry, Sabbie, I don't usually go on like this."

"'S okay with me." I liked the way he was opening up; he had been quiet among the pushy, downright combative males at Stonedown Farm.

"My family didn't want me to come back to uni. They thought I'd fall sick again, but I've been fine."

"Were you all boys in the family?" I asked, remembering the model planes.

"Two older brothers and a sister a bit younger than me." He paused for a long time. "Babette," he said at last. "But we all called her Babe." And then he closed down, locking his hands together and tucking them between his knees, as if that would keep his thoughts together. I knew something was bothering him. We had all watched Alys drop to the ground, but I didn't think it was entirely to do with that. I recalled his grim face, staring out from under the shared duvet, while Shell's hand rested on his thigh. I'd've loved to get Ricky's version of what had gone on there. Shell should be careful if she wanted to keep Wolfsbane; he was flighty with girlfriends, tiring of each one as soon as they demonstrated any trend he didn't like. And he definitely didn't like girlfriends who flirted with other men.

Not that I was quite able to think of Ricky as a man. His boyishness clung to him, a kind of inculpability.

The sun was fierce on my left side as I drove in a straight, northbound line. It had not ducked behind cloud for the entire solstice day and a golden evening looked certain. Gloria and Philip might be eating on the flagged patio at the back of their house tonight; it faced west and would catch and hold the balmy weather right up to sundown. I should find a local shop and arrive with some chilled white wine.

I came off the motorway and Ricky directed me through the housing estates of north Bristol. "Take this little road coming up on the left and we're there ... this house, with the high blue gable. That's my room, under the gable."

I pulled up to the kerb. "Sounds lovely."

"Yeah ..." He drummed his fingers on the dashboard again. "Sabbie," he began.

"Tell me."

"I've wanted to ask you something since ... since I met you yesterday ... but now I've held you up long enough."

I cut the engine. "Never leave with regrets."

He gave a brief laugh, though he was close to tears. "I promised myself I'd ask you. I lost my nerve."

"You've found it again now."

"Yeah." He put his hand over his chest as if afraid his heart might jump right out. "Five years have gone past. Would that make a difference?"

"That depends. Is this something you've lost?"

"My sister." He'd been staring straight out through the car windscreen, but now he turned to me, unashamed of his wet face. "My Babe."

"Your sister is lost?"

Ricky dashed the back of a hand over his face, smearing his eyeliner. "She was sixteen. A bit spirited, you know?"

"You ... lost her when she was sixteen?

"She disappeared. Wretched, wretched time."

"I'm so sorry."

"They started this countywide search. Didn't find a button."

"Had she run away, Ricky?"

"We'll never know. Never. It wrecked my parents. We thought they were going to split over it. Mum did blame Dad, for a while. Babe was the only girl and he gave her less freedom than we'd had. I mean, like, going into town, clubbing, that sort of thing." He reached over the seat back and swung his bag onto his lap, ready to leave. "Telling you feels bloody stupid. It's so long ago."

"Ricky, do you have anything of Babe's? A small keepsake?"

"Mum might. I dunno." He rubbed at his wet eyes. "Oh! I've got her sketchbook. Is that the sort of thing?"

"Ricky, that's perfect."

———

I followed Ricky into his house, a typical student residence darkened by forgotten curtains and smelling of ancient socks.

"Eijaz," Ricky called. "Eijaz?"

A lanky boy with sharp-nosed Asian features and a two-day dark beard appeared at the top of the stairs. "Wass-a-time," he asked, peering hard at his own watch.

"Time you were up. Try being awake for the solstice dawn."

"I was up half the night, working on my thesis. Dawn musta come, but I didn't take no notice." Eijaz was in crumpled lounge pants and an inside-out t-shirt. His face had a crushed look too but nothing would have mussed his hair; it was clipped short on top and shaved short at the sides. To add to his trendy look, he fished a pair of sunglasses from the pocket of his lounge pants and pulled them on, as if ordinary daylight defeated him.

Ricky ushered me up the stairs and into his room. I'd expected the usual student riot, but Ricky's bedroom was tidier than mine. On the small wooden table which functioned as his desk was a laptop, a writing pad, a ruler, a row of pens, and a folded pair of spectacles, all positioned so neatly it made me wonder if he'd used the ruler to lay the rows out. Stacked against the wall were tall piles of philosophy books in order of size. The walls were covered with posters of old men—philosophers, I had to assume—but between these were photos of Glastonbury, Avebury, Stonehenge, and other sacred sites, Blu-Tacked with geometric precision. There was still the fusty smell of closed-down living; stale beer and ancient dust, and I could see a greying pile of old jeans and smeared tops had been pushed under the bunklike bed, but the room would still take a medal if there had been one, for student sleep/work environments.

"The photos are lovely."

"Yeah, I took some of them myself. But I must get on with my dissertation. I have a tendency to fall behind and I can't let that happen this time. I've got my ideas all lined up; I've just got to start writing."

"What's it on?"

"'The Concept of Light and Darkness in Plato's Analogy of the Cave.'"

"The what?"

"That's the title. It's about perception of goodness. Plato uses a cave as an analogy of lack of virtue. He associates goodness with the sun—knowledge of The Good. The sun can't be seen directly from the cave. That's the point, you see. My tutor suggests I compare him to Locke, who says the sun differs from other objects because light comes directly from it and reveals all other objects to us, but I've decided to bring in someone more recent. Iris Murdoch. She was an atheist, and wanted us to rethink what goodness is without the inclusion of God—"

He broke off, realizing his student brain had gone into overdrive. "Sorry, I should be looking for Babe's sketchbook."

"No hurry. No one's expecting me at any particular time. What do you think goodness is, Ricky?"

"Me?" He ran a hand through his upright hair. "Doesn't matter what I think. I'm just a degree student. My job is to work out what the philosophers thought."

"Surely you have an opinion."

"I like the idea that goodness has something to do with love. Murdoch says—" He clamped his teeth together to stop himself.

"I like that idea too."

Ricky pulled a sports-bag out from under the bed which was filled with things from home; things maybe he'd never unpacked but didn't want to throw away. "This was Babette's." He passed me a standard-sized sketchpad half-full with pencil drawings and some watercolour paintings.

I turned the first couple of pages, taking in chalk sketches of woodland, studies of trees and butterflies. "Where is this?"

"New Forest. The four of us were given a lot of freedom in the woods, with our bikes and that." Ricky sat down on the bed as if his legs couldn't support him any longer. "I was in Bristol, of course, when Babette disappeared, first year of my business degree. It was easy for me to get back, but Claude was stuck into his finals and Jacob was working in Dubai. Still is."

"So you had to contend with your parents' distress."

"I had to contend with my own! Babe and me, we'd been inseparable when we were kids. You know how a family of four can split off into two? Well, it was always me and Babes."

"Were the woods … I mean, they're quite extensive, aren't they?"

"Yeah, they were searched." He held himself rigid and stared at wall opposite.

"Was it … was it after all that you fell ill?"

"After she went, business studies seemed pretty lame. Not worth the effort. I guess I had a bit of a breakdown."

"That's not at all surprising," I said. "You've recovered really well."

"Yeah." He got up from the bed, as if to demonstrate his renewed energy. He found a crumpled carrier bag and we slid the sketchpad into it.

"She's a talented artist," I said.

"I hope she still uses that talent," said Ricky. "If she still can. If she still *is*."

————

Ricky did not ask me what I was going to do with Babette's sketchpad, which was as well, for I had not yet worked that out. I knew I should study it more carefully; possibly journey with it as my lodestone, but for now I took a quick look through, turning the pages with care until I came to a pen and ink sketch of a girl. It could have been one of her friends, of course, but I decided it was a self-portrait, partly because the girl had the same buttony mushroom-shaped nose as Ricky.

Babe clearly loved to paint and sketch, and the passion behind her talent showed through. Most of the work was conventional, orthodox.

The things you'd expect a teenager to study were all there: the family dog, the New Forest landscape, the view from her window. Later on in the book were pictures of her brothers. It was easy to spot Ricky, and fun to see him without his gothic makeup and gelled hairstyle.

Nothing was revealed through the pictures in the book. Nothing that whispered *I am here…* or *I am gone…*

I lay it on the passenger seat and drove to the grandly named Oak Villa—actually a narrow terraced house with no front garden—where my foster parents lived. I knew the Davidsons would welcome me in; they were as generous to me as they had been the day I went to live with them, eighteen years back. Right that moment, I was driving along in the continued proof of their generosity—a couple of months ago my foster dad Philip upgraded his car and donated his ten-year-old Vauxhall Astra to me.

I'd once had a wonderful car, a classic Morris Mini Minor with the original racing strips and metal wing mirrors still intact. I wept when I sold her, but I'd got into debt and thanks to an eBay auction, she netted me enough to reduce my outgoings.

I parked outside Oak Villa and was brandishing a Pinot Grigio, straight from the local shop, when Gloria opened the door.

"You look done in, girl."

"Yep." I entered the house and flopped onto the sofa in the living room. The telly was on low, the curtains half-pulled against the sun. It felt like heaven. "Been a ghastly day."

"Want to stay the night?"

It was an offer I couldn't refuse. My next-door neighbours had been commandeered to feed my hens while I was away; they weren't expecting me back yet anyhow. I smiled my acceptance.

"Supper's in an hour."

"That sounds wonderful. Can we eat in the garden?"

"Why not?"

"Is Dennon in?"

"He's in his room, packing."

"He's going on holiday?"

"Moving out."

"What's he done now to get the old heave-ho?"

"I mean, he's moving in ... to a flat of his own."

I sat up. "Ye gods. This I have to see. It might even cheer me up a bit."

———

Up in Dennon's bedroom, things were at hurricane level. I closed the door tight and leaned against it to prevent any flying objects sailing past.

My foster brother stood straight as I came in, knuckles in the small of his back, and grinned. I laughed—Dennon's smile has made me do that ever since I first encountered it. I was twelve then; he was thirteen, and I knew soon as I looked at the guy that he intended to cause even more trouble than I did. Now he was thirty, and, until this moment, still living with his parents. He looked groovy, though. Better dressed, now his job had become regular, and he'd clipped his hair short enough to see his scalp, although this evening he'd pulled a baseball cap over his head. He was wearing a loose, grey marl t-shirt over Diesels and his forearms showed bare sinewy muscles beneath skin the colour of an Americano coffee.

"You do understand the principles of packing, right, Den?"

"Get it in the boxes somehow?"

"Fold flat. Neatly wrap against breakage. Stack to allow maximum room. Wedge to prevent sliding and knocking. Not stuffed so full you can't lift the package."

"Hell … all that? I haven't left the family threshold yet and already I'm useless in the wider world."

"Where you going, anyway?" I took a drawerful of socks and started sorting and balling them into pairs.

"Northville. Me and a mate."

"I'm impressed. Does this mean you're sticking to the promotion you got?"

"They've made it permanent. Not bad, eh?"

"Shocking." I continued to ball the socks. "Den, do you remember those so-called legal highs you had once?"

"Er …" Dennon looked me over, trying to spot the trick in my question. "Sort of."

"How much do you know about that drug?"

"Come on, Sabbie, you were the one that was all over the Internet about it. You're the one with the facts."

"I'm trying to remember. Para-meth-something? PMA, and lots of pretty names for it too. Pink Lady?"

"Dr. Death, we called it. Some guy round my mate's place, he had some. We bought half a doz each. Thought they'd be the same as E."

"Weren't they the same?"

"Yeah and no. They were bloody amazing, but mad. One minute there's nothing there at all, and the next, you're trippin' balls."

"So you did take it?"

"We all popped one and sat round, waiting. Waiting and waiting. Bark, he couldn't wait no longer, took another … two, maybe. I didn't bother, I was on the beer. Then I started feeling really horny."

"Eugh," I said. "Too much information."

"But not high, is my point. Not for a bit. We stuck the music up on max and suddenly I was smashed, right along with all the others. We was flyin' round Kyle's house to the sounds. Then Bark went onto his knees. He was sort of retching, y'know? I took his pulse."

"*You*? How did you know where to find it?"

"I watch *Casualty*, don't I? Anyway, it was fast, man, racing like a pro."

"Was he hot?"

"Yeah, and he knew it. S'if he had rabies or something, he was scrabbling at his clothes, stripping them off, panting. We got him under the armpits and he sort of squealed, like a pig, but we dragged him into the garden."

"Cool air. Good thinking."

"Yeah, 'cept my heart was doing about a million to a minute by then. It made me panicky. I could see why Bark was squealing all the time, just layin' there on the patio, making these piggy noises."

"And you didn't think to call an ambulance?"

"Are you kiddin', man? This was Kyle's house, his mum would've killed him!"

I shook my head. I'd forgotten about balling socks; they lay limp in my hands. "What happened in the end?"

"He was okay. We all came out kicking. It was the scariest experience of my life."

"And that's saying something."

"It was the panic. You go totally down the rat hole. I'm not 'xactly a panicky person, would you say?"

"No, Den, I'd say you were generally mellow."

"For ages after that, slightest thing would set me off. Sweatin' and dizzy and not seeing proper, like club lighting strobing into my brain."

I remembered Stefan, his eyes red hot. Had Wolfs been right about spiking the flying tea?

"It kinda did make me think some," Den was saying. "After, I mean. Like, what is a high, really?"

"D'you mean, what is real ecstasy? For me, it's the joy of being a shaman. That's as close to the divine as I reckon I'll ever be getting."

"Yeah, sort of that. And you—God, Sabbie—you're such a good role model for me."

"I *am*?"

"Yeah, like, you got your head sorted, and you went and did your degree, and like … you're *happy*."

I paused. Happy? Not this day. "I've just watched someone die."

"Shit, no!" Dennon rocked back. "Did they take something?"

"I'm sure we'll find out. They'll be doing the tests. They'll be examining the body. Awful thought. Alys had a lovely face, you know? I hate to think of them examining her body, stretched out and totally naked. Cutting her with a scalpel. Taking samples. I hate it."

I thought about both of them. The Hollingberrys. Alys has wanted to dance, so Brice spent a night on the Tor even though he thought it was "purgatory." How must he feel about that now?

"I can't believe it only happened today." I stoppered the light, folding my hands over my eyes. "It seems years have gone past. Decades. And seconds, at the same time."

"Fucking unbelievable," said Dennon. "Come here, sis."

He put his arms all round me.

SIX

LAURA

I GOT HOME AROUND eight the following morning. It had come onto rain in the night. The brilliance of the sun's zenith had passed. It was the twenty-second of June already. I felt something wrench, deep inside. It was almost physical, as if I'd torn a hole in my body. Death and sadness.

I needed Rey. I reached for my phone. I put it down again. He'd be on his way to Bridgwater Police Station to start his day as detective inspector. As soon as he walked into his office, the pressure would begin. He would not be pleased to have a call from his girlfriend.

Girlfriend. That's what I was. The girl he dated. The girl he came round and bonked when he had a spare evening.

For quite some time now, that hadn't been enough for me. I wasn't pushing him; I wasn't even mentioning it, but I wanted more. Rey lived in a microscopic studio flat—what was the point in that?

He could move in with me whenever he liked. I had two bedrooms—the spare one could be his den (if we cleared it up a bit), or office, or whatever coppers need in their life.

I hadn't asked, and he never raised the subject. I don't think he ever considered it. The extent of our relationship was the toothbrush he kept in my bathroom.

Usually, I left the phoning to him. I knew he would call me; that or turn up on my doorstep after work, holding a couple of bottles of Merlot. He initiated the moves and I let him, because cops worked antisocial hours and had their heads totally immersed in the job, and because I was afraid that a nagging girlfriend might quickly become an ex-girlfriend.

I went out into the garden with the hens' breakfast. I stood in the rain, letting it trickle over my face. I wanted something to soothe me, cool me. Alys's death was a heartache. I touched my neck, half expecting to feel an open sore, my throat felt so raw.

The cock, Kaiser, didn't come near me as I checked the nesting boxes. He sat on his favourite post, watching his flock get under my feet. There were three eggs, still warm. Suddenly, my appetite was back. Scrambled eggs, maybe with one of my greenhouse-ripened tomatoes. I just loved this time of year in my vegetable plot—there was food sprouting in every direction. Even if the therapy business I ran from my front room went a bit slow, I knew I'd eat dinner.

Only three eggs from six layers. The two old Warrens, Ginger and Melissa, didn't lay so often, but Jessie, Emili, Rihanna, and Florence were still young and—

I stopped. Florence was not under my feet. She was not anywhere at all.

"Florence," I called, even though she had no idea that was her name. "Flo, where are you? Chuck-chuck?"

Panic welled up. I didn't understand this; none of the other hens were missing. They didn't even seem perturbed, which they would have been if a fox had come near them. I'd already experienced a fox in the night. It had wreaked havoc, blood and feathers everywhere. I thought of other, more stealthy predators. A polecat, even a sparrow-hawk, might have snatched her away if she'd escaped from the run.

I worked around the perimeter of the garden, chuck-chucking.

Florence was my secret favourite. She was a curious hen, bright eyed and comical. I'd had her and her siblings for over a year, a farmer had given me a recently hatched clutch of Sussex hens and they'd been productive and so beautiful to look at.

I went into the lane at the back of my garden. My house was on the edge of a sixty-year-old estate. Behind the lane was a patch of scrubland. I half slid down the slope to the stream that was almost a drain, filled with rubbish and old bikes. I clambered back up, still calling, over and over. "Florence? Flo? Chuck-chuck-chuck?"

Florence wouldn't go missing by choice. As soon as dusk fell, my hens took themselves off to bed. My neighbours, the Wraxalls, were happy to feed them in the mornings if I was away. The only tricky bit was checking they didn't escape the fox-proof run as they fed them. The Wraxalls had said nothing about a missing hen when I'd popped in to thank them after I'd got back.

"Damn. Damn!" I kicked at the water-butt, making it slosh and spill. It seemed a shitty thing to happen, as if the spirit world was reminding me that the loss of a hen was not to be compared with the loss of a partner. Brice must feel a hundred times worse than I, a million times more heartsick.

There in my garden, I sobbed for the deaths of Florence and Alys.

———

I waited until I'd recovered my composure before I rang my boyfriend.

"Hi," I said. "S'me."

"Hi, Sabbie. I'm in a meeting."

"Okay."

"I'll come over later, okay?"

"Okay."

"Bye, then."

"Bye."

That conversation rather summed up our relationship: me passive and ill at ease, him busy and distracted. Rey was at the near-centre of my world while I was at the edge of his.

I wasn't sure how I'd let it get like that.

I rewound the thought, because I knew exactly how I'd let it get like that. When it came to men, my solid perspective on life goes all distorted. Like I've picked up the wrong spectacles. At least with Reynard Buckley, I knew I had a good guy. He wasn't abusive. He wasn't using me as eye-candy (fat hope!) and he wasn't a two-timer—he was still officially married to Lesley, but she was living with another man and I wished that relationship a long and happy existence.

I flicked a duster and a floor mop over the house, which looked crumby after two nights away. I checked my phone diary. I knew it would be empty, as I should've been at the workshop, so I had a free day. As I stared at the screen, the phone buzzed in my hand.

"Hello? Is that Sabbie Dare?"

"Speaking."

"Oh, er … a friend gave me your card."

The caller sounded a bit frantic. "You'd like to book a therapy session with me."

"Er, yeah, that would be great."

"Reiki, reflexology, aromatherapy, or shamanic therapy?"

"Uh, I dunno. The last? Yes, the last one."

"Okay. Usually, people book a prelim appointment and then think about taking a course of therapeutic shamanism once they've met me. Would you like to do that?"

"Er … yes … I don't suppose you're free now, are you?"

"I am, but you—"

"Would it be okay if I saw you this morning? I have your address. I could come straight away."

"Well, okay, if you're sure." I took a breath. Her urgency was catching. "Can I have your name, please?"

"Laura Munroe. If I set out now, I could be there soon."

"Don't rush, Laura. You need to give me an hour to prepare for you."

———

I changed into my black shamanic gown which fitted my figure from shoulders to hips then flared out to my ankles, bright embroidery swirling round the hem. I loved pulling on that dress; it transformed me. I brushed my hair, merciless as I tugged the bristles through the tight curls which had a tendency to boil out of my scalp. I brushed and brushed, eventually it shone like a halo of black gossamer.

The therapy room felt chilled after two days of inactivity. I lit candles around the entire room. I held a flame to a charcoal disc until it fizzed with heat and laid a sprig of garden sage across it, throwing a pinch of frankincense resin on top. The grey smoke spiralled up, filling the room with secret scents. When the room was ready for work, I sat on a cushion and meditated for a while, trying at first to empty my mind, but actually recalling the journey I'd experienced at Stonedown Farm—the land of worms, the ancient black man, and the clearing in the woodland. I had a strong desire to use my drum to journey again, but in the scurry to get out of Stonedown Farm, I'd left it behind.

So instead, I pressed the remote to start the drumming CD, lay back on the floor cushions and rested a scarf over my eyes.

When I'd guided the workshoppers yesterday, I'd told them to find their shamanic portal. Every shaman should have a haven of safety—the place where, if possible, they begin and end their journey. For me, this is the bank of a fast-flowing brook. I have never been to the Highlands of Scotland (I've never been to the Lowlands, for that matter), but I've seen photos of the burns that flow there. Like Scottish streams, my haven is green with moss and blue with heather, which makes a cushiony place to sit.

I dangled my bare feet in the stream now. The water rushed over them. My otter came splashing out, shaking his coat like a dog and scattering droplets over my black dress.

"What is your purpose?" he asked.

"I'm here to touch base. To check out two new possible clients and to calm myself for the day ahead."

"You should go to the Lady of the River."

I always felt wary of the Lady of the River. I wouldn't disrespect a guardian, but she was a hard taskmaster, more strict headmistress than goddess. She never quite seemed on my side. Or, rather, she gave the impression that my best life choices were not the ones I tended to make. She was prone to offering difficult advice and I'd avoided her since the last time she'd insisted on helping me, which was half a year back.

"I don't know how to find her."

"True," said Trendle, as if he also thought it my excuse.

He trotted ahead on his short paws, leading me along the bank. As we walked, the brook altered. The bank became high and slippery, the water below wider and deeper and muddy brown. Every so often a tiny wave of frothing white slipped and skidded along.

On my right hand, the woodland had grown deep and Trendle was weaving through the trees while my bare feet glided along the country path. I felt the hazy sun struggling to shine through a layer of cirrostratus. All at once, I stopped in my tracks. A tantalising scent came at me on the breeze. "There's honey in the air," I said. "As if someone is pouring it from warm combs."

I quickened my pace. Ahead was a single massive lime tree in full leaf, shaped like a green heart. Standing under the tree was the Lady of the River. Her grey eyes were as sad as forgotten lakes.

I bent my head in humility. "Lady of the River ... I witnessed something. Something terrible. A young woman's death. I ..."

"You have done well," the Lady interrupted.

"Have I?" I shook my head, even though she would not want me to disagree.

"You are a support to friends, new and long-standing, in this world and in the apparent world."

"I can't be of help to Alys," I whispered. "She's gone…"

"I see such tenacity in you, Sabbie Dare. You do not let go until you have your answer."

"Yeah. Hell or high water."

"Tenacity. Commitment. Love. Hell and high water. You have faced those things and you will again."

I hadn't expected such a generous response, and it heartened me to ask further things. "I am about to take on a new client. Laura Munroe. What should I know before I begin?"

"Use your silken braid to journey. Seek out mirrors, masks, and symbols that turn things upon their own heads."

"And… what should I do about Babette Johnson? Ricky has asked me find his sister."

"Such a search might help you in ways you cannot yet imagine. Examine all that comes to you. When you eliminate that which you no longer need, one possibility will remain."

I was going to ask, "examine what things?" but she spoke again. "Soon, you will have to face your past."

She caught me unawares. I didn't want to discuss this subject. I never had seen the point in chasing after my own past.

"I know it is the hardest thing for you."

The longer I worked with spirit, the more I understood that past was everything. It wasn't the opposite of future. It wasn't dead and gone. The story already told was as crucial as the story not yet known. Ancestors were as important as friends around the table. Knowing this made my past all the more difficult to come to terms with. I'd been a motherless child in the state care system, pushed from foster home to children's home for years before I met the Davidsons. Yet for all that lonely time, I'd recently discovered, I'd had blood relations.

When I'd been a child, I had no idea that there was anyone out there who might have rescued me, cared for, loved me. Six months ago, someone who thought they were my cousin came into my life, and with her came an unbearable thought: if this family been informed of my existence earlier on, things might have been so different.

I hadn't been able to hack the sudden immersion into a new family. I'd told them not to contact me again. That decision still had the smell of shame about it, like a rude word spray-painted on a concrete wall.

At the back of my throat came the scent of honey. It made me feel positive, reinforced. It shored me up, as if the Lady knew what I needed most at this point. I'd experienced hardness from her; she often stonewalled my questions and took me to grim places. This time she was filled with honey.

"Tell me what you saw, when you descended the realms," she said, out of the blue.

I forced a shudder away. Too many images. "A plague of worms and dry ground, nothing growing…"

"Yes," said the Lady. "A wasted land, stagnant, despoiled."

"I met a guardian, an ancient black man, beside a fire. He showed me a powerful totem—a red hind. What did that mean?"

"It would be better if you asked him yourself."

I shook my head, violently. I had no intentions of returning.

"There are roots that penetrate deep. That bind tight. You will find them at the hut of the old man."

"Lady of the River, please tell me what you mean."

"Sabbie Dare," she said, and her voice was firm. "When will you call me by my true name?"

"I don't know your name, Lady."

"Indeed?" She glanced towards the river, which, as always, tumbled along, breaking white as it hit surface boulders. "I am the river, Sabbie…" Her voice was fading. She was leaving me. All that remained was a shimmering, a rippling of blues and browns and foaming whites. I heard her voice in my head, and as I did so I realized that the call-back sign from the drumming CD had come and gone and that I was lying on cushions in my therapy room.

I am the river of cool, translucent waves and treacherous, violent tides. Only when you call me by my name can I truly be of aid…

Recording that journey in my journal gave me pause. I hadn't been expecting such specifics; the Lady of the River usually spoke in enigmas. I wrote down her suggestions, and it turned out they were enigmas after all. *Mirrors, masks… turn things on their heads* was her guidance for Laura Munroe, and she'd said Babette's sketchpad would help *in ways you cannot yet imagine.* She'd told me to confront my past, insisted I called her by her true name.

I didn't know how to do either of those things. I stashed my journal away as I went to answer the doorbell.

———

Laura Munroe looked flustered as she stood on the doorstep, but I was used to that. People keep my card in their wallet for weeks, until they reach a peak of distress. On the phone I'd guessed she wasn't much out of her teens and now I could see I'd been right. I took her jacket, damp from the rain, and her motorbike helmet. She was almost entirely in blue denim, tight jeans perhaps a size too small, and a baggy shirt buttoned over a camisole. I showed her into the therapy room and directed her to the two wicker chairs by the desk.

"You got here without trouble, then."

She managed a nod and a smile, but didn't speak. I held my hands steady in my lap as a calming gesture; her hands were wringing each other. Her fingers were plump, her face a little puffy, while her ankles and wrists were narrow, almost sinewy.

"You need to catch your breath. Shall I put the kettle on?"

"Oh, I'm okay, really."

"Tell me what attracts you to shamanism."

"Oh ... er ... well, I ..." Her voice was soft. Her hair was parted in the centre, clipped to fall just below the nape of her neck and hang like open curtains at either side of her temples. She wore hoop earrings, the sort that are used as starters.

"Look, let's go and have a cuppa. I'm gasping, even if you aren't."

I got up and led the way out of the therapy room. I could see Laura was not going to tell me why she was here until she felt more relaxed, and I reckoned the best place for that was the sofa in my kitchen.

———

"D'you live around here?" General questions were best, as if we were chatting in a pub.

"Weston."

"Weston-Super-Mare?" She gave a nod and I added, "My family have a caravan at Brean Down."

"Oh, right."

"Been there long?"

"Yes, all my life. I live with my mum and dad."

"No shame in that; my brother's only just moving out and he's older than me."

"I did live away. For four years. I joined the Royal Navy when I was sixteen."

"Sounds an interesting career."

"Yeah. I loved it. I did all sorts. I got my able seaman certificate and saw loads of countries—the Philippines, Libya ... seven seas, and all that. I left it a few months back."

I thought navy life would suit her. She looked beefy enough to haul ropes around capstans, and smart enough to read sensors. "What made you leave?"

"I got ill. A virus, something a bit foreign, I think."

"What was it?"

"It didn't really get, sort of *diagnosed*, you know? I just kept getting these symptoms. The Royal Navy don't like you being sick. I had to work twelve months notice."

"If you were ill, surely they'd discharge you."

"I dunno," said Laura. I could feel the distress coming off her like a scent.

"Sorry—none of my business, I suppose. I'm just curious about how such things operate. What is it that makes you feel ill?"

"Sometimes, I just ... can't breathe. It gets so bad I think I'm going to suffocate."

"But you don't?"

"And this buzzing. Inside my head. It stopped me doing my job."

A silence grew between us. We were at opposite ends of my sofa, leaning against the squidgy arms. My mind went back to Dennon's experience of PMA. "Laura," I said, at last, "this didn't start with taking ... something ... like on shore somewhere, some night club?"

"Definitely not. We like our grog, us ratings."

"Can you pinpoint a moment it all began?"

"No," said Laura, and although I was sure she wasn't lying to me, for some reason I didn't think this was the entire truth, either.

"What's happened since you've been home? Are you feeling better now?"

"Not really. It's getting worse, if I'm honest."

"More buzzing and shortness of breath?"

"Then there's the spinning. The room spins and I'm shaking."

"Have you seen a doctor, Laura?"

"Er ... yeah. They're rubbish, aren't they?" Laura held her mug like a child, two hands around it. She blew on the surface before drinking the coffee in one go. I reckoned that might be a sailor's habit; get it down you before it slides off the boat. It had also occurred to me that coffee might be the worst thing she could drink.

"Is this why you've come to me today?" I asked eventually. "Because the doctor couldn't help you?"

Her eyes filmed with tears, but she held her mouth firm.

"I'd better let you know my rates, and how I work. And I'll ask you to fill out the form I have, just a general info and health check. Okay?"

She managed a nod. I got up from the sofa to fetch the papers without looking back. I took my time doing this, because Laura had started crying properly; silent sobs were choking out of her.

I came back with a big box of tissues and the paperwork. I explained my fees to Laura as she mopped her eyes. She seemed calmer after her good cry; she concentrated on what I was saying and happily filled out my questionnaire.

"I won't ask for a fee this visit," I said. "You were distraught when you made the decision to come today, and you may very well decide a more regular treatment is better for you."

"What d'you mean?"

"Okay; I'm betting your doctor told you that you were having panic attacks."

"I get pains in my chest, everything. I can feel my heart beating!" She tapped her hand on her breast bone, a fast rhythm that was close to the speed of the drumming on the Tor. "I get awful sick. I vomit, sometimes."

"I know that sounds physical, but these things could still be related to a full-blown panic attack."

"I don't have anything to panic over!"

We both thought about that. I asked her about life in the Royal Navy, how close to action she'd got, what sort of boats she'd been on. At some point in her career, I was betting, she'd been terrified and the feeling hadn't left her.

"I loved my job," she said, in reply. "I was never afraid as a rating—not like this. Not sickening fear over nothing."

"I'm just wondering if the fear comes after or before the rest of the attack. Perhaps there's an element of anticipation?"

She bowed her head. "That's what the doctor said."

"Coming to me needn't interfere with what your doctor might recommend. There's medication, and some good techniques you can learn if you see a psychotherapist." Laura had no job; she was probably not well off and she could ask for Cognitive Therapy on the NHS. I could teach Laura those techniques myself (my counselling certificate gave me plenty of practice), but I wouldn't want to take her money unless she was sure.

"My friend said you were good. She's had massages with you and said she'd really trust you."

"That's kind." I let out a long breath then explained how I would travel as a shaman into her otherworld to search for the deeper problems that had given rise to her symptoms. "Finding out what triggered this might be a tremendous help. And seeing as it started when you were abroad and at work, once you've discovered the trigger, you'll probably be able to totally dismiss the fears about it."

"Do you think?"

I looked at her carefully. "That's one possible scenario, Laura. Only the spirits know what the others might be."

"Okay." She took her mobile out of her jeans' back pocket and examined it, as if it might ring at any second. It was switched off.

"If you want to call anyone, you could go into the therapy room to give you some privacy."

"There's no one I want to ring."

I had a sudden thought. "Did you tell you parents you were coming here?" I watched her gaze swivel away from me and knew I'd guessed right. "Do you think you should let them know?"

"I'm not a child."

"No. 'Course not." I gave her a broad grin and hoped it didn't look too false. "Maybe this is enough for one day, though. At our next appointment, we can start working properly. If you've got anything on you now that might help me journey into your otherworld, that would help us both."

"On me?"

"Yeah, like anything you might carry that really means something to you, that you wouldn't mind me having for a while."

"Like what?"

"Something that represents the inner you. A little object that has a nice memory, or something you wear constantly, perhaps."

Laura looked at her hands. They were bare of rings, and her neck looked bare of chains The little hoop earrings were her only jewellery. "I might have something at home."

"Okay, next time will do."

"Could I come again tomorrow?"

"That seems rather quick, Laura."

"Don't you have any appointment time tomorrow?"

I shifted my position, crossing my legs. I had plenty of time tomorrow. "Okay. We could say eleven, if you like."

"Eleven it is. Thank you."

I leaned and grasped her fidgeting hands. "You can see your doctor as well as me, Laura. It won't affect what we do together. Being calmer will only help. I'm more long-term. After all, you don't want to be on tablets for too long."

"Yeah." It was hard to catch Laura's gaze, but finally she looked at me. "Tracey was right; you're really nice."

"But I'm not cheap, am I?"

"That's fine. I've got money saved." She gave a proper smile. "It's easy to save when you're in the Royal Navy."

Once Laura had gone, I went into the therapy room and started a notebook for her. I put down everything everything we'd talked through, but also the impressions I'd picked up; all those presentiments that passed through my mind. I sat, thinking about Laura Munroe. She'd managed to pack a lot of life into twenty years. At her age, I'd only just got going. Somewhere along the way, she'd encountered something that was making her life unbearable. It's always horrid if you don't know why you feel the way you do. When I'd squeezed her hands, I'd been hoping for a more subtle contact with her energies, but all I got was what I'd already worked out from her body language: tense, vaguely unhappy, defensive. She seemed uncomfortable in her own skin.

I copied her next appointment into my phone and clipped her questionnaire into her file. She'd truthfully listed the symptoms she'd spoken of. Apart from that, she seemed perfectly healthy.

Like Alys.

My central candle was still flaming, strong and steady. I blew it out, thinking of Alys. She'd danced like a demon all night, full of vigour, exploding with joy. Then she'd dropped to the ground, as if she'd worn enchanted slippers which had danced away her life.

I picked up my phone and dialled for Wolfsbane. "Hi, Wolfs. How are things?"

"Things are shit. Brice phoned me. Apparently there will have to be an inquest and as next of kin, he can call witnesses."

"That might be so."

"He wants to call me."

"Does he know about the problems with the flying tea?"

73

"There are no problems with the flying tea, right?"

"What about Stefan?"

"What about him?"

"Something went on between the two of you, after the Tor. You were at each other's—"

"Sabbie. Don't talk about that now. It's over. Forgotten."

"Wasn't it about … you know … the tea?"

"It was about his rental fees. The man's crazy if he thinks he can charge over the odds at a time like this, when there's precious few bookings."

"We ought to get together and talk about doing the workshop."

"Okay, Sabbie. One thing will be different though."

"What?"

"We won't be using Stonedown Farm."

I wished I'd spent more time with Brice Hollingberry while he was at Stonedown Farm. Wished I hadn't been put off by his shiny new car and the way he'd carried a laptop bag up to his room, as if he didn't intend to leave work behind him. Now it almost felt too late, as if I shouldn't poke my nose into his desperate business.

In the end I put my reservations to one side and rang him.

"Hello?"

"It's Sabbie Dare here, Brice. How are you?"

"I'm … er … I'm good, thank you."

"I just wanted to ring to say how dreadfully sorry I am about Alys."

"Oh, I should say thanks to you. You were the one that phoned the ambulance, weren't you?"

"Yes. Brice . . . I hope you've got your family there, supporting you."

"Yeah, my mum and dad are staying. And Alys's parents, well, they've gone back now, but they'll be, yeah, I guess, in touch, you know? There's a lot to sort out. A lot to do."

"Brice, I'm so, so sorry. It was—she was—"

"It sucks, Sabbie. It fucking sucks."

"If I can help, please tell me. I know I'm miles away, but is there anything I can do?"

"Er, no . . . not anything. Well, yes, actually. You could come to the inquest. Apparently it will just open and adjourn, but I want to be there and I don't think my parents fancy the long trip in one day and my mates will be working. I wouldn't say no to some local support. It's going to be held at Wells."

"Okay. I can do that. When is it?"

"Friday at midday. Do you know Wells?"

"A bit. I can't think where inquests are held, but I can find out and meet you there."

"Thanks, Sabbie, I appreciate that."

"It will be nice to see you, Brice."

He hung up then. I hadn't expected him to say it would be nice to see me.

I laid my mobile flat on the kitchen working top and stared at it. I felt shaky as I thought of Brice, of being left without the one you love, the one you thought you'd be with always.

I remembered how Alys had sat up in bed, ill with cramps before going up the Tor. Her head had seemed a bit too big for her body, and the skin across her cheekbones had shone, as though it was stretched and thin. I'd brought her blister packs of painkillers from Esme's bathroom cabinet. She'd taken two ibuprofen and clipped the rest of the packet into the purse on her bed. Could that be part of the possible causes of her death? Probably it was nothing at all.

A nausea welled up in me. Death was like stage magic, it seemed. *Poof!* and you're gone—solid matter, flesh, bone, pulsating blood. So horribly vulnerable to attack. So easy to destroy.

SEVEN

REY

AT ALMOST NINE THAT night, Rey turned up with a couple of take-away curries, lentil for me, beef for him. I watched Rey has he un-wrapped the food, lining the naan bread, yogurts, and pickles up on the coffee table, savouring him as if he was part of the goodies. A heavyweight kind of guy, with finger-width, shrew-colour hair clipped tight, his scalp showing pale beneath. The lights were dim and his eyes looked their greenest; they flashed at me as he straightened from the coffee table. I took a step towards him and put my hand on the day's growth of beard. It felt as bristly as a teasel. My head reached his chin, and I had to lean back to touch his cheek. As I did so, he drove his arms round me and kissed my mouth, hard, urgent, long, and rough.

"Food'll get cold," I pointed out, a problem we'd encountered before.

"Yeah, I guess."

We poured the wine and chose a TV channel and snuggled up on the sofa with our plates. It was bliss; an hour of normality. I didn't even mention Alys, but I couldn't stop thinking about her and Brice, and the aborted workshop.

The ten o'clock news came on the telly and the realization came over me that the headline might be *Death on Glastonbury Tor!* I zapped it off.

"Hey, I was watching that!"

"I've got something I want to talk about."

"What?"

"The solstice?"

There was a pause. Rey was a policeman—he didn't like questions he couldn't readily answer. "That was ... yesterday, yeah?"

"Yes. I was supposed to be in Glastonbury for the next three days."

Another pause. "You're back early?'

A little screw of anger drove into my belly. He hadn't noticed I was home early, that I was not my usual chatty self.

"Sorry, Sabbie. I should have realized."

Apologies always disarm me. The anger slipped away and I felt like crying. "Didn't you hear in the station? About the Tor ... as the sun came up?"

"No." He sat up straight. "Criminal activity? Don't tell me your friend Wolfsbane was involved."

"A girl died."

"How?"

"We don't know. She just ... dropped."

"Hell. And you witnessed that?"

"She was there with her husband, Brice. They're Londoners, in their thirties. Bankers. Pretty loaded."

"You knew her?"

"She was a member of the workshop, Rey. Someone new, as well. We cancelled the entire thing."

"Don't you have any idea why she died?"

"She was fit, underweight if anything, certainly not the sort who'd have a heart problem. And she was having fun! Dancing, laughing..."

"Drinking?"

"No. Well, not unless her sports bottle was full of vodka. She said it was isotonic stuff."

"That's a shitty thing to happen."

"I wondered if they'd be doing a postmortem."

"Perhaps. This doesn't sound like a suspicious death, so the police wouldn't be directly involved. And it's outside my patch."

"Brice said the inquest would be in Wells."

"That sounds right. The coroner's court have their own co-oped police department to investigate such things—or rather, the word I should use is *enquire*. They don't investigate, as such."

"Wolfsbane said that Brice can choose who gives evidence at the inquest."

"Now that's *not* the case. Only the coroner can summon witnesses, and anyone so summoned must attend if they live in this country. They'd listen to what Brice had to say about the circumstances and if he mentioned Wolfsbane as an interested party—"

"*Interested?*"

"Someone who might have information relevant to the death."

"No one really knows what's relevant yet."

"People do know, Sabbie. They know if they've done wrong, or if they saw something untoward."

He pulled me into his chest and I rested my forehead on his jumper. I'd bought him that jumper for his birthday in May. It was a Fair Isle pattern and very warm. I didn't think Rey looked after himself in his cold, bare, rather grubby flat. I sobbed into the complex pattern, wondering if the colours might run. Rey found a hanky in his trouser pocket and dabbed at the wetness around my eyes.

"Brice has asked me to go with him to the inquest," I said, sniffing. "I was surprised to be asked. He must have tons of people he knows better than me."

"He's taking advice. He'll have spoken the liaison officer, they always recommend someone not directly involved—emotionally involved, I mean. He'll need someone like that when the inquest is resumed and all the evidence is heard."

"When will that be?"

"They have to gather their findings. It could be six weeks. Complex cases can be six months."

"That's awful. You'd want it over and done, wouldn't you?"

"It's like everything else, Sabbie, there's a shortage of staff and a waiting list."

I wondered if Brice had realized this, and if I was going to be the one that would have to explain.

"How long do toxicology reports take?"

He gave me the look I knew so well. "So she *had* taken drugs."

"She didn't honestly look the type, but they were all over the Tor. There were people screaming out, asking who had what." It was possible drugs were all over Stonedown Farm, but I kept that to myself.

"Sounds like death by misadventure to me."

I'd always loved that word. *Misadventure.* It summoned up nineteenth-century explorers in pith helmets, striking out through unknown jungle territory, or people dangling off mountains by ropes. Now I knew what it meant. The death of someone dancing.

Dancing, dropping, dying.

Misadventure.

"Brice sounded very stoic. Probably bankers are. They try not to let their feelings be shown, or at least known."

"Bankers don't have any feelings at all."

"What, like policemen, you mean?"

He laughed. "No, not like us. We're full of feelings, us. It's why there are guidelines to good policing nowadays. Because we used to let our feelings show . . ." He trailed off.

I lifted my head from his jumper and stared at him. His mouth was a straight line, the lips sucked to thinness.

"What is it, Rey?"

"God, nothing. You've got your own worries."

"Don't be daft." I sat properly up. "Here's me going on about this and I didn't even pick up that there's something wrong. There is, isn't there?"

"Not at all. I just hate corruption cases. The evidence is all over the shop . . . what one person said to another person, overheard by someone else about what some burke expected to be paid . . . And Pippa likes to play things by the book, which I can understand, but the old ways were . . . well, quicker, if nothing else."

"You're a maverick cop. Can't change that."

"An old dog who likes the old tricks."

"That's my Rey." I backtracked through several beats. "Who's Pippa?"

"She's the new DS."

"You didn't mention you had a new Detective Sergeant."

"Must have. They've finally replaced Gary Abbott."

"Pippa as in …"

"Philippa, I suppose. Pippa she likes to be called. Pippa Chaisey."

"Good name for a cop. *I chaisey the baddies.*" I was summoning up images of Pippa Chaisey, chasing the baddies, and in my mind, her big breasts flopped as she ran on legs that went up to her polished uniform buttons. I tried dismissing this fantasy from my mind. With any luck, she scraped her hair into a bun and had a complexion like a Worcester apple.

"It's a tricky case is all."

"You've had them before, eh?"

"Once or twice. Nothing to worry about. I'm really sorry about this Alys."

"And to top that, one of my hens has been taken. Florence. She was my favourite."

"Taken?"

"Yeah, maybe by a fox, Mr. *Reynard* Buckley." I'd met Rey the morning after a fox took three of my chickens last year. In my mind, I'd named the culprit Reynard, after the fairy tale fox. When Rey knocked on my door, I wasn't at all sure what the universe was trying to tell me—sometimes I still wasn't.

"That's the pits."

I got up and cleared the food away. It meant I could compose myself, get rid of the lump in my throat. I didn't want Rey thinking I was maudlin over a hen. Meanwhile, he stretched full out on the sofa and put the news back on.

I took my time, swilling the disposables ready for collection and washing the cutlery. I came back with two fresh glasses of wine and leaned against the breakfast bar, right between him and the screen.

"Sabbie, I'm wa—"

"Yes, I know. You're watching that. Like you live here, or something."

I had his full attention. "You're a bit sore. 'Course you are. Nasty business witnessing a sudden death. Important night of the year for you, the solstice. It must have shaken you up."

"It's made me think, yes."

He didn't reply, but he did have the decency to reach for the remote and turn the TV off.

"I love seeing you, Rey, you know I do. I love you coming here like this, bringing food, sharing normal stuff."

"You're saying we're getting a bit too settled? A bit too 'telly on the sofa'?"

"I don't dislike that. We both lead unsettled lives. Neither of us knows when work will finish for the day; heck, I don't even know when mine will begin. But ..." I trailed off. I was hoping he'd start guessing.

"Sabbie, are you trying to tell me something?"

"If you like, yes."

"Only, I thought we were good. I mean, I thought we were okay, seeing each other whenever we can. I know we don't go out a lot. I don't do 'wine and dine', you know that. Aren't you happy? You have to tell me if you're not happy."

"Yep. I'm happy. Really—I'm happy."

"Right." His hand fingered the remote.

"I see you a lot of you, for a cop. And I'm good with you being here; your place is so small it's not fit for canine habitation. I love it when you get up in the morning and shower for work, but you're using up all my toiletries and the team at work must be thinking you smell a bit … flowery."

He frowned. "You want me to replace the stuff I used? Of course I can—"

"What I want is for you to bring your own."

"Shower gel?"

"Suitcase."

"Huh?"

"God, Rey, however do you solve crimes if you can't unravel the clues? Oh, yeah, of course; you leave it all to Chaisey."

He frowned. He was still not getting it. "This is about Pippa?"

"Most certainly this is not about Pippa," I lied. "It's about us. I'm asking you, oh Detective Inspector, if you fancy moving in with me."

"Move in?" I watched his face. There was genuine surprise in his eyes. He had not suspected I would ask, had not considered this. I peered closer, looking for some sign that he was pleased. "Well, ah …"

"It would be cheaper."

"Yeah, I guess …"

"Two can live as cheaply, etcetera, etcetera."

"You might be right."

"But I'm not on the nail, am I?"

"What? Oh, well, Sabbie, give me a second to get my head around the idea."

I waited, one moment, two. Rey didn't mean a "second." He meant proper time. Twenty-four hours … a week.

"Do you like the idea? I mean, on principle?"

"Yes." Finally, I'd squeezed a smile out of my man. "The principle is tempting. Indeed. It's just … it's just I have, well, ties."

And there we had it. The thing I'd suspected all along. Rey was thinking he would have to discuss this with Lesley, who had not been his wife for almost three years. Who had her own life and a partner she lived with. Yet Rey thought of himself as still married. He liked having a girlfriend. He was allowed a girlfriend. Living together was a step too far.

I sat on the sofa and picked up his hand, the one loitering by the remote. "It's okay. It was just an idea. You know, like in a brainstorm. You put crazy ideas into the pot and throw most of them out again. So just... throw it out."

"I don't know if it works like that."

Something crawled up my spine, something that felt like apprehension. What had I done?

"The thought was there. We threw it out. Gone!" I flashed a smile.

Rey laid his head on my shoulder, then slid it down so that it was resting on my breasts. "Let's go to bed, huh?"

———

In the morning, I got up earlier than Rey, before there was any light in the sky. I didn't even wait for my phone to alarm; I'd been awake for a little while.

I put on the bread machine and took a shower before Rey stole all the hot water. I meditated for twenty minutes. Dawn began to break as I went into the garden. It was going to be a glorious day, I could smell it in the sharp air.

I fed the hens their pellets. There was still no Florence. A pang went through me. I'd been hoping I'd made a mistake about her disappearance; that she'd been hiding under the straw all the time. I

85

recognized the sensation of expecting a miracle to occur and the overwhelming disappointment in remembering that miracles don't happen. Not this sort, anyway.

I was to blame. The hens were my responsibility, and I was always fobbing them off onto the Wraxalls.

She was one hen, I told myself roughly. *Get over it.*

I waited until there was full light in the sky before I did the thing I'd so missed doing on the Tor; the Salute to the Sun.

I was in the middle of the yogic postures and the chanting, when I realized Rey was watching me. I jumped as I saw him, staring through the open back door.

"Hi."

"What's that you're doing?"

"Saluting the sun." I held out a hand. "Join me?"

To my delight, he came out. I showed him the moves and their meaning, and he copied my words, coming in just half a second after me all the way through.

"Oh, shining one, radiant one."

"… radiant one …"

"Dispeller of darkness and bringer of activity."

"… activity …"

"Who illuminates, all-pervading, bright one."

"… all-pervading …"

"Giver of nourishment. Giver of fulfillment. Giver of light with infinite rays."

"Like me. Infinite Reys!"

"Whose golden brilliance is friendly to all."

"Friendly to all," chanted Rey. "Hmm, all, yeah—good and bad alike, I'm sorry to say."

I put my hands on my hips. "Can you forget being a copper for two sorry seconds?"

Rey thought about this. "Nope. Don't think so." He pulled me to him. "I enjoyed that."

"You were taking the piss out of it."

He kissed my forehead as if I was a child. "Sabbie, get used to it. I always take the piss."

EIGHT
LAURA

AT FIVE TO ELEVEN, Laura Munroe was outside my door.

"Hi. Come on in."

Candles guttered as we entered the therapy room. The scent of sage came into my nostrils. I took her over to the wicker chairs to let her get settled. She looked pale, but she was a natural mid-blonde, with eyes a faded blue, like late hydrangeas. Yesterday, she'd highlighted them with a little makeup, but today she wore none, which might have been the reason she appeared so wan.

"How are you?"

"Okay. Well, it hasn't been long, has it?"

I laughed. "You're right there." I told her about the dream diary I wanted her to start, then I asked, "Did you find anything for me to get close to your otherworld during my journeys?"

Laura's face went a little blank. I was sure she hadn't even bothered to look, which surprised me because it didn't tally with the desperation coming off her. She dug into a pocket and pulled out her key ring. She detached a little mascot and passed the toy to me. It was made of stuffed felt, with a yellow body, a pink smile, crescent-moon ears, and a little apron of white. The short loop of ribbon which had kept it on the key ring grew from its head. The creature was worn and a little grubby. Loved, in other words. It felt weightless in my palm.

Suddenly it clicked. "Pokémon!"

"Yeah. I was potty about it when I was a kid. This was my favourite, Raichu. Don't know why, except it took me a long time to get this one evolved, so maybe that's it."

I was trying to remember how the game went, but it probably didn't matter too much.

"He used to hang above my bed. When I packed to go away, I knew I couldn't take kids' stuff, but I reckoned Raichu didn't count; he was small enough to get hidden somewhere. Hitch a ride, like. Will he do?"

"Definitely. You chose him above all others to accompany you on your adventures."

"Oh, yeah!"

"Sixteen is early to leave home. What made you go?"

"Er ... poor exam results, mostly. I hated school. I only did well in sport and I've always loved boats. All my happiest memories are of boats. Living in Weston, you see a lot of them, mostly out on the Channel, moving towards Avonmouth to unload, but people have Ribs or motorboats, so I was always able to cadge a trip out. I got good at it. It seemed a natural way to go."

"What did your parents feel about the Royal Navy?"

Laura was silent for a while, not because she was refusing to answer, more that she was remembering and it had stoppered her.

"They didn't want me to go but they had to sign, because I was a minor."

"They must be relieved to have you back safe."

A spasm crossed her face. "I'm not safe, am I?"

I nodded slowly. I didn't want to diminish her fears as groundless. "I'd like us to undertake a journey together, to start our work." I gestured to the sets of floor cushions I'd arranged and explained to Laura how I would use my plaited cord, as the Lady of the River had directed me. I held out the white, green, and brown silk plait to show her.

"We will both go into the otherworld. Linked to you, I will be able to find your otherworld and start working out what the spirits want us to do. Linked to me, Laura, you might find your power animal."

"I don't think I've got a power animal."

"You've probably got more than one. I believe we all have otherworld guides and guardians, right through our life. When I tell people this, they often say, well, yes, I do have an affinity with this animal or that; they remember moments when an animal tried to communicate with them. So today, when we journey with my silken cord, I'd like you to see what happens."

"Wooo, scary," she said, leaning back. Then she thought for a moment. "Why should that be scary?"

"It's not, but it's good to be cautious." I spent a little time explaining how she should build a safe portal into her otherworld. "I want you to flesh it out, add to it, explore it. Don't forget to look behind you, as new journeyers often do. Don't go wandering off, though. Stay safe. All you have to do is wait for your power animal to arrive. They mostly come up from the Lower Realms, so knocking can help summon them, or stamping with your foot. Ask any animal who arrives, 'Are you my power animal?' When you get the right response, you'll know."

"Okay. Let's go for it."

I gave her a scarf to cover her eyes and draped the cord round both our wrists. I settled myself by placing the little Pokémon mascot on my solar plexus, one hand over it. The drumming CD led me into my shaman's portal, the stream glittering and chattering over its bed of stones.

———

"Trendle?"

I caught the brightness of my otter's eyes in the thicket of willows on the other side of the brook.

To get across, I would have to feel my way through the rush of water. I pulled my black dress up high and stepped in. It was almost up to my knees, especially where it pooled around and spat at me. The bottom was uneven; gravel that cut into my soles and slippy stones that were poorly balanced. As I contended with this, a tune song came into my head, deep gritty guitar chords with a slow beat.

I had to let go of my skirt to scramble up the bank, and the hem got wet. I could feel it slap against my ankles as I made for the thicket of thin willows. I blamed the tune revolving in my mind. I shook my ears to get rid of it.

In the thicket I passed an old-fashioned wooden fingerpost, the outline of a pointing hand with a single finger reaching out. I was sure it hadn't been here before. I pushed through the willows in the direction it pointed, bare twigs scratching at my arms and tangling my hair. I kept going until I found a path leading alongside the stream. I was sure this was the same stream that flowed through my safe haven, but here a wall of rocks rose up, as if the stream lay at the bottom of a gorge. I spotted Trendle's strong tail, flashing as he trotted ahead. The same catchy tune was in my head, people singing, their harmonies close and the guitar riffs powerfully measured to a drumbeat that worked well with the drum on my CD.

I often heard music in my journeys. Sometimes it's the music of the spheres, but this was off-putting—a pop tune I couldn't identify and I couldn't get rid of.

I rounded the bend. Ahead of me, water gushed down a crevice into the stream. To go farther, I would have to cross the foaming waterfall. I looked up, hoping for some help. Almost hidden by the fall of water was a slashed opening in the gorge wall, as high as a man and only slightly wider than my shoulders. I eased myself in and looked around. Daylight fell on sheer stone walls; no moss or ferns on damp ledges, no stalactites or odd-shaped boulders. No bats leaving their sleeping space.

"Trendle?" His yellow eyes flashed in the darkness. The tunnel of the cave curved slightly and after a few more footsteps the light disappeared. I could see nothing.

"Far enough for today," said Trendle. He turned and made for the entrance, swift on little legs. His silhouette flickered like a shadow against the dull cave wall. Then he was gone, leaving me in total darkness.

"Trendle," I called. "Trendle come back, guide me out. Trendle!"

In my distress I called his name aloud. The trance lifted. I lay on my back for a few seconds, waiting for my heart to steady. I pulled the scarf from my eyes and unwound the braid from my wrist, but didn't disturb Laura. I sat crossed-legged for a minute or two, thinking about the journey, my fingers laced round my toes to keep them warm.

I'd never found the waterfall and cave before, and I believed I'd successfully reached Laura's otherworld.

I tried to get the tune I'd heard back into my head, but it had gone. In Laura's notebook, I wrote out the few lyrics I'd hummed but could not place.

———

Laura stirred herself naturally and came over to the desk holding the cord out to me. I passed her a notebook. "The account of the journey is in here."

She sat with a thump, staring at the book in her hand but unable to open it. "What, is it like a story?"

"I don't always experience a story, sometimes I see an imaginary landscape, or have a long conversation with a spirit guide. This time my journey was chocked full of symbolism. I'm hoping some will mean something to you. And I'd like to blow the images I have into your subtle body ... what some people call their aura ... so that you can intuitively start to make sense of them."

She didn't open the notebook. My account was the unknown, and that was a fearful thing.

"There were four symbols," I went on. "A fingerpost—I've drawn a representation on the page for you; a waterfall—the thin, mare's-tail type, falling a great height; and a cave right behind the waterfall. And a tune—I only picked up a snatch of the lyrics. I didn't know the song and I've already forgotten the way it goes."

Finally Laura opened the notebook. I gave her time to read through what I'd put, but she looked up almost immediately, and her face, which had been pinched with uncertainty, lit up. "'Shape Shifter!'" The smile glowed from her eyes.

"Pardon?"

"I know this song. It's by one of my favourite groups. Local Natives."

"I've never heard of them."

"They are still a bit underground over here. Big in the States. I just love their sound, sort of fusion of pop and folk and soul. I used to play that album, *Gorilla Manor,* over and over on board the ship. You need slowish stuff because there's no room to dance about."

"Local Natives." I felt relief that the song was real and delight that Laura recognized it. It meant I could be certain I'd been in Laura's otherworld.

"I got to see them in Portugal, while we were stationed at Gibraltar. They were mammoth."

"Laura, are you saying the song is called 'Shape Shifter'?"

"Yeah, why?"

"Would shape shifting mean anything to you, outside that song?"

"No, nothing."

It felt far more than a coincidence, so soon after the aborted shape-shifting workshop, and I wondered if the lyrics had been offered to me simply to bind me and Laura closer, make us a team.

"What about the other symbols ... fingerpost, waterfall, cave?"

"Sorry, no."

"Okay, I'll gift them to you shamanically, see if that helps prompt anything."

We went over to the floor cushions and Laura lay on her back, eyes closed, as I visualized each symbol in turn, blowing them through the funnel of my cupped hands into her solar plexus. I left her lying there, hoping that her mind would settle and clear, and that the images would become implanted within her deep psyche, but after a moment or two, she got up and joined me at the desk.

"Even if there are no associations right this minute, they may come to you in the week ahead. Be sure to jot anything that comes to mind in the notebook."

She nodded, but her lips were clamped together as if she was afraid to speak.

"How did you get on in your journey, Laura?"

"Dunno. This ... er ... a baby chicken came to me, yeah. It was all ... fluffy ... yellow ... cheepy ..."

I thought of the chicks I'd had a year ago and had to control my chuckles. "What did it say?"

"It said it was my power animal." She made a scoffing sound. "Not much power there, if you ask me. Not much *animal* to be honest."

"Right." Even I wasn't entirely sure how to take this result. "Let's just see how it goes. This spirit animal might appear in dreams, now. Keep a dream-eye open and write down anything it says or does along with any other dreams you have." She looked at me with a solid expression, as if not sure about this, so I battled on. "There's something else that has occurred to me. If your doctor offered you a diagnosis you're clearly not happy with, maybe you should ask them to go through the standard tests for your breathing and your heart. Maybe your parents could back you up with that."

"I guess ..." She checked her big fat watch, noting she'd had an hour. She prized herself out of the wicker chair, slid her fingers into her back pocket, and put the right money in cash on my desk. "I wish I could be better for them. They worry too much."

"You've told them about me, haven't you?"

Her face was full of alarm. "If I look at it through their eyes, I must be a pain to them. I don't come out my room, except to raid the kitchen. I've put on pounds, eating crap. I don't really blame them ..." She turned away, stopping in front my altar, looking at things but not touching. Sailors must be trained not to touch unless they know what will happen if they do. "Mum never stops going on at me. So then I start to row, and then I yell, and then I slam my door again."

"Sorry, I didn't mean to push. It would be useful to know if a doctor has been of any help to you."

"They got Daniel. He's a nurse. He came to the house."

"What did he say?"

"Oh, just ... panic attacks ... depression."

Her face was like sand. I felt my heart fluttering under my shamanic dress, as if copying Laura's attacks. "Daniel left you tablets, perhaps?"

"Uh, yeah. He made an appointment for me to see this doctor. Waring. But, uh ..." She lifted her hands in supplication. "What good would it do? I didn't want it! They were all getting at me. Nag, nag! Mum, Dad, Daniel, Dr. Waring. Getting at me!"

"They didn't mean you any harm, Laura."

"They did! They did! I couldn't think how to stop them! I got on my bike and drove here!"

She put her hands over her chest and dragged fast breaths in, one after the other, shoving them out again as if her windpipe had narrowed. "Ugh!" She bent forward as if about to puke. "Ugh, ugh!"

I got out my of chair, making my movements steady and smooth. I stood behind her because I didn't want to crowd her in. I put my hands over her shoulders and gave them a steady squeeze, as when beginning a Reiki treatment. "I'm channeling some energy into you, Laura, some calm feelings," I whispered. "Breathe out; breathe out, as well as in. That will help. Empty your lungs, fill them with fresh air."

I could see she was trying, but the hyperventilation had overcome her now. She was heading towards a full panic attack.

"Think where you are, Laura."

"Where—I—am?"

"You're in safety. No one is nagging. No one is telling you anything. No one is..."

"Coming—for—me!" She twisted round. Her face was layered with sweat. "They—were—coming for me!"

"Pardon?"

She shook her head, unable to speak as the breathing rose to a crescendo.

"Would you like to lie down?"

She flung herself onto the floor cushions, curling onto her side, whimpering like hurt dog.

I dropped the fleece over her and touched her forehead with my hands, cleansing her with Reiki. "Don't be afraid. It's almost over, isn't it? Just keep remembering to empty your lungs and gently fill them. It's almost over, now."

The minutes it took for Laura to be calm again felt endless. Eventually she let her body relax and her breathing steadied and she precipitated into sleep, as if a great release had come over her.

I moved away and began writing my notes—everything I knew and everything I wondered about Laura Munroe.

Five minutes later, I heard her suck in a waking breath and roll onto her back.

"It was Mum, mostly." She spoke to the ceiling. "She wanted it. She said it would sort everything out. Just a week, and I'd be better. And, I'm like, 'How? Exactly?' She got Dad on her side. They phoned Daniel and told him I'd agreed, which was a fat lie, of course. They packed my case. I felt like a child again, like when your parents come into your room and you're in bed and they're up and dressed and they're moving around you, telling you how your day will be and putting out the cutesy clothes they've chosen for you to wear. They said Daniel was coming at eleven o'clock and he'd explain things to me and then they'd drive me in. Just for a week. Then I'd be better."

"Where did Daniel want you to go?"

She was quiet for so long that I didn't think she was up to answering. Then she said, "Juniper Ward, HDU, Weston General Hospital. It's only up the road. It's got a sea view. They said I'd like it." She shuddered. "I found your card, that Tracey gave me, and rang you. I had to get out. I did leave a note."

I tried to get my head around what she was saying. "You came here because you were due to be admitted into an acute psychiatric ward?"

"Yeah." She sat up, crossing her legs. She shook herself as if trying to mask a shudder. "How horrible would such a place be? Filled with ghosts, that's what I think, what I'm imagining. Looney zombies, walking around with glazed eyes. Mumbling to themselves. Accosting you—the sane one, you'd have to think—with crazy notions. It's a black-and-white horror film, isn't it? It can't really be like that nowadays, can it?"

"The unknown is always terrifying."

"Stupid, though."

98

"The thing that strikes me, Laura, is that you didn't have an attack. Not in that particular case. You got me on the phone, wrote out a note, got on your bike. You acted. You didn't panic."

"Not ... badly, no."

"Is that surprising?"

"I guess if I was honest, I've known from the beginning that it's inside me, what causes this. When Mum got chili in her eye, I was fine. Like I was in the Navy. Capable and quick thinking." She smiled. "That was on my report: 'Competent and destined to go far.'"

I shook my head. Maybe Laura should have stayed in the Navy. Things had not got better at home, and surely there had to be facilities for sick people in the armed services.

"What happened when you got back yesterday?"

"I didn't go back. I stayed in a B&B."

"You haven't seen your parents since yesterday?"

"I texted to say I was okay." She took a deep breath. "I have to go back to it, don't I?"

"I think your work report was right. You're a courageous person. Clear-headed. Perhaps better when things are right in front of you. Like an emergency to deal with. But this isn't clear cut; it's impossible to *see* what the problem is."

"Could you find that out? My problem?"

"I'll try. In the meantime, you should go home. Talk to Daniel. I don't think you've done that yet, have you?" She shook her head, and I continued. "Tell him about me, about where you've been. Tell him you feel capable now of being treated at home. He won't make you go into the ward if you can persuade him you won't hurt yourself and you will take the treatments offered."

"Okay." Her face cleared. "Yeah. They can't force me, can they?"

"I'm sure they can't. So, from now on, if you want to keep on seeing me, we should probably arrange a weekly appointment. We would make six appointments, over six weeks. At the end of that time we can evaluate how things are going. How does that sound?"

"We can't do it quicker?"

"You can't hurry the spirit world. If you try, guides and guardians tend to get annoyed and less communicative."

"Oh. Only … I feel …"

"Despairing." It was vibrating off her. "Do you remember me saying how shamanic therapy would be a long-term solution? Every time I work with you, you'll go home and do some further work yourself."

She nodded. "Okay."

"If you don't mind, I'll keep your Pokémon for a while."

"Raichu," said Laura. She got up and went over to the desk. She picked up her toy and gave him a snatched kiss. "Call him Raichu."

NINE
THE RED KNIGHT

THE GREEN KNIGHT IS not dead.

The acolyte has scoured the papers for news reports—nothing—
no account of a mysterious death or even a short piece on a mugging. The Green Knight has disappeared into oblivion. Yet the acolyte
can clearly recall the roughness of the stone in his grip, the wrench
in his shoulder as it flew. He'd seen the Green Knight fall. And Morgan had whispered, *your work here is complete.* Hadn't she?

Today he's back in Glastonbury, his first time since ... since the
day the damsel fell. Since the dolorous blow was struck. The thread
pulled and pulled at him until he could stay away no longer.

Morgan le Fay is standing outside the grounds of Glastonbury
Abbey. Almost at once, his head is plugged up with her. She takes a
hard, long look at him and pain slices through his scalp.

She disappears into the abbey grounds, unheard and unseen,
shifting her shape from visible to invisible.

The acolyte waits in a short queue and pays at the booth. He's given a little map of the grounds, which he holds before him. High Altar, Lady Chapel, Fish Pond, Abbot's Kitchen. He moves away from the constant stream of tourists … or perhaps they move from him, as he mumbles the things he needs to be ready to say to Morgan.

All at once, he's at the edge of a cool, green space. Monuments crumble over the lawns. It should be a place of deep peace, but the ruins of the abbey are filled with a shocking clamour. There's bedlam in his head, a noise like dentists and blacksmiths, full of screech. It splits his aching brain into molecules, into atoms; it splits the atoms.

Morgan is waiting beside what must be the Holy Thorn, a magnificent hawthorn, so old it has crutches propping up its boughs. The acolyte lurches towards his mistress.

"You are found lacking, acolyte." She is seething with anger. "A knight rapes a maiden until she lies there, lifeless. Your only duty was to strike him down. *Not* make him falter. *Not* watch him stumble. Strike him down! *FALL!* Life from life!"

The Green Knight cannot die. That is the story, the legend. However many times you slice through his neck, he returns. He tries to explain this, spurting words out of his plugged up, tortured head.

Someone skirts by them, then doubles back. "Are you okay?"

A tourist guide, dressed for the part—medieval costume of a rusty red cloak pinned at the neck and beneath it a belted tunic with a heraldic design, a red dragon.

"There's a terrible noise," the acolyte says.

"Yes, we're sorry for that. They're doing some repairs to the Lady Chapel. Reconstruction work on the crypt. We're trying to prevent winter flooding."

"Are you a monk?"

"I'm a knight, actually." The man smiles. "I'm here to answer any questions…"

The acolyte only half hears, his hands over his ears against the dentists and the blacksmiths drilling on and on, dark and bleak. He glances at Morgan. Her face is ablaze with irritation. She mouths at him. *Red Knight.*

The Red Knight is a thief who steals even from King Arthur.

She wants him to take down the Red Knight, he knows it even before she demands it. Strike him down. Not make him falter. Not make him stumble. Fall. Life from life.

The acolyte follows Morgan over the clipped grass and the Red Knight comes too. In fact, he's ahead, talking talking talking as he walks backwards, gesturing with his hands, explaining the disaster of the flooding in the crypt, leading them between galvanized crowd barriers and into the Lady Chapel.

There's no roof. Just the high stone walls and a bridge that spans the chapel's depths. The acolyte clings to the rail, looking down at men in helmets and yellow jackets like something out of a kid's cartoon. There are pneumatic drills, chisels, mallets, and long sharp poles that lift the flagstones laid five hundred years ago by monks, pulling them apart, piece by piece. Above, a scaffolder is building his cage of poles and planks up the walls of the chapel, dangling off his platform, working with a series of thuds and clunks and clangs. An electric hand drill buzzes; he can feel it boring down into his teeth.

And in his ear, the Red Knight, talking talking talking.

He feels shitty. Nauseated, shivery as a newborn pup.

"I know why is the crypt flooded," he tells the Red Knight. He's shouting, but he only knows this because his throat is raw from the words. "It's the wasteland! The dolorous blow. The land ravaged. Neglected. Everything will die in the land of Britain. It's the story of the wounded king, and the wasting of the land of Logres!"

Morgan slants a look, a message without words. *Get rid of him or I'll toss him over the bridge.* And she could. He knows well the extent of Morgan le Fay's sorcery; she can trap a person with her mind and play with them, using a level of control that allows her to alter bodily movements, speech, even thoughts. For entertainment's sake, she uses her magic on the random herd of humanity, compelling the pedestrian ahead to trip over his own feet, forcing the woman browsing the shop window to weep without warning.

The acolyte uses his shoulder and hip to pin the Red Knight to the bridge rail. "Go now, before she tosses you over," he hisses.

He means it as a fair warning. He closes his eyes on them, contending with the throb in his head. When he starts awake again, he's alone. Morgan some way off, staring at a metal sign imbedded on a pole in the grass.

"Read it!"

Her constant edge of impatience makes his headache worse. He swallows over a dry throat. He tries to breathe, but he can't. In the end, Morgan has to read it.

"'*The site of the ancient graveyard where in 1190 the monks dug to find the tombs of Arthur and his Guinevere . . .*' King Arthur Pendragon. The only marked grave of the Sleeping King."

Selkie walks over the grave, which is invisible in the grass, as if bored by this, as if Sleeping Kings were threepence each. His bright cat tongue licks each side of his mouth and his blue gaze stretches away, over the wall of the abbey, over the tops of the green trees. He can see the Tor rising in the distance. The place where the maiden died.

Morgan le Fay lifts the cat from the grave by its underbelly and strokes its head with ring-glinting fingers. "This surely must be the place."

"Place?"

"That day is enshrined in me. The journey across the marshes with Arthur, mortally wounded." Her eyes glitter. "We sat around him, you know, in the bow and in the stern. Nine maidens of Avalon. Slipped from wetland into roofless tunnels. A river inside the hill, wide and black, deeper, deeper, and then—a vaulted basilica with gilded pillars. Arthur resting on swansdown under silken canopies, his crown bright gold in the light of our flares. His knights hoisted the Bell of Doomsday."

"The Bell of Doomsday," the acolyte whispers.

"They lay down, still wearing their arms, feet pointing towards the sarcophagus, and slept. We left him there, his cool cheeks damp with our tears."

Out of the corner of his eye, the acolyte watches the Red Knight. He's with a party of babbling kids. He leads them into a stubby building with an octagonal roof. The acolyte checks his map. The Abbot's Kitchen.

Inside, the kitchen is garish; paint-and-plaster food, raw meat, and bread. The acolyte stays at the door, where the flagstones are loose and broken. A good-sized corner chunk snapped off, flat as a book and as easy to hold, but with a deadly edge.

The babble of kids move on, shepherded by their teacher.

"Excuse me?" They signal to the Red Knight as he leaves the Abbot's Kitchen. "We're looking for the gateway to the Tor."

"Not far. A mile in that direction. Make for the Chalice Well—"

"We don't want the route for tourists," Morgan spits. "Any fool can find that for themselves. We search for its nucleus. The basilica in the hollow of the hill. The place of the interregnum of Arthur Pendragon."

The Red Knight gapes. The acolyte remembers that the Red Knight is here only to answer questions. "Where is the tunnel that can take us there?" he asks. "I've read that the old monks used it."

Since the acolyte warned the Red Knight off, he's been less talkative with them. He tries to walk on, but the acolyte takes a leaf from his book and steps in front of him. "The tunnel to the Hollow Hill?"

The man laughs. "There was a tunnel uncovered, oh, forty years ago. It was nothing but a medieval drain."

"Monks used it to go into the hollow of the hill!"

"Okay. Well, it was blocked up. Health and safety."

The acolyte snatches at his russet cloak. "Show us."

"Look, please, sir; I'll have to ask you to keep your voice down. This is the abbey grounds." The Red Knight says no more. He walks away, fast, glancing behind to where they are watching him.

Morgan leans in. "I say we should follow the Red Knight, and in a quiet place, take the thing that is to hand, and pound and pound until he drops like a stone."

The acolyte looks down at the doorstep below his feet. He eases the corner of the broken slab from its place. Yes. It feels right. "Life from life," he whispers.

Loving Morgan le Fay is like stepping on hot coals. Like lighting a garden fire, watching it grow fierce, and, on the opposite side, visible through the flames, there she is. Silent but calling. He would just … walk through … over the hot coals … there's no alternative. It had been like that from the beginning.

He first saw her at the library. He'd been taking out his usual pile of books. She'd asked if he needed the one on the top, a book on astrology. Sun signs. How to understand the age-old method of reading destinies.

"I'm hooked on that sort of thing, aren't you?" she'd said. "I have the sun in Gemini and the moon in Libra. It's a combination that makes me glow bright, but makes me also a little ethereal. What is your ascendancy?

"I … I'm not sure. I won't find out, will I, if you pinch this book."

She had laughed, so infectious. "I like to travel. I do so all the time. Life is never dull with my chart the way it is."

The paving stone digs into his palm. They're both moving fast, now, and when the Red Knight glances back, he sees that they are following. The Red Knight begins to run.

"Go!" Morgan whispers. "Life from life!"

He doesn't think about it. He can't, his head is too full of clang. His teeth are throbbing with the drill. He keeps his shoulders low and the bit of paving slab behind his back and sprints, full at the tilt. The Red Knight slips out of sight between low-lying bushes. They burst after him into a small copse of trees.

"*Pound and pound,*" Morgan screeches.

The Red Knight glances round. His brow furrows, as if he can't comprehend what is happening and yet knows all too well. The cloak swirls out like a girl's dancing skirt. The acolyte makes a heroic dash and snatches at it, pulling the Red Knight full under the darkness of the trees.

"Whatchyu-watchyou-gerrofff …"

The cloak tightens around his neck until the pin that secures it springs away. The guy unbalances. He thuds onto the ground. He lets out a strangled "ugh," but he's winded only for seconds, then is struggling up.

The acolyte steps in and uses his elbow as a club. The knight topples backwards. His eyes have gone wild, he's swatting his hands at the acolyte, eyeing the corner of paving stone. He lets out a shout of alarm—high—almost a scream. For a second, they are looking at each other. It's a connection. All along the Red Knight set out to mislead and prevent them from finding their way into the Hollow Hill.

The acolyte drives the point of the paving stone into the man's scull. There is a soft sound. Wet. There is a lot of red. It smears his hands and the knight's face. The smell makes him heave. He wipes his hands on the man's red cloak.

"My work here is achieved," he whispers. He doesn't care if Morgan hears him or not.

TEN

ESME

ALYS'S INQUEST WAS OPENED, using formal terms and legal confir-
mations, and then adjourned. The Coroner's Office was still waiting
for the full outcome of the autopsy and the toxicology tests. As soon
as those were complete, Brice could start to arrange the funeral.

"It's taking a heck of a time," Brice said to me, as we left the Town
Hall. His voice was as thin as a washed-out rag. When I had spoken to
him on the phone he sounded bright and in control, but face-to-face,
he was grey, his eyes pulled back into their sockets. "I need a drink."

I led the way into the Crown. I thought a nice hotel would be better than some dingy watering place. Brice was kitted out in a suit and
tie, and it felt right to take him somewhere civilized. Besides, I didn't
want to face the possibility that he'd get too wasted to drive. I made
him order a sandwich to accompany his drink.

"Glad to get this over with?" I asked as we found a quiet corner.

"That was the easy part, wasn't it?" He bit into his chicken and ham on wholemeal and chewed as if it was transforming into cardboard in his mouth. "I'm now contending with rumour. All this talk about toxicology; people are hinting that Alys must have taken something. That wasn't her. She was into her fitness. At the gym three times a week. She ran marathons, you know."

"I didn't, but looking at her figure, I should have guessed. Very toned."

"Whatever she did, she gave it the full wellie."

"Did she work for the same bank as you?"

"Yes, but not in the same department, or even the same building. We met at orientation. It was my first day and hers too. She's in the auditing department. I'm a manager at a branch on the South Bank. She actually earns more than me, not that it ever mattered to us."

"She sounds an amazing person."

"She is. Was. No, *is*. Amazing. You can still be amazing after death, can't you?"

"I think the memories of Alys will always be amazing."

He nodded for a long time. "They will."

"Are your parents still staying with you?"

"No, they've gone back now. It was a bit cramped in our flat and hotel prices in London are silly in the summer."

"Yes, of course."

"I told them to go. I have to get back into the groove, haven't I?"

"The groove?"

"Work, seeing mates, living my life, I guess."

"Can't be easy."

"Nope." Brice was picking the sandwich apart. "They've given me this pamphlet thing. 'The Stages of Grieving'. I've never read such crap in my life."

"I don't think it's supposed to dictate how you should feel, Brice, just give you a route—"

"I don't want a route, thank you."

"You're not finding the pamphlet a help, then?"

"No, because it's trying to tell me that, in the end, it will all be better. I don't want that. I don't want *better*."

"You said yourself you had to get back in the groove."

"Yeah. Earn money. Keep a roof over my head. Eat to stay alive."

"I didn't know her well, Brice, but maybe Alys would want you to do that."

"And I *am*. I *am* doing that. I just don't want to be told that right now I should be feeling fucking depressed or fucking guilty or fucking angry."

I tried a smile. "Even if you are fucking angry, eh?"

"Yeah. Even if."

"Some people find those pamphlets quite a support."

"I can't believe that anyone actually wants to feel better. To 're-cover.' I want Alys back. If I can't have her back, I can pretend, at least. Talk to her. Dream about her. I love it when people talk about her. Not that they do, much."

"People don't find it easy."

"Correct. D'you know what I think? They should make those pamphlets for all the others. The people who know the bereaved 'loved one.' Tell *them* what to do. Because mostly, people are fucking useless."

I nodded. At that moment, I had great sympathy with anyone who felt useless.

Brice directed a morsel of chicken towards his mouth. "It was her idea, of course," he said, having finally managed to swallow. "The whole stupid Tor experience."

"Shell said something about that. How Alys had been wanting to spend summer solstice on the Tor for ages."

"What else did Shell say about her?" I felt his eyes bore into me. Did Brice know that Alys hadn't felt well that day? Surely the pathologist knew that. "Did you speak to Alys? What did she say to you?"

"Mostly that Anagarika was a jerk."

That made him laugh. "I've started to think what Alys would like at her funeral. Naturally, Alys didn't think she'd *need* a funeral. I know she'd like some ritual elements to it and I want to be inclusive of people she thought of as friends."

"Who you invite is up to you."

"Anag got my fucking goat."

"He's a dickhead, Brice."

"Even so, I guess I'd include him. For a start. I need to clap eyes on him again, because ... well, did he look to you like the practical joke sort?"

My heart gave one big thump. "What d'you mean?"

"I was sitting in that bloody hospital. We weren't being told much, at first, but then they put us in a room. There were flowers in a vase and a tray of tea and I'm thinking—uh-oh. Then they tell us. They ask if I'd like to view the body. They don't ask if I'd like to be sick, but, hey. Fucking awful. Shell's let off that; she'd gone back for my car. So I go in, on my own, and Alys is lying there. Like she's asleep, Sabbie!"

He began to study his phone.

"So then Alys's parents go in and I'm back staring at the four walls and vase of flowers on my own and ping, an email arrives." He tapped the screen to its side and pushed the phone towards me. "Fucking bizarre."

I felt oddly shy of reading his email. The wording was in a fancy font, as if written with a calligraphy pen.

It has begun. The dancing damsel, the maiden from the well, was cut down on the hallowed hill with a dolorous blow. The wasteland is upon us, a desert of death. Those who laughed—those who pushed forward to gloat—have been punished. The Green Knight has been taken down and others will perish likewise if they bring opprobrium to the ancient land of Logres.

Morgan le Fay

I looked up, blinking in the sun pouring in through the pub window. The words felt like lead in my mind.

"What's that about, Sabbie?"

I shrugged, perplexed.

"You know … about these things."

"Who sent you this?"

"Not a clue. I almost deleted it, but I'm glad I didn't." He took back the phone, adjusted the screen, and pushed it back to me across the table. "Because, today, day of the inquest, of all fucking days, ping!"

The Tor needs no sacrifice. This utter waste of blessed life signals doomsday. The wasteland creeps over Logres. We are all witnesses to the slow destruction. Before it is too late, we must

113

wake the Sleeping King, yet the passage from the abbey grounds into the Hollow Hill has been blocked. The Red Knight is both thief and liar and has been fatally struck.

Morgan le Fay

"These are appalling," I said. "You should report them."

"I don't want to show them around. Actually, I've shown no one but you."

"The police could find the source faster than it takes to swallow a pint. There's probably some Internet law this 'Morgan le Fay' could be questioned under."

"I don't want to involve the police in Alys's death. Frankly, I don't plan to do anything about this. That's what this Morgan wants. She want me confused … I dunno … upset." Pain stretched across Brice's mouth. "The email leads nowhere. I got one of the IT guys at work to trace the address; she had no success. I tried a Google search, but that was crazy. Morgan le Fay is all over the Internet."

"A lot of pagans take names like that."

"One of them has a dumb perception of a very stupid gag."

"You don't know who might have sent this?"

"No. I thought you might. You mix with all those Glastonbury types."

"You think this is someone Alys met on the Tor?"

"Or in that house."

"Stonedown Farm?"

He pushed his plate back and looked steadily at me. "You might as well know that I hated the entire experience. I hated almost every-one I met during it. Even if Alys and I had got back … unscathed … I would never have wanted to repeat it. Alys asked me to go with her, and I did. I will regret that I didn't dissuade her for the rest of my life."

"Brice, could you forward those emails?"

I passed him my business card, which had my email address on it, and he fiddled again with his phone. "Done. Now I can delete the vile things. I don't understand a word of them anyway. What is all this knight shit?"

"The Green Knight is a legend, an Arthurian myth. And Morgan le Fay was King Arthur's half sister. Logres is an old name for England, I think. I've never heard of the Red Knight, but I bet some scholar in medieval literature would be able to tell us."

"I'd better hit the road." He stood, patting his pockets for his car keys. "You were the only one, Sabbie. Of all the people at Stonedown, the only one knew I could trust."

—————

When Brice had left the bar, I got my own phone out. The two emails were sitting in my inbox. I read the words again, then again. They were crazy; senseless, yet, horrifically, they made plain sense. I wondered if a crime had been committed in their sending. I was sure Rey could tell me. Maybe he could get some tech nerd at the station who owed him a favour to trace the email address to a computer.

I got in the Vauxhall and drove the five or so miles that separated Wells from Glastonbury. I planned to collect my drum from Stonedown Farm before going home. I'd texted Stefan to that effect. There'd been no reply, but I had a feeling Stefan and Esme were less than rigorous about locking doors, so even if they were out, I could still pick it up if I left a note.

Twenty minutes later I was parking by the pillared front door. Stonedown Farm hadn't lived up to its farming title for decades. Stefan McKiddie had inherited the entire thing from his uncle, the last in a line of local farmers. He'd immediately put the two hundred acres of land up for auction, leaving a little copse of native trees with an ancient pet cemetery at its centre, an acre paddock wherein Esme kept a wild-eyed but well-groomed Arab, and a pleasant bit of lawn at the back of the house. Stefan had lived on the proceeds of that auction ever since. Not that he and Esme didn't work. Stefan ran his psycho-spiritual and counselling services from an outhouse in the garden and Esme was a potter whose bowls and jugs fetched good prices. She came out of the house when she heard my car roll over the gravel.

"Did Stefan get my text?"

"He's not here."

Esme was what Gloria would have called big-boned; her shoulders loomed over averaged-size individuals like me. From well-muscled arms dangled big hands that were ideal for controlling the fast spin of the potter's wheel. She hid her high forehead with fringed scarves tied as thick bandanas. Oddly, her cumbersome figure was the one thing that endeared me to her and helped me forgive all the bitchy asides and cold stares.

"I'm hoping you found my drum." Actually, I didn't think Esme would have spotted it; she wasn't the sort who tidied up immediately after guests. She turned without further communication and stood, almost holding the door open for my impending departure, while I scurried into the workshop and gathered it up.

"I'm sorry to miss Stefan," I said as I returned to the hallway.

"I thought he'd be back by now. I suppose this sort of thing does take time."

"Business deal?" I asked. Stefan and Esme would never admit they engaged in "business," or ever did "deals," so it gave me great pleasure to watch her face.

"Actually, a friend of his was rushed to hospital."

"I'm sorry to hear that. Not serious I hope?"

"You could say so. He had his head bashed in."

"Goddess! That's awful."

"When I say 'friend', of course, I don't mean close friend. Just an acquaintance." She gazed past me as if hoping Stefan would roll down the drive and rescue her from hostess duties. "Between us, I'd say we know almost everyone of significance in Glastonbury. Wouldn't you?"

"Huh? Oh, sorry, yes, of course you do, Esme. You're part of almost every event."

"Stefan is the sort that can mix with all comers—pagan, Christian, Buddhist ..." She nodded a couple of times, to confirm the statement.

"Nice of Stefan to support this guy."

"Hmm. I can't see why he has to spend all day hovering over the chap's bed."

"Will he pull through?"

"Who knows? I certainly don't. This chap does voluntary stints in the Glastonbury Abbey grounds. The story runs that they found him in some bushes, bleeding from a head wound." A smile flickered. "Not good for the abbey's image, methinks."

"That's shocking."

"It's the world, though, Sabbie, isn't it. It's a nasty world, out there."

I was thinking about the nasty world inside Esme's head, but I kept my peace, giving her a sweet smile. "I haven't asked how you are."

She sighed and leaned against the doorpost. "I've been trying to persuade Stefan to stop the workshops. I hate having our home invaded."

"Okay, Esme. I'm sorry we walked in on you. I had no idea you were all rowing in there. Maybe you don't know, but Wolfs was worried that Stefan might have been trying to sell drugs to the workshoppers."

She narrowed her eyes. "Stefan isn't a pusher. Or a handler of any kind."

"I'm sorry if I've got the wrong end of the stick. I don't know why that row blew up." I paused. "But you do. You were there. What *was* it about?"

Esme had a pale complexion, as if she avoided the sun wherever possible. Her cheeks turned rosy now, and she couldn't hold my gaze. "If you must know, Wolfsbane said something unforgivable."

"What about?" I shook away my instinctive response and managed to stay polite. "I'm sorry, Esme. I can't imagine Wolfs insulting anyone."

"Why are you sorry?" Esme adjusted the yellow scarf encircling her head. "It has nothing to do with you."

———

I drove away from Stonedown Farm with a lot to think about. I wasn't sure whether to believe Esme's version of events, because the

Wolfsbane I knew would never make an insulting comment about any person. I was wondering if they'd started out calmly discussing legal highs or price hikes, and, as things got heated, the insults had started flying. Esme would certainly want her two-penny's worth. Perhaps Wolfs had said something in the heat of the moment, something like *keep your bitchy nose out of this...* a phrase I'd had to swallow before now in Esme's company.

I was guessing that, once upon a time, Esme had been nice enough. Okay, perhaps the sort schoolgirl that would break friends with you and then taunt you from her position as gang leader, or the sort of roommate that asked to copy from your work when her hangover and her deadline clashed. Nice enough, in respect to, as she would put it herself, *the nasty world out there.*

Shortly after Esme hooked up with Stefan, her ceramic work had gone viral. Stonedown Farm was an ideal place to hangout if you were a potter, and Esme had always made pots. She'd decorated them with images of the Green Man or Cernunnos, the wild-wood god, and sold them in the shops along Glastonbury High Street for enough money to keep her in clay, at least. When she widened her designs, using more abstract images and bolder colours, she was offered exhibition space in a small London gallery and before she knew it, her pots were reaching silly prices at auction.

Almost imperceptibly, Esme changed. When she'd first met Stefan you could enjoy her company. Since then she'd developed a sneer that presumably extended to most of the human race, excluding only Stefan and any artist reaching more at auction that she was.

I was still trying to like Esme, but she didn't make it easy. If the victim with a bashed head had been a well-respected painter, she would have gone with Stefan to sit at his bedside. As it was, we were all just scum, now.

There was something else about that conversation knocking around at the back of my head. The guy in hospital had worked at Glastonbury Abbey.

I stopped in a lay-by and reread the second email.

The passage from the abbey grounds into the Hollow Hill has been blocked.

The wording was just as strange as on first read, but that strangeness suddenly felt chilling.

Until now, I had wondered why Morgan le Fay, whoever she was, picked out Brice for her nasty little joke. With a jolt, I saw that it might not be a joke at all.

Two mentions of the abbey grounds in less than two hours. There's an old saying I read somewhere, probably Facebook. *Once is happenstance. Twice is coincidence. Three times is enemy action.*

I thought it through as I sat in the lay-by and came to the conclusion that was all it was. Coincidence. Not weird enough to get me buzzing. I would wait for the third thing.

———

Or at least, I thought I would ... until I found myself in the abbey car park. I wasn't going to be long, so I left my flashers on in the hope any traffic warden would think I was seeking change for a ticket. Even the car park asphalt glowed in the sun and the dusty smell of the hot afternoon came into my nostrils. I went up to the pay booth for the abbey and hailed the chap inside. "Hi there!"

"Just one ticket?"

I'd already studied the entrance fee and knew I couldn't afford it. I'd been inside a couple of times in the past and was hoping I'd get away with some free information. I started out with a nice, fat lie. "I was here earlier, with my family, d'you remember me?"

"Not really, I wouldn't, I'm afraid. We get thousands passing through on a day like this."

I flashed him a glance, hoping it didn't have too much gratitude at the edges. "I was just wondering if you had any news on that poor volunteer who got attacked."

"Gerald Evens? Sorry, I don't. Bad business, wasn't it."

"Awful," I said, filing the name away. "I know he was taken to hospital. Stefan McKiddic is with him. I've just been talking to his partner, Esme, you know, out at Stonedown Farm?"

He nodded. "I don't know Stefan personally, but—"

"I suppose you see most of Glastonbury in here," I said.

"Oddly, no. We see the rest of the world—Americans, Europeans, Japanese…"

"Does someone called Morgan le Fay take an interest?"

"You mean as a Friend of Glastonbury Abbey?"

"That or someone who comes here on occasion?"

"I know a Morgan—a bloke."

"This is the full works. Morgan le Fay."

"Typical of the hippie types in the town. They're all Mikes and Johns, really, but they're not satisfied with the name they were given by their mothers. They all have to choose some fancy alternative."

"Not like Gerald."

"No. He was a solid churchgoer. That's why people volunteer, mostly. To give back to the church. He was a nice person."

121

"Was? He's not—"

"I don't know for certain. He wasn't saying much as they took him away." The man smiled at me, as if that thought would keep him going until Christmas.

"Do you mind if I ask you one more question?"

He inclined his head, offering a flash of female-pattern balding. "Please."

"Did Gerald have an argument or disagreement with anyone? Here in the grounds?"

"Someone called Morgan le Fay?"

"Yes," I said, my hope flaring.

"Gerald Evens couldn't have an argument with swarm of wasps. He's one of the gentlest persons I knew."

"I was more thinking, did someone pick a fight with him?"

"He never said."

"He wouldn't be able to, would he?"

He paused, observing me carefully. "Is there something you know about the accident? Because if there is …"

"I'm just shooting in the dark. I wish I did know something. Except, well, it was no accident, was it?"

The man folded his hands and I did the same, both of us contemplating that fact.

ELEVEN
BABETTE

I FELT EXHAUSTED WHEN I got home. I was hungry, but not in the mood for heavy cooking. I went into the garden and picked a bunch of salad leaves. I straightened my back, standing in the middle of the salad bed, and put my free hand on my brow to shade my sight from the long shafts of sunlight and shadows that come before a June summer dusk. I thought I'd detected some movement ... a crackling sound within the pea sticks. My heart was in my mouth as I crept forward. My pea sticks are all snaggy ends of branches and right in the centre of them I could see something white and grey. "Florence?" I called. My voice cracked as if I hadn't used it in days. "Flo, pretty Flo? Chuck-chuck-chuck?" I took one step too close and the bird flew up, with a heavy clattering of wings, landing in the big apple tree in the Wraxalls' garden. It was a collared dove, after my baby peas. I roared at it, waving my fist, as competent gardeners are supposed to do. In my heart I knew Florence had been a tasty meal for a nest of sparrowhawk chicks.

I put the salad leaves in my basket and pulled up some baby carrots and beetroot, thinning the rows as I went. These took ten minutes to scrub and head and tail, but once they were ready, I threw them into light oil with crushed garlic, some black pepper, and a final squeeze of lemon, knowing they would taste heavenly, hot or cold. I made an omelette, lavished the lot in mayo and wolfed it at the breakfast bar.

My eyes strayed to my drum, newly back from its adventures. I had experienced the most vivid and surprising journey at Stonedown, and I was convinced that was because I'd been drumming at the same time.

The Lower Realms were the place of the ancestors, where shamans are likely to find the spirits of the dead, ancestral souls who are waiting to move on or even staying to communicate with the spirits of the living. Shamans most easily access these realms by falling—into a well, down a drain ... or into the bole of an ancient oak. Why had Trendle led me there? Was it to communicate with the dead? *A wasted place, stagnant, despoiled*, the Lady of the River had described it. I *had* seen a wasteland, no doubt of that.

The message Brice had been sent by the enigmatic Morgan le Fay was imprinted in my head. ... *the wasteland creeps over Logres*. If there was a connection between the emails and the attack in Glastonbury Abbey, then it hardly surprised me that my otherworld journeys had already touched on this link.

I got up smartly and washed my dishes. I had to be kidding myself. Glastonbury could be uber-crazy, but even I couldn't believe one person would attack another because of a belief in the Wasteland of Logres.

I knew that legend well enough. It's a deeply symbolic story, seeped in ancient myth, from a time when plenty and starvation were hairsbreadths away from each other, back when man worshipped Earth goddesses and gods and believed that if a king was wounded, his land would also sicken. In the Arthurian tale, the wells of the land dry up when the maidens who look after them are raped or killed. Such wells held the people's drinking water and in such long-ago times, losing them would have led to famine and thirst.

One of King Arthur's knights searches through Logres for the grail, in the hope the land will become fruitful again. He reaches the castle of the Fisher King, who has been wounded and so is unfit to govern his kingdom. No branch holds a leaf. No field ripens with corn. The farmer's nightmare, then as now. In the story, the knight has to ask the right question of the Fisher King to heal the wasteland … but he doesn't know what that question is.

Did the Lower Realm I had seen in my journey link to Morgan le Fay's wasteland? Did I need to find the right question to heal it?

I was unsure about the new otherworld spirit I had met. In the light of the fire, his face had glowed deep bronze. A guardian, I was sure; an African shaman of great age and wisdom. The brew on the fire had been waiting for me, ready to add power to my silk braid, so that it could stretch out of the Lower Realm and glimpse the woodland I'd seen.

A red deer in a glade slanted with sun. So beautiful—the sort of scene people capture in art. I looked up from the sink. I *had* seen a picture just like that one. Where had I been? Not a gallery. I never go to galleries. In a magazine or book?

In a sketchpad.

Babette Johnson's sketchpad was lying in my desk drawer. I sat at the desk and turned the pages. My original evaluation that Babe would become a fine artist did not diminish this time round. I turned another of the wide pages and stopped in my tracks. A woodland sketch brought to life in pastel crayons—full summer, the sun setting. An awesome picture. And almost the exact scene I had witnessed so fully. Except there was no red deer.

I turned every page in the Babette's sketchpad, looking deeply into the pictures. She had drawn the forest creatures within her landscapes—ponies, butterflies, the odd bird overhead, sometimes herds of deer in the background—but nowhere had she depicted a solitary red hind with the imploring eyes that I had seen in my journey.

I went over to my bookcase and pulled out one of my books on shamanic symbols.

> The red deer, in its female form, is better called the hind. In ancient times, the Celts considered them sanctified. It was believed the fairies milked them and sometimes took their form. The skin of a hind deer was treasured and would alone be used to make the clothes of their high-status womenkind. A meeting with this magical beast could lead to enchantment. It could also be a harbinger of doom.

A sharp awareness hit me. This journey to the wasteland had occurred shortly before Ricky had told me about Babe—I could bet he'd been thinking about her in that circle, trying to psych himself up to ask me for my help. It made me wonder if I had descended to that Lower Realm simply to find Babe. And if Babe was in a Lower

Realm, that meant she wasn't of this world anymore. Except, I'd shifted realms when I'd stepped onto the threshold of the African shaman's hut. It was why he'd connected me to my silk braid, to stop me wandering. Maybe the woodland glade was Babe's otherworld—which meant Ricky was right to wonder if she could still be found.

I booted up my laptop. Of course there would be news reports about a missing girl. I tapped in "Babette Johnson" and waited. Suddenly, the search page was littered with sites, all on the subject of Babe. I closed my eyes against them.

They were full of loss.

MISSING NEW FOREST SCHOOLGIRL

Hampshire police put out an alert for a missing schoolgirl yesterday evening when she failed to return home from visiting a friend. It has now been disclosed that she did not reach the friend's house. Police have issued a recent photo of Babette Johnson, and ask that anyone who may have seen her in the last twenty-four hours contact them on the following helpline ...

MISSING GIRL: POLICE STEP UP SEARCH

Missing teenager Babette Johnson had not rowed with her parents before her disappearance, it was revealed today. At a press conference, Richard Johnson, nineteen, appealed for his sister to return home. "We love you so much. Every day without information is heartbreaking. Please, if anyone knows anything, phone the hotline." Police state that they are extending their search to the wider New Forest area ...

RECONSTRUCTION OF LAST KNOWN MOVEMENTS

A reconstruction of the last known movements of missing schoolgirl Babette Johnson was staged in the New Forest village where she lives. The 16-year-old was last seen walking through the village and down Pigend Lane, towards the home of a school friend. Police hope the reconstruction will bring new information as they continue their search. Babette's last movements were acted by a police cadet from the Hampshire Constabulary…

BABETTE JOHNSON; FIRST ANNIVERSARY

The first anniversary of the disappearance of teenager Babette Johnson has resulted in a fresh appeal for information from the public. The photograph that was released during the original search for the bright student features in the fresh appeal. Her family remain adamant that something has happened to her. "Babette would get in touch if she possibly could," her father said in a statement today. "And we are still asking people to be vigilant."

I sat in contemplation of this puzzle almost until it was time for bed. An early night would do me good. Tomorrow there was a full diary of clients plus my evening shift at a local drinker's pub, the Curate's Egg, and that mean a late night and a busy one.

———

Saturdays at the Curate's Egg didn't feel like work anymore. I'd grown fond, in an exasperated way, of Kev, the landlord, and Nige, the other member of the bar team. It was like getting paid for a night out—I knew all the regulars and they were mostly a laugh, and my mates would pop in on the way to somewhere else, or stay to listen to the live music. Tonight my friend and shamanic partner Marianne came in with her boyfriend, Geoff. They stayed for one drink; they had an office party to go to.

"I haven't been to a good party in ages," I told them.

"You can go to this one instead of us, if you like," said Marianne. "Our office parties are horrid. It is all about who will end up shagging whom, behind which photocopier."

Geoff laughed, but I was quite shocked. Marianne's first language is Dutch, and although her English is impeccable, it's also usually untainted with anything close to a rude word.

"The band's good," said Geoff.

"Yeah, one of Kev's better choices."

"Sort of a fusion between pop now and pop way-back-when."

We looked over at the group; singer, three guitars, and a drummer. They were way-back-when themselves, with Mick Jagger lines scored in their faces and a general lack of hair on their heads. They were giving us up-beat tunes and had balanced their speakers so that you could hear the lyrics. The crowd responded by getting up between the tables and bopping.

I started to talk about the solstice night on the Tor. It was good to share with someone who would understand; Marianne and I were part of a small group of pagans called the Temple of Elphame, and last midwinter we'd held a ritual in my garden to watch the dawn arrive. It would have been nice to do the same thing for the midsummer, but Juke and I had chosen to be in Glastonbury. We'd invited the rest of the group, but Garth and Stella had a very new baby and the others hadn't fancied it. I imagined they'd now be glad they'd stayed away.

"It is a dreadful thing," Marianne said.

"I actually hate the idea of ever going up the Tor again."

"Then you should go. And soon."

With that disquieting advice, Marianne and Geoff went on their reluctant way.

I kept my eye on the door as I worked, and at nine thirty I was rewarded. Rey pushed his way in, still wearing his work suit and looking dark under the rims of his eyes.

I hadn't seen anything of Rey since he'd brought the curry round, and I hadn't texted him since. Six months into being Rey's proper girlfriend, I was sanguine about his lack of spare time. He knew where I was if he was free of the demands of Avon and Somerset's Constabulary. I tossed him a toothy smile and was rewarded with a tired grin.

As he made it towards the bar, a woman came into the pub. Every eye in the room turned to her; every male eye, that was.

She strutted in, shrugging her shoulders out of her summer jacket and tossing her hair. Her hair took my breath away—a mass of waves the colour of pennies when they're newly minted. She'd parted this curtain of hair to one side to soften her high forehead. Between the curtains were eyes of unachievable deep blue that took your glance and refused to give it back, and a wanna-kiss-me mouth slashed with orange lippy.

The one good thing was that Rey hadn't noticed the woman at all. He got busy searching his inside jacket pocket for his wallet, but before I could say hi, I was shoved aside as Nige moved into action.

He leered at the woman. "What can I fix for you, miss? I don't believe I've seen you in here before. Would you like one of our on-the-house introductory cocktails?"

My mouth fell open. We didn't do "on-the-house introductions"—ever—and Nige had no idea how to mix a cocktail.

"I'll get these." Rey had found his wallet and was turning to the woman as if he'd known she'd been there all along. "Shiraz, isn't it?"

"Perfect," said the woman and stretched her fuckable mouth into a smile.

"Oh, Sabbie, this is Pippa. Remember I told you? Thought I'd bring her in to say hi."

"Hi, Sabbie," said Pippa, reining in the smile.

"What're *you* having?" Rey asked, as if I cared. "Usual vodka and tonic you never drink?"

"Er …" I wanted to squeal, *you are Pippa Chaisey?* and tip a pint over her Titian locks. I turned my back on them, since Nige had taken charge. I put up the big order for the band members, who were heading towards their halfway break. I carried the tray of drinks over and when I got back to the bar, Rey and his sidekick were gone. They'd miraculously found a table (I guessed Rey had flashed his ID or perhaps just bounced the previous occupants out of their seats). Rey lifted a hand and waved at me. I couldn't work out if he was hailing me as the barmaid or calling me over for a chat.

He surely knew I wouldn't have time to chat. I didn't *want* time to chat. What sort of conversation could you have with a woman who should be on the front cover of *Cosmopolitan* rather than sitting opposite your boyfriend?

"Isn't it time you went out for a ciggie?" I said to Nige.

"What? Okay, if you can cope."

"Don't worry about me, Nige. I can cope with anything."

I knew he'd be twenty minutes minimum, and as Kev was now chatting to the band, I could keep myself flat out busy. Even so, I found the time to cast a glance over to Rey and his new detective sergeant now and again. They certainly didn't need my small talk. They were engrossed in conversation. When Rey spoke, Chaisey listened with care. When Chaisey spoke, Rey nodded, earnestly. Once, he laughed at something she said.

I saw so little of Rey, and foolish thoughts ran through my head when he was away. I already had a pair of rivals. Number Two was his wife; fair enough, she'd been around a long time. Number One was his job. Nothing kept him from that. I hadn't reckoned on a Number Three, but here she was, drinking in my pub. A sensation washed through me, forcing me to lean against the beer taps while I controlled my breath.

"Sabbie?"

I started. Rey had come to the bar and was examining my face, as if I'd printed my thoughts over it.

"Are they working you too hard here? You've lost your sparkle."

I couldn't tell him that Pippa Chaisey was sucking all the sparkle out of me. I was lovesick, was all. Love ill.

"Sabbie, I'm so sorry I haven't been around more. Things are difficult."

"What things?"

"Oh … meetings and that. It's complicated. Anyway, how are you?"

"I'm still reeling, if the truth was known."

"The death on the Tor? I picked up something about it on the grapevine, but it's certainly not being handled as a criminal case."

"I went to the opening of the inquest with Alys's husband, Brice Hollingberry. I told him what you said about it all taking at least six weeks. He was cut up by the idea, so I hope you were right, Rey."

"He could try phoning the support service at the coroner's office to ask about the autopsy result. As he's the next of kin, they might give him a bit of a feeler up front."

"Really?"

"It does depend on the coroner, so I can't guarantee."

"I'll tell him that. You can guess how on edge he is. He didn't talk about what he thinks Alys died of, but he's always emphasizing her fitness and her ethical way of life. Perhaps he has suspicions he won't articulate."

"Recreational user?"

I shrugged. I had wondered if Brice had found out about Stefan's stash of tablets, and was waiting to pounce—to lay the blame at someone's door once he was sure of his facts.

"What hasn't helped is that Brice is receiving poison pen emails."

I passed my phone across the bar. Rey read both messages then gave me a slanted look. "When did he receive these?"

"At shitty times, when I think about it. The first came while he was still in the hospital with Alys. The second came before the inquest opened."

"There are a lot of weirdos out there. How many people witnessed Alys's death?"

"Gosh, maybe a hundred." I watched Rey's mouth curl into a smile. "Yeah, okay ... *maybe a hundred weirdos.*"

"Did I say that?" He raised his hands to ward off blows.

"Want to know the oddest thing about this?"

"I'm not sure. When it's you asking that question, I'm wary of what will come next."

"Well you might, Mr. Detective. Because the day the second message arrived, someone was attacked. They had their head bashed in.

133

They're still in hospital in a coma." I knew this because I had rung the hospital, pretended I was a friend, and checked up.

"And the connection is …"

"They were a volunteer at the abbey grounds."

"What?"

I tapped my finger on the screen. "'The passage from the abbey grounds into to the Hollow Hill has been blocked. The Red Knight is both thief and liar and has been fatally struck down.' This chap, Gerald Evens, was attacked there in the grounds."

"At the abbey?"

"Yes."

"There you go. Case solved when witness fingered alluring woman in gem-encrusted cloak."

"The police are investigating," I said, ignoring his sarcasm and hoping I was right. Rey shook his head. I knew that gesture and what he would say after it, so I said it for him. "I'm not going to get involved, Rey."

"Good. You always see harbingers and innuendoes."

I checked over to where Pippa Chaisey was steadily sipping her wine. Her legs were pushed away from the table, crossed above the knee. The heels on her shoes made a starting point that took the eye up and up. "That's because there often *are* harbingers and innuendoes."

"Huh?"

"You're not working tomorrow night, are you? Come over and I'll cook. You always say it helps the thinking processes to put some distance between you and a difficult case."

"Not tomorrow. Sometime soon, but … I'm not brilliant company at the moment."

I choked down the reply that he was here in the pub, being very good company to his companion. "You don't have to be brilliant company, Rey. That's not what our relationship's about."

"Hope not, with my low social skills rating."

"Do you want another round?"

"Not for me, and I think Pippa just has the one, before she turns in."

"Turning in now, are you?"

"I'm knackered. And there's paperwork waiting at home."

"Could you do one favour for me?" I searched his face. "Is that a 'no' before I've even told you what the favour is?"

"I'm a cop, Sabbie. I'm perceptive, astute. I don't have to ask. You want me to investigate these emails." He drained his glass. "I can't. That's the honest truth. Right this minute, there's no chance."

I could see Pippa was not going to wait any longer. She unwound her legs and came towards us. For the first time, I noticed she had freckles. They were dotted around the top of a neat nose, pale against her creamy skin. She arrived at the bar and gave me a caricature of a smile as she flicked her flaming hair out of the way and slung her big shiny bag over her shoulder. Just the right size for holding a big shiny gun.

"It's okay," I said. "I understand." I leaned over the bar, grabbed his jacket lapels, and lavished him with a lusty, possessive kiss. I kept it going for as long as I could then pulled away, leaving Rey lipstick-slavered and disheveled. "You go." I gave his lapels a shove. "Go home, both of you. Get some beauty sleep."

TWELVE
LAURA

TUESDAY MORNING I PREPPED my therapy room early. I had appointments all day, and I was keen to get to work. Laura Munroe
would be my first client at eleven, and I intended to work with the
little mascot she'd left me—the Pokémon figure. I set it on my palm.
Most Pokémon fans had an entire collection of cards and stuff; it
was odd to love just one figure. I'd missed out on the craze, so I'd
gone online to find out about Raichu. Apparently, he was the evolved
form of Pikachu, but he was neither a strong nor useful player.

I took a long drink of water, got changed into my shamanic gown,
and called power into my therapy room, lighting the candles and
incense. I lay on my back, rested Raichu on my stomach, and pulled
a scarf over my eyes. The drumming CD was already playing, but I
was slow getting settled into a deeper place. There was nothing making me feel uncomfortable as I lay on the cushions. Everything was as

it should be—the scarf wasn't tickling and I didn't have a sudden urge to scratch my leg or anything.

I tried my meditation technique, counting breaths until I forgot to count, then starting again from one. I was almost up to fifty when I finally lost the room and could feel heather beneath the soles of my feet. I took a breath of damp country air. There was a mist over the far meadows, a fairy-breath of whiteness, but when I looked more closely, I realized it was not mist. A gauze veil had been thrown over my vision. And Trendle was nowhere to be seen.

I opened my eyes and the trance lifted like the fairy mist. There was no point trying to continue. The journey had aborted because Trendle hadn't wanted to take me on it. I trusted my otter implicitly. Without him, I was no more than a wanderer on a rainbow bridge. I lay still, trying to think, stroking the tiny Pokémon mascot with one finger. Raichu wasn't a pretty thing. Like all loved toys, it was the worse for wear. Its yellow had faded, and one ear, which must have come unstitched, had been reattached with the wrong colour thread, as had the white patch of felt that constituted its apron.

There was something stuck under the apron. I could feel it with the pulp of my thumb. I sat up and looked closer. The inexpert stitching around the patch meant I could ease the foreign body out. It was nothing—a skinny bit of pink plastic. I rolled it between my fingers. Nothing at all. I got out Laura's notes to refresh my memory. Last appointment, she'd been given an odd little power animal—a fluffy chick. I had visited a cave in my journey and brought symbols back with me; a waterfall, a song, and a fingerpost. I looked at the sliver of plastic more closely. It did look eerily like a finger. I slid it back under the apron.

"How have things been, Laura?" I began. "D'you want to bring me up to speed?"

"Okay." She took a couple of deep breaths, in through her nose and out through her mouth. "I have seen Daniel."

"Good."

"Actually, it *was* good. We had a proper chat. With the stuff we'd done here, I didn't feel so scared of him. I asked if I had to go into hospital and straight away he said, no—no, not if I could successfully manage my medication at home. I asked him what the medication would do, and he said I could have antidepressants and a small dose of Valium, but I'd have to come off the Valium after a while. That sounded okay to me, so we've agreed on a sort of programme. I've got this plastic drugs dispenser so that they come ready to take and we're going to give that a month or so to see if it will work." She stopped for breath, but the emotions coming off her felt controlled and far more confident.

"Did he mention anything like cognitive therapy?"

"Yes, but there's a waiting list. He gave me exercises ... *strategies* ... to use when I panic. I told him about you, and all the certificates on your wall, and he said that you might help a lot."

I asked her to lie on the floor cushions so that I could I rattle her.

"Do what?"

I passed her my rattle, and explained that it was made of calfskin and beechwood by a craftsman called Freaky.

"Weird name, Freaky!"

"I've no idea what his real name is, but that's what everyone calls him. If you ever went to Glastonbury for the day, you'd probably see him. He sometimes sells his things from a blanket spread out by the church. He's lived there for decades. Since the end of the Swinging Sixties, you know? According to Freaky, the town was filled with hippies and they all lived under canvas around the Tor and spend their days drinking the spring water and communing with nature spirits. I guess Freaky must have been in his twenties then, but he still has lovely long dreadlocks. All the others have left over the years; finally joined the rat race, I guess, or bought houses in Glastonbury. Freaky lives in a caravan. He's a marvellous craftsman."

"Yes," said Laura, handing back the rattle. "It's beautiful."

"He wove his journeys of me into it. That makes it special and tremendously effective."

"What does it do?"

"Tells me things I'd never see with my actual eyes. When I rattle it over someone's prone figure, it works like a sort of subtle metal detector."

Laura burst out laughing. "What, you going to find gold inside me?"

"Maybe. We've all got some treasure, hidden away." Without further bidding, she lay on the cushions. I draped her with a fleece. "Just close your eyes, breathe naturally, and let your mind go wherever you want it to."

I stood for half a minute, to let her become still, and to attune myself to the rattle, which would speak most clearly if it and I were already working in harmony.

At first, I passed the rattle over her without direction, waiting and watching for a shift in perception, for movements in my mind. It was like dowsing; when water was hiding, the rod could tell you where. After a while I could see Laura's outline, floating under water, held steady by a sort of membrane. She was in a net, trapped like a dolphin. I couldn't see her breathe. I couldn't see any part of her vibrate with life.

I held the moment so that I could understand what I'd seen through the energy waves of my rattling. Then I put the rattle on my altar and dragged a cushion over so that I could perch next to Laura. She opened her eyes, sat up, and looked across at me.

"Is that it?"

"I'd like to tell you what I found in the rattling. It's to do with what Shamans call 'soul.'"

"My soul?" she asked.

"Yes. The spark of the divine within us, is how I'd put it."

"Isn't it the part of you that continues after death?"

"And continues through birth, if, like me, you believe in reincarnation."

"I think I do. Feels like more of a solid bet to me."

"In my mind, having a soul is tantamount to being alive. When we're born, we have enough energy to power us through our lives. The body and the soul work together, driving off each other. When someone as young as you loses that drive, I think that's because, somehow, their soul isn't fully operational. I think you've lost a part of your soul."

She gripped her hands together. "Sounds weird."

"It's a plausible explanation for feeling so out of control, so lacking in energy, and so ..." I ran out of words.

"So scared of nothing?"

I nodded. "Perhaps you're not scared of nothing. Perhaps you're scared because part of your soul is missing."

"That would scare anyone!"

"Instinctively, you arrived at my door. Because that's what shamans do. They search for shattered soul parts and retrieve them."

"Blimey," said Laura. "Like fishing?"

I thought of her, weightless and deathlike in her net. "I'm positive that this is my role now. To go in search of the part of your soul which is missing and retrieve it for you."

"Are you taking the piss?"

"No, Laura, that's how I work!"

"Okay. Okay, cool."

I stopped and breathed several times. "I was working with Raichu again this morning and noticed something about the little apron he wears."

"That's a part of his evolution—Raichu is an evolved Pokémon creature. His ears and his white belly are part of his evolved state."

"The white bit fell off, didn't it? Along with an ear."

"Yeah. Poor Raichu got some seriously bad treatment in the past."

"Who sewed him back together?"

"I did. I wasn't a great sewer until I joined the navy, though."

"There's something trapped in there."

"No there's not."

"See for yourself."

"No."

"It's easy to get it out because the stitching's broken."

She shook her head. "It's nothing."

"It certainly isn't much." I gave the toy a shake and the sliver of plastic fell into my palm. "But it is something. Isn't it, Laura?"

Two spots of red appeared over her cheekbones. She took a shuddering breath. "It's a thumb."

"Pardon?"

141

"A doll's thumb. From a Barbie."

"So it is! I knew I recognized it; I just couldn't figure where or how." I smiled at her, but my smile faded. Her plump shoulders had drooped forward. Her gaze was fixed on the floor between her knees. She was trembling, her entire body shaking, her face was burning with internal heat. I held her hand steady. "Remember your strategies."

"Strategies," she said. "Yes." She put a hand in front of her mouth and retched into the palm. Her breathing was wild. She scrabbled to get up, as if she couldn't find a comfortable position to breathe from.

"Why don't you lie down again."

"It … might …" Even her teeth had begun to chatter. "Might … help."

She rolled into a foetal ball and I covered her with fleeces. Her cries came through the inhalations like the whoops of a child with croup. "Oh! Oh!" I sat beside her, gripping her hands. She clung to me as if I was on dry land and she was dangling over deep water.

"Something's bubbling up, isn't it? So many clues. We should follow where they lead."

She took a slow, controlling breath and blew it out between pursed lips.

"There's Raichu, a cave, and a song. And a fingerpost—that reminds me of the Barbie doll thumb. Was she your Barbie?"

"Uh, yeah."

"Did you love her same as Raichu?"

"No. I hated Barbie."

"Is that why you cut off her thumb?" It seemed full of meaning, to me. She'd disfigured her doll—butchered it. "When you were small?"

"Laurie did it."

"Laurie?"

"What I used to call my pretend friend. You know, like little kids have."

"An invisible friend."

"Yeah ..." The squeeze of her hand stung mine. Her shoulders were shaking under the fleeces. "I'm so cold," she said.

I didn't want to leave her, even just to turn the heating up. I just held onto her hand.

"Do you remember cutting the thumb off?"

"I didn't! Laurie did it!"

"Okay, that's okay."

"It was just a thumb! Skinny, silk-haired creature."

"You didn't like her skinny body?"

"Laurie didn't like Barbie. We cut off all her hair. I chucked her under my bed. It was just a stupid *doll*, Sabbie."

She was quiet. I wondered if she'd fallen into an exhausted doze. Then she said, "You're right. I do feel a part of my soul is missing." Bit by bit, her colour returned. Her breathing quietened. The pressure from her fingers was firm, but the chill in them struck at me like steel.

THIRTEEN
SHELL

I⊤ was boiling ⊤he following day. I met Wolfsbane and Shell at a pavement table outside Heaphys where we could watch Glastonbury parade along its streets and in and out of the abbey gardens in summer finery.

Wolfsbane had promised to treat me to lunch and I thought it was only what I deserved. I didn't feel very supported by my long-standing mentor at the moment. I would have told him exactly how I felt about walking into a blazing row between him and Stefan so shortly after the entire workshop membership had witnessed a death at a sacred time and sacred place, but there seemed no point going over painful memories. Maybe it was the weather; it was too hot to quarrel.

Wolfsbane got us paninis and plates of carrot cake and a tray of cool drinks, and we tucked in.

"Best place to eat in the entire universe." Wolfs waved the food on his fork at the market cross. "Hub of the universe, in fact."

"Centre of its own zodiac," Shell pointed out.

"You're learning, gorgeous."

"I *can* read, actually," said Shell. "I bought some secondhand books while we were here for the solstice. I even spent an hour in the Glastonbury library. Which is amazing, by the way. I'll know more than you, soon, Wolfsie."

I hid a grin. Wolfsbane chose his girlfriends from outside the pagan community so that he couldn't be accused of mixing business and pleasure. He certainly hadn't made a play for me when we'd first met. Not that I'd assumed he would, or wanted him to. I don't like heavy smokers, and Wolfs's breath always smelt of tar products. And I've never fancied guys with goatee beards—Wolfs's habit of stroking his made me cringe for no reason. It was good that we weren't physically attracted; this was a man with astounding skills as a shaman, and our robust pupil-teacher relationship had grown into something close to a junior and senior partnership.

Wolfs tried to mould each of his girlfriends like raw clay, starting with a foundation template of buxom breasts, piles of dark hair, and uniformly empty minds chocked full of ga-ga-ness over Wolfsbane. But Shell was proving different. She was displaying a mind of her own in lots of ways. She'd recently chopped her hair into a thick bob and henna'd it until it flamed red. Also, I'd seen her flirt with Ricky. Wolfs wouldn't have like that one bit, had he known.

Not that I was going to tell him.

"Dion Fortune had the idea, didn't she?" Shell was saying. "About the zodiac on the Glastonbury landscape."

"Dion Fortune *ran* with the idea," said Wolfsbane. "She wasn't the instigator. That was Katharine Maltwood."

"I've been reading the stories, too," said Shell. "Balls of lights hovering over the Tor, people meeting strange beings when they're alone on the summit. I bet it's the place to find ecstasy."

She was staring at Wolfs intently and I remembered what she'd said about tantric sex on top the Tor.

Wolfs refused to take the hint. "You got the wrong idea, Shell. It's impossible to see the zodiac from up there."

"Whatever." Shell shrugged. "It's cool. I want to walk the labyrinth to the top of the Tor like Sabbie did. Then lie down in the cool grass, under moonlight ..."

As she talked, her earrings swung. They were the size of poker chips but finely enamelled to resemble the bright eyes at the end of peacock feathers. To set them off, she sported the shortened end of a peacock feather in her raffia sun hat.

"I love your earrings."

"Thanks. I make them myself."

"Wow! That's amazing!"

"I could make you a pair."

"Sounds good. How much d'you charge?"

"For you, they'd be complimentary."

"Thanks, Shell. I'll offer you a massage in return, if you like."

Wolfsbane drew a fresh ciggie from his pack and tapped it several times on the table. "Can we get back to the subject in hand? We have to decide when to hold the workshop ... and where to hold it."

"Is everyone committed to coming? Apart from Brice, obviously." I was determined that Freaky and Anagarika would not both be at the next workshop, but I did want a few more women, to prevent it from positively minging of football changing rooms. While I tried to find a way of putting this, Shell said, "Brice rang me yesterday. He's in absolute bits."

Wolfsbane inclined his head. "It's still very fresh."

"He said some cutting things about the workshop."

"There was no workshop."

"He didn't like the dynamic," Shell reported.

"He should have told me, not burden you."

"I was one of Alys's best friends. He can tell me what he wants."

"Yeah, but if he has criticisms "

"He is grieving, Wolfsie. Hurting."

"Of course."

"The memories are raw and we don't have a place to hold the workshop anyway," I said. "Have you considered just refunding everyone?"

There was a pause. Wolfsbane lit his cigarette and inhaled deeply, blowing the smoke gallantly away from our food.

"Darling," said Shell, "she has a point."

"I don't have enough left to give everyone their money back."

I found myself sharing glances with Shell. Naturally, finances were tight, but I'd assumed Wolfsbane made a reasonable living out of being a well-respected shaman.

"You could try holding it Bridgwater," I half joked. "It's better value."

"Might as well use Chippenham, in that case." Wolfsbane and I both lived in market towns in neighbouring counties and they were quite similar in some ways; neither big nor bold, but both proud of their history and their rivers. Chippenham was charming and perhaps a bit posher than homely Bridgwater. "I might attract punters from London, it's a direct run."

"At the very least, we need to get in touch with all the participants, talk them through the idea of holding the workshop elsewhere, and get some dates out of them."

"Good thinking, Sabbie. I'll action that to you, then."

"Right." Was I his employee, of sorts? It was a simple enough desk job. I looked away across the town square, trying to get on top of my vexation, shading my eyes from the sun. A familiar figure was sitting on the steps of the market cross, hugging his knees.

"That's Freaky," I said. "I'm going to say hi."

I walked the short distance and plonked down next to him. He glanced at me briefly but went back to turning a leather friendship bracelet round his wrist.

"Hey, what's up?"

"I'm good. Just catching my wind."

"And catching the sun?"

"The light has gone out of the sun for me, Sabbie. Midsummer, and I grieve for it."

"I know. I still feel the same about Alys."

"Alys is in the Summer Isles, now. The living is where the trouble always lies." Freaky took off his glasses, a tortoiseshell-rimmed pair that he'd had for longer than I'd known him, and wiped his eyes. "There is no homeland. No solidarity. No bond of communal feeling."

"What's happened, Freaky?"

"My caravan. I believed it to be a song to the god and the goddess. According to Stefan McKiddie, it's a sore sight for any eyes. A blot. He towed it out onto the road."

"What? Why did he do that?"

"My friend..." said Freaky. He trailed off. His lips were moist. I could see he was close to giving way. His hand went to his eyes again. I took his spectacles from him and gave them a much-needed cleaning with a tissue.

"Has this anything to do with the row Wolfsbane had with Stefan?"

"I think not. Except that it left Stef... vulnerable."

"Vulnerable! You mean cold-hearted."

"The Plods towed the caravan off the highway. Impounded. Fine to pay. Impossible, my dear, dear, friend."

"Look, Freaky... have you eaten today?" I got up and slid my hand under his arm, easing him into as standing position. We walked like an old couple over to the others. "Wolfsbane, will you get Freaky a panini?"

Wolfs didn't move for several seconds, as if he had to compute my words to make sense of them. Shell was already on her feet. "Fruit juice with your food, Freaky?"

"Could I plump for a hot chocolate? It's kinda warming."

Shell disappeared. I brought Wolfsbane up to speed and he finally woke himself, slapping Freaky on the arm in camaraderie. "That's the pits, mate. Pits. Sodding cops."

"Sodding Stefan McKiddie!" I added.

"Yep. Not filling the universe with love and light at the moment, is he?"

"I have a theory," said Freaky. "He's under the influence of a very malign spirit."

"From what plane?" asked Wolfs.

"From this one." Shell had returned with the hot chocolate and he sipped at it fast. "I speak of Esme Hall."

I thought about Esme. Stefan had met her at a Pagan Craft event at the Town Hall and in weeks she was living with him at Stonedown. Her pots were popular in an underground, person-to-person sort of way, but it was when Stef offered to set up a website that her work took off. Was she a malign influence on Stef? Had he changed for the worse since they'd been an item?

"He is supportive of some mates," I said. "You know, the chap attacked just after the solstice?"

"What chap?" said Wolfs.

"Gerald Evens. He was bashed on the head in the abbey grounds."

"Bloody hell," said Shell.

"Esme was the one who told me. Although, to back up Freaky's assumptions, she wasn't very nice about how Stefan was spending time with him."

Freaky's food arrived and he tucked in with the vigour of the recently starved, saying nothing more. We all agreed that he should try to get his caravan out of the pound, and that Wolfs, who had a tow bar on his ancient estate car, would find somewhere off-road for it. We threw some tenners into a kitty.

Freaky stuffed the last of his food into his mouth as Wolfs eased himself up from his chair using his staff, which was as tall as Wolfsbane and took up its own sacred space at the table. Wolfsbane never appeared in Glastonbury without his full pagan regalia of bright cotton trousers, Celtic knot tunic, and full-length cloak. Freaky had carved the ash staff with runes and triskelions way back—it had to be twenty years old.

Once they left for the police station, Shell and I ordered teas and sat soaking up the sun.

"Slightly gender-ridden division of labour."

"Don't knock it," said Shell, fishing sunglasses from her bag. "Personally, I'm glad to get a bit of me-time."

"Wolfsbane's too full-on?"

"Hmm. Not in every department, I'm afraid." Her eyes were shielded by the glasses. "He's like Jupiter, you know?"

"What, you mean a seeker after intellectual and spiritual wisdom?"

"No, a massive, shining star … full of nothing but gas." I couldn't help the snort that came down my nose. Shell took a tiny sip of tea and masterfully changed the subject. "Brice wanted me to thank you, Sabbie. For going to the inquest with him."

"That was not the inquest. Believe me, when it gets going, he'll need all his friends there."

"Brice is really worried what the outcome will be." She turned her teacup round its saucer, using a single finger. "He's terrified, actually."

"Is it drugs?" My voice came out in a sort of choke. "Does he think Alys took something?"

"No, Sabbie, and don't you dare mention that to him. He thinks Alys will be found to be pregnant."

I felt my eyebrows shoot up. "He's not thinking that she died because she was pregnant, is he?"

"Maybe. He's not thinking straight, to be honest."

"Had she lost a baby or something?"

Shell gave me a sharp look. "Why d'you say that?"

"Because she'd been having bad periods. I remember wondering at Stonedown if she was miscarrying that day."

"No, Sabbie, you're way off beam." She took a couple of minutes to drink her tea and let me think about that. Then she said, "I may as well tell you. Wolfsie says you're good at getting to the truth anyway."

I felt an inward preen go through me, as if my feathers had ruffled pleasantly. It was nice to know Wolfsbane thought well of me as a shaman.

"Alys and I met at school, did I say? So I know her better that any other friend; better than Brice. Do you follow? I know things Brice does not."

I gave a nod.

"She was always mature for her age, you know? She sneered at the boys in our year. We were doing our GCSE courses when she started seeing this older bloke. A specific older bloke, actually. A teacher."

"Goddess!"

"This chap was new in the Humanities department and to be honest, we wouldn't think of him as old at all now, I guess he was two, three years out of university. He was a fantastic looker and Alys wasn't the only girl with a crush on him, a gaggle of girls used to follow him around on the pretext of their history studies. It was Alys who got him in the end." Shell smiled. "She wasn't especially pretty or anything, but back then she had a big, cheeky personality. She knew what she wanted and usually got it."

"So she got this teacher."

"It was the worse thing that could have happened. She fell so heavily. It couldn't end in anything but disaster, could it? She got pregnant and he paid for her to have an abortion in a private clinic, in the hope of keeping it quiet. In fact he put a lot of pressure on her to have the abortion, although I don't suppose she had many other options. She'd left it late telling him, so by the time she went in, she had to have the drip and everything and it went horribly wrong. The bleeding wouldn't stop and she was rushed into the general hospital.

Naturally, it all came out at school. Alys was sixteen, over the age of consent, but the bloke got the sack. She never heard from him again. She messed up her exams and we didn't see her all summer holidays because she refused to come out with the rest of us."

"She was probably depressed," I said.

"And how. At the start of the next year she looked a wreck. That cheeky personality was in bits. The weight had fallen off her and she still wasn't eating. I was scared for her, Sabbie. I'd been a rubbish friend too; all summer we'd gone off partying and do you know what she'd done? She'd joined a sort of club called the 100 Day Fast."

For some reason, although I'd never heard the term before, it made my skin go cold.

"For one hundred days, you drink only water."

"*What*? That's crazy. Dangerous."

"Yes, it was horrible. She was still doing it, and trying retake her GCSEs and start her A levels all at the same time. I thought she was going to break down and end up in hospital, but I rallied the gang round and we gentled back into eating. By the end of the school year, she was okay. Not eating well—to be honest she's never eaten well since—but she'd put on half a stone."

"Where does Brice come in?"

"They met four years ago. She'd just had her thirtieth birthday. Within six months, Brice had spent his banker's bonus on a big meringue wedding. They started trying for a baby from day one."

"Did Brice know …"

"He doesn't know any of this. And I don't want him hurt, Sabbie."

"Don't worry, I'm not a tale-tat."

"She couldn't pin down why she failed to get pregnant. Whether it was the years of being super skinny or the thing that happened in the clinic. Brice went for a sperm test and confronted her with the result, which was positive—good sperm count. She phoned me up in a panic, scared he was going to insist she go in for investigations."

"Poor Alys," I said. I thought again. "Poor Brice."

"Why did you mention drugs?" Shell asked.

"Oh, nothing. No reason."

"Really?"

I pursed my lips together as if that would prevent me saying more, but I'd've needed duct tape for that. "Was Alys a user? Sometimes anorexic behavior goes with that sort of lifestyle."

"I don't think so. I never saw her take anything on a night out while we were kids, let alone later. And Brice is a pretty staid guy; he'd never touch anything like that. Anyway, we might soon know for sure."

"Has Brice heard?"

"He's been promised an appointment with someone from the Coroner's office. As soon as the labs are done with their tests, I think."

"That's good. Isn't it?"

"In my experience of life, things never quite turn out like you think they will. That's the trouble." Shell pushed her chair back and crossed her legs. She was wearing a salmon pink top and a shape-hugging sherbet-lemon mini skirt. A fat leather belt with a rhinestone buckle clinched her soft waist. She had purchased an armful of bangles in a shop on Glastonbury High Street that chimed as they fell together. Their colours picked up the pink and yellow, and the turquoise from the peacock feathers on her hat and earrings. I'd sort of assumed that, like a lot of Wolfs's girlfriends, Shell didn't do anything much, but I now knew she made jewellery. I was about to ask about this when she said, "Heard from Ricky since the Tor?"

"No … I think he's in touch with Juke."

"They're old uni mates, aren't they?"

I gave her a girlie look. "You've heard from him?"

"Er … we've been chatting. Facebook … the phone …"

"Just be careful, sweetie, okay?"

"What d'you mean?"

"Wolfs likes—er—solidarity from his ladies."

"Solidarity?"

"In plain text: he can be the jealous kind. You know, doesn't believe men and women can sustain a platonic relationship … ergo …"

"*You* have a platonic relationship with him."

"Trust me, this isn't *logical* reasoning."

"What the heck. He can believe what he chooses."

"Isn't Ricky a bit young for you, Shell?"

She flicked me a grin, her eyes hidden behind the shades. "Cute, though. And far less gaseous."

FOURTEEN
FREAKY

I WASN'T SURPRISED THAT Wolfsbane and Freaky returned empty-handed.

"They won't let it out until it's roadworthy," said Wolfsbane. "The handbrake's broken and the wheels are ripped to shreds."

"I hadn't planned on going far," Freaky said. "As I explained to the Plods."

"Can it be repaired?" Shell asked.

"Yes, but it will cost."

Shell got up and spontaneously hugged Freaky's narrow frame. "I know a mechanic. Maybe he could help if we gave him a day out in Glastonbury."

Wolfsbane was jangling his car keys. He wrapped his arm round Shell. "We have to split, I'm afraid. All the best, Freaky, eh, mate?"

"I'll be in touch," Shell called as she was led away.

I looked at Freaky. "Where are you staying?"

"I did ask the Plods if I could sleep in the caravan in the pound."

"That was a no, then?"

"Maybe the Backpackers Hostel will cut me a deal."

"You've got no cash?"

He pulled the kitty out of his pocket. "I've got this, but it's not strictly mine. Otherwise, I'll have to wait till my pension's due."

I knew that Freaky made the few pounds he lived on with his sacred painting and craftwork, and recently he'd begun to receive his state pension. He'd commented that it was enough to live like a king. I doubted other pensioners would agree, but finance is relative, I guess.

"Put that away and come home for the night with me. In the morning, things will look clearer." I wondered about phoning Rey and asking if he could have a word with his Glastonbury colleagues, but the facts wouldn't change; the caravan was still not roadworthy.

On the walk back to my car, Freaky was very quiet, which wasn't like him. I gave his arm a squeeze. "It will be all right, you know."

"I've never sponged off my friends. I respect them. I'd never use them. You understand that, Sabbie, don't you?"

"I've got a spare room, Freaky, it's no bother."

"It hurts like hell, nevertheless."

———

We got going, heading west across the Somerset Moors, Freaky still in morose mood. He gazed out of his window as the countryside slid by. It was late afternoon. The sun was golden on the land. It was mostly dairy farming round here; although the fields had been drained generations ago, they still got boggy in the winter and didn't hold grain well, or sheep, for that matter.

"You don't see so much withy growing nowadays do you," I remarked.

"True. Used to be the big commodity on the Somerset Levels. You could stick willow wands into the wet soil and in a year or two you had trees to coppice for basketmaking or wattle fencing. Not much call anymore."

"That's sad."

"It's all peat now."

Out of sight of the roads were the excavations, tonnes of ancient peat bagged as growing medium for gardens. I had many reasons to hate that scourging of the land, but all I could do in practice was never buy peat-based compost.

As we crossed the Polden Hills, my phone rang. "Bugger," I said, without thinking.

"Want me to get it for you?" Freaky dived into my shoulder bag. As someone who lived off-grid, he was always delighted to demonstrate his ability with modern technology. Freaky didn't own a phone or computer or even a TV, but seemed to know his way around receptionist duties. "This is Sabbie Dare's phone," he began, "Freaky speaking."

He listened carefully to the caller, nodding as if they could hear, while I mouthed, "Is it a client?" at him.

"Did you want to make an appointment?" he asked, and I could hear a tinny reply, but Freaky didn't scrabble for paper and pen or look to me for directions. "Okay, my friend, I'll tell her." He took his time finding the right buttons to cut the call, then dropped my phone back into my bag. "That was Marty-Mac."

I didn't recognize the name. "What did he want?"

"He said he knew you knew Reynard Buckley."

I frowned. "Like, in what way?"

"In a getting a message to him sort of way."

"Well, for goodness sake, why can't this Marty get his own message to Rey?"

"Apparently, they're not speaking."

"Oh, great. Sounds like one of Rey's cronies wants me to be intermediary. Did he say what the message was?"

"Yeah ... sort of." He didn't go on.

"Sort of what?"

"Sort of confusing. The man was confused."

"He must have phoned with something on his mind."

"Why not phone him back, it might make more sense to you."

"Give me something to go on, first."

"I remember he said he was in dead shit, excuse the French."

"He said that?"

"I put the French bit in."

I spent the silence of the journey trying to make sense of this, alongside wondering what sort of houseguest Freaky would make. Although I'd only mentioned a one-night stay, I had a horrible feeling he would not be going anywhere for a while.

As well as shredded wheels, Freaky's caravan had no electric wiring. He used bottled gas to cook his food and to run an evil-looking wall-mounted fire that gave out little heat but could burn you to blisters if you got too close. I knew the caravan was getting leaky, damp, and full of drafts, and Freaky, in a similar manner to his home, was becoming worn. His hair was turning from pepper-and-salt to pure white. His cheeks were hollow, but you couldn't see that because his beard grew in a haphazard fashion wherever it pleased. I believed Freaky kept it from hiding his entire face by using nail scissors, something I might be subjected to in full if he decided on a trimming in my bathroom.

"Can I ask you a personal question, Freaky?"

He turned to me and raised one eyebrow, a trick that always make me chuckle with delight as it transformed Freaky's face. "I'm twenty-one."

"Yeah, you and me both. Seriously, you've never thought about settling more permanently?"

"Where, my friend? Why, my friend?"

"Living in a totally sustainable way is great when you're young and fit. But … well … you've been twenty-one for quite a long time, and … it can't be easy anymore."

"I will not ever leave Glastonbury. Your offer is kind, but no."

"That's a relief, then!" I laughed, hoping he would too. "I was thinking if you went to the council now, with the loss of your home, they'd probably help you find a one-bed flat."

"With neighbours tolerant of long hours of chanting and drumming, I presume?"

"You won't know till you look, Freaky."

He shifted in the seat. "They all went, in the end."

"You're talking about the hippies?"

"Nineteen sixty-nine. There really was peace and love. We gave each other our hearts. Our bodies too." He raised his eyebrow again and I giggled.

"I bet you were a total love machine, Freaky."

"We were called the Freaks. That's how everyone knew us around Glastonbury. Elsewhere, it was 'hippies,' but if you stayed on permanently under the Tor, you got that nomenclature and you were proud of it. We had a commune. We squatted in a big old house not unlike Stonedown Farm. We used to dance all night tuned in with acid, up on the Tor or in the chambers of the Chalice Well."

"What chambers?"

"They got bricked up, I think, but back then they were perfect for chilling out. The White Spring's the same, far out. We lived chilled and cool. We had no possessions. We ate no meat. Some only ate raw food, until Astral nearly died eating uncooked red beans. We got moved on eventually, of course, and some drifted away before the end. I shared a geodesic dome then, with a girl and her kid. That was into the eighties, I believe. She was a wonder. She called herself Seren, which is the Celtic word for *star*, but her real name was Tracey. The little girl, Sky, was a brilliant kid. She must be, oh, your age or more now."

"Was she your kid, Freaky?"

"Who knows? Seren certainly did not."

"They moved on, too?"

"One dark and stormy night—you might laugh, but really   the dome lifted off in a gale. We watched it from our sleeping bags. It flew like a kite, and the wind took it right over the top of the Tor. We found bits of it, the following day; some of the metal connectors, some rags of tarp. We fought; Seren left with Sky. We fought about a crazy thing—about the storm and the loss of the dome, which was no one's fault, not even the gods."

"So you became the very last Freak in Glastonbury."

"Yes. I've had the caravan since then. I bought it off a touring family who got to Glastonbury, parked up in a campsite which was part of Stonedown Farm's land at the time, and saw a brighter, shinier model on a show site. I gave them a fair price."

"We're here," I said, pulling into the kerb. "Welcome to 43 Harold Street."

"My friend, it looks most welcoming." Freaky leaned over and pecked a kiss on my cheek. His white bristles tickled my skin, making me smile.

———

Freaky rushed to the loo as soon as we got in; it had been a long journey. I took the opportunity to ring Rey. Usually I get voicemail, but he must have been on a quick break because he answered immediately.

"Hi, gorgeous."

Well might he call me nice things; he had a lot of ground to make up. I hadn't seen this so-called boyfriend since he brought his detective sergeant temptress into the Curate's Egg four days ago. The vision of red-gold locks and freckly, porcelain skin hadn't left me.

"Hi, big boy. You okay?"

"I'm surrounded by bloody paperwork. Nightmare."

"Aw, poor you. Not out on the beat?"

He gave a snort. "Get your roles sorted, Sabbie. It's the humble police constable that walks the beat. Your detective's main skill is brainwork."

"No running after felons?"

"Absolutely. Abseiling walls, leaping from roof to roof, that sort of thing. Got to stay in peak condition."

"Mmm, I know you're in peak condition."

Having got the flirting out of the way, I told him about my staying guest. A little imp poked me with its trident and I made sure he realized that this was a male visitor, a pagan I had great respect for.

"What's his name?"

"Freaky."

"*Freaky!*" He didn't speak for several moments, and I knew he was laughing, the sort of laugh that bubbles up from a giggle and gets you right in the solar plexus, so that you can't stop, can't even draw breath. "What sort of name is that?"

"A descriptive one. He's a Freak."

"And a Freak is ..."

"One of the original Glastonbury hippies."

"Cool."

"Very cool. Rey, come and say hello. I'm sure you two would get along famously."

"Yeah. I will. Soon as I have a second to spare."

I paused to digest this. I was never sure how to take what Rey said, which did make for a less than candid relationship at times. Probably all my fault, because I was the one reading things into his words, and he was the one who was straightforward to the point of bluntness. Now I was wondering if "a second to spare" meant he would be rushing round as soon as he'd put down the phone in a lather of suspicion, or that all his seconds were taken up with chasing Pippa Chaisey.

"I had a phone call, Rey. From someone trying to get in touch with you."

"Who?" He sounded cautious. "What did they want?"

"Name of Marty-Mac. I didn't speak to this guy, Rey, but if you know him, perhaps you could give him a ring back. Freaky took the

163

call. He's my PA at the moment." I heard the flush go upstairs. "Better get back to my guest. Help him settle in."

"Sabbie, what—"

I cut him off. Always leave before they want you to. I felt quite lighthearted as I went up the stairs.

I found Freaky exploring the second bedroom. And by *exploring*, I think I mean *nosing around*; every drawer was open and showed disruption (quite a tricky thing to accomplish in the existing mess) and now he was lifting the bedding, as if checking for lice. He didn't jump or drop the duvet when I arrived, but turned with a grin and said, "Ye Gods, Sabbie this is the Ritz in Paris compared to my van!"

Freaky had an oversized backpack stuffed with things salvaged from the caravan, so I cleared a drawer and a shelf (mostly by cramming things into another drawer and onto another shelf). He pulled off his boots to display sockless, grimy feet. I gave him a demonstration of how the shower worked, but he said he'd leave that to the morning.

We went downstairs and I put the telly on for him and made a pot of Darjeeling, which was one of the things Freaky had stuffed in his backpack. Apparently he drank little else, apart from the odd pint of beer.

"Make yourself at home," I instructed. Freaky took the hint. He put his feet up on the coffee table and let out a ringing fart.

The doorbell went while we were downing the teas. My insides immediately wrung themselves into knots. Rey had found a second; he was here to look my visitor over. I tore along the hallway like a five-year-old expecting presents, but as I opened the door, I realized that neither of the figures waiting outside were Rey-shaped. In horror, I almost slammed it shut and hurtled back down the passage, but it was too late.

I was wavered between *What are you doing here?* and *Go away now!* but in the end I plastered on a smile. "Mrs. Mitchell, hello. Hi, Lettice."

Lettice grinned at me as if all this was a great hoot. "Hi, Sabbie!"

"Good afternoon," said my aunt, unable to raise even an artificial smile in return.

I had not seen my aunt or my cousin Laetitia for six months. They had last stood on my doorstep in the deep midwinter. It was now the high midsummer, but I was no more pleased to find them here.

"Would you like to come in," I said, finally, "for a moment?" I stood aside for them and a thought flashed through my mind: *Oh heck! Freaky!* I swept that away and replaced it with, *Freaky—yippee!*

My aunt spotted Freaky almost the instant she entered the kitchen. It would have been hard to miss him, a mass of white dreadlocks, a tobacco-brown grin, and sooty feet sticking up between the tea mugs.

"Freaky," I said, "I don't believe you've met my aunt, Peers Mitchell, and this is Lettice, my cousin."

Freaky, ever the gentleman, swung his limbs into a standing position and advanced on the pair, his hand extended, his nails pointing like a series of little black lances. "Pleased to meet you, my friends."

Mrs. Mitchell turned solid. Her ivory court shoes came to a neat halt and she swayed backwards as if some form of floor glue was the only thing preventing a retreat. Her daughter was made of sterner stuff. She stuck out her hand and pumped Freaky's up and down. "Pleased to meet you, how do you do?"

"I am at peace, my young friend. How do *you* do?"

"Well." Peers Mitchell shook herself. Actually, it might have been a shudder. "We won't hold you up. We will deliver our message and leave you to ..." She waved a hand. A single massive diamond glittered.

"Grandma Dare wants to meet you," said Lettice. There was triumph in her voice.

I had not expected this. "I didn't think she knew anything about me."

"No. I ..." Lettice pinked up around the cheeks. "I sort of let the cat out of the bag. As Grandma might say."

I eyed my cousin. The cunning little minx had engineered this. She'd longed to get me and our shared grandmother together. Since the winter, she'd steadfastly remained a Facebook friend, occasionally directing chatty messages at me. I liked Lettice—genuinely liked her—but I could hardly have a relationship with my thirteen-year-old cousin without also having one with my aunt and my grandmother. Seven months ago, I had no idea of their existence. They hadn't known about me, either. Peers Mitchell had been horrified to discover I was her niece and made it clear enough she'd prefer it if her mother never met me. I couldn't help but agree with this assessment. I guessed Grandma Dare would have to be in her eighties. The news might've floored her.

"What did Lady Dare say?"

"Lady Savile-Dare," Mrs. Mitchell corrected. "She was intrigued."

"She said, 'I cannot now live without casting my eyes upon this grandchild,'" said Lettice.

"Heck."

Mrs. Mitchell inclined her head. "Precisely."

"You'll have to come, Sabbie. When Grandma issues a summons, you simply must obey," Lettice said cheerfully.

"Which is why we are here," her mother said uncheerfully.

I glanced over my shoulder. Freaky had disappeared to the other end of the kitchen and was making himself useful, swilling the empty mugs in the sink, trying not to overhear. I gave a brief nod, desperate to get them out of my house.

"Eleven in the morning is a good time for my mother. She is breakfasted by then, but not yet tired by the day."

"Okay, eleven. Which day?"

Mrs. Mitchell dipped into her crocodile handbag and brought out a leather-bound diary, opening it where the red silk bookmark was placed.

I got out my phone.

"Friday next week would be convenient."

"Sorry," I said, trying to keep the delight out of my tone. "I have ongoing appointments for the whole day."

"Saturday then," said Mrs. Mitchell.

I checked. There was nothing until the afternoon, when Juke had one of his regular sessions. "Okay. Eleven on Saturday next week is fine."

"You can recall where Lady Savile-Dare lives?"

"Oh yes," I said. I was never going to forget where Lady Dare lived, or the fact that I'd been a fast-food deliverer when I'd arrived at the Hatchings for the first and only time.

"I'll be there, Sabbie," said Lettice. She gave me an apologetic smile and I returned it.

"Thanks. Appreciated."

Mrs. Mitchell wasted no time in leaving, her arm tucked into her daughter's as if she was concerned Lettice would be beguiled by me or Freaky and ask to stay forever. I didn't do the polite thing and follow them to the door. Peers already thought I was the scum of the earth, nothing I did would change that.

I flopped onto the sofa and cried out in anguish, "Bugger! Bugger, bugger!"

Freaky gave up pretending to rewipe the mugs and came over. "I've never heard you talk about your family."

"Last year I didn't know I had a family. It was a double whammy; they didn't know about me, either. My mother had been sent packing from the family home—the family pile, really. You wouldn't believe the size of my so-called grandmother's house. Mum and me lived in squalor until she died of an overdose when I was six. Izzie had done a good job of disappearing; none of them knew she'd died. Peers Mitchell almost fainted when Lettice told her I was her niece."

"How did you find each other?"

"Synchronicity."

"Ah! That old surprise package."

"Yeah. I turned up on a scooter with their take-away order."

"Ye gods."

I closed my eyes. "I don't want these people as my relations."

"You don't like them?"

My lids popped open and I fairly gaped at Freaky. "Did *you* like them?"

"I thought Lettice was sweet."

"Yes." I sighed. "Lettice is extremely sweet." That was the problem. Lettice wanted to be a cousin to me; it oozed from every pore of her lovely teenage being. "Sadly, Freaky, her mother is a demon, a Grendel who eats people like me for supper. And I've never met *her* mother, but it looks like I'm going to."

"Grendel's mother was a hag from a deep swamp," said Freaky, raising his eyebrow.

I groaned. "Granny, the hag from the swamp. I'll need a magic sword and an invisible cloak."

"That would be cheating," said Freaky. "Beowulf fought the demon bare-handed."

Although he was teasing me, Freaky had a point. Lady Savile-Dare was my very own nightmare beast. I'd have to face her with only my wits.

FIFTEEN

DENNON

WHEN MY FOSTER BROTHER Dennon rang on Friday morning, Freaky was still lodging in my house. In fact he was mowing my patch of grass at the time, so I climbed the stairs with my phone to get away from the roar of the lawnmower. It was surprising how many of my calls were enquiries about therapy work, and I couldn't afford to miss a single one.

Dennon was calling from the landline in his new flat. "Sis," he began, "it's my housewarming tonight. You coming?"

"Not really. I got someone staying."

"Bring them too—we're low on girls. We're low on people. And we're low on beer; bring some of that."

I felt myself weakening. Hadn't I bemoaned to Marianne that I never went to parties? I was curious to see Dennon's accommodation. Plus, Freaky was always good at a party. He'd start a debate with anyone and danced like a dervish.

I texted an invite to Rey. He hadn't been around since I'd told him about Freaky, although I didn't think it was Freaky keeping Rey away. An image kept nagging at me—a hand, rough and browned by the sun, caressing a soft mass of wavy auburn hair. How could Rey resist such hair when my coiffure still resembled a labradoodle after a bad shampoo experience?

For the party, I tackled it with hair straighteners and zipped myself into the scarlet dress Marianne had given me because it was a size too big for her. I reckoned I looked the biz and even Freaky had scrubbed up well; he'd shampooed his dreadlocks (or, at least his scalp) and changed into colourful trousers straight from the Summer of Love.

It was a cloudless evening and the run up the motorway was a cruise, which meant we arrived early, so we dropped in on Ricky, seeing as he'd left an open invitation.

Ricky's flatmate Eijaz came to the door, sliding on his famous shades as he opened it.

"Is Ricky in," I asked.

"You wanna go up?" Eijaz waving a hand at the stairs. "Ricky's bedroom is last on the right."

By way of introduction, Freaky swept the surprised Eijaz into a shaman hug. I left them to get acquainted and went up the stairs. I tapped on the closed door. There was a rustling and thumping. I'd caught him having an evening siesta. "It's Sabbie," I called out. "We were just passing…"

Ricky opened the door a crack. I could only see his face which was covered in his usual gothic makeup, but it had run, the black into the white, and he looked vaguely clownlike, with his lacquered hair in spikes. "Hi, Sabbie," he said and closed the door. I heard a muffled conversation. I took a step back. His girlfriend was in there. I had just made the decision to call out that I'd be downstairs with Freaky when the door opened again, fully this time.

"You'd best come in," said Shell.

She'd pulled on what looked like Ricky's bathrobe, belting it tight around her curves. She sat down on the tousled bed and gave me a rueful grin, which had *I couldn't resist* plastered all over it.

"Shell's been helping me collate my course work," said Ricky, in a monotone that suggested he didn't think I'd fall for that line, except he was booting down his laptop and his notebook and text books lay open so he might have been telling the partial truth. "I'm a bit behind."

"You know about philosophy?" I asked Shell.

"No, but I know how to get through end-of-year exams. All the same, really."

"Er ... yeah."

I was flabbergasted at the speed Shell worked. While I was thinking of a way I could imply that their secret was safe with me, Freaky bumbled into the room.

"Greetings, my friends." He didn't bat an eye at Shell's presence, hugging them both to him before starting his usual regime of exploring his environment. He reminded me of all the dogs I'd ever lived with at Gloria and Philip's house. They would scamper around any new place we were visiting until they'd got a map in their head. It was disconcerting for non-dog lovers, and I could see that Freaky had disconcerted Ricky.

"Sorry." Ricky rubbed his face with his sleeve. "Sabbie didn't say you were here."

"I love this," Freaky announced. "It's a quest for truth. Your spirit is guiding you." He had opened the wardrobe doors and was standing there, peering in. "My friend, you have found peace."

I went over to see what he was talking about. Ricky had created an altar inside his wardrobe. Now I understood the jumble of clothes I'd spotted on my first visit, pushed under the bed; he'd taken them out so that he could hang ritual objects from the clothes rail—some wind chimes, a dreamcatcher, a yew branch tied with red ribbon. He'd spread a silk scarf over the wardrobe floor and a bodhran, two candlesticks, and a bowl of various crystals were arranged around a framed pen and ink representation of a goddess.

"That's my sister's work." Ricky's closed glance warned me to say no more.

It was Babe's style, and beautifully realized. She'd defined the goddess without tipping over into clichéd beauty.

"A sacred altar," said Freaky. "May the goddess bless your awakening."

"That's it—awakening! As from shadows. All my studies are about awakening. Paganism, shamanism—they're so akin to philosophy. See, when you philosophize, you reach amazing new conclusions about old arguments."

"It's the same when you walk between worlds, my friend. Conjunctions. Associations. Parallelisms. They show you how to navigate the living truth."

"I'm developing my shamanic work." Ricky nodded at the glossy posters pinned on his wall. The pictures of philosophers were becoming invisible behind images of sacred sites and sea eagles. I could feel them whisper to me, hushed murmurs that told me Ricky had been working in a sacred way, regularly and with deep intent.

"I want to get a good connection with Sea Eagle," he was saying. "It's amazing what I've found out about them. They were worshipped as totems thousands of years ago."

"You should travel to Orkney," Freaky said. "The wonderful tombs. You'd love it."

"I mean to," said Ricky, and glanced at Shell as if asking her if she'd like to go too.

Freaky wandered out and Ricky went with him. Shell and I followed them down the stairs. I'd gone up to Ricky's room with the intention of having a private conversation about Babette and her sketchpad, but that wasn't going to happen now.

In the kitchen, Eijaz was in the process of pulling cans of lager from the fridge.

"We're heading off to a party," said Freaky. "So I won't imbibe, thank you."

"You can all come, if you like." I knew Dennon wanted bodies, and I fancied the idea of arriving with my own little posse.

We waited while Shell disappeared to get dressed and Ricky refreshed his makeup and otherwise transformed himself into a Goth.

Eijaz got started on the cans, snapping one open and taking a long pull. "You two are the shamans, innit?"

"If you like, my friend," said Freaky. "We are all shamans, deep inside ourselves."

"Not me, man. I don't want nothin' to do with all that."

"Everyone fears the unknown," I said. "If you talked to Ricky about it—"

"I only get crazy answers. This stuff gives me the jitters."

Eijaz had a North London accent that rose to a pitch as he tried to make his point. He was standing by the fridge while we'd taken seats at the kitchen table and his posture was a bit "gangland." I glanced at Freaky, to see if he was in the least fazed, but he was cleaning his pointed fingernails with a paring knife that had happened to be on the table and seemed to have bailed out of the conversation.

"What d'you have against the idea of learning about shamanism?" I asked, keeping my voice calm.

"I guess I'm not in a position to judge. Ricky would say if you don't know nothing about something you should shut up till you do."

"Are you doing philosophy like him?"

"No! I wanna make money in my life, thank you. I'm doing the MSc in Business Management. Ricky's definitely a philosopher, I admit—that stuff goes over my head."

I laughed. I had a feeling it would go over mine, as well. "How did you get to know Ricky, then?"

"We were both there day one on the business degree, but he flagged badly. Had to go home."

I was wondering if this had been after the shock of his sister's disappearance. That would have thrown him well off course. And perhaps he'd set to thinking about life … the meaning of it, which might have spurred his interest in philosophy. Another thought came to me. "D'you remember Juke Webber then? From the business degree?"

"There was a big student intake in our year. Juke never was my mate. Ricky's linked up with him again and, suddenly, they're seeing a lot of each other."

I flashed an uncertain smile. "That's what old mates do, though, isn't it?"

"Not sure about this Shell, though. She looks like she's been round a few times."

I said nothing. It was clear Ricky hadn't told his flatmate that his new woman was also the partner of his erstwhile workshop coordinator. Ricky lived in a philosophy-filled bubble; these small issues probably floated above his head.

Finally, Shell and Ricky reappeared. Shell had transformed herself into a vampiress, and I had to admit, she looked stunning. We squashed into the Vauxhall and drove to the address Dennon had given me—a block of purpose-built flats on a small housing development.

Dennon relieved Eijaz of his bag of lager and me of my wine. "I was hoping more of the neighbours would be here. I don't dare put the music up until I've cleared this floor of possible complainers. Anyway." He waved his arms towards the interior. "What d'y think?"

Dennon had one biggish living room. A miniature kitchen area was incorporated at the windowless end of the room, but the units were lit well and the rows of bottles and beer cans glittered. On the island surface that separated the kitchen from the rest of the living space, big paper plates were piled with Iceland freezer party food, which Dennon could get at a staff discount. In daylight, I suspected the room would be faceless with its magnolia walls and the white ceiling with a central bulb hanging on a short cable, but Dennon had festooned the place with balloons and streamers and glittery wreaths.

"It's great!"

"Yeah; finally, somewhere I can bring tasty chicks!"

"So … where are they?"

"What?"

"The chicks."

His face dropped. "I was hoping people would bring chicks with them. I need to polish those old chat-up lines."

"Bit of information, Den: people who bring chicks are usually hoping to hang onto to them."

He was right, though, even with the addition of five extra guests, the place was not buzzing. His mates from the Iceland store were there, but the younger ones were chickless and the older ones had brought their wives. The usual suspects—Dennon's mad-bad mates, including Bark and Kyle—were chatting in one corner, cheap lagers in their hands. Eijaz had taken some cans over to them and I could hear him regaling them with tales of Newham, which was where he'd been born, he was explaining, of Pakistani parents. Den's gang, all nearing the big three-oh, carried their rough reputations with pride, but clearly thought Eijaz, in his sharp suit and tight-fitting t-shirt, was awesome. He'd dismayed me, with his sudden attack on Ricky's interest in shamanism. I'd wanted to tell him he wasn't his flatmate's keeper, but I'd kept that opinion to myself.

I spotted Dennon's sister, sitting in what must have been Dennon's only easy chair, her husband, Chris, leaning against the back like they were posing for a sepia photograph. I scooted over and perched on a chair arm. "Hi, nice to see you both."

"Couldn't let Dennon down after the big move, could we?" Charlene leaned towards my ear. "We've had to buy in a babysitter for this. We'd rather be in the Taste of Delhi down the road, tucking into a curry."

"Don't you dare desert us."

"I thought Dennon knew more people than this."

"Don't knock it, Charlene. The ones that aren't here are probably in the nick."

Charlene burst into giggles. She'd put on a comfortable layer of weight since having Rory and Kerri and it suited her; she wore no makeup except cherry-coloured lippy and her dark skin glowed tonight like slightly padded satin.

Eventually, some of the neighbours on Dennon's floor arrived, and he notched up the sound to danger levels. Charlene covered her ears. Dennon was stuck in a bit of a musical time warp—he only liked the music of his reprobate youth—but that happened to be my reprobate youth, and I found my fingers snapping.

"Want to dance? I asked Charlene and Chris, but they shook their heads, like the old married couple they were. I got up and began to sway, all alone, in the middle of the room. "C'mon," I yelled at Ricky and Shell. "Time to groove!"

They sauntered out onto the floor, by which time Freaky was bouncing around, arms at all angles, legs kicking and stamping, whipping up a frenzy with the stationary drinkers. Freaky's dance display was irresistible. People put down their drinks and joined in. Dennon and his mates ground their hips, Latino style. Charlene and Chris got up and smooched, and even the elderly neighbour, who'd arrive with a good bottle of wine he'd been steadily working through, swayed from side-to-side. Eijaz flashed past him, narrowly avoiding knocking the glass out of his hand. I fancied Eijaz was trying to outdo Freaky, who continued to windmill around the entire room, wailing a high-pitched version of the song coming from the speakers.

"*Voolay voo cooshay avay mwah, saaaay swah,*" he warbled in a terrible French accent.

The party sparked into a new dimension; we all lobbed about over the carpet, arms aloft, yelling out the words to the anthem. It had become a competition. The longer Freaky danced like a windmill, the more everyone else had to keep up. The entire flat was rock-ing. Ricky had moved away from Shell and was showing off a technique, jumping on the spot to the beat of the music, his knees bent like a Russian dancer with each lift-off.

The tracks blended into each other so that there was no time to stop, no moment to catch your breath, and Freaky knew the words to every song.

It seemed as if we'd been dancing forever when Ricky came to an abrupt halt. Sweat was running down his temples and his face was tomato in shade. I heard him cry out, anguish that could be heard over all the other noise.

"No! Nooo!"

He pushed through the dancers. The front door was ajar and he fled through it.

We all came to a halt, but Shell was the only one to pursue Ricky. Dennon turned the sound down a bit, and people renewed their drinks.

"What was that about?" asked Dennon, coming into the kitchen area.

"He's been messin' with his mind," said Eijaz, looking at me as if to say it was all my fault. He scratched at the back of his knee. "You wanna check him out?"

I looked out into the corridor, but no one was there, so I took the stairs. Ricky and Shell were sitting on the little patch of lawn that came with the apartment block. They weren't smooching or any-thing, so I waved and went over.

"Are you all right, Ricky?"

"I'm fine. I'll have to go in and apologize for wrecking everyone's good time, won't I?"

"Don't be daft. To be honest, I think people were really glad to get a break. Freaky can get high with not much help."

"That was the trouble." Ricky picked at the grass, almost orange under the streetlights. "It reminded me … you know?"

Then I saw. "Alys," I said.

Ricky took a great sniff of air. "It took me right back there."

I sat beside them, the grass cool on my bare legs.

"All that panic came into my mind—trying to revive her. Hopeless."

"I don't think either of us are in a party mood anymore," said Shell.

I'd half forgotten that Shell was also sorrowing for her lost friend. I wondered if Ricky was trying to share some of the burden of grieving.

Shell stood and put out her hand. Ricky levered himself up from the grass. "We'll walk back home," she said. "The moon'll be up in a minute. It's a waning quarter. I love that phase."

I wandered back to the main door of the apartment block and was halfway up the stairs when I heard my name, called softly behind me.

It was Ricky, standing in the shadow of the stairwell. His shoulders were bent low. I came back down.

"You think I'm stealing her away, don't you? Like chocolate bars."

"Uh?" I wasn't sure if Ricky was comparing Shell to chocolate or recalling a teenaged nick-fest. "Is she …"

"I told her I was going for a pee." He moved slightly, checking Shell was still where he'd left her. I could see her on the grass, staring at the stars. "I won't hurt her, you know."

"Trust me, Ricky, that was not my first thought." I was far more worried about what Wolfsbane might do if he found out. "Have you got time to talk about Babe's sketchpad?"

"Oh." He faded from me, his still-pink face turning grey. He fell back against the corridor wall.

"So far, I have one strong image. A female red deer. The ones with the whitish rumps. Do you have them in the New Forest?"

"Yes, we do."

"Did Babe ever sketch one?"

"Probably. That wasn't her only sketchbook, it's the one that has survived through the years. Because I clung on to it."

"I guess they searched the forest when she went missing."

He took such a deep breath through his nose that his chest juddered with it. "We all did. We searched the entire countryside."

"Ricky . . . this must be hard to talk about . . . but can you remember the time around her disappearance?"

"I only want to know if she's okay. That she survived. I think that would help my parents too. Just to know . . ." He was staring at his lace-up boots, which were shiny black patent leather. "I haven't told Shell about her."

"Okay."

"It's something my family don't talk about much. It used to upset my mother so badly. I got out of the habit." He raised his head. The rims of his eyes were inflamed where he'd been rubbing them hard. His kohl makeup was smeared. "Doesn't mean I don't think about her."

"I'll get that sketchpad back to you as soon as I can. It must mean so much."

"I should pay you. A fee or something."

I shook my head. I didn't want money. Ricky was a friend. Besides that, I wanted the freedom to hand the sketchpad back and tell him I'd made no progress. I increasingly believed the project to find Babe was a poison chalice.

Ricky walked out on the grass, triggering the powerful security lights. Shell turned, smiled. She lifted her arms above her head and did a short, graceful imitation of Freaky's dance. Ricky seemed to grow in stature, as he went towards her. His shoulders came up and his footsteps lost the flat-soled shuffle they often had. It was as if he was shaking off the bad dreams of the past.

There on the lawn, they danced to silent music.

SIXTEEN

LAURA

By Tuesday morning, Freaky's established status at Harold Street had moved from temporary houseguest to something worryingly permanent. When I shuffled out into the early morning air to feed the hens, they were already strutting round their run and Freaky was scattering corn in every direction. He waved at me. "I know you like them up with the sun."

"You found their food, then."

"Just nosed about until I did."

"Okay ... only the corn is their supper treat. They have layers' pellets first thing. Anyway ... thanks."

Freaky was next to no trouble. On Saturday, we had spent all day in the garden, and Freaky had put his back into things, weeding and pricking out the rows of vegetables now bursting from the soil. I'd stood him a couple Wild Cossacks at the Curate's Egg, and he seemed to think that was payment in advance because on Sunday he'd cleared and tidied the greenhouse to give the tomato plants more room, and he was back out in the sunshine yesterday. While I was seeing clients, he'd used his skills to build me a firepit in the centre of the lawn, where our group, the Temple of Elphame, met in ritual circle.

Freaky and I had a grand fire-pit opening ceremony. We cooked a fresh-picked garden paella—broad beans, peas in their shells, baby beets, carrots, chopped spring cabbage, a mix of herbs, the first of the shallots, and some canned tomatoes from the store cupboard all bubbling away with short grain rice, served with a tossed salad. We were into early July, and the strength of the sun played on our backs right into the evening.

Freaky let himself out of the chicken run with a basket. "There's eggs . . . still warm. And I put flour, yeast, and water in the machine too."

"Freaky, you're a star. Whatever time did you get up?"

"With the sun, Sabbie."

"I suppose in the caravan you have to take advantage of the light hours."

"Up with the rising sun and to bed when it sets."

"I try to follow the same adage, but that's not much sleep during summer."

"It's more than enough in winter. I'm hibernating by then. Like a bear." He bent, pulled a dandelion from the cabbage patch, and smiled at its sunny face. I went over to the standpipe and unwound the hose. There had been no rain for days. Freaky handed me the egg basket and took the hose. "Allow me."

"You don't have to do everything!"

"I only respond with gratitude. Your bed is of the Ritz and your food is of the Fay."

"Let's hope not. You get stuck in fairyland if you eat the food of the Fay."

I was enjoying Freaky's company, but I'd only invited him for one night's stay. It was over a week now, and as I watched him create rainbow prisms with the water spray, I knew I didn't want him in a routine that meant he'd never leave.

"Any sign of Florence?"

"Sorry … no."

I turned away. It was surely daft to be this upset over the disappearance of one hen.

———

At seven fifty, Rey pulled up in his Citroën. I spun out of the front door.

"Only stopping for breakfast, I'm afraid."

I snatched at his hand. "Come and meet Freaky."

I'd always known that my game of tease-the-boyfriend would be up as soon as Rey clapped eyes on Freaky's reedy frame and lined features. In fact, they got on well enough. Rey could be charming, when it suited him, and he tolerated Freaky's orations with half-hearted laughs.

As the three of us ate breakfast together, the conversation stayed neutral, chatty. Actually, the conversation seemed to revolve entirely around me. We'd discussed the thankless task I'd been allocated by Wolfsbane—unpicking the mess of the shape-shifter workshop.

"Why do it, if you don't want to?" Rey asked.

"Only do it if the stars are in the right places," said Freaky, who always knew what his chart advised.

Then they started advising me on my visit to Grandma Dare.

"Why go, if you don't want to?" Rey asked, like an echo.

"Don't go," said Freaky. "The conjunctions in your houses are all wrong for looking back into the past."

"How can you tell?"

"Because families always mean trouble. Wouldn't you agree, my friend?"

In answer, Rey turned his eggshell upside down and tapped its empty bottom with his spoon. "My dad always did that when I was kid," he said. "He'd pretend he'd been given extra rations and be all disappointed when there was nothing inside."

Rey mostly kept his childhood to himself, and I dived in while I had the opportunity. "You father sounds great fun."

"They're good people, my mum and dad. In comparison, I'm a very bad son."

"Oh, I'm sure you're not ..."

Rey stood to clear the breakfast bar, as if talking about his family was something best done on the run. "I haven't seen them since Christmas. Didn't mean for that to happen, it just did. When I was with Lesley, we'd spend every third or fourth weekend with them, but since the break-up ...."

"Where do they live?"

"North Petherton."

"A hop away!"

"I know. Okay, at the moment, Mum and Dad have each other, they have their neighbours, and my brother and his wife live in the village. They don't nag me."

I chuckled. "You're busy, that's the trouble. You should make an appointment with yourself to go and see them."

"I'm not keen to do that now..."

"Why?" I asked as he trailed off.

"Like you said, I'm busy." He ran hot water into a bowl.

Freaky twisted on his bar stool. "Rey, you'd probably know where I'd have to go to talk about finding accommodation."

"I'd start with Citizen's Advice. They're the people with all the answers. They'll point you in the right direction. There's a branch on the High Street."

Freaky patted his few pockets. "I'll be off, then. Bus due any minute, might as well be on it, get things sorted. Nice bumping into you, my friend."

"You too." Rey watched him go, his hands held fast in the washing up bowl. "Interesting character," he said at last.

"I bet you say that about your snitches too."

"My what?"

His tone alerted me. "Sorry. Whatever you call them, your informers."

"He's effectively homeless, isn't he?"

"If you like."

"That means he'll be hanging round here for months, doesn't it?"

"He wouldn't be on his way to Citizen's Advice, if he was thinking like that!"

"Okay, wind your neck in, Sabbie." He turned and began scrubbing at the yolky egg cups.

"Have you told them about me?" I asked, quietly.

"What're you talking about now?"

"Your parents. Do they know you have a girlfriend?"

"Not as such."

"Any reason why?"

"No! No, really. I should tell them."

"You're not ... you don't think I'd embarrass you? Like, you don't want to tell them you're seeing a shaman?"

"I'm not embarrassed," Rey barked. "I'm proud of you. I'll phone soon. It would be good. Something positive." He balanced the egg cups on the drainer. The sight of them reminded me that I had one less laying hen. "Florence is dead; I told you, didn't I?"

"Sabbie! That is awful! I'm sorry—I'm so sorry. After this Alys thing and all." He snatch my hand. His was covered in soap bubbles. "What a blow. How did it happen?"

It was wonderful to know he empathized so deeply with the pain I felt. He'd never taken much notice of my hens. "She went missing while I was in Glastonbury. Not a fox. He would have left carnage behind. Like the day we met, remember?"

"Sorry? Met? Fox? Who is Florence?"

"One of my Sussex hens."

"God, Sabbie! Heck—I was thinking of—what's her name? The Dutch girl."

"Marianne," I said, my voice flat. "That's Marianne, Rey. She's alive and kicking. It's Florence who's dead." I felt my eyes water up. I snatched my hand from his to rub at them. "Why on earth would I think you'd remember the names of my hens?"

"I do know you're attached to them."

"Good. Good. I'm glad you know that."

"Look—sorry. I'm tired, that's all. My brain's fucked up. Didn't get to sleep until almost three."

"Is it this case you're working on with DS Chaisey?"

He didn't reply. Suddenly, I wish I hadn't asked. Perhaps he'd been getting to sleep at three a.m. after a night out with Pippa. Worse, a night *in* with Pippa. I got off my stool and went to put my arms around him, desperately thinking of some neutral territory I could use to move the subject on. "Did you ring Marty-Mac, Rey?"

He shrugged.

"Only, yesterday afternoon, I popped into Facebook for five minutes and found a friend request from him."

"You what?"

"I declined, of course."

"I bloody well hope you did. The man is trouble. And I know what you're like with trouble. It usually blows up on you."

"Is he a..." I struggled for the right word. "A felon?"

"He should not be hounding you."

"Stop it!" I tried to laugh. "You're scaring me."

"That'll be the day." He put damp palms on my cheeks. "Marty-Mac plus Sabbie Dare equals disaster. If you hear from him again, contact me directly."

"Okay." My voice sounded unsure—I'd have liked a bit more explanation, but dared not interrogate him further. I was rewarded with a kiss. It wasn't as deep or as long or as passionate as I'd hoped, but I knew I should be grateful for that kiss; that I should savour it.

———

Laura arrived for her fourth appointment a little harassed round the edges, as if the scooter ride had blown her about. "It's not such a nice day, is it?"

"It wasn't going to last forever," I said. "This is an English summer after all."

"Yeah." She huffed, catching her breath. "I do forget, sometimes."

We sat across from each other in the wicker chairs. "I want to start with those bits of homework, Laura. Are you managing recording your dreams?"

"Right. I did have a good think about dreams. I honestly can't remember having any dreams since last Tuesday."

"It would help to keep the book beside your bed."

"I guess." She turned down her mouth, suggesting she wasn't keen on the dream diary.

"What about coping with your panic attacks?"

"They haven't been so bad. Thanks to you."

"Thanks to your Community Psychiatric Nurse!"

"I think the medication is helping, but mostly, it is down to you. I would never have faced up to Daniel if you hadn't held my hand like you did."

"We should keep moving on with our work too. I'd like to start some soul retrieval. Would you be up for that?"

She gave an energetic nod, but I couldn't help notice that her cheeks paled, as if the idea of soul retrieval made her slightly faint.

———

With the silken cord connecting us, and the Pokémon toy in my hand, I knew that I would find Laura's otherworld again.

"Trendle, my faithful companion. How will we do this?"

"By fishing in the dark," he said, reminding me of how I'd detected a net around Laura as I'd rattled over her body.

We pushed through the willows, passing the fingerpost. Trendle slipped into the mouth of the cave and I followed, taking judicious footstep across the gritty floor until even the last glimmers of daylight were left behind. As I turned the bend in the cave, I began tracing the cave wall with my fingers. I could feel the warmth of my own fast breathing. I screwed my inner eyes up, searching the blackness, and saw a jagged crack shining brilliantly in the distance—a space in the cave wall large enough for the sun to shine through. A shadow moved on the cave walls, as if there was activity just outside the narrow exit. I heard the sound of waves. Of course. There would be sea in Laura's otherworld. I watched the shadow and made out limbs, a blurred head. I was watching the reflection of some sort of spirit being.

"Please! May I ask you, are you Laura Munroe's guardian?"

The shadow moved on the wall in a kind of dance. "I am guardian to many. I have watched over Laura since she came into this soultime." The voice was buoyant, like the song of a boat.

"I saw a kind of caul around her. Was that a true vision?"

"Human souls are crippled with misunderstandings and obsessions," said the shadow. "They have many and varied burdens."

I let out a sigh. "Laura is burdened. I can tell. I just don't know how, or why."

"Laura's affliction jolted her soul from its axis. This judders every thought and wipes away peace of mind."

"Her soul is out of kilter?" I asked. "Like a dislocated shoulder?"

I heard the being laugh. It was a shocking but glorious sound. It was like choirs; like symphonies of laughter. It was almost more than I could bear. I kept my eyes away from the blaze of light outside the cave and concentrated on the shadow form.

"A wonderful correspondence, Sabrina Dare. It will hold good for you. Yes, dislocation and a jail of netting."

"Please … you know my name … can you tell me yours?"

"I have many. Ask Laura what she calls me."

I felt my eyes grow wide. "You are Raichu! How…bizarre!"

There was silence. I felt the spirit distance itself, but only when the brilliant light faded completely from the cave exit did I lurch outside. There was sand beneath my feet, the chill of a breeze on my skin. High summer, and Trendle and I were on a beach, leaving trails of footprints in wet sand.

The tide shushed in and dragged out again. Behind me was a low sea wall. Ahead of me were the dark legs of a pier which stretched out into water. This was familiar territory.

"Weston Super Mare," I called to Trendle. "Laura's hometown."

I'd been to Weston many times as a kid. I'd been on the pier for the rides and the slot machines. I shaded my eyes against the sun; I'd noticed a flicker of red which burst from the pier's platform. "What is that?"

"Come." Trendle quickened his pace.

The flicker was growing as we ran. I could see individual flames licking the sides of pier booths. I heard a whooshing sound and in an instance fire ran along the wooden slats of the pier walkway.

"Fire!" I yelled. "Fire!"

It took hold fast, consuming the wooden structure. Even though there was nothing I could do, even though the flames were scorching my arms, I ran towards the blaze. I could feel the heat on my face and the smuts in my eyes. Trendle shot ahead, like a dog, and nosed under the pier structure. I ran to him and stopped dead.

Despite the fire above us, it was cool under the pier—cool, dark, and a little mysterious. Trendle was sniffing out something in the flotsam and jetsam, snuffling at some fishermen's nets tangled in the surf.

There was a bundle wrapped inside netting ... *trapped* inside it. I touched it and it felt cold.

"Is this the juddered piece of Laura's soul?" I whispered. I pulled at the netting, but whichever way I tugged, I only made things worse, tightening the knots.

A rending creak sounded above our heads. We were surrounded by the falling sparks of the fire above us; red rain in the summer sky. A board collapsed through the walkway and fell, hissing as the charred shape hit the sea.

"Help me, Raichu!" I called.

For a moment nothing happened, and I fretted that Raichu had felt dishonored by my comment in the cave. I stood my ground, waiting.

Through the curtain of raining sparks and burning beams came a figure as tall as the pier. A garment of plain white hung like a sail over its limbs. I saw a glorious face, ablaze and formless as molten rock. Laura's guardian was ageless and genderless, almost bodiless, and yet it was holding the bundle of netting safely within its luminous form.

"Please? Please tell me what this means!"

The guardian dissolved through the fire, carrying the bundle away, floating high against the clouds. Raichu held Laura's soul safe, the fishing net trailing behind, suspended by nothing but air.

SEVENTEEN
GERALD

I HAD PLANNED TO spend the afternoon doing some deep inner study, meditation, and path-working. But after Laura had paid and left, I couldn't resist a visit to Facebook. I checked my friend requests. No further contact from the chap who called himself Marty-Mac. I went into Twitter and couldn't find him there. I entered my email inbox and my back rammed straight.

Three emails from Brice. One had arrive late last night, as if, like Rey, he couldn't sleep. The following two had arrived together an hour ago. I clicked on the first to arrive. It was an open email to all the workshoppers.

This Friday, I need to come to the West Country again. I would like to take the opportunity to see everyone. Shell tells me the Chalice Well Gardens in Glastonbury are worth a visit and I propose we all meet there at midday. There are things to lay to

rest about Alys's death. And I'd like to talk about the funeral,
which will be next week on Friday.

Brice Johnson

Shell had already told me that Brice had an early appointment with
the Coroner's department in Wells; the toxicology results were back.
It looked like Brice was willing to bring everyone who'd been at
Stonedown Farm in on the updates.

What if the truth turned out to be that while at Stonedown Farm,
Alys had been sold drugs which had killed her? Was Brice planning
a sort of Agatha Christie revelation where he'd point a finger at the
perpetrator? I envisaged Stefan rising from his seat and leaping from
an upstairs window rather than be arrested and put away.

Luckily, Brice wanted to use the gardens, not the house, so there
was no likelihood of suicidal leaps. In fact, he'd chosen one of the
most restful spots in Glastonbury—perhaps guided by Shell. Just
walking through the turnstile of the Chalice Well had a calming effect. We'd certainly need magical tranquility if Wolfsbane and Stefan,
Freaky and Anag, were going to meet face-to-face, not to mention the
twisted triangle of Shell, Ricky, and Wolfs.

I clicked on the second message, which had been sent solely to
me. It was short.

I've had another one. Sick and tired. Don't want to look. Haven't
opened it. Forwarding directly. Tell no one.
Regards,
Brice

Suddenly I was his storm gauge, the one who would stand outside
and take the lightning strike, should it come. Of course he was sick

and tired. I didn't blame him for being curt, although it felt as if, now I'd agreed to take these messages from him, he was blaming me for their arrival.

I opened the third email and studied it, reading it several times. The address was *morganlefay@* an obscure server. The Subject was, as always, *Morgan le Fay*. No marks for original thinking.

Earthly knowledge is but adumbration. People are weak; fools not to be trusted. Humans are responsible entirely for the coming of the wasteland.

Blood runs deep through the Hollow Hill and bubbles to the surface, spilling out into a vast, undiscovered cavern. On that day we will gird our loins and walk through blood. Anyone who does not stand to protect Logres is pusillanimous. Foolish knights abound and will be pounded down into the ground. It is presaged.

Morgan le Fay

I looked up the definitions of *adumbration, pusillanimous,* and *presaged* (shadowy, cowardly, and foretold). I checked online, to see what sensible people said about the centre of the Tor. Turned out, no one knew anything much, not even where the springs that ran through the hill began.

I pressed print. I had hard copies of both Morgan le Fay's other emails. I'd read them so closely, I knew them by heart, but I took out those copies and compared them with this new one, treating them as three chapters of one story.

I felt a ghostly tap of the shoulder. I jumped and slammed my hands over the printouts.

"What's up, my friend? You're deep into something here," said Freaky.

I lifted my hands. Brice had said, "tell no one," but I'd already told Rey and it was going to be hard to hide anything from my guest.

"If I show you, can you keep it to yourself?" I waited for the one raised eyebrow, which was followed by a single nod. "Brice has been getting these."

It was a relief to tell someone who would not scoff at my theories. Freaky read the printouts slowly. "This woman is some nutter, that's for sure, but she has a point. *The wasteland is upon us . . .* She couldn't be more right, could she?"

"No, but—"

"Just ask Yew. He'd tell you about the wasteland. It's still evident in our modern world." He waved his sharp fingernails in the air. "Petrol fumes poisoning the air. Industry poisoning lakes and rivers. Intensive agriculture poisoning the land, washing topsoil away, and the only answer they want to come up with is to genetically modify our food."

Freaky had a point—although Morgan le Fay talked about ancient legend, threat of famine was perennial.

"You know the story of the wasteland of Logres," Freaky asked. "The rape of the well maidens?"

I nodded. "It's the story of the Fisher King and Sir Percival."

"Ah," said Freaky. "A good knight."

"Yes. He's determined to save the land by finding the grail. The Fisher King shows Percival a strange procession—a bloodied lance and a candelabra, both carried by boys, and a golden cup, held by a maiden. It's clear to everyone except Percival that he must heal this wounded king to restore the land's fruitfulness. But he's too uncertain and the following morning, when he wakes, the castle is empty."

I thought about that. Percival was an innocent abroad who got everything wrong.

Foolish knights abound and will be pounded down into the ground.

"This Morgan le Fay must be doing Brice's head in," Freaky was saying. "Surely he's gotta let it go."

"He can't let it go. These emails are grisly ... and Morgan le Fay isn't kidding."

"What d'you mean, not kidding?"

I didn't stop to think further. I told him what I knew about Gerald Evens. "Every time I read the second email, the message screams out at me. *The Red Knight has been fatally struck.* I don't think it's coincidence there was an attack at the abbey. But this latest email is less clear. I'm just hoping someone else hasn't been attacked. A 'foolish knight.'"

Freaky read aloud. "*Blood runs deep ... on this day ... ... a vast cavern.* That's the red spring, surely. The Blood Spring. The cavern spilling with its water. She's talking about the chambers from the Chalice Well that used to go into the hill."

"You told me about that, a while back," I said, remembering. "Something about dancing all night?"

"Yeah, man. The white spring and the red spring were far out in those days. We Freaks loved the chambers; deep, echoey, perfect for hanging loose. There was no paying to go into the Chalice Well back then." He paused, thinking things through. "Could we find out if somebody's been attacked at the Chalice Well?"

As soon as Freaky said it, I could see. Patterns and markers jumped out. Not clear, or precise—more a tingling in my body, a gripping of my intestines. A firewall rolling down. My forehead prickled with cold heat. "That's what's different. The other two emails made announcements. This one ... it's a warning. For a future event. *On that day we will gird our loins and walk through blood.*"

"What day?" said Freaky.

"Three days from now. Brice has asked us all to be at the Chalice Well Friday midday. He's sent us all an email and I reckon Morgan le Fay is on Brice's list. This is her response to the invitation."

— —

In the garden I bedded out all the forgotten trays filled with leggy seedlings. This was the sort of gardening that allowed my mind to wander until I was somewhere else—searching for connections. Freaky's input had really helped and for the first time, I had a glimmer of how Morgan's mind worked. His questions about Gerald Evens made me realize I should have chased things up. Before I realized I was doing it, I'd swilled the mud from my fingers and was dialling for Stonedown Farm. Stefan answered.

"Hi, there!" I struggled to sound upbeat and friendly. "It's Sabbie. How are you?"

"I'm okay," said Stefan in a tone that suggested he had also received Brice's invitation to the Chalice Well and was wary of anyone connected to it.

"I'm actually phoning for some information on your friend. The one that was attacked."

"Er ..."

"Gerald Evens. The volunteer at Glastonbury Abbey."

"You saw it in the paper?"

"No," I said, making a mental note to check this up. "Esme told me. What did the papers say?"

"Oh, you know … no clear sighting of assailant … no motive for attack …"

"I was wondering how he is."

"Gerald? D'you know him then?"

I'd like to, I wanted to say. "How is he?"

"He was bad for a couple of days. They ambulanced him to the Head Injury Unit. I had to drive behind with his things. Out of the woods now, I think."

"Brilliant news, Stef! Can he talk to people?"

"Er … I guess. I've not seen him for a while. I do ring up, but Bristol's a long way. Tomorrow, he's being transferred to West Mendip Hospital."

"He's coming back to Glastonbury. That has to be good, doesn't it? Has he talked of the attack?"

"Glad to say he can't remember the attack. He's a bit … sluggish, you know? Not the full shilling yet. Why ever do you want to know that?"

"I … you know me, Stef. Always looking for auguries. I wondered if he'd let me introduce myself."

"You?" His tone became suddenly enthusiastic. "Could you go tomorrow? Visiting's in the afternoon. It would save me the trip."

"Yes, of course," I said, immediately irritated that my visit would prevent Stefan getting off his butt. "Thanks, Stef. Send my blessings to Esme."

———

Gerald Evens stared out from under swollen eyelids. Nearly a fortnight had not lessened the signs of his brutal attack. His eye sockets
were yellow and blue from bruising and his lips were swollen into a
rounded ball. His forehead was hidden by a dressing. The front of
his head had been shaved so close his hair was just a shadow, but it
hung in a greasy tangle at the back. There was a nasty split high on
his cheek, closed up with stitches. He was sitting in a winged chair
next to his bed in clothes that no longer seemed to fit. Every so often
his hand would reach up and touch the stitches, visible under their
plastic coating, then stray to his forehead to finger the bandage.

I managed to get my facial expression under control as I walked
into his room, wipe off the horror. I held out my hand. "I'm Stefan's
friend, Sabbie Dare."

"Hi," said Gerald. He took my hand with caution, as if touch still
mostly hurt. He tried to smile. One of his front teeth was missing.

"I was in town and wondered if you'd mind me visiting."

"To be honest, people are not forming queues. My partner's in
every evening, but people are at work in the day."

He was trying to speak clearly, but it was hard to pick up every
word Gerald said. The vowel sounds felt whispery, as if his voice box
had been wrecked in the attack, and the consonants that needed
tongue and lips were muffled.

"I was shocked when I heard what happened."

"The abbey people came in, but they haven't been back." His
mind was still on visitors. "I've brought them bad publicity."

"Surely not!"

"Want to sit down?"

I sank onto an adjacent hard chair. I was still clutching my carrier
bag. I'd piled some old magazines together, before I'd left the house.

I laid it on the bed. "I brought this for you. Didn't know if you were up to grapes, so ..."

Gerald pulled the magazines out and flicked through the pile.

"They're a bit specialized. Wasn't sure what you were into. There's a couple of old *Avalon* issues, and the latest copy of *Current Archeology*, but most of them are gardening mags."

"These will take my mind off things."

"I'm sure you'll—well, make a full recovery."

"That's what they're saying." He swallowed. "I work in the Glastonbury library. Quiet job. They say I'll be back in no time."

"Does it hurt?"

"Bit of a headache." He touched his stitches again.

"Don't think you have to talk. Not if it's difficult. I just thought you might like some company. Although ..."

Gerald opened a *Gardener's World* and flicked through as if my comment on not talking was an instruction. I held the pause for a bit. He didn't seem to wonder why I'd come to visit. Maybe his mind was too fogged. He'd taken me at face value, and now I was going to have trouble explaining that I'd come for information.

"Are you into gardening?"

"Not much. Tiny town garden. I like to keep the front nice. People see that."

"I grow vegetables, mostly."

"Don't have room for vegetables."

"I love flowers too, but I'm not overfussy. I weed my veg rows more often than the flowerbeds."

"Weed is a plant in the wrong place, eh?" He turned a page, perhaps so that he didn't have to look at me directly all the time. He must have been aware his face was a mess. "At the abbey grounds, we're careful about the wildflower areas; no mowing and that."

"I've seen the wildflower meadow. It's spectacular. And the Fish Pond. I loved that."

"Where the monks kept their supply of supper."

"It was covered with lilies when I was there. Trout making bubbles. Dragonflies drinking with their tails. Peace, deep peace."

He gave a tiny smile and I knew I'd hit the spot. "That's what I can't work out. Glastonbury Abbey is a tranquil place. People come to be quiet. That's why I love volunteering there."

"D'you recall someone who might have been ... I dunno ... accusatory ... aggressive ... suspicious?"

"I get these flashes. Like I'm remembering a dream. It was odd, that day. I remember that." He reached to his table and took a sip of water, moistening his mouth. "Sometimes, you feel out of sorts, don't you? With your day. Like someone up there has it in for you. I remember feeling that. Bad feeling. Something out of place."

I tried a grin. "We are talking about Glastonbury, y'know. Odd things happen."

To me, Glastonbury was a core of power. Those energies were neutral and the overwhelming majority used them for good. But someone out there, calling herself Morgan le Fay, was using that power with malicious intent.

"Occasionally I remember some little snippet, then realize it could be something from another day."

"Has anyone talked to you about the weapon that was used?"

"They said it was a loose stone—a piece of masonry from the abbey. Normally that would be almost impossible. We make sure everything is safe for the general public. We don't have loose bits of masonry. So much building work is going on right now … I don't know."

"Did your assailant bring it with them, perhaps?"

He looked at me through the bloated tissue around his eyes. I got a sense of finally being assessed. "You're not police, are you?"

"No. Nothing like that."

"What d'you want from me, then?"

I wasn't going to deny I wanted something. I just wasn't sure how to explain. "Did you hear about the death on the Tor? Midsummer Eve?"

"I read about it. A girl collapsed."

"I was there. The girl who died—her husband's been getting what amounts to anonymous emails from a woman called Morgan le Fay. Does that ring any bells?"

"I don't know punks like that." He closed his eyes and appeared to doze for sometime.

I knew he wanted me to leave. I rested my fingers on the back of his hand, being careful not to touch the drip he had in his arm.

He felt the pressure and looked at me, bleary-eyed. "I don't think they'll want me back," he said, as if he'd been dreaming this thought.

"Maybe you won't want to go back anyway. After this … after what happened."

"I loved volunteering. I loved it better than my job, if you understand that."

"Talking to people?"

"Yes. I like to give something back. And I'm a graduate in medieval history."

"The abbey's so full of history, isn't it?"

"Certainly. Starting in the early medieval period, of course, what people call the Dark Ages—a misnomer because plenty of writing went on at that time, mostly in monasteries like Glastonbury Abbey."

I nodded enthusiastically. "I guess."

"I'm wondering if I did anything to provoke."

"From what I've heard, you aren't the sort to goad anyone."

"It's my job as a guide to be chatty, but sometimes I can go on a bit."

"That's what you are, a guide?"

"Yes. I'm Sir Walter of Somersetshire. We all have names, but to be honest we're not asked for them a lot. I usually get called Dragon Man by the kids."

"Why?"

"There's a dragon on my tabard. At the centre of the red cross."

"So ... you dress up."

"We do. I'm a knight at arms. Jenny is a serving wench called Maid Myrtle, and Tyrone is a peasant. Then there's the monks. The punters like the monks."

"You're a knight? In red?"

He closed his eyes again. "Sir Walter of Somersetshire."

I was staring at my shoulder bag, in which was my phone. The image in my mind of Gerald in his red knight's costume confirmed to me that Morgan le Fay had been at the abbey. Had she witnessed something? Or been involved in something?

"You might have seen her," I whispered. "The terrible attack has blocked it from your mind."

I stood up and put one of my cards on his bedside locker. Gerald opened one eye. "You off? Thanks for coming in. Kind. Sorry."

"You're exhausted. Of course. I just wanted to say ... well ... memories can grow. Flashes, yeah? They might grow. Would you tell me?"

I think he nodded a reply. He might just have been nodding off to sleep.

EIGHTEEN

YEW

The trustees kept the Chalice Well gardens neat as a pin by taming nature, as all gardeners do. That set it apart from other Glastonbury sites like the Tor and Wearyall Hill, which had powerfully wild aspects. At the Chalice Well, the lawns were clipped and the flower beds weeded to within one centimetre of their lives. The red spring bubbled beneath an ornate metal cover and its flow was landscaped via flumes, little waterfalls, and still pools. There were quiet corners where one could meditate and light a votive candle.

It was not a place where violence could happen. But then, neither was the abbey. Neither was the Tor.

On Friday morning Freaky and I drove to Glastonbury, where Brice had arranged to meet everyone from the shape-shifting workshop.

Brice and Shell were standing on the forecourt of the Chalice Well when we arrived. Freaky strode up, dreadlocks flying behind him, and hugged them both. "We are early, my friends, thanks to clear roads and the lure of my hometown."

In fact, we were early because I wanted to grab Brice before anyone else arrived. I'd sent him a long email yesterday bringing him up to speed on my visit to Gerald Evens and explaining my worries about the third Morgan le Fay email. He hadn't responded, and now I was wondering if he'd read it.

He looked as if he'd been strung up by a windlass. He did not even smile a greeting. Shell was pale around the mouth, which accentuated her pillar-box lipstick. I swooped forward, taking Brice unawares, and wrapped my arms round them both. "How did it go at the coroner's?"

"You don't actually get to see the big man himself." Shell glanced at Brice as if for confirmation. "It was a bit of a shocker."

"I'm still processing it." A muscle in Brice's cheek moved as he ground his teeth. He'd wait until the full party was assembled before spilling his news.

I felt my belly screw and couldn't help look away from him; from his pain. The Chalice Well lay quietly behind its fencing, dulled by the grey July day, and a frisson of chilled darkness moved through me. "Please? Brice? I emailed you to say we should not go into the Chalice Well."

"What?" said Shell. "Why?"

There was a silence. "I've had a hate email, Shell." Brice flashed me a glance, as if to warn me not to mention the other two emails. "Sorry, I didn't want to tell you. But we might as well show it to them both, Sabbie."

I passed across the printout of the third email. Freaky and Shell bent their heads over it, Freaky doing a very good job of pretending he'd never seen it before.

"What the hell is this?" Shell snapped.

"Some punk, some pond scum who gets a fancy kick from winding me up."

"When you sent the email about today to everyone on the workshop list, did it occur to you that Morgan le Fey would read it?" I asked.

"Let me tell you, this woman is fucking with my mind." He gestured towards the entrance gate. "She's in there, isn't she? Morgan le Fay. If she's in the gardens, I want a fucking look at her."

Shell took him by the wrist. "Let's take a moment to think about this."

"Please, Brice. Don't let's go in. She dangerous."

"She's a crazeball. D'you think that makes me scared of her? Quite the opposite."

"No one is saying you're scared, Brice." He didn't want Shell to know about the other emails, but he surely could see the connections I was making. "In a few minutes, everyone will start arriving, expecting to go into the Chalice Well. I'm asking you to tell them—somehow—that we should not go into the gardens. Must not go in."

Brice nodded, his chin jerking with determination. "I have things to say to them."

"We could just go to a pub, instead, I suppose," said Shell. "Doesn't have to be here."

"Feels cowardly," said Brice. "Not to go in."

"I think Sabbie's saying that it would only mean trouble," said Freaky.

"Who cares? It's just …" He found a handkerchief and wiped his mouth. He'd dressed as casually as he knew how, in blue jeans and a powder blue jumper. "We never got to see the Chalice Well when we were here. Shell said Alys would have loved it."

"It's glorious," I agreed. "Do spend time in there. Just not today. Something is shouting at me—this thing—shouting at me."

"I don't want anyone else knowing about this."

"Then we'll concoct a good reason," Shell said.

Freaky put out the flat of his palm. "Looks like it's going to chuck it down, eh?"

"It won't, though." I peered up at the thin layer of clouds.

"Yeah, but who else is gonna to know that?"

———

Juke and Ricky were first to arrive, Juke striding ahead of his mate. His face was dark, almost tinged with grey. Moments later Ricky wandered into view. I think he would have walked past the gateway if Shell hadn't run to him, her hands stretched to touch his. She drew him into the group.

He gave a brief nod. "Everyone's grim." He'd picked up the atmosphere hovering round us like bonfire smoke. "Everyone's in pain."

Shell put an arm tight around his waist, under his unbuttoned raincoat, a full-skirted affair last seen on a funeral director. "We're together," she announced. "Me and Ricky. We're keeping it quiet, though."

"You haven't told Wolfsbane," Freaky stated.

I didn't comment. Although I'd never stop a girl from running two guys side by side—I'd probably done it myself pre-Rey—it felt a like a murky thing to do to someone as exceptional as Wolfs.

"There is a reason we're so grim, Ricky." Shell was staring hard at Brice. She wanted Ricky to know about Morgan le Fay. Brice shook his head, a strong double jerk, his mouth a thin line.

"It's the results isn't it?" Ricky put in, too eagerly. "They've done an autopsy. You've got the cause of death." Ricky shook his head as if something had flown into his ear. "I don't want to think about it. The cutting…"

A hush fell. The tick in Brice's cheek returned.

"Honey…" Shell whispered.

Ricky stared at his feet. "You won't need gifts, at least."

"What?"

"It's what Aeschylus said. Only the god of death does not desire gifts."

"Ricky's a philosopher," said Shell.

"I am not. Only the great thinkers can call themselves that." He scuffed at the gravel with his glossy boot. "But I did see her spirit rise."

Moments later, Wolfsbane and Yew arrived. Ricky and Shell sprung apart, Shell offering a secret smile, but Ricky was still staring at the ground, where his boot had made a pattern in the gravel. Shell slid her arm through Brice's and hung on to it in a supportive manner.

Wolfs thumped Brice on the back with a consoling fist. "How are you?"

"Work keeps me busy. Shell's been a godsend, Wolfsbane. She's in touch most days."

"Right. I'm glad. Glad."

Wolfsbane didn't look glad, and it made me wonder if Shell had been using her friendship with Brice as a smokescreen for when she was with Ricky. She knew how to throw out a confusion of messages.

Brice stuck out a hand towards Yew, clearly not keen on any further pagan hugs. "It's good that you could all come. I wanted to tell you some things—ask you some things. We're going to find a pub—not sure where …"

"We'll go to the Rifleman's Arms," said Freaky. "I know them in there, I'll swing us a discount."

"I thought we were going in the Chalice Well," Juke snapped.

"You okay, Juke?" I asked. He'd been standing slightly outside the small group, unsmiling. With attention moving between Shell and Ricky's news, and Brice's clammed-up posture, maybe he felt a bit unwelcome.

"I've had to pull a sickie to get here. Exhausted before I begin, that's all. And I was looking forward to a bit of peace in the gardens, not a cider-swilling dive."

"I was looking forward, too," said Ricky. "I've never been in. But perhaps it's nothing special. Like *The Phantom Menace*."

Brice gave him a dagger look. "What?"

"*Star Wars: Episode One*. I'd seen the DVDs of all the others and I was dead keen when it came out. It was rubbish."

"The Chalice Well isn't like that," said Shell, softly. "It's the sacred red spring of Glastonbury Tor."

"Wherever we go … this has to be good, yeah?" said Freaky. "Find some closure."

Brice gave a robotic nod, reminding me that he might not be here for closure at all. "Is anyone else is coming?"

As he spoke, Esme Hall maneuvered her heavy car in through the Chalice Well entrance, stuck a "permission to park" card on her windscreen, and peeled herself out of the driver's seat.

"Juno's peacocks," I heard Yew mutter.

Esme was resplendent in a prism of colours—a shoulder cape of rich teal over a tight turquoise basque top and blood-red sateen crop pants. Her hair was backcombed into purple spikes and her earrings glittered as they coursed the distance from earlobe to shoulder.

"Hi all. Were you waiting for us? Stef sends his apologies. He's meeting with the bods from Town Hall this morning, I'm afraid."

Brice took her hand and I reminded myself that he'd met Esme for brief minutes, during which time both she and Stefan had probably been charming. "That's all of us, then, except for Anagarika. I invited him, but true to form, he hasn't showed."

Freaky huffed a breath. "Thank the gods."

"We should carry on without him," said Yew. "He wants us to wait and be irritated. The same as when a small child is naughty for attention."

Esme leaned into our rough circle, tucking chummy arms through Freaky and Wolfsbane's elbows so that the bulk of her breasts half-fell from her basque. "I found out his real name. It's not Anagarika Dharmapala at all. It's Woody Choke."

The men shouted with laughter, even Brice.

"Well, I think it's sad," said Shell. "Most people choose names that mean something to them, that will represent what they've become, not to hide some godawful given name. Like Wolfsbane. That plant is powerful; used carefully, it can heal."

"It can poison, too," Ricky mumbled.

"The guy's from Melbourne," Esme went on. "Before he came over here, he ran a video porn shop in the city."

Juke's mood had lifted dramatically with this news and he was having a full fit of giggles. "How did you find that out?"

"Sorry, can't reveal my sources."

I glanced towards the road, worried that Anag would turn up while we were giggling over his name.

"Are we going in, then?" said Esme.

"We're going the Rifleman's Arms," said Freaky. "Looks like rain."

"What—are you all made of sugar?"

"I haven't brought a coat," said Brice. He strode off along the narrow stretch of pavement with Shell still attached to his arm. Wolfsbane hurried behind them. Freaky and Yew walked together in deep conversation. Ricky and Juke followed, seemingly both lost in their own thoughts.

Esme sidled up to me. "How're you enjoying having Freaky in your house?" It was as if she was talking about some vagrant who had pushed his way in.

"He's bloody lovely, if you want the truth. Extremely helpful. Excellent gardener. He even makes bread for us. And gets up early to feed the hens."

Perhaps it was the reflection from her turquoise basque, but she seemed to go a bit puce in the face, so I carried on joyfully in the same vein all the way to the pub.

The Rifleman's Arms had a strong following among Glastonbury locals. It was a low-lit watering hole with a Hobbit-like feel and I wouldn't have been surprised to spot Strider smoking a pipe in one of the quiet corners.

Freaky hailed the publican with an ease that came from propping up the bar here for the last forty years and helped Brice get in a round of drinks. Wolfsbane pulled a couple of tables together. I went to grab a seat, but Yew caught my elbow and eased me out of earshot.

"Wanted to say ... Freaky just told me about Gerald Evens. I mean ... the Red Knight thing."

I closed my eyes in despair. How could I have forgotten that Freaky rarely resisted the impulse to gossip? "Brice wants it all kept quiet."

"Lips sealed with superglue. It's just ... what happened to this Gerald chappy rang a bell. One of my residents was mugged round that time. Felt a bit similar."

"A resident? Of your hostel?"

"Yes. Anthony Bale. He was on the Tor, solstice night. I'd invited him; thought he'd enjoy it. On the way back to the hostel, he was attacked."

I could feel my eyes widen. "What happened?"

"Well, nothing much, to be honest. He was extremely lucky. Someone threw a brick or something at the back of his head. He felt this hard whack—he lurched forward. If he'd fallen onto pavement, he might have hurt himself, but he fell onto the grass verge by the side of the road."

"This didn't happen *in* Glastonbury."

"No, but he was there. Anthony had got extremely upset when Alys collapsed. Almost hysterical. Some of the residents have very bad histories; nasty memories. He caught the first bus back to Yeovil." Yew often talked about his residents, all of whom would be homeless if they didn't have the hostel, and Yew had a passion for his work there. His lavish covering of tattoos and piercings, and the plait that reached down his back, gave him the strong street cred such a job needed.

"Hysterical? Sort of … laughing?"

"Yeah, if you like."

I remembered him, now. A guy with his hand over his mouth; that embarrassed reaction to death that you sometimes see.

"Did Anthony see his attacker?"

"Not by the time he'd scrabbled up and regained his wits. He didn't want to report it."

"Why ever not?"

"He has a homeless mentality, Sabbie. When you've been through that sort of existence, you're expecting attacks each and every day, and you take it as your due."

"Did *you* report it?"

"Yeah, but to be fair, Anthony hardly had more than a nasty bruise and his attacker had disappeared. I guess all the cops did was complete the paperwork."

"Yew, can you remember what Anthony was wearing?"

"Why?"

"Can you?"

"I honestly doubt even he'll be able to, to be fair. You can ask him, if you want." Yew raised his hands to make quotation marks. "Who do you think 'Morgan le Fay' is?"

A tray of drinks had appeared and I slipped into my seat without replying. I didn't want to get Yew any more involved. Besides, I had no answer to his question.

———

There were nine around the table—me, Wolfs, Shell, Ricky, Juke, Yew, Freaky, Esme, and Brice—and every eye was focused on Brice.

"I guess I should start. Do what I came here for. I feel you deserved to know what happened this morning."

Brice gripped his glass too tight. The surface of the beer trembled. His tension was infectious; Wolfs's future as a well-respected shaman depended on the pathology results. The silence lengthened, as if Brice couldn't find the words.

"I've been to Wells. Shell and I. Coroner's court. They've—"

He broke off. No one moved. He glanced at Shell.

"They're releasing Alys's body. That's it, Brice, yeah?"

"We can have the funeral. I'll be sending invitations to all of you. I'd love to miss a certain person out, but I don't see how I can. Anyone can come to a funeral anyway, I think."

"That's really strong of you," said Freaky.

"I've asked Shell to provide a eulogy. She's known Alys a long time. Longer than me."

I caught Shell's eye and she gave me a saddened smile. I was remembering what she'd said about Alys's early teen years; about getting pregnant by a teacher, and the botched abortion.

"I've already been in touch with a funeral director. I wanted things ready to roll. He said anyone can lead the celebrations. So I thought of asking Wolfsbane and Sabbie to be joint celebrants; to officiate the order of service. We hardly know the ministers round our way, and Alys would have loved you two to do it."

"Brice," I began, "that's such a huge honour..."

"It'll be at the Aldersbrook Crematorium, Friday midday. You're thinking London's a long way away. I'll help with travel costs—buy you all train tickets, accommodation. I'm happy for your partners to come. So you can enjoy London a bit, as well. You could stay all weekend, if you like. Apparently the ashes will be ready to scatter on Monday. I'll find a hotel, book you all in. No problem."

He'd thought this through and sorted it already—thrown money at it straight away.

"It would be a privilege to lead the ritual," said Wolfsbane. "Thank you, Brice."

"Alys would be so delighted," said Shell. She had her hands wrapped over Wolfsbane's, but under the table I'd noticed she was playing footsie with Ricky.

"That's a lot of expense, my friend," said Freaky.

Brice turned his beer mat round as if it would open a secret code. "You know, I didn't understand Alys's interest with this shaman lark. Obsession, I'd've called it. I thought the lot of it was rubbish; animals and journeys and, above all, goddesses. And I did presume that everyone else in the business was flaky. Actually, I thought you'd all be completely whacko. I've got to know some of you better … you're good people. Certainly no more nuts than most of my colleagues."

There was a pause as people digested his words.

"That's kind, my friend." Freaky showed his brown teeth. "I don't think I've ever been compared to a banker."

"They've finished the forensic tests," Shell said, half prompting Brice. "That's why they could release Alys."

"I had hoped knowing would help," said Brice.

"Did it help?" I asked, keeping my voice low.

"It's not good. About as bad as it could be."

"Wha …" Apprehension caught at Wolfsbane's throat. "What d'you mean, Brice?"

"Alys had taken something."

"Ecstasy?" whispered Yew.

"No. No."

"PMA?" I blurted out. All eyes turned me. "Pink Lady?"

"No … nothing like that at all. She was jacked."

There was a long silence. Apart from us, the pub was almost empty; our conversation had filled it. Two old men sat at opposite sides of the bar on high stools. When my gaze strayed their way, they quickly began to study the pints of dark liquid before them.

"Jacked," said Wolfs, eventually.

Brice gave a Gallic shrug. "It's a fitness supplement. Keeps you going—through a marathon, for example. You pick them up in the gym. Although I had no idea that Alys used them."

"She did tell me," said Shell. She coughed and turned to Brice. "For her marathons. She said it gave her energy. Like a bonus of glucose sweets."

"DMAA. Don't ask me to give you the full medical name, but they called it Jack3d for short. Jacked, with a three for the E. They've found it in her blood."

"An overdose or something," I said. "Enough to kill you?"

"It shouldn't kill you, Sabbie," said Shell. "It's supposed to be a harmless supplement … that's what she told me, anyhow."

"She should have discussed it with me," said Brice.

"Yeah." Shell's voice cracked. "So should I."

Wolfsbane visibly relaxed, leaning back in his chair. Brice would not be hauling Spirit Flyers over the coals. It was no relief to me. Alys had brought something to the Tor and died because of it.

"I think they're working along the lines that it weakened her heart." Brice shook his head. "Straight up, I guess we'll have to wait for the full inquest."

"Brice," said Esme. "I do wish to offer my full condolences. Stef and I are so very sorry about what happened."

"It was nothing to do with you," said Brice, which was exactly what Esme wanted. "It was nothing to do with any of you. You're all nice people and I know Alys would love you to come to her funeral."

Esme threw her cape tightly around her shoulders, rose from her chair. She embraced Brice, offering stalwart advice into his ear in a stage whisper we could all hear. She air-kissed everyone else and made her getaway.

Brice picked up his laptop bag. "If you don't mind, I'll head off. I'll be in touch about the arrangements."

"We'll keep everyone informed," said Wolfsbane. "And, yeah, I'll ring you soon about the funeral, shall I?"

We sat for about a minute, almost mute. Then Yew and Juke made their farewells, saying they had to get back to work.

Ricky disappeared towards the toilets, so distracted he hardly said goodbye.

Wolfsbane got to his feet, manhandling his chair out of his way. "Let's split," he said to Shell.

She looked around her, as if unsure how to respond. "I'm not coming back tonight, Wolfs. I might stay in Glastonbury for a bit."

He didn't argue. Wolfsbane hated not being in the know and it was clear something was up. He walked off quickly, as if to catch the others. Shell sat tight, watching his ignoble retreat. She gave me and Freaky a wonky smile, then slid off, in the same direction as Ricky.

"You in a hurry to get home?" Freaky lifted an eyebrow.

"Well, no—"

"Fancy one of their veggie pies? I'm not trying to butter you up or anything, but Shell's mechanic friend has been working on my caravan. It's good to go, my dear Sabbie, and I need to a lift to the cop shop."

———

I knew getting Freaky's van released would to take up the rest of the day, and I was right. We waited some time to sign the papers, but then it became clear that the van would have to stay put. I had never towed a caravan and didn't fancy starting now. "Unless you park it somewhere secure, the cops will take it straight back to the pound," I told him.

"Can't think of any place except Stonedown," he muttered. "I've lived there for so long."

"Have you tried apologizing to Stef?" I asked.

"There's nothing to apologize about."

"I understand that, but a 'sorry' can make all the difference."

He sighed. "I could try, I suppose."

I bit the bullet and drove him there. The Tor rose above us, sometimes invisible, sometimes looming as we wound along the lanes to Stonedown Farm. The afternoon had moved into early evening, and as I'd predicted, the blanket of cloud had lifted without a drop of precipitation. I drove with the windows down to catch the birdsong—a snatch of blackbird here, the shout of a wren there—and a flash of a monk's grey habit wandering up a rough driveway, like an apparition from past times.

"Look at that," I said, slowing. "An abbey friar. Maybe a guide from Glastonbury Abbey?"

"Not exactly." Freaky barked a laugh as a flash of mint green showed under the grey robe. "I recognize those trainers! That is Woody Choke, no less."

He was right. The grey robe was stock from a High Street pagan shop. I bet Anagarika had paid dearly to kit himself out in that ritual garment.

"Whatever's he doing?"

"Heading towards Gog and Magog, it seems. No concern of ours. Drive on, Sabbie. Drive on!"

Minutes later we were pulling up in front of Stonedown Farm. Even before we'd slammed the car doors behind us, I could hear raised voices.

I frowned across at Freaky. He didn't hesitate. He pounded round to the back of the house, where he knew the doors would be open. I followed, my curiosity getting the better of me.

The voices grew louder as we came close to the back rooms. A shriek rose on the air. Freaky disappeared through some French doors. I was on his heels. We came to a stop in Stefan's lounge.

Esme was curled on the floor, her knees up into her belly. She was still shrieking, but as we arrived the cries were diminishing to whimpers. Stefan stood, legs astride, bending slightly over her, as if he was about to assist her. When he saw us, he straightened up and took a step away.

"She's fine," he said. "She's good."

"What've you done to her?" said Freaky, his voice breaking.

"She's an emotional woman at the best of times."

"You hit her, you fucker."

"I barely laid a hand." He looked at his hands as if to check for signs of guilt.

I didn't believe him. Stefan was exuding savage fury; it burned the air between us. I kept my eyes on him as I knelt beside her. "Esme?"

She groaned, but not in a way that worried me. She was perfectly conscious and able to move. She was that saddest of things; a terrified drama queen, diminished and trembling on a floor. Her pride had taken the worst beating. I took her hand and helped her stand.

No one spoke as she pointed a long finger at Stefan. I stared at the finger—it reminded me acutely of the pointing hand I'd seen in the shamanic journeys I'd made for Laura. My heart gave an unexpected thud and I knew Esme's words would be crucial to my client's problems.

"All men are savages at heart. I have no wish to live with a brute."

"I love you," said Stefan. "You know I do. But you drive me wild."

"Never a need for violence, dear friend," Freaky pointed out.

"I lost my temper." Stefan scratched his hair. "I had a right."

"You are weak to the point of uselessness." Esme began to sob.

"I had a *right*. You drive me wild. *You* drive me into savage acts."

Esme spun round and directed her drama at the witnesses. "Will you go now?" she said to us. "Will you go and leave us in peace?"

"One moment, my friends." Freaky eyeballed them. "I want my spot back. I want what's been rightfully mine since before you inherited this crumbling wreck of a house, Stefan."

"That's impossible," said Esme.

Freaky kicked at an easy chair with his toe. "Don't see why."

"Because it was the local council who chucked you off the land. And they're not going to let you back."

"It was your bloody partner who hitched my van up and left it in the lane and it was you nagging him to do it!"

223

"That's not the case at all. The caravan *was* a problem. Stefan kept getting letters from the Planning Office. They clearly stated that your caravan was a 'residence without planning permission.'"

Stefan nodded, but he looked perplexed, as if the sudden change in dynamics had thrown him off course.

"I showed the letters to you, Freaky. Maybe you can't read, or something."

"That's unfair, Esme," I said, breaking in without thinking. "Freaky's not a dunce."

"Who asked you anything? What are you doing here anyhow?"

"Good question. I'm sure you're going to settle everything a lot sooner without me. Freaky's caravan is good to go. All Stefan has to do is tow it back."

I left through the French doors as fast as I could without running. I had a feeling that without me there, Freaky would be able to negotiate a lot more successfully.

———

A mile or so down the country road, I reached the place I'd seen the grey monk. I pulled in and got out of my car. I was desperate to check that our eyes hadn't deceived us. I left the car unlocked, in case Freaky's negotiations were a failure, and followed in the direction we'd seen Anag taking. The driveway led into a touring park, but at the top of it was a short path, which I could see would take me onto the lane Wolfs and I had walked the morning of Alys's death. I continued up it.

The hooded figure was standing between the two brave and ancient oaks, Gog and Magog. His habit was tied at the waist with a loose cord, and the hood was thrown well over the face. He held a wooden recorder to his lips. The notes were soft, if not tuneful—the instrument was forgiving of clumsy fingers. I couldn't help but slow my pace to watch the spectacle.

"G'day, there."

He lowered the recorder from his lips.

"Anag, why didn't you come to see Brice?"

"I did. It was you lot that didn't turn up."

"No, we were all there. We waited for you."

"I was in the Chalice Well Gardens from before the meet time to way after it and I didn't see any of you."

"Ah. Right. We were in the forecourt. We … er … went to the Rifleman's Arms in the end."

"Why d'you do that?" He threw back his hood. There were burrs and bits of goose-grass attached to it.

"We though it might come on to rain."

He looked upwards. "It didn't."

"Ah … no."

"Bit of a lame excuse, ain't it?"

"It's not an excuse, Anag—"

"Don't worry, it dawned PDQ. You'd told me different 'cause Brice didn't want me at his little get-together."

"That wasn't it at all. We had no idea that you were in the gardens. You must have been early."

"Yeah, well, I was playing on my flute, wasn't I?"

Then I saw it. Anag had hoped we'd all arrive to find him, positioned strategically under the yew trees or by the chalice wellhead, engaged in his music and garbed up like something out of *The Mists of Avalon*. Sad thing was, we didn't turn up to see the spectacle at all.

"I know when I've been sucked in, Sabbie. You all knock at me, think I'm a fastie. But I can have out-of-bodies with the best of them."

"You what? Oh, yes, Anag, of course you have a spiritual side."

"I've been in the otherworld today, for sure. I saw things I did not believe." His expression was startled, as if he expected wild things to fly at him. "It's the zodiac. You know about the zodiac?"

"The Glastonbury one?"

"Each sign has a different energy and takes you to a different place ... you can be drawn in." He took his time sliding the recorder into a phallic-shaped bag that hung from his waist. "On the zodiac, the Chalice Well Gardens is the beak of the phoenix. The phoenix is Aquarius, the archer." I'd never heard him speak like that before. It sounded like he'd remembered this from a book. "And—okay, yeah—you can be seduced by the Age of Aquarius. But y'know what? You Brits gobsmack me."

I blinked at his change of tack. "Sorry?"

"The lot of you are yobbos. Defaming the sacredness of Avalon." I felt my mouth slacken. Anag's "out-of-bodies" had sent him a little crazier than usual. "Guys here are pretty keen to have a lend of someone else's sheila."

"*What?*"

"I saw them with my own mud pies. In the field above the Chalice Well."

"The cress field."

"In the grass like a couple of teenies. Ask me, there's something crook about having a cheeky root in a revered place like that."

I didn't respond, but I couldn't help see Shell's unshod foot creeping up Ricky's trouser leg under the pub table. Two people making love in the cress field.

"I went over that fence, yelling at them. Was right into my power, Sabbie. Told my truth. She called me a dipstick. Laughed at my chosen name. That was unforgivable, Sabbie!"

I felt my cheeks warm. Woody Choke, owner of a porn shop. I wondered if he'd had to leave Melbourne fast. Was he hiding out in Glastonbury, using his search for enlightenment as a cover?

"It's important to me," said Anag, watching my face carefully. "Anagarika Dharmapala is my hero. He was from Sri Lanka but he studied under Madame Blavatsky. He took a vow of celibacy and cared for the Temples of his country. I've read every one of his diaries—full of wisdom."

"So you came out here, to Gog and Magog."

"What? No, I just happened on the trees." He looked up into the dying branches. "You're not indiscreet, like I am. I am indiscreet, I confess. Had to snitch."

"Snitch?"

"Seemed right at the time. Now, not so sure. Messed it up. I know that. But it felt wrong. Couples cheating. They should think themselves blessed."

He'd witnessed things in the Chalice Well Gardens, at the beak of the phoenix of Aquarius, that seemed to have broken him. I wondered if there was an underlying jealousy behind all this.

"What's the matter, Anag, really?"

He picked a bit of twig off his robe. "He was as mad as a cut snake about it."

I gave up trying to process what Anag was saying. "Come on. I'll give you a lift back to town."

He hitched his robe above the knees of his jeans and climbed the fence. Head down, hands clasped, he looked more like a monk than perhaps he realized as we walked the driveway. "We've all been invited to Alys's funeral," I said eventually. "That's what Brice came to say. It's in London, this Friday."

Anag paused, but only for a second. "No good for me. I'll be at the workshop I'm taking. I'll be walking the Tor Labyrinth!"

We came out from the lane. I dug in my pocket for my car keys. Anag stop in his tracks. "Uh oh. That's a pig's bum."

On the opposite side of the road a khaki-coloured vehicle had pulled in—Stef's jeep—with Freaky in the passenger seat. He rolled down his window and called through it.

"All's well that ends well, Sabbie! We're off to get my van."

I crossed the road and came up to the open window. "That's great news. Thanks, Stefan."

"Best thank Esme. It was her idea."

"We're going to put the caravan inside the Dutch barn," said Freaky. "We've measured up already; it'll fit easy."

"It won't be visible from the air, that way," said Stefan. "Which was the problem, you understand."

"We think it'll be snug when the winter comes," said Freaky. I noticed that he'd invited himself back into the family, using the familiar *we*. "And as I'm closer to the house, Stef's going to run a cable."

"He'll be kitted out with electric light and power."

"You'll be able to paint your drums and rattles in the evenings," I pointed out. "You could even have a radio."

"He could have a laptop, whatever, so long as he pays his share of the bill."

"The generosity of my friends overwhelms me. First Sabbie takes me in like a stray dog—"

"I don't think you're a dog, Freaky."

"Then Shell's friend gets me roadworthy again. And now, Stef … you've reforged our old solidarity. I am humbled."

Stefan coughed into his fist. As he raised his eyes, he focused on the road ahead. "What the fuck's he still doing here?"

I glanced round. Anag was racing along, his robe flapping at his heels. Stefan pressed his horn. The sound was loud, rude. It made me jump and it made Anag pick up his skirts and break into a sprint.

"You!" Stefan was out of the jeep in seconds, chasing Anag as he fled into a field. "You!"

At first, it all appeared comical, Stef waving his arms in fury and Anag checking behind him and tripping on the hem of his habit, tumbling in the tussocky grass. Freaky and I pursued them, but Stef was fired up; halfway across the field he floored his quarry with a rugby tackle. Anag hit the ground so hard he seemed stunned. Stefan straddled him, rolled him over, pulled him up by the collar of his habit, and fisted him in the mouth.

Freaky proved himself fast for an undernourished man of older years. He reached Stefan and yanked him away from Anag, holding him tight by both arms. I arrived moments later. It seemed we were constantly destined to watch Stefan's headstrong urges.

"What are you thinking, Stef?" I screamed. "What is going on?"

"Calm down," said Freaky. "Calm down and explain yourselves."

"Don't bother on my account." Anag flailed around on in the uneven grass inside his robe until he'd got himself upright. He smoothed the folds of the habit and checked his recorder bag for breakages. A drip of blood splattered onto the back of his hand. He put his hands to his face. They came away stained scarlet. To be fair, it was not much more than a trickle from a cut lip, but he looked at the smears in horror. His voice broke with the emotion of it. "You are all bastards!"

He turned and hobbled away. We watched him reach the far boundary hedge and walk alongside it, faced with the choice of finding a way through or returning, tail between legs. He must have found a gap, because he disappeared from our view.

"What was that about?" demanded Freaky.

Stefan shrugged. "What a complete dunce neck. Good riddance to bad rubbish. D'you want your van towed or not?"

"I do, mate." Freaky laid his arm over Stefan's shoulder and they crossed the field together.

I caught a glimpse of Anag in the distance, jogging between the trees, reduced to a miniature monk. A mile or so further on, the Tor rose from the flat land.

While I had been persuading people not to step foot in the Chalice Well Gardens, Anagarika had already been inside, wandering the paths, playing his flute. Surely he could not have anything to do with Brice's emails. And yet, as he'd stood beside the ancient oaks, I'd seen something in his eyes—something secret and powerful.

I shook my head and went back to my car. It didn't feel right. Anag was a pathetic figure, moving through the world in search of a truth he couldn't find because his search map was wrong. He was throwing huge amounts of cash at it too, without discrimination or common sense.

I've been in the otherworld today, for sure. I saw things I couldn't believe.

He was an innocent, and I was persuaded that he had nothing at all to do with Morgan le Fay.

NINETEEN
MORGAN LE FAY

"EXPLAIN," SAYS MORGAN LE Fay. "Why is it your intention to study the magical arts?"

She's testing, testing. Every question is a trick. *I love you.* Wrong answer. *I will do anything for you.* Wrong again.

"I want to learn how to change."

"Ah ... transformation. Well. We'll make a magician of you yet."

A spasm moves across the front of the acolyte's head, as if Morgan has placed electrodes on each of his temples and flicked a switch on some pocket-sized transformer.

Transformer; transformation. He's unable to work out the truth of her words. Does she mean it will take a transformation to make him a magician? Or that knowing change is the deepest magic already gives him an edge?

"Wearyall Hill," says Morgan le Fay, unnecessarily. "Where Joseph of Arimathea planted his staff. The Holy Thorn has grown here since that day. Twice yearly it flowers, once in May and once in at Christmastide."

"A miracle."

"Dead now, of course. Desecrated. Growing here, son and daughter, for two thousand years, then cut to its trunk."

"Toxic idiots!" The bitter feeling is like bile in the throat, like scissors on the skin. That the land is in such a desperate state. The migraine quickens, a deep core of ice in his forehead with ice chips spreading outwards. Fingers freezing on this hot summer's day. He stumbles slightly, already more breathless than Morgan as they climb even though Wearyall Hill is nowhere as steep as the Tor.

The dead thorn tree is smothered by clouties; ribbons draped over it with veneration, some faded and ragged, some satiny-bright. They make the poor stump look alive as they move in the light breeze.

"Crazy. Pointless! Who cut down the Holy Thorn?"

"Don't you know who performed this defilement?" She leans in, flirts a little, drops her voice.

"Was it the foolish knight?"

"Fool yourself! It was the Black Knight."

The acolyte squirrels the fact away until he can get to his books and learn about the Black Knight. "Morgan, you could raise one finger and speak the word, and not ever again would any person destroy a beautiful, hallowed tree."

She laughs at him, delighted at the compliment, and removes an earring, a long strand of white crystal, slipping its silver back inside the knot of a ribbon on the dead tree.

"Let's walk."

It's wonderful, walking the length of Wearyall with her. The cat tugs them along the path and Morgan talks, staring out towards the River Brue, explaining how it was once part of that sea that extended over the Somerset Moors. When she's a mellow mood, the acolyte can sometimes get her to reminisce about her Georgian-Cornish parentage, how her father was a cultural attaché to the British Diplomatic Mission in Tbilisi and her mother one of the catering staff that doubled as a spy. When the diplomat's post was peremptorily terminated and he needed to disappear, he brought his small child home to his native Cornwall, setting himself up as a watercolour artist in St. Ives.

"When did you first know?" he asks. "That you were Morgan le Fay?"

"When I was but eleven."

Her father had taken her to Tintagel, and there, on the island of legends off the Cornish coast, she had her first visions showing her the lives that she had lived before this life.

"Imagine a blinding flash of light," she explains. "The world moves into black and white around its edges and at the centre is the most beautiful, stately, supreme being you might ever encounter."

"The first Morgan le Fay? Your ancestor?"

Morgan's mood sours. "We need to get in." She points in the direction of the Tor, rising from the valley on the other side of the town. "What are you doing to get us in?"

"I've put everything in order of the zodiac," he says, before his mind closes down in panic. "Twelve perspectives of the land."

"And?" She puts her face to his. "Nothing! Nothing!" His throat is dry with panting. Stomach cramped, waiting for her screech. "The Green Knight barely faltered in his step. The Red Knight refuses to die. And the wasteland is upon us!"

"I get it. I do get it! The land *is* wasted. Ravaged, overused, dried out, and dying of neglect. A sacred tree cut down—forests denuded —fossil fuels ransacked!"

"Why can you not do this simple thing?!"

She does not tolerate impertinence. He'll never be able to ask Morgan le Fay the obvious thing… *if you were there when the Hollow Hill was first closed upon the Sleeping King, why don't you know where the entrance is?*

Millennia have passed. Fifteen hundred years, to be exact. Things change. Morgan may be twelfth descended from a goddess, she may be a sorcerer of high esteem, but she is, actually, human. Flesh. Blood. Beating heart. Weaknesses show through. She can be petulant, impatient. Incandescent with rage. At times, reckless, blinkered.

The acolyte takes a breath. Steadies himself. "Even your deep magic has not triumphed. I've searched all over. Every entrance is sealed against us. I need help." Morgan towers over the acolyte, fuming, but she is silent and that empowers speech. "There is someone."

"Someone!"

"Someone who can help." Agreeable. Patient. Someone who *strives.* "Someone who can offer assistance."

"And where, pray, do you intend to look for such assistance?"

"Bridgwater," says the acolyte.

Selkie lets out a wide meow. They both look at the cat. It lashes its tail.

"If we take a visit, acolyte, you will promise one thing."

Careful, now, he thinks. Careful what you promise Morgan.

She doesn't wait for the promise, because she doesn't need it. It's not a promise; it's a condition.

"A slaying. The Black Knight. A chivalric slaying."

TWENTY

GRANDMA DARE

MEETING TROUBLE HALFWAY HAD been my problem since I was old enough to know where halfway was. It was going to be the same when I met my grandmother, I just knew it, even though the Lady of the River had encouraged me for my own good.

As I left Bridgwater for Zotheroy on Saturday morning, little flappy insects were invading my stomach. Being dropped without warning into a family fold was disconcerting. I was used to my own status quo. I was not a family person. Anyway, I had a family, thanks very much—Gloria and Philip, Dennon and Charlene. I didn't want another, especially one with gargoyles on their house.

Twenty minutes later, I was crunching over the expansive sweep of driveway that led to the Hatchings, deciding which door I should use. The house was vast and centuries old, set in acres of garden with some woodland behind. It was built from stone, but there were newer parts knitted onto the original, some in red brick and some rendered and painted. The last time I'd been here, it had taken me all of five minutes to walk around the side of the house to the kitchen entrance with the takeaway order. I didn't want to start off as Lady Dare's servant, so went up to the front door and pulled on a cold iron knob. Deep inside the house, a bell jangled.

It was Lettice who answered. She was in Saturday jeans, her hair held back with a band. She leapt at me, wrapping her arms around me. "Sabbie! I'm so relieved. I wasn't sure you'd bother."

"I keep my promises." I was in the hallway, but this hall wasn't the narrow corridor people like me had to manage with. It was a huge room with high ceilings and walls mounted with—I checked I wasn't imagining it—the heads of stuffed animals. Mostly antlered deer and foxes but I saw a leopard's head as well. Between the mounted beasts were portraits in elaborate frames. Some were old, I could tell by the clothes the people were wearing. I stopped in my tracks. "Are these your … ancestors, Lettice?"

She made a face. "Gross, huh? They're yours too!"

"Let's not get ahead of ourselves."

She bounced on the spot. "I can't wait for you to meet Grandma!"

I didn't even want to think about it. "How are you, anyway?"

"I'm very happy now the hols have started."

"That's early, isn't it?"

"Yeah. We break up for almost twelve weeks at Millfields."

"Ah. Lettice."

Mrs. Peers Mitchell framed a doorway I hadn't spotted before, it being painted the same colour as the wall. I eyed her without smiling. I did not want this woman to think for one moment that I liked her, or that I was pleased to be in her mother's house.

"Why don't you saddle up Abacus and take him for a canter?"

Lettice looked at her mother, her body primed for an argument. "I'd like to stay here, please, Ma."

"I think not. Off you go."

My cousin shot me a look of solidarity then thumped along a corridor that lead towards the back of the rambling interior. I was left with my nemesis.

"Perhaps you'd come with me."

Mrs. Mitchell didn't wait to see if I was going to follow. By the time I'd skidded thought the camouflaged door into a smaller room, she was disappearing from it into shadow, her ash blond French pleat lighting the way like a beacon.

I crossed the small room and stood on the next threshold. Now I was in a private, personalized part of the house, a sort of sitting room. It felt smaller than it was, thanks to the navy flock wallpaper and the fact that the woodwork was varnished a deep brown. It was dimly lit, despite the bright day outside, because velvet curtains fell half across the window, tied back at their waists by fat lengths of cord. The carpet was spongey under my feet and of a pale, intricate design. Carpets that couldn't be bought for a song from Ikea were outside my radar, but I thought this might be Turkish or Chinese. It reached across the floor, leaving a margin of polished wood around its edges.

My grandmother sat in a winged chair plumped with all manner of cushions. Her feet were raised onto an upholstered footstool; black house shoes with a small heel peeked from under her lap rug. I had somehow imagined she would be boney, delicate as a bird. She was instead matronly. A vast bosom—all I could think to call it—was covered by a tailored outfit straight from a high-end but rather out-of-date fashion establishment. Her hair, which she still possessed in all its glory, resembled a swirl of marshmallow. She was in full makeup—powdered cheeks, coral lips... I even detected a flash of eyebrow pencil.

I was captivated by her eyes. They were the same blue as my mother's, a summer-flower shade. I had loved my mother's eyes. Almost twenty-four years after she died, these are the only feature I can clearly recall.

Grandma Dare looked at me for a moment or two without speaking, or even moving. Then she said, "Peers, dear. Some tea, I think."

My aunt's lips sucked into a point, but she flounced away to attend the request. I guessed that was how they spoke round here... *attend the request... matronly bosom...*

"Would you move a little closer, please?"

That made me jump. Because she hadn't said hello in any fashion, I hadn't thought that she had even noticed I was in the room. I came closer, as I was bid. Her hand lifted from under the rug. She held it as if she wished me to take it. I hoped she didn't expect me to curtsy and kiss its back. The hand was plump and slightly freckled with old-lady marks, and the fingers each wore a ring. They glittered with bright gold and gemstones. I put my own hand out and she grasped it firmly. Her hand was cold, despite being kept under the rug.

"So," she said. "I hope you don't mind tea. I rarely drink coffee now. It doesn't have the flavour it used to have."

It occurred to me that one of us should open this conversation with some modicum of politeness; if she wasn't going to do it, I'd better.

"Good morning. I'm Sabbie Dare." Perhaps I should have addressed her as Lady Dare, but it was already too late.

"Sabrina."

"Yes." I'd've loved to tell her that I had hated my full name since I was little, but I wasn't brave enough.

"My own mother's name."

"Really?" I was genuinely shocked. My mother had given birth to me far away from all this pomp—far away from all this wealth. I found it hard to believe that she'd chosen a family name.

"My mother's family were shamefully theatrical, unfortunately," said Lady Dare. She took in a breath, and began to recite.

Sabrina fair,
Listen where thou art sitting
Under the glassy, cool, translucent wave,
In twisted braids of lilies knitting
The loose train of thy amber-dropping hair...

"That's beautiful," I said.

"Milton, of course. 'Comus.'"

"Oh, right."

"You have had some form of education?"

"Er ... I've got a degree, if that's what you mean."

Lady Dare shook her head, as if that was not what she'd meant at all. "You should sit."

"Er ..."

"The chair in the corner. The light one. Bring it over."

The chair was what I'd call a carvery dining chair with a padded seat; heaven knows what Lady Dare might have called it. Hepplewhite or something. It wasn't light at all.

I positioned it a metre away from her and sat on it, crossing my ankles primly. I'd made a nod towards decorum and worn tights and a summer skirt for this occasion and now, for a reason I couldn't have explained, I was glad I looked more ladylike than usual.

"I think we've shot ahead of ourselves, Lady Dare," I said as I settled into the seat. "I've not made any claim to being your granddaughter. I haven't done any research into it, either. I was happy to leave all this well alone."

"Laetitia made that perfectly plain. It was I who instigated this meeting. I wanted to see you. I knew, if I set my eyes on you, that I'd be sure, one way or the other."

"Right!"

"It is plain to me you are my daughter's daughter."

"Even though I must look a good deal like my father?"

It was a bold thing to say; I wasn't sure how she'd react. According to things Lettice had told me, Lady Dare had refused to speak to my mother, or welcome her into her house, once she had taken up with a black man from Bristol.

"Yes. No doubt you do have some features that might come from that side of your bloodline, but what I see is the shape of your chin, which must be drawn from my own heritage, and the line of your nose, which is not at all African."

When it came to barbs, this matriarch was perfectly able to duel with me and win.

"You are my granddaughter, Miss Dare." She caught my gaze and for a second, the corners of her lips turned up. "However much either of us dislike the idea."

At that moment the door opened with a sort of hush. I assumed it would be Mrs. Mitchell, but a woman I hadn't seen before was managing the tray of tea. She was dressed in a brushed cotton blouse, a pair of lightweight slacks, and comfortable lace-up shoes.

I hadn't bothered to wonder what happened to Lady Dare when her sole-surviving daughter was not here, but it was obvious now; she had a care worker. Except I imagined this woman was never called that; she'd probably be the housekeeper or companion or suchlike. She placed the tray on a sideboard that stood at a far wall and brought over a small table, placing it between us. She poured the tea and brought over the two china cups on their saucers. She added a milk jug and sugar bowl to the mix, and the sugar bowl had lumps of sugar and a set of silver tongs. Finally, she brought two little plates and an assortment of posh-looking chocolate biscuits on a raised cake stand.

"Thank you, Shreve, we will manage."

Shreve left the room, but first she bobbed her head as if in the presence of royalty.

"Sabrina, would you please add one lump for me and a little milk?"

It took me several seconds to get my head round that, because something had occurred to me as I'd watched Shreve do her bob, that perhaps I should have thought about long ago. What sort of lady *was* my grandmother? I hadn't even researched what sorts of ladies there were. If you married a lord, were you a lady? That stood to reason. And if you became a member of the House of Lords, but were a woman, surely then you became a lady. Some women got called it from birth; how did that work? I had no idea, and although this was the opportunity to find out, I couldn't think how to start. At last I managed to pass Lady Dare her tea. She took a sip and held it out again. The cup rattled on the saucer and I grabbed it.

"I'll have a Viennese, if you'd be so good."

I stared at the cake stand. This was the bit of my education that was patently missing.

She pointed with one finger.

"Those are Viennese." Her finger shook and the ruby on it glittered red. "Those are mint crisps. And those, Florentines. Try one."

I thought I detected a flicker at the corners of her lips again, but it might have been my imagination. I lifted her cake by the little paper towel underneath it and passed it to her on a plate. I picked up a mint crisp. It was so thin and light, I didn't bother with a plate; probably be hounded out of society, but, hey. I nibbled its edges. It was exquisite.

"I have a selection box of these sent from Fortnum's every twenty-eight days. They are the best." Lady Dare took a bite from her Viennese and moved her mouth round it, like old people do. She lifted the cup without spilling, although her hand shook very slightly, and took another sip. As she placed the cup back on the saucer, she spoke again, and this time, there was no stopping her.

"My husband was a baronet of the realm. Sir Sebastian. The baronetcy was granted to the Savile family by great Queen Anne, the last monarch of the Stuart dynasty, in 1712. He was Sir Simon, first Baronet of Zotheroy. He built this house and had a large family, creating an extended lineage. My husband, twelfth Baronet of Zotheroy was his direct descendent down the male line. This is my point; heritage moves directly and solely down the male line. My husband and I, as you must be aware, were unfortunate enough to produce only girls. The eleventh Baronet of Zotheroy is Sebastian's second cousin, Guy Dare. He inherited this house immediately my husband passed away. However, he is, at this moment, living in South Africa. He owns several mines. Diamonds, I believe. I stay here, as Dowager Lady Savile-Dare. Here I will remain, until my death, which, God willing, surely cannot be far into the future. At that time, Guy must decide what he will do with The Hatchings. Perhaps he will return here, retire here. Perhaps he will put the old thing on the open market. I sincerely hope he will not, as this house has been in the family since its construction in 1720."

She took a breath—her first, I think, since she'd begun. I couldn't have spoken even if someone had goaded me to do so with the point of a Jacobean dagger. "I have brought you here, Sabrina, to inform you of these things. As my grandchild, it is only right that you know; that you do not go about the countryside in the belief that, as the only child of my elder daughter, you are in line to inherit anything."

There was a pause. I heard her breathing, a settling of breath after exertion. My own breath had almost stopped. My head spun. It felt as if my grandmother had directly responded to my earlier thoughts—everything I wanted to know about being a lady but was afraid to ask.

"If you have any questions, Sabrina, you can pose them."

"Lady Dare, there is one thing I'd like to ask you."

"Laetitia calls me Grandma. I rather like that. You should do so too."

"Can I ask you about my mother?"

She sighed, as if that was asking for the world. She took a couple of sips of cooling tea. "Your mother was, I'm afraid, not a perfect person."

"Who is?"

"There are some things that are expected. Isabel was…" She coughed into her fist. "She was promiscuous."

"Oh."

"You do know what that means, I assume?"

"Even thirty years ago … well, it feels an outdated description for a woman."

"Perhaps." Lady Dare's lips thinned. "This modern world is not for me."

My mother hadn't been brought up to be a woman; she'd been brought up to be a lady.

"So that's why you didn't speak to her, ever again?"

"It's not an attractive trait, Sabrina. She was my eldest daughter, and I was fearful that if I gave into her waywardness, Peers might similarly be afflicted."

I shook my head. I didn't believe that Peers Mitchell would ever be attracted by anything that might afford pleasure, or even a bit of fun.

"I did not give that final ultimatum. I did not say the words 'never darken our door.' The girls' father was alive at that time, and it would have hurt him deeply. She left of her own free—of her own promiscuous—will."

"So it was Izzie that decided to break off from her family?"

"Yes. And for Sebastian's sake, I was glad. He was in failing health and he was my primary concern during the years after she left. I felt it was better that he should know as little as possible. And, after he had died … I felt it better that things should continue like that."

She drained her cup. I lifted my own, leaving the saucer where it was, and drank the tea, trying not to let the cup chime as I put it down. Her words had been carefully chosen. Almost as if she was leaving me to decide what she'd said.

"What was it that my grandfather was better not knowing about?"

"Perhaps you could pass me my pashmina. It's over there, folded onto that chair."

It was of the softest cashmere in the deepest shade of rose. I longed to put it to my cheek, but I resisted. I opened it wide and she pulled herself forward a little so that I could drape it over her shoulders.

"I still don't understand, Lady Dare."

"Grandma, please. Or Lady Savile-Dare, if you insist."

"What was it that you didn't tell your husband about? Or Mrs. Mitchell? Or anyone?"

I knew, of course. I'd worked it out from things she hadn't said, and the way her shoulders shook as she didn't say them.

I stepped back, knocking my legs against the carvery chair. "You knew my mother had died, didn't you? You never told your family, but you knew. They always find next of kin and inform. Always. You knew she'd had a child before she died. That's what you didn't tell. You didn't tell about me."

TWENTY-ONE
JUKE

SOMEHOW, I WAS IN Bridgwater. I must have driven on autopilot from Zotheroy while my thoughts frothed, as if my grandmother had thrown a sachet of brewer's yeast on them. A lorry hooted as I trailed blindly into the middle of the road and I found it utterly impossible to drive any further. I swung into the next car park, turned off the ignition, but forgot to go into neutral. The car jumped forward as I took my foot off the clutch. I was going to sob. No; I was going to scream.

I'd slipped away from the Hatchings. The thought of clapping eyes on Mrs. Mitchell had made me shake, and Lettice had still been hacking over the hills. If she'd seen the state I was in she'd have gone straight to her grandmother and got our conversation out of her with those beguiling eyes. I didn't want Lettice to know the truth about her family. Even so, leaving without saying goodbye to anyone felt like running away.

How stupid to think that my grandmother might welcome me into the fold. I'd met her daughter—the daughter who had stayed a daughter and taken on the family mantle of indifference to the world. Peers Mitchell should have been a lesson to learn; a shallow, repugnant woman who had never even thought to search for her own sister. Why had I allowed myself to believe for one moment that her mother would be different—in any way nicer?

Six months ago, it had been plain to me. I'd made the decision not to link up with this new family. I'd all but broken Lettice's heart when I'd told her. And I could remember my words, clear as day … *we've been quite happy not knowing each other up to now …*

Finally, I gathered myself up and looked out on the day. I was parked on the edge of town, opposite the Angel Shopping Centre. Clouds hung like a bruise. I pulled my shoulders back and took a shuddering breath.

I turned the ignition and the car fired, almost masking the tap that came at my window. A man was standing right outside the car. He tapped again, bending so that I could see his face. He was somewhere between forty and fifty and his pate was almost hairless, just a few brownish curls above each ear. In substitution he wore a mustache that was a slash of brown across his upper lip. He had a squat head, as if someone had taken a cricket bat to it sometime in the past. A cigarette burned between the fingers still resting on the glass.

"Could I have a word?" he mouthed.

I went to wind the window down, but thought better. For no reason I could put my finger on, I didn't like the look of him. I turned off the engine and shoved the keys deep in my coat pocket. Then of course, I couldn't operate the window. Instantly, I felt a fool.

All the guy wanted was a word—which would probably be that one of my tyres looked a little soft—something like that.

I opened the door and got out. The man stepped back to let me do so.

His black jeans were low slung and baggy and he wore a black open neck shirt over a black t-shirt, the better to display the concentric circles of heavy gold chains wrapped round his neck.

"Yes?"

The guy moved into my personal zone. I shuffled away and my back hit the car door. As our gazes met, his face transformed from living flesh into grey stone.

It was one of my "moments"—I was seeing the man's otherworldly presence—a stone gnome. The bald head was polished granite and the mustache was a line of dark lichen growing beneath the gravelly pits and dents, lumps and bulges, that made up his features.

Gnomes are a part of the Middle Realm of the otherworld. They love working with metal, often draping themselves with the glitter of gold. You never know which way a gnome will jump. Maybe they'll help you on your journey … maybe they'll throw a rock that catches your shin bone and trips you up.

The alteration in the man's features occurred for a few spine-tingling seconds and in that time, he'd said whatever it was he'd wanted to say. He stood there, expectant, waiting for my reply. I hadn't heard a word.

"… your face?" The stone mouth was transforming into soft flesh. All I could do was gawp.

"Er—what?"

"I recognized your face." He gestured behind him. "From right over there. You're Sabbie Dare, aren't you?"

"Uh…"

"I knew it was you."

"I don't think we've ever met."

"That's right." His voice had the local growl of West Somerset. "No, you don't know me."

"Can you tell me what this is about?"

"Heard all about how you're so kindhearted, like."

I felt behind me for the door handle. He watched the action, his eyes trained. He ground his cigarette out under his foot, like a cue to action, and took my elbow. His grip was hard, stonelike. I shrugged him off and in doing so, moved away from the car door. He eased into my place. Now his back was at my door. "Please move. Move away from my car."

"Only want to talk. That's all. Little talk."

I didn't take my eyes off him as I fumbled at my remote key and zapped it from my pocket to lock the car. The lights flashed on, off.

He made towards me. He was almost upon me, about to snatch at me. I swerved out of his path. His stride became wider, breaking into a jog. I could hear him pounding behind as I dodged between cars. I aborted my bright idea—to escape from the stone gnome by heading back to my car—and was running wildly, barely knowing why, taking the exit from the car park and sprinting over the road between traffic. I thought the hammering in my ears was his footsteps, but it was the surge of my own pulse. I glanced behind. He was stuck in the centre of the road, a fresh stream of heavy traffic moving through. He raised his hand as if that would stop me in my tracks.

Nothing was going to stop me. I made it through the doors of the shopping mall long before he'd dodged the vehicles in his path. I ducked into Bon Marché, fleeing to the back of the store, and hiding behind high rails of party frocks. I calmed myself by pretending to flick through the goods. Even a girl in negative financial equity has the right to browse. I separated the dresses on the rails and peered through the gap. The man was standing in the central open space of the mall, turning a full circle. His pebble scalp glowed under the lights.

In the relative calm of the shop, it began to occur to me that maybe I should have asked him what he wanted. What harm could he mean, here in the middle of town? What harm could he do? After what I'd been through at the Hatchings, I was extra receptive to the vibes coming off him. Was that a warning?

My phone beeped a message.

JUST WONDERING ABOUT SESSION TODAY? ONLY ...

I heard a humph come out of my mouth. Juke! I'd forgotten his afternoon appointment. The meeting with my grandmother and the stone gnome had robbed me of my usual routine.

I checked the time. Juke's session should start in fifteen minutes. He was probably outside my house, wondering where I was.

He answered directly when I rang him.

"Sabbie," he began, "I've got a bit of a problem."

"I've got a bit of a problem too," I kept my voice light. "I'm not at the house, not right this moment, Juke—" My voice broke as my throat closed over. "I'm kinda trapped. It's stupid, honestly, but there's this guy following me and I ... well, I don't like the look of him."

"What? In what way."

"Daft ways. Just ... intuition. He presented his otherworld face to me. He's a gnome."

252

"You're scared. I can tell it in your voice."

"He's searching for me in the Angel Shopping Centre. He'll give up any moment and go. Can you give me half an hour to get back to my house?"

"Absolutely not. Sounds like you need help."

"I'm sure I'm not in any sort of danger."

"What you need is backup. Once this man sees you're not alone, he'll give up."

I tried to insist that I could cope. He didn't want to hear it. All at once, he was in alpha male mode. "We're on our way. Won't be more than ten minutes. Keep in touch."

As much as I hated the thought that some random male friend was rushing to my rescue, the knowledge was reassuring. I took another peek through the clothes rail. My follower had disappeared.

I moved to the shop entrance, cautious but in control. No flat-headed gnome. I was about to make a run for it when the doors to the lift opened and let him out. He'd done a recon of the upper-floor café and not found me there. I peered through layers of Bon Marché plate glass as he got into the queue outside Greggs, waiting to be served a lunchtime pastry. Each time the queue shuffled forwards, he turned and did an appraisal of the mall. I had the blinding flash of a great idea. I should go up to the café. I waited until he was putting his pastry order in and dashed towards the lift. The doors opened, a mother with a buggy stepping out. I shot in and pressed the button. He'd looked upstairs and I hadn't been there. He wouldn't check again.

The café was spaced over the upper floor, which meant even when it was busy there were seats available. It was one of those "tweenie" affairs; perfectly clean and respectable but lacking any imagination. I don't drink coffee, but I suspected theirs wasn't very nice.

There were two women at a table close to the counter, talking furiously. There was family with a baby in a high chair, eating lunch. A gaggle of young girls sprawled over the sofas, but by the time I'd purchased a cup of tea they'd left. I texted Juke … In Angel Café. I took the sofa and waited.

You'd've thought I'd've had the sense to sit facing the lift, but I felt secure, now; Juke was on his way and the gnome had given up his search. I took a sip of tea. Weak and not all that hot. I stared at the wide-rimmed cup, where a shadow reflected in the thin brew. A scent came into my nostrils; a toadstooly smell of damp, underground places.

"Shouldn't leave your card around. Not if you don't want to be recognized."

Tea flew from the cup, splashing across the coffee table. A thumping sound came from my mouth, my shriek muted to an *aagh*.

The man walked around the sofa until he was opposite me. At close quarters, I could see that one ear was disarranged into a cauliflower shape, possibly due to the same swing of the bat that gave him his flattened head. His eyes were concealed behind puffy lids, but the pupils penetrated and pierced from their hiding place, like laser gun sights.

"I'm waiting for someone." I snatched at my phone, which was drenched in tea. "He'll be here any moment."

I couldn't believe I'd just used the "a burly bloke is on his way" technique. I'd proved time after time I could look after myself. I didn't need to simper and whimper to a guy who did not yet threaten me. The only thing he had against him, apart from improper use of social networks and a taste for Greggs sausage rolls, was that I'd observed his inner, subtle features. Gnomes are not entirely evil, but they're not entirely trustable, either.

"Name, address, phone number ..." He was moving my business card between his fingers like a poker ace. "Seen your picture on Facebook. Nice photo."

"You gave me a fright, chasing me like that."

"I heard you weren't easily frightened."

"What ... look, I don't know you ... *what*?"

He flicked the card onto the table and lifted an unused chair from another table. He wasn't a tall man, but his physique was thick and wide and he dangled the chair by one finger. "Can I sit down?"

"Just tell me what you want then go, please."

The chair was wrong for the low table between us. His knees stuck up above it. He took a bite of his pastry, half inside its paper bag. "I rang you," he said through the food. "Some chap fobbed me off. You never rang back."

Something slotted into place. "You are Marty-Mac?"

"That's what they call me." He finished his food and screwed up the bag, dropping it onto the table. "You're close to him."

"Close?"

"Rey Buckley."

"What? I ... what?"

"He's your boyfriend, right?"

What had Rey said? *I don't want Marty-Mac anywhere near you. Let me deal with it.* "Okay, Marty. I told Rey you phoned. He'll contact you when he's ready."

"He's never gonna be ready." He stared at my spill of tea. He put his index finger into the puddle and pulled a trail of milky fluid over the table.

"Why don't you simply walk into the police station and ask to speak to him?"

Marty-Mac gave me a long stare, at the end of which he barked a single, acerbic laugh.

"Please go, Mr. Mac."

"I only want you to have a word. He'll listen to you."

"How would you know that?"

"He told me. Like, he said what you mean to him."

"He did?"

"Yeah. Everything."

"Everything?"

"'Cause we're mates. All I want is a message passed."

I couldn't pretend I wasn't curious. I'm always curious. It was never beneficial, but there it was. And something else—a tang on the air—the way his finger trembled as he played with the puddle of tea. Marty-Mac was scared. Not of me or the impending arrival of Juke. Not even of Rey, for it was Rey he needed to sort out the fear eating away at him, which had driven him to seek me out.

"What message?"

"I done him a disservice."

"What?"

"Everything is down to me. Due to me. And I'm sorry. You tell him that. Say, 'Marty's sorry, but he's in dead stick.' Dead stick. They're gonna put me down. Lotta time. Rey Buckley has gotta speak up, tell the truth. Well. Not *truth*. It's gonna be complicated."

"I bet it is," I whispered.

"I'm in deep."

"I bet you are."

"I'm not 'xactly asking him to tell whoppers!"

I stood up. "I don't want to hear any more. Rey doesn't want to help you. He's warned me about you."

He grinned. His front teeth were chipped and yellowed from tobacco. "I got you rankled, eh?"

"I'm not asking again. Just go!"

In a blink, his grin vanished. The camera angle changed. Juke had burst out of the stair well and was sprinting between tables like he'd just transformed into a superhero. He stood legs astride, arms folded across his chest. "You heard the lady. She wants you to leave." It was what superheroes said inside their speech bubbles.

Marty pushed up from his chair. "We're having a private chat here."

Juke hesitated. "This is the man who followed you, yeah?"

I nodded once.

Marty swung round to me again, as if Juke was no bother at all. "I thought Rey was a mate. All he is, is a bloody copper."

"Look," said Juke, "look, excuse me, but I think we've established this lady has asked you to go."

Marty raised his voice. "Butt out, right?"

Things were shaping badly; escalating. I stared at Juke, trying to indicate that he should do exactly as Marty-Mac advised. Juke had to be a lot less experienced in thuggery, but he stood his ground. "You're the one who's leaving, you *gnome.*"

Marty's yellow grin faded. "What d'you call me?"

Marty lifted his chair and tossed it as if it was no more than a cushion. It knocked against Juke's knee and clattered to the floor. He dusted his hands. For one, chilling moment, I thought he was squaring up.

The family and the two women looked across at us, still chewing their lunches. The family man kept staring when the others had all looked away. He put a soft hand on his baby's head.

"It ain't a lot, what Rey's gotta do. Is it?" He gave the fallen chair a push with the point of his trainer. "They're gonna put me down!"

"Walk away, Sabbie," said Juke. He sounded sure of himself. Maybe he knew about situations like this because of his work with displaced persons. He put both his flat palms on Marty's chest, the sort of gesture bouncers use. Marty, bigger all round, copied the action with a rough push, heavy, both hands, sending Juke spinning over the width of the coffee table.

"Stop it!" I yelled. From the corner of my eye I could see the waitress talking on the phone.

Abruptly, Marty-Mac turned on his heel. He'd seen the waitress and decided he needed to split. He took the stairs, moving fast.

Seconds passed. Juke scrambled up. The waitress put the phone down. The family man went back to his chips.

I sank onto the sofa. "I should apologize. I didn't want to get you involved."

"Not a problem." Juke tugged his jacket sleeves as if to steady himself as he turned a full circle, looking into every corner of the bar. At one point, he seemed to spot something and raise his hand as if to gesture, but the hand fell to his side.

"He is gone, Juke," I reassured. "You got rid of him, all right. You were great. Superman!"

"You okay?"

"I am okay, but I'm wondering if I'm in a good place to work with you this afternoon."

"Rescheduling would suit me. It was why I texted. I'd be happy to postpone this session."

I shook my head. "That's not why you texted. Some goddess transformed you into Superman and sent you my way."

Juke laughed. But he didn't disagree.

———

"I have this double-barreled gran." I wiped another chunky beer mug and hung it above the bar at the Curate's Egg. "Lady Savile-Dare. She's a monster. Forget knitting and cosy slippers. This woman can lacerate you with a look."

The pub was full, sweaty with noise and inebriation. The local punk rock band was finishing its first set. Juke had settled at a bar-stool and was already down to the bottom of his first pint as I spilled out my personal soap opera. The other drinkers solemnly lining the bar were also conspicuously listening in, but I was past caring.

"Anyway, that was why I found myself at the Angel Shopping Centre."

"Coincidence," Juke hazarded, "that he approached you?"

How long had I been parked up in front of the mall? Long enough for Marty-Mac to pass by on whatever was his business and do a double-take as he spotted me. I didn't want to believe Marty-Mac hung around Bridgwater waiting to spot me.

"Yes. Pure luck. He tapped on my car window. He was all draped in his gold, with this gnomish head."

"A gnome with attitude. Not pleasant." Juke placed his beer mug on the bar towel, which was already sopping and stinking of malt. "I'll have another jar of your finest ale, please."

He seemed wired-up. He was drinking fast and jerking his head around each time a punter came in. Since I had seen him that afternoon, he had trimmed his golden beard so that it appeared a little more bushy than it did when it grew to the maximum four or five centimetres. He was all scrubbed up, wearing his favourite suit jacket with the artificial daffodil in the lapel, a plain violet shirt, and a pair of stonewashed jeans.

I played responsible barmaid by pulling him a half of Wild Cossack and waving away his tenner. "This is on the house. For my Superman!"

"Let's hope he'll leave you alone now." He jerked again, looking towards the street door. It was propped open on this balmy evening. Rey sauntered in, giving me one of those grins that don't turn up the corners of your mouth. I held my breath, waiting for Pippa to make her entrance. He was alone. My spirits lifted.

"Juke, this is Rey. My boyfriend."

"Right, hi. I'm one of Sabbie's shamanic apprentices." Juke stuck out his hand and waited, leaving Rey no option but to shake it. I'd flicked a beer tap on while I'd been talking, assuming Rey would want his usual pint.

"I'll have a short with that," he said, pointing to the whisky bottle clamped upside down behind me. "What about you? Can I get you a chaser?"

"Why not?" Juke aimed a wink at me. "Guess I deserve it."

I shot Juke a look he didn't choose to see. I'd planned to tell Rey about my encounter with Marty-Mac in my own sweet time, but

Rey hadn't missed the flick of Juke's eyelid. "What is that supposed to mean?"

"It's nothing, Rey."

"It's never nothing with you."

I clamped my mouth shut and turned to pour their whiskies. When I turned back, Juke was in full flow.

"... rang her. She was in the mall, being hounded by this guy—"

"What guy?"

"I didn't get his name, but Sabbie thinks he's a gnome." Juke gave me another wink and swallowed his whisky in one.

"Sabbie thinks she's beset by supernatural beings. Gnomes, elves, Morgan le Fay ..."

"It was Marty-Mac," I said, quickly.

Rey's eyes lasered onto mine. "You've spoken to Marty?"

"It was hardly a conversation," said Juke.

Rey shifted his body and spoke directly to him. "Tell me what happened."

"He was basically harmless. I dealt with it in moments. Told him to go and off he slunk, tail between legs."

"You ... *dealt* with it?"

"Rey," I put in, "Marty's in trouble."

"Too right he's in trouble. He's been arrested and charged and is out on bail, stirring up a mess."

"He told me he was in dead stick. He called you his mate."

"I wouldn't describe us as mates. Yeah, we knew each other at school, but if I saw Marty right now, I'd probably slam my fist into his jaw."

"I'd be careful," said Juke. "All I did was put my hands on his lapels and he got angsty. I thought he was going to hit me with that chair."

"Exactly how does that equate with your previous estimation that he was harmless?"

It occurred to me that Juke deserved to know the fuller facts. "Rey's with the Bridgwater Police, Juke."

"Oh." His hand went to his beard, now a bit too well-clipped to stroke properly. He looked stymied, a reaction I frequently noticed on introducing my boyfriend. "I spoke out of turn, didn't I?"

"Don't let it concern you," Rey grunted.

"Maybe he has something to confess." I took a deep, shuddery breath, as if I'd just finished a bout of crying. "Why don't you just give the guy some time?"

"Marty-Mac will be getting time ... when he's sent down. He's a pest. He's due what's coming to him."

I really was hoping Juke would go, if only for a trip to the gents, because I needed to tell Rey what had happened at the Chalice Well—all of it, from the things Brice had learnt about Alys to meeting Anag under the oaks. But my phone was vibrating in an annoying way in my back pocket. I didn't feel like speaking to anyone this evening. I let it ring itself out, but then started up again. I didn't recognize the number.

I took a step away from the bar. "Sabbie Dare."

"I hate you! I *hate* you! You loathsome, loathsome fiend!"

"Lettice. That is you, Lettice, isn't it?"

"What have you done to my grandma?" Lettice screeched. "You walked out on her! She was in such distress and you just left! You didn't get Ma—you didn't even get Shreve!"

"Something's happened to Lady Dare. Is that what you're saying?"

"She's a little better now. Now—now we've calmed her and put her to bed with warm milk and called the doctor."

"What did the doctor say?"

"Nothing." I heard the teenaged sulk behind the word, as if I'd caught her out. "Just ... her pulse was a bit high and it would settle with a good night's sleep."

"When I left, Lettice, she was fine." *It was me who wasn't fine.* Things had been inverted in the Dare household; for some reason, I was the culprit now.

"Don't lie! I got back from my ride and went in to see her because I thought you might still be there, and ... "

"Lettice? Tell me what you found."

"Grandma was in a state! She's *never* in a state. She's the one that snaps people out of states! She was moaning, half out of her chair. She was so pale and breathing so hard." I heard the gulp in her throat. "I thought she was dying."

"It's dreadful that you had to witness that, but—"

"What did you *do* to her?" Her voice dropped to a hiss. "Something despicable. Ma says it's because you are not family and never will be." I heard Lettice sob at the end of the line. "She says I should've known from the beginning. She says it's my fault that I let you into our lives."

"This is not your fault. Nothing is your fault, Lettice. You are the only one who has nothing to blame yourself for."

"I need to know. Why did you do it? Make Grandma collapse, then just disappear?"

"I wouldn't ever hurt your grandmother," was all I could say.

"She's your grandma too."

I couldn't respond. There was no solution to Lettice's sorrow. I was never going to tell her the entire truth—*Grandma dearest is an unpleasant, bitter woman whose understanding of life is diametrically opposed to my own. If she had taken me as six-year old I wouldn't have spent my life in the care system.*

"I'm so sorry, Lettice."

"You are not," she snapped. "You are *not.*"

She cut me off. I looked up. Rey and Juke were gawping. Nige was stock still with a glass of red in each hand. Then a punter flashed a ten-pound note and yelled out an order. I made up his drinks as if nothing had changed.

Something *had* changed. The sense of losing a thing I'd never had. My aunt had been right to say it: I was not of that family, and never would be.

TWENTY-TWO
THE BLACK KNIGHT

"A CHIVALRIC SLAYING," SAID Morgan. "It was promised."

The acolyte had brought them here. It was his plan to find Sabbie Dare. He didn't expect to witness such distress.

Such magic.

For there he is. Ready for the taking. The Black Knight.

The man in black hurtles down the stairwell. He goes straight past them. A door bangs below.

He can do this. He wants it. First time. A line of cold steel straightens his back. His hands are steady; rock-hard fists.

"The Black Knight cut down the thorn tree," he says, realizing. "The Black Knight struck the dolorous blow."

"Don't let him get away."

Pulse in the ears, he runs through the Hall of Angels. They will never catch him if he has a car, but the Black Knight is on foot. The encounter will be a true, chivalric combat.

They cross the town, over the great river bridge, through the back streets. Morgan is ahead on her four-inch heels, snakeskin leather with a peep toe. Selkie can no longer keep up, the little white paws slide on the tarmac. Morgan whips the cat into her arms.

"Don't let him get away."

Finally the Black Knight turns into a narrow alley. High fences on either side leads to squat back yards. A gate swings on a single wretched hinge. The Black Knight travels through a weed-infested yard and a back door slams shut.

"The Black Knight was called Pride," says the acolyte, staring at the door. "His arms and legs were severed. He was dispatched with a blow to the neck." The story from the books. From the film too. The Black Knight had not let King Arthur pass.

He looks at Morgan's belt, at her gem-encrusted dagger. "I'll need a weapon."

"Fate always brings your weapon."

The yard is filled with the detritus of bad living. Bins overflow. Broken microwave thrown onto piled rubble and broken bricks never disposed of. Here, just as Morgan said there would be, are weapons aplenty. He chooses a brick, severed across the middle to form a sharp corner. It's comfortable to hold. He *longs* to use it.

He almost laughs, exhilarated; this is true chivalry. Pursue the enemy of the land. *Raison d'etre.*

Silently, the acolyte tries the handle of the back door. Locked already. This is the fortress of the Black Knight.

"We can wait." Morgan drapes her silk shawl over a low breeze-block wall further along the lane and sits, crossing her leather-clad legs. She brushes her hand along the weed heads growing up by her feet. Dock and nettles. The stings don't bother her. The cat settles near her feet, sitting as upright and alert as any mouser. The acolyte sits at a cautious distance. Late afternoon passes, moves into shade.

"He's in there for good."

"Patience."

"We could knock."

"No."

Selkie stretches his body and opens a pink mouth wide, licking the surrounds with a long tongue. He yowls.

"Pretty baby," says Morgan. "You've missed your teatime."

Each day, the cat has single cream and flaked white fish at five in the afternoon. The cream comes in a saucer and the fish in a soup bowl, both items from a 1936 art deco dinner service that originally had square tea cups and a hexagonal soup tureen. Being a full pedigree seal-point Birman, he laps up every last drop of the cream, but takes only the centre portion from his bowl of fish.

"Poor Selkie," says the acolyte. He's never liked the cat, or trusted it, but he hides this well. Morgan le Fay adores her pet—his lineage is from the incense-fogged temples of Burma, part of their myth, and their art of transmigration—the oracle cat of the saffron Burmese monks. When courage was needed to stand firm against warriors from across the Burmese border, the temple cat transformed himself. His dark eyes became sapphires and his white coat became gold—all except the tips of his pure white paws, which had touched the high altar of the temple. Seeing this transfiguration, the monks had found their ultimate courage. They took up arms and defeated their enemies.

The acolyte worries that this is a story impossible to live up to.

The sun sinks into low cloud. It's cool now. Morgan wraps the shawl around her.

They hear the click. Door opens, door closes, door locks.

The Black Knight has an errand. He takes the cluttered path to his back gate. He sees them. How can he not? They are inside the yard.

"Stand aside," says the acolyte.

"What?"

"Stand aside, worthy adversary!"

"Piss off."

"He is not worthy," Morgan snarls. "Take him down."

"He must say the words. 'None shall pass.'"

The Black Knight shrugs. He's not afraid. Not at all concerned. This is easy for him. Fun. To prove it, he laughs, once. "Piss off before I smack you one."

The acolyte tries to breathe. There is no air in his lungs. No blood in his heart. No thought in his mind. Only the brick, gripped hard, and Morgan's voice soft as a breeze … *be swift, be swift, my little apprentice … pound and pound …*

"You fight with the strength of many men, Black Knight."

"You're asking for it, you are."

"I must cross, though you tell me none shall pass."

"Get out of my garden, you nutter."

"Stand aside I say!" In his mind he sees the Holy Thorn, cut down by this man like a blade of grass and tied up with red ribbons. Blood behind his eyes. He's found his mettle. He swings his arm. Bowler in the crease. This time, there is no faltering. The right implement to hand. Heavy hand. Pound. Shriek of pain. Black dots. Black Knight. Black death.

The acolyte is on the offensive. The sharp, red brick fisted tight makes its mark, once, twice. Brilliant red. The smell of blood is sweet as a come-hither scent. He's doused in it, fired by it. The third blow misses its mark. Black Knight is staggering upright, hands to his face, yowling, swearing, "Shitbastard! Fuckfuck ..." He lashes out, catches the acolyte on the shoulder, sending him down onto his behind. Pain shoots through his spine; the ground is littered with rocks. The Black Knight aims a kick, going for the ribs, but blood is pouring into his eyes and his aim is poor.

Morgan screams at them like a tart at a wrestling match. "Get up! Fight on! Slice him to pieces! Life from life!"

The brick is in his hand and he brings it down on the man's knee, the sharp point driving home.

He's scored. While the knight is dazed with pain, the acolyte throws himself into a rugby tackle, powering the man into the wall of the house, powering the brick down onto the knight's bald scalp.

He hears a crack. Brick on bone. He powers again. His hand is glued to the brick, his shoulder is programmed to lift, swing, pound again.

Chivalric blows. Hard. Accurate. Measured. Unflinching.

DEATH of beauty. DEATH of grace. DEATH of love.

The wound grows large. Blood and mashed flesh. The splintering of bone. Something inside, grey, glistening. The body twitches twice. Then it stills.

He drops the stone. In his pocket is a handkerchief to wipe the blood from his jacket. He retches, once, bringing up only a little strand of green bile.

"Severed through. Limbs then neck," says Morgan.

There is no severing, not with a brick. A grim sight—crushed skin and exposed bone. A blood vessel at the temple spurts red, slower and slower, until it runs empty.

"I've done it." He's breathing so fast he puffs the words. "Life from life."

269

The Green Knight—he had to run. Run and run until sickness overcame him. The second one—the Red Knight—he'd gone into town and sat with a whisky in a dive down Benedict Street. Then he'd found some alley and burnt his throat with the vomit.

This time, his mind is singing. It's like leaping from a cliff; running through fire. Like an orgasm.

"You are my best pupil to date."

"I am?"

"Oh, yes. The very, very best. You have long shown your mettle." Morgan slides the dagger from her belt. "Kneel."

He kneels in the mud and rubble of the back yard. Blood is oozing in a trail through the gravel towards him, but he doesn't shift or flinch. "You struck the chivalric blow." Morgan taps both shoulders with the naked dagger. "Rise, companion-at-arms. You have won your spurs."

He has won his spurs. He's a companion-at-arms. Surely now, the Hollow Hill will open and they will walk in and wake the Sleeping King.

"The Bell of Doomsday," she reminds him. "It must be rung. You must ring it. You must be the one to wake the Sleeping King. You will heal the wasting land. You are the one, my companion-at-arms."

"I am the one."

The back door creaks. A hand, clawed, it seems, pushes at it. It opens a crack.

"Marty? You all right, love?"

He puts the handkerchief away and sees a man pulped to death in his own yard.

"Now we run," he says.

For the first time, he is ahead of Morgan le Fay.

TWENTY-THREE

LAURA

LAURA HAD THE NOTEBOOK in her hand as she came in that Tuesday. After our last session, I'd felt too full of what I'd seen in my journey—the burning pier, the section of Laura's soul trapped in a net, the name of her guardian—to want to talk about it until I'd processed it. I'd sent her home with a full account and asked her to work with the images herself. Even before she pulled off her jacket and helmet, she cried out, "You found my soul-part, Sabbie!"

As soon as she was seated, she opened the book and read through my last journey notes, as if to recheck. "What you wrote about the cave was amazing. Remember how you told me to find my power animal? Go to a nice place, you said. Well, I chose a holiday we went on as a family. Mum and Dad liked something a bit different than Weston Super Mare. Cornwall. Kynance Cove. There's a lot of caves in the cliffs, sort of interconnected? So while you were in a cave, I might have been in one in my imagination too."

"And that's where you saw the chick."

"Yes. Quite a surprise. I thought beside the sea, it might turn out to be, I dunno, a seal or something. It was suddenly there in front of me."

"Have you seen it since?"

"Everywhere!" she laughed. "On the telly, in a kid's picture book, you name it. And then there's the part where you watched Weston pier burn down. Well, that's perfectly true. Someone had left a deep fat fryer alight. You could see the smoke from miles off. Loads of people went down to the front, half our street set out. It was like some massive fireworks display. Come to think of it, fireworks did go off; they'd been left in storage, I think."

"It must have been a disaster."

"Apart from the odd lungful of smoke, you could watch safely from the promenade. No one got hurt, not even the firemen, thank God. The owners had insurance of course, so the revamp was even better than the original."

"Win-win?"

"Ghoulish, I know." There was such energy about her; she was rubbing her palms in anticipation. "What are we doing today?"

"I'd like to do another joint journey, Laura, as the last one was quite productive."

Laura knew the drill. She lay, business-like, on two floor cushions. I lay close to her, with my silken cord wound round our wrists. I set the drumming CD for fifteen minutes in real time—I find most clients can't take any longer—and made straight for Laura's cave in the hope of a dialogue with her guardian. I moved through the darkness of the cave, feeling with my hands, until I reached the turn of rock which led to the far exit and the beach. Something blocked my way. I waited, listening. Trendle's rough coat rubbed at my bare ankle. A shadow flickered on the wall of the cave. Some logical part of my mind told me there could not be a shadow in such total darkness, and yet this was what was happening. An impression flickered there.

"Raichu?"

The shadow moved. "You have come to reclaim Laura's soul-part." The reply was as ghostly as the image, as if it came from the sky outside the cave, which was hidden from me. "I'm sorry, Sabbie. I cannot let you have it. Not yet. Only when you know the answer will Laura accept it from you."

"I don't know the answer!"

"I have spoken of this before. And your own guardian has offered advice. You must allow our reflections to manifest in the apparent world. When all is clear, Sabbie, you may offer the soul-part."

"Why not now?"

"Laura would reject it. That is my fear."

"I see."

And I did see, but that didn't help one bit.

Deflated, I followed Trendle back towards my portal. I passed the fingerpost that directed me to Laura's cave, and recalled a memory of the previous day; the way Esme had pointed at Stefan. *Men are savages at heart ... I have no wish to live with a brute.*

I came out of the journey with my heart thudding in time to the call-back drum. I pushed aside my fleece and looked at Laura, who already had her eyes open.

I was going to have to ask her about previous boyfriends, even her relationship with her father. Had she escaped on her bike, the morning I'd met her, because she was scared of her dad?

We stayed on the floor cushions, writing our accounts. "You go first," she said, not looking up from her notebook.

"Okay, well I went to find Raichu to ask when you should have your soul-part back."

"Oh yeah. You're supposed to give it to me, aren't you."

"I'm afraid he feels you're not ready for your soul-part just yet."

"Why the hell not?"

"We have to get closer to the underlying problem, I think."

"The problem is my shitty life! The problem is I don't have all my bloody soul!"

Laura's breathing quickened. It struck me forcibly that telling Laura the problems I'd encountered with her guardian had only made matters worse.

"I'm not really sure what a guardian is," she said, steadying her breathing.

"As a shaman, I think they are rarified beings on the spirit plane, usually from an Upper Realm."

"What does mine look like?"

"I mostly see his shadow. I saw his face, briefly. He's very grand."

"I know why my guardian is called Raichu." She hugged her knees. "Or rather, why I love my Raichu so much. I think he showed himself to me."

"The … guardian?"

"Yes. I was sitting on my bed, just before I left home for the Navy, and I was holding Raichu. A sort of … brilliance came into my mind. It made me feel light, like a winter leaf … floaty." She grinned. "Weird."

"A nice feeling?"

"More than nice. Whole."

"You don't always feel whole?"

"No, but right then, I did. Just for a moment."

"Your guardian communicated through the toy."

"It's the real reason I took him with me. I hoped the feeling would come again."

"Raichu's been looking out for you from your birth."

"He's kinda been on vacation, then, hasn't he? And now he seems to be hanging on to a bit of my soul."

"Tell me about your journey."

"Oh, it was lovely. I love this journeying lark. I went back to the beach and the chick was there. And he told me to call him Laurie. You know, my invisible friend from when I was tiny. Is that okay?"

"Absolutely. The chick's in charge! Did Laurie say anything else?"

"Yes! It said it was maturing, as I was, and that soon it would have all its feathers. It already had a few, on the wings."

"Oh, good sign."

"And then it said"—she bent over the notebook, where she had written—"'Not until I am fully formed will you become you own self, true to what you must be.' Does it mean when it becomes a proper hen, I'll be cured of my attacks?"

I gave a brief smile. I sincerely hoped that.

"I wondered about going back to the night of the fire, but the drumming changed and called me back."

"Did you want to relive the event?"

"No. I hoped it would be the scene you saw. With my soul-part under the pier. I was never under the pier on the night of the fire. No one was, not even idiots."

I remembered the signpost, and took my queue. "I'd guess you hung out under the pier as kids."

"Yeah, good place for playing chase games."

"And later for first kisses."

"I guess."

"It might be a place where you'd come across someone up to no good."

"I'm not saying stuff didn't happen. Stories would go round the playground. Nothing scary ever happened to me." She stopped, barked a laugh. "Worst I ever saw there was the little boy."

"What little boy?"

"Nah. I'm kidding you. This boy—he must have been about eleven, twelve, I guess; older than me at that time. I was on the beach with my mum and sister and I went under the pier and there he was, peeing."

"Peeing."

"Yeah, against one of the uprights. One of those silly things you remember from your childhood."

"I wonder why you remember it."

"Well, we weren't really a very open family, not in that way, and I don't have any brothers, so I'd never realized until that moment that boys pee standing up."

"That sort of image does get stuck in your mind."

"You're curious at seven or eight, aren't you?"

"About men's bodies? I still am, frankly." We both laughed. I let a beat pass by then said, "Boyfriends certainly can be a mystery, can't they."

"I guess."

"What I'm wondering is … were all your relationships good ones, Laura?"

She shrugged. "To be honest, I was a bit of late starter—in the Royal Navy at just sixteen, concentrating on all the new stuff to learn…"

"Did you leave someone behind when you joined the service?"

"No." Her answer was so brief, I was alerted.

"You maybe had a fling… one that left bad memories."

"No." She looked directly at me, as people do when they are sure of a thing. "I didn't leave someone special behind. And all my memories are good."

"What is your relationship with your father like, Laura?"

"He's cool. A bit under Mum's thumb, you know! Like, it was her idea I should be admitted to the psychiatric ward and he went along with it. Turns out, even Daniel hadn't actually suggested it. Since then, Dad's apologized to me, and that was really good."

She hadn't understood the implications of my question, and now I was glad she had not. I thought about the netting I'd sensed around Laura. "Do you ever feel trapped?"

"In my life?" she asked, her eyes closed.

"In any way."

"Since the attacks started, yes, they trap me. Stop me from doing what I want."

I could have kicked myself. Of course Laura felt trapped. "You've now got quite a few shamanic symbols," I said. "I think we should draw a web."

I scrabbled under the desk for the roll of wallpaper I use for this process. Laura helped me weigh down a length on the laminate floor and we got going with felt tip pens, drawing our way through the things we'd seen on our journeys.

When it was complete, we connected the symbols to create a web.

"Cave," said Laura, counting up. "Pier, fingerpost, beach, waterfall. Little Raichu and guardian Raichu. And my chick … Laurie."

"Shadows," I added. "Glimpses. A net. Flames. The song, 'Shape Shifter.'"

We rolled up the paper and Laura put it under her arm.

"Pin it above your bed and see what your dreams bring this week," I advised, as she left.

She frowned and shook her head.

"You're not sleeping well, are you?"

"No. I keep imagining they're coming to get me. Take me away."

"That won't happen, Laura. You're not a threat to anyone."

"Even so …" She was halfway through the door as she spoke, and her words were half lost. "It would be nice to have one full night of untroubled sleep."

TWENTY-FOUR
MARTY-MAC

"Could I have a word?"

"Pippa?"

The woman was standing, like the police officer she was, respectfully outside the porch-way. My voice sounded hollow within it. She put out her hand and I shook it. It was cool and steady.

"Could I come in, please?"

"Er..."

"It's official, I'm afraid."

"What?"

"I need to ask you some questions. I'll only take a few moments of your time."

That was what the police said, wasn't it, when actually they had brought handcuffs and a search warrant.

I took her into the therapy room. I'd done an aromatherapy massage after Laura had left, so it smelt of lavender and chamomile.

We sat at the desk, as I would with a client. She didn't have anything on her; no notebook or recorder. She sat comfortably back in the wicker chair and crossed her legs, which today were hidden under a pair of pinstriped suit trousers with a sharp crease. Her blouse was off-white, open-necked but buttoned high, with short sleeves as a nod to the weather. She'd left the jacket in the car, perhaps. Her hair—that glorious tumble of penny-bright curls—had been slicked into a tight bun. She looked the biz. She looked scary.

"I need to ask you about your movements on Saturday the eighth of July."

"What?" I gave myself a shake. "I'm sorry?"

"Last weekend. Where were you on the afternoon and evening of Saturday?"

"You think I did something wrong?"

"Of course not, Sabbie." She offered her professional smile. "If you could answer the question, please."

"Er … well, as always I was at the Curate's Egg from sixish onwards. I usually get home about quarter to midnight." An image came into my head; the phone call from Lettice.

"Oh, goddess! Oh, no!"

"Yes?"

"Is this about my grandmother? Lady Savile-Dare? Has she died, is that it?"

Pippa's head went back, as if she'd braked at speed. I'd thrown her. "I don't know about your grandmother, I'm afraid. I'm here about Martin Macaskill."

"Who?"

"You might know this person as Marty-Mac."

For no good reason, my heart clunked into a faster rhythm. "I do know him as that. He's been bothering me. Is that what you want to talk about?"

"Can I establish that you had contact with Martin Macaskill on Saturday, July eighth?"

"*Contact?*" It felt like the wrong word. Like Marty-Mac and I had trumped up some plan together.

"Where were you when you saw Macaskill?"

"In the Angel Shopping Centre. Well, no—in the car park. He gave me the jitters and I ran off. He followed me into the café."

"What time was this?"

"Sort of two-ish. Yes, because I was late for an appointment..." I trailed off.

"Can you recall your conversation with Martin Macaskill?"

"Er..." I hesitated. Marty had talked a lot about Rey. Rey was Pippa's boss. I didn't think it would be good to discuss this behind his back. I was quickly deciding not to say anything that Pippa didn't drag out of me.

She closed her eyes, a slow blink, as if forcing herself to have patience. "Anything at all, Sabbie."

"He had my business card. And he'd found me on Facebook. He scared me, a bit."

"So what happened in the end?"

"He went."

"You asked him to go and he complied."

"If you like."

She recrossed her legs. "I don't like, Sabbie. Because that afternoon the station had a call from the Angel Café to report there had been an altercation within the premises. An officer took a statement. So we know a third party was involved."

"Marty didn't touch him. Not at all."

"Him? That would have been Reynard Buckley?"

"No, it wouldn't."

"Would you make a statement to that affect?"

"Pippa! It was just a friend who was passing. Will you please tell me why—"

"Can I have the friend's name, please."

"Eh?"

She pulled her iPhone out of her trouser pocket. No wonder she didn't carry a notebook. She held it in readiness.

"Justin Webber," I said, on my out-breath. "Known as Juke. He works at the Agency for Change, near the river, above the Polska Café. It's a small charity that supports displaced persons."

"Did you see Martin Macaskill at any time after that?"

"No, I didn't. I haven't. I'm glad to say he's left me alone."

Pippa lay the phone on her lap. "Have you spoken to Reynard Buckley since that time?

My heart flapped wildly. "We're both busy people, you know? I … I don't recall discussing Marty." That was what politicians said, when they wanted to lie. *I don't recall.* I hoped Pippa hadn't noticed. "I thought it was over."

"Can you clarify what you thought was over?"

"Nothing." I trailed off. "What d'you mean, *Reynard Buckley*? Like, you don't know I'm his girlfriend?"

"I'm sorry. I didn't mean to give that impression." An irritated smile flashed across her face. "Please go on."

"You need to tell me why you're here, Pippa."

She sighed. She shifted again, uncrossing her legs and placing her neat almond toes together on the laminate flooring. "Martin Macaskill was found on Saturday evening at just after seven. Dead."

"I'm ... uh? Sorry? *Dead*?"

"He was found in a garden on Brendon Way, where he had been living with his mother, since being arrested, charged, and released on bail."

She sounded so sure. Like the information was already imbedded in her memory. "How did he die?"

"Blunt weapon injury. I can't reveal more than that, Sabbie, at this time."

"Rey has asked you to question me about this?"

She favoured me with her professional version of a smile. "What makes you say that?"

"Well, if he's heading up this investigation—"

"He's not heading it up. I'm reporting directly to Chief Inspector Horton." She stopped short and looked at her phone screen, although I could see that she wasn't reading anything. She was buying herself some time. I felt my forehead wrinkle into a frown. Why would Pippa ever need time to think? "Rey is a suspect, I'm afraid."

"Don't be stupid!"

"You didn't know." I felt, rather than saw, the sympathy in her eyes. She was sorry for me. I gripped the wicker chair, locked into position, unable to move. "You did know that Reynard ... Rey ... has been suspended?" she asked.

"Suspended? From duty?"

"I'm sorry to be the one to break the news." She tried another smile. It was cracking her lips.

"That's nuts. That's a lie."

"Reynard Buckley was suspended two weeks ago, on suspicion of becoming personally involved with a case of corruption and theft."

"Stop calling him Reynard Buckley!"

I'd raised my voice, but she didn't respond to that. "I'd no idea I'd be bringing you this news. It must be hard for you."

"Piss off, Pippa."

She processed that, filing it away. "You understand that if you hadn't been approached by Martin Macaskill, I wouldn't be here. We found Macaskill's phone on his body. He had entered your telephone number into his contacts. You were also a match with the description the café staff gave us." She looked delighted with her good police work.

"Whatever you think Rey has done, he hasn't done this. He's as incorruptible as a ..." I trailed off. Rey was incorruptible. But he had been angry when I'd seen him in the Egg. And by that time, Marty-Mac was dead.

"It was noted and recorded that Rey had dealings with Martin Macaskill, who was sourcing unpaid items within his previous working environment. It is possible Rey had become involved with the ... with what was going on."

I looked at her. It was the first time Pippa Chaisey had been the least bit vague. "So, what was going on?"

"We are still investigating that."

"You mean *you* are."

"Yes. I am."

"Bit of a leg up for you, this, isn't it? I mean, you've only just become a DS, haven't you? Rey was years a DS before he got his promotion."

"I don't think that's any concern of yours. If you must know, I'm fast-tracked."

"You're what?"

"Fast-tracked. I'm a university graduate."

"Oh, please. Let me congratulate you. You're one of millions."

"Not in the police force."

"And you think that gives you the right to go snooping around my boyfriend, who has served the Avon and Somerset Constabulary meticulously for over twenty years?"

"This time isn't the first time, Sabbie." The compassionate tone was back in her voice. "Even before I arrived at Bridgwater, there had been some dodgy business with Rey Buckley. In fact, it was station gossip. A station joke, if you like." She shook her head. "Unbelievable."

"I'm sorry?"

"Six months ago, he took part in some sort of sting." She paused. "Beg pardon, you probably don't know what a sting is—"

"Any fool knows what a sting is. Rey's not like that. He wouldn't do that. His methods got results. All his results are good. They led to his promotion."

"Really? If you like. All I know is what I heard around the station, which, of course, I had to pass onto my superior."

"Your superior is Rey."

"Not when a colleague has legitimate suspicions. I had to report what I'd found to be the truth. Reynard Buckley had taken a uniformed officer into a municipal car park late in the evening and involved him in a private affair. He proceeded to accost a family as they were about to leave in their car. To achieve this, it is a possibility that he had previously smashed the back lights of the car involved. He did this, apparently, as a favour to a mate."

She gave me a look that was so satisfied, so triumphant, I had to dig my fingers into the woven cane of the chair to stop myself from lunging at her. I wondered if she knew everything. Did she know I had been there, in that car park? That I was the "mate" in question? Did she know Rey had smashed the lights to help me rescue someone from dreadful captivity? Did she have any idea how good a man Rey was?

"Because of this small thing, he's been suspended from duty?"

"Reynard Buckley is prone to acts that are outside the professional conduct of an officer of the law. This time, it's far worse that just a smashed light, I'm afraid."

I wanted to tell her to stop calling Rey by his full name again, but I couldn't. I couldn't speak at all.

———

I dialled Juke's number as I ran around the house, collecting my bag, finding my car keys. "Juke—sorry, but something's come up I need to tell you about—"

"Is it Marty-Mac?" I heard Juke ask.

"He's dead, Juke! He's been killed."

"Oh God. How d'you know?"

"The police have been here—"

"Oh hell."

"It happened on Saturday after we saw him."

"Oh shit!"

"They already knew the three of us were at the café."

"How? How did they know that Sabbie?"

"Okay, Juke, calm down."

"I'm sorry; sorry. It's just so awful."

"I'm afraid they might come and interview you."

"Oh hell! Not here at work I hope!"

"Maybe usurp them by going into the station to give a statement."

"Yeah. Good thinking. What did you tell them, Sabbie?"

That made me stop. I was halfway to the door. I slashed my hand across my eyes. "The truth, of course."

"Right."

"You didn't touch him."

"No. No! I didn't."

"Tell it like it was, Juke, because the staff reported the incident to the police."

Juke sighed. "I could do without this, Sabbie."

"Yes. My fault. I got you involved. Unnecessarily."

"No ... no, I was pleased to help ... "

"Go and make that statement. Tell them I've rung you. I know how cops' brains work, and this will only look good for you."

"Yeah."

"Well, *you* didn't kill him."

"Yeah. No. Nothing to worry about."

I cut us off and sprinted to the Vauxhall. I swung out of my street and tried to keep my speed down as I cleared the estate and crossed the River Parrett. I couldn't get Pippa Chaisey out of my mind. I had thought she was a threat to my relationship with Rey. Turned out, she was a threat to Rey himself. And how was I going to break it to him—that I knew? An entire fortnight had passed with him suspended from work, pretending to me that he'd been so busy he couldn't even see me. I'd thought he was going off me. Now I knew that he hadn't been able to face me.

The nineteenth-century terrace of houses loomed as I came to a halt, one wheel on the pavement. Most of these houses were now divided into flats. Rey's quarters were so tiny they could not be described as anything more than a bedsit, but I knew that he was crippled by keeping up repayments on a house he owned but didn't live in; the house of his marriage. I pushed at the front door. It was usually left unlocked, so the inhabitants could come and go, locking their own doors independently. I took the stairs, flying round the turns. I couldn't stop myself from crying out, as I got to his floor.

"Rey! REY!"

"Sabbie?"

Rey was standing there. He hadn't shaved. He was wearing lounge pants and a t-shirt. I saw his unmade bed, duvet rumpled and pillows flattened. I realized this was his sleeping attire, something I didn't often get a look at. His expression wasn't entirely shock; there was some guilt there too.

"I'm a bit … er … yeah, off work with some sort of virus … best not get too close." He wasn't making much attempt to lie convincingly, perhaps because he'd been caught so far off-guard.

"Man flu, is it?"

"If you like."

"Rey, you never take a day off."

"Been a crackdown on bugs. They force us to work from home, now. I don't want you catching it."

"Women can't get man flu."

"I'm sorry you've … found me like this. I look shit."

"Nah … I like you in bedtime gear and stubble. Sexy."

He regarded me, taking in my words, not breaking into a smile. His eyes were bleary.

"I need to sit down, Rey. If I don't, I'll drop, I swear it."

By the cold radiator was Rey's single comfy chair, piled with open files. I lifted them from the seat, trying not to disrupt things.

"Yeah—just—on the floor is good."

"What are you working on?"

"It's nothing."

He looked done in ... sucked dry. For the first time, I realized that I could sometimes be the stronger one in our relationship.

"I have to talk to you about Marty-Mac."

"What?" Rey was instantly on alert.

"I've been worrying about it all, Rey."

"Marty-Mac won't be bothering you anymore. He's dead."

"You're ... glad he's dead."

"No, don't get me wrong—"

"You wanted him dead."

He took three steps and was across the small room. "'Course I didn't want him fucking dead."

"Swearing won't help, Rey."

"I'm a law enforcement officer. I protect the innocent."

"Marty wasn't exactly innocent, was he?"

I let the moments tick on. Surely he trusted me enough to tell me what was going on. Surely if there was one person he might confide in, it would be me. As you would confide in your partner. But we weren't partners. I was his girlfriend, *a* girlfriend, someone to meet in a pub and take home for a hump in the hay. Not someone to confide in.

I wondered if his wife knew. Had he told Lesley of his suspension? Had she come round to clean the bedsit and found him in bed late into the morning?

"You think I got him killed," said Rey. "It's my fault? You think that?"

"How could I think that? I don't even know your connection to the man."

"Yeah you do. I said. We knew each other at school. I knew lots of people at school. Most of Bridgwater and surrounds. I've never been friends with Marty-Mac, but no one is listening."

His hands brushed the arm of the chair I was in, as if afraid to touch me. I so longed for him say it, get it out in the open. *I am under suspicion for his murder.* I snatched at his hands and held them tight. "What you've got to do, is work out who killed him."

"Yeah." He tried a grin. "Not a difficult case, for God's sake. Mac had friends who would quickly change to enemies. Who would happily get someone to go at him with a bit of house brick, if the circumstances allowed. I don't know why they can't see that."

"They?"

He stared at me for almost a full minute.

"Rey," I repeated. "Who are 'they'?"

He snatched his hands from mine and turned on his heel. I think I made a sort of sound, not a word, not, "please" or "no, don't go", but rather, a wail of distress, knowing he'd rather walk away than tell me. He swung away into the kitchen area of the bedsit. It was not anger. He'd walked away from me in shame.

He reached into a wall cupboard and drew out a beer, flipped off the top and took a swig from the neck. "You can tell me," I said, without moving. "Unload whatever there is to unload. I love you."

That unnerved him. I'd told him I loved him before, several times—I knew because I was keeping count—but he never responded. He didn't seem to be able to say "I love you" back. Didn't mean he didn't love me.

There was a pause that grew and grew.

Finally, Rey put his beer down, quite gently, and drew himself up, as if this was the superintendent's office and he had been called there to give his account.

"Marty-Mac has been a petty criminal from—well, from early days, I suspect. He'd been in prison a couple of times, and from what I can make out he didn't like the experience. He's weak, a loser, the sort that always comes under the heel of someone else. Prison would be hell for him. He came out the second time and tried to go straight. He got this job on a building site. Something with a county council connection—the firm who got the tender for the work had given the mother of cheap quotes. Stupid. Cheap tenders always attract the cowboys and criminal elements."

"Marty-Mac was the criminal element?"

"Not at all. He's trying his utmost to go straight, right? Do a bit of roofing, a bit of bricklaying, that sort of thing. It's not easy to go straight for an ex-con. The only people who will think of employing you are people who want something from you."

I got up. It was silly to carry on this conversation with metres of space between us. I went over to him and slid my hands around the waist band of his lounge pants. "What did they want with Marty?"

"A factotum, I think. A runner, a driver, that sort of thing. A go-between. Years back—ten, fifteen years back, before he did his first stretch—Marty had been my man. My snout; my informer. In those days, we'd do things on the quiet. Just a word, just a fiver passed over for beer money. Now, things have changed. We have to document the lot; there's a fund we use to pay informers. *Informants,* they're called." He lay his cheek against mine and I felt the dry chuckle in his throat. "They're still snouts and grasses, of course."

I'd been holding my breath. I let it out with my words. "You did it on the quiet."

"Yeah. Just this once. He knew materials were being passed into the worksite which were poor in quality—dangerous in quality— and that certain officials had enabled this to happen. He came to tell me and I started asking round. That was a bad move."

"You had no written records?"

"No proof of evidence obtained. Only the tip-off from Marty, who is not my documented informant."

"It seems so insignificant."

"We're talking major investment. People with a lot of money looking to make further killings. If they didn't like how I was asking my questions, it would be relatively simple to get me out their way."

"If you were easy to remove, how much easier would Marty-Mac be?"

"Trouble is, I don't have an alibi, not for early evening Saturday. And I do have the means, motive, and—"

"Opportunity." I'd watched the crime series. I knew that didn't make him guilty. "Can't the powers that be at the station see that you'd be the last person to want him out of the way?"

"Apparently not. And although it looked like a random attack, there were a lot of wounds."

"A lot of wounds?"

"Yeah. Extremely vicious."

"*The Green Knight has been taken down.*" I could barely hear myself over the buzzing in my ears as I thought about Morgan le Fay. "*And others will perish likewise.*"

"What're you on about?"

I shook my head, thinking how Marty-Mac was beaten to the ground with a bit of brick. Gerald Evens had been attacked with a paving stone. Not a mugging, I was thinking—it was clear Gerald wouldn't have money on him.

I looked up. "Marty-Mac wasn't mugged. He still had his phone."

"How do you know that?"

"Pippa let it out."

"You've seen her?"

"She thought she'd get something from me. She was wrong. She's brutal, Rey. Ruthless. The sort of stickler who has to do everything by the book. She wants your job."

I heard him swallow hard. Silent moments passed, then I felt his chest shake. So tight was it to mine, that I shook with it. He was crying, keeping the silent wracked sobs inside him in the hope I'd never know.

I clamped him to me and hung on. My eyes stayed dry. I felt steely. I was prepared to fight to the death for my man. I was prepared to scratch the bitch's eyes out.

TWENTY-FIVE
ANTHONY

THE KAISER WOKE ME on Wednesday morning with the dawn. How *could* he? I'd had barely four hours sleep. Immediately I was awake—bright-eyed and alert and infused with cockeyed promise.

It was crazy to be so happy and hope-filled, but I couldn't help it. Rey's difficulties were not one wit removed, but at least we could face them together, as a couple. I couldn't solve his problems, but I could support him.

I shifted with care over the mattress, so that I could feast my gaze on the shorn head lying next to me. Rey was on his back, his head lodged between the pillows. We'd driven to mine in the Vauxhall and picked up a bottle of something deeply red on the way. Once that was all finished up, we went to bed.

It was the first time we'd made love in a while, and it felt wonderful … it *was* wonderful—renewed and thrilling.

Even so, a tiny spasm of disappointment trickled through me as I gazed at Rey's sleeping form. As far as I understood, relationships start out with two people wound round each other's necks. Eventually that developed into compromises and home-sharing. We had not reached that stage yet, and we wouldn't, until we'd resolved the unfinished business of Rey moving in with me. I didn't dare reintroduce the idea at the moment. He'd said, "give me some time to think" and since then, we'd both had other things to think about.

I was zinging from our lovemaking ... his fingers on my skin, the way he, too, closed his eyes as our kisses got deeper . . I knew I should count the blessings the goddess had granted me before wanting more.

Rey let out a bellowing snore. He was in that deep pattern of sleep that comes with REM and vivid dreams. If I woke him now, would he tell me the dreams he'd forget later in the morning? Would he confide his nightmares to me?

Probably he'd bark at me, roll over, and go back to sleep.

The Kaiser crowed again. I pulled back the curtains. A glimmer of light was rising in the east. A good time for a garden meditation.

———

It was ten before Rey staggered downstairs. His eyes were full of blear. Mine were summertime bright; my buoyant state of mind had driven me to make pancakes for breakfast and while I was flipping them in the pan I had done a lot of thinking. More and more small pieces about Marty-Mac's death had fallen into place. I'd put the pancakes to warm and dialled Brice's number to ask him if he'd had any further emails.

"I've put her on my spam list, Sabbie," Brice had said. "I never want to hear from that woman again."

"Please … could you check your junk mail? I need to know if she's sent another."

He had not asked why. A minute or two later, an email dropped into my box. When I'd read it a tightness wound round my stomach that was almost elation. I couldn't wait to discuss my thoughts with Rey, but I didn't want to bombard him with them, as soon as he sat down to breakfast.

I slid a two-cup cafetière over to him. I had a pot of mixed herb leaves. "Rey, why don't you stay for a bit? Let me feed you up. You need all your strength to fight this thing."

"Yeah? Well … if I got pancakes every morning…"

"Except, I have to go to a funeral on Friday."

"Is this the girl on the Tor … Alys, wasn't it?"

"I've been asked to officiate, with Wolfsbane."

"What's a pagan funeral like?"

"Wolfs has done a couple of them. He's lent me a transcript of a ceremony he uses. It's nothing scary, or heavy. There won't be many surprises. Nowadays, most funerals are more a celebration of the life lived, aren't they? Brice wants lots of music and a slideshow screening of pictures of Alys from when she was born onward, that sort of thing. We'll be using the presence of certain deities and spirits to help Alys's soul move on. If we decide to stay, we can help Brice scatter her ashes."

"Stay?"

"It's in central London. I was going to ask the Wraxalls to look after the hens, but if you're here I'd come straight back."

"When are you leaving?"

"Early Friday morning. It will mostly be over by early evening. I could jump on a return train."

"You're not worrying, are you? I will be fine, Sabbie. I've done nothing wrong."

"No. Nothing." I could wait no longer. I slid the printout of the fourth email over the breakfast bar.

Rey groaned. "Is there any hope that this isn't what I think it is?"

"No hope at all."

Rey took his time drizzling honey over his pancakes. He read the email, and, I could see, was reading it a second time. When I dropped the other printouts beside his plate, he took his time with those too.

"You're tying up your gumshoe laces," he said. "I can detect the smell of amateur sleuth from over here."

"You want to hear what I've been thinking?"

"Do I have a choice?"

I flashed him a pretty smile. "Nope."

"Fire ahead, Miss Marlow."

"There are patterns. I'm not sure Morgan le Fay means there to be, but I can see them."

"Okay; good. An investigating team would start off, if they had nothing else, with that."

"Morgan le Fay sends the emails at distinct moments. The first arrived only hours after Alys had died. The second as Brice drove to the inquest. The third one in response to Brice; he'd emailed the entire workshop group, asking us to meet at the Chalice Well."

"And this one?" Rey picked up the fourth sheet and waved it. "The funeral?"

"Maybe ... just hang on in there, I'm getting to number four." I took a breath. I wanted to do this my way. "There is one knight per email. Green Knight. Red Knight. Foolish Knight."

"Black Knight," Rey read aloud.

"Then there are the locations," I went on. "The Tor first, the Abbey second, the Chalice Well in the third email. *Blood runs deep through the Hollow Hill.* It felt like a warning. The Chalice Well is sublime, a haven of peace—Brice wanted us all to meet in the gardens—I made them go to the Rifleman's Arms instead. Blood had already been viciously spilt, and I didn't want it to happen again."

Rey concentrated on pouring himself a dark coffee which smelt so luxurious I almost wanted a cup. But he stayed silent, and I pressed on. "However, one of us did go into the Chalice Well. Anagarika."

"Ana-*what*? Christ, Sabbie, your friends have some seriously strange names."

"You should meet the guy. Apparently, Anag did see something while he was there—he ended up with a split lip because of what he saw. That does makes me wonder what might have happened, had the rest of us gone in."

Rey lifted his cup and stared into it as if it was a black mirror that held the answers. "A team will investigate the 'mights', it's true. But they'd keep them to one side. Fact is, Sabbie, you will never know whether you'd've been safe in the gardens. In fact, despite these patterns you've detected, you still haven't proved a thing."

He lifted the printout of the fourth email and read aloud.

The Black Knight was a butcher. His name was Pride. He cut down the Holy Thorn. He raped a maiden of the well. And he has been dispatched. Limbs sliced through. Head taken with a single sweep of the sword. In blood we are revenged. His slaying was expedient. Side-by-side I will walk with my companion-at-arms into the Hollow Hill. Angels flank us. We are ready to ring the Bell of Doomsday. The knights of Avalon will wake. The King will raise his sword. Each hurt shall be avenged and Ogres will be healed.

"A new knight," I said, ticking my points off on my fingers. "Black. A new location. And a new reason to alert Brice. It's not just the funeral, Rey. It's because finally, someone has died. Marty-Mac."

Rey stared at me for half a minute. He wasn't laughing, trying to shut me up or even coming back with a counter-argument. Finally, he said, "Haven't you noticed? Each email is written as if to mollify pain. Morgan le Fay seems to think Brice will be pleased to hear from her, as if she's reporting in, bringing the director of operations up to speed."

Rey was right. The letters didn't threaten; on the contrary they were saying all would be well; that Alys's death would be avenged. That the land would be saved from destruction.

"Brice is trying to cope with the death of his wife. It's possible that his mind has got scrambled. Losing the woman you loved might turn you crazy, lead you to invent answers, lead you to search for retribution, even if no one was to blame." Rey pushed his final forkful of pancake into his mouth. Honey oozed from one corner of his mouth.

"Yes…" My voice sounded faded. Perhaps Brice had suffered more psychological damage than I'd seen him show, but I could not believe he had gone as far as creating an untraceable email address to send messages to himself. "If he has invented Morgan," I asked, "why have people been attacked? Died?"

"No one has died because of these emails. Marty-Mac was already in jeopardy. He was in above his head. He could have asked for police protection, but he grabbed the chance of bail and left himself wide open. He was eliminated for having a big mouth which was about to flap wider under cross-examination. His death isn't linked to this at all."

"Let me just explain the pattern in this last email. A Black Knight. Marty-Mac was all in black when I saw him the day he died. And new location, the Angel Shopping Centre. *Angels flank us,* according to Morgan." Something flashed at the back of my thoughts as I remembered what had happened in the Angel Shopping Centre. It was like a child's torch, a beam of light directed through a dark window after bedtime. A signal—on, off, and on again. Not an idea, more an awareness. Rey interrupted it, and it flew away.

"The angel connection is tenuous. Marty-Mac was killed in his own back garden."

"But the Red Knight *was* attacked at Glastonbury Abbey. Gerald Evens was a volunteer all kitted out in a knight's costume to show tourists round the abbey grounds. He nearly died in that attack."

Rey wheezed out a breath, as if throwing in the towel. "Okay, Sabbie. I do recall you mentioning this guy's name. But at the most you only have two knights. There are four all together."

Rey thought he'd stumped me, but I hadn't told him yet about Yew's story. "Anthony Bale was attacked with a stone as he walked back to his hostel. He was returning from his night on the Tor. This was solstice morning, at around the time Brice received his first email. And I honestly can't see how Brice would ever have known about that incident—"

"Slow down here. Who is Anthony Bale?"

"Anthony Bale was so distressed at Alys's death, he had one of those giggly reactions. People do sometimes laugh at death, don't they, an automatic response. He caught an early bus from Glastonbury to Yeovil, where he was attacked. Not badly. Got up, walked on."

"You know this person?"

"No, but Yew does."

"Who? You?"

"Yew. His chosen name is a tree, Rey. A sacred tree of the dark winter. Grown in churchyards because of its association with death."

Rey raised his eyes to the ceiling. "I can't keep up. Really, it's beyond my simple capabilities. One moment we're discussing grievous bodily harm, the next we're on to death trees."

I grinned. This sounded more like the old Rey. "Yew is the tree of great age, death, and reincarnation, because it regenerates itself each year of growth. Oak is the tree of the druid, solid and host to many. Ash is the tree of the world. Odin initiated himself into wisdom on it, although he did lose an eye to the crows as he hung there…" I trailed off. "Sorry."

"So, what is the tree of the lover?"

"Oh! The honeysuckle."

"That's hardly a tree."

"It's a woody shrub, but it lives to embrace another. If you bring the blossoms into your bedroom, the scent gives you erotic dreams."

"Then you are honeysuckle, Sabbie."

Rey caught me completely be surprise. He took my hand and buried soft lips into my fingers, my wrist, my palm.

My pulse raced, yet I didn't seem to need breathe. Each kiss suspended me in delight, holding me between this plane and a higher one. The kisses went on forever, as if time was suspended while Rey held me to his lips.

We're on our way...

The last words of a brief dream. My eyelids scratched as I forced them open. I was in the passenger seat of my own car. I checked the dashboard clock. Yeovil was a longer drive than I anticipated; I'd been asleep for the best part of an hour.

"You okay?" Rey was easing the Vauxhall round a street corner, searching for the hostel.

I shifted in my seat and sipped from my water bottle. *We're on our way.* It had been the fleeting though that Rey had earlier driven away, the something that had sat unnoticed on the edge of my mind—a hidden thing, crucial, dropped into place like a card trick in my car dream.

I thought back through all the subject matter we'd covered since I'd turned up at Rey's yesterday: Yew's story about Anthony, Pippa's stab in the back, Brice's relationship to his emails, Marty-Mac's death and its connection to the other attacks, Juke's appearance in the Angel café—

Juke. It was Juke's voice in my head. His words in my dream. *We're on our way.* My chin snapped up. In my mind's eye, I rewound that moment—Juke squaring up to Marty-Mac in the Angel café. He'd looked round, searching for someone. I'd thought he was worried Marty-Mac would return.

Hadn't Juke been alone, when he'd arrived? If someone had been there with him, they'd chosen not to show themselves. They'd watched from the wings.

A chill moved over my back. It was the chill of daytime sleep, but it felt like the hand of death on my shoulder.

"I've been using my driving time to think," said Rey. "And I have a question. Why would Morgan le Fay attack anyone?"

"Because she believes she's a powerful magician and likes to prove it? Because it's a thrill?" I paused for a beat, Juke's words in my ears. *We're on our way.* "I'm wondering if there are two of them, working together. She's started to talk about this *companion-at-arms.*"

"The attack on Macaskill was brutal; it needed strength." Brice slowed the car; the hostel was ahead of us. "Three scenarios. One, Brice is sending emails to himself, and the link to the attacks is chance. Two, someone is looking out for attacks, maybe on social media, and then sending Brice prank emails to wind him up—someone who wants to see him off work for a long time, maybe to grab some contract or another. Three, Morgan le Fay is attacking people in the belief that this will atone for Alys's death and that Brice would be pleased to hear about it."

"I don't want it to be number three, Rey. I know you think I meet trouble halfway, but number three involves everyone who was at Stonedown for the Spirit Flyers' Workshop."

"Don't tell me you haven't already considered that it might be one of them."

I was fond of then all, underneath—Wolfs and Shell, all the workshoppers, even Stefan and Esme. "Yes," I admitted. "I've considered it."

"Who was there? Was Juke there? The Juke I met in the pub?"

I turned my water bottle round in my hands and listened to the gentle slosh. "Yes."

"The Juke who accosted Marty-Mac at the Angel Café?"

"Ye-es." My voice broke. "Okay, Juke is sometimes a little too earnest for his own good, but ..." I raised my hands in submission. For once, my spirit-based instincts were falling foul of what I could see with my own eyes.

I'd phoned Juke straight after my foul interview with Pippa, to warn him Macaskill was dead. Had he sounded surprised? Had he sounded guilty? In the shopping centre, we'd parted company on the grounds we were both too shattered to work shamanically. To commit this crime, he would have had to follow Marty out onto the street. Clock where he was headed. Maybe work out where he lived. None of that sounded anything like Justin Webber to me.

———

There was a girl at the reception desk, a key-worker I supposed, sifting through some paperwork. She looked up as we pushed through the main door.

"We'd like to speak to Anthony Bale," said Rey, "if that's possible."

"We texted Yew Merrick earlier, asking if we would could," I added.

The girl looked us over. "Anthony? Er ... yeah. You can talk to him in the communal area, if that's okay." She smiled. "One of the Residents' Rules."

"That's fine."

"Who shall I say?"

"Sabbie Dare and Rey Buckley," said Rey. I expected him to get out his police ID. When he didn't, I realized it had been taken it away from him.

She got up from her desk and disappeared. Rey instantly leaned over her desk and eased the computer screen towards us until it was legible.

"Rey!" I hissed.

He flashed a wicked grin. "Nothing of importance anyway."

While Rey was snooping, I took in the hostel surrounds. The magnolia walls were covered in posters and a few cheap prints in frames. The woodwork was painted white. It had been a while since a redecoration; the paint was chipped and scuffed, but the place was tidy. Clean, warm. Welcoming, to a point. There was a smell, though. Nothing like the perpetual ammonia scent of homes for the elderly, but not particularly pleasant either. It was tempting to think the place smelt of misfortune and hardship, but it was probably the dampness that lingers around things that have been kept outside for too long. A musty, sporal scent.

"Rey!" I hissed. Yew was pushing his way through some far doors. He spotted us and waved, walking at a fast pace, his plait bouncing between his shoulder blades. Rey moved away from the desk and put out his hand, introduced himself.

"I hope Anthony is okay about seeing us."

"I think this will actually help him," said Yew. "He's fallen into a depression since it happened. Talking about it might put things in perspective."

Rey shrugged. "He was hardly touched."

"When you're homeless, you lose friends in the outside world, but you gain enemies. We cope with a lot of hate attacks; there are people out there who think everyone down on their luck is a beggar or a wastrel."

Rey nodded. "I guess that's depressing enough."

"Exactly. We even see grudge aggression. Anthony could have been attacked by someone else from the hostel."

"That's a horrid thought," I said. Nevertheless, if that's what had happened, we could eliminate Anthony from the Morgan trail of victims. I wasn't sure if I wanted that or not.

"Yep," Yew was saying, "hostels are like boarding schools. Full of rules, hierarchies, and bullies."

"Sounds like you know the system!"

"I was a Westminster boy. Boarded from the age of nine."

"Your parents must have been loaded!" I screwed up my face. "Sorry, that wasn't meant to come out like that."

"No offence taken. I was on a scholarship. A chorister."

I giggled. Surprisingly, it wasn't hard to imagine Yew in a red cassock with a white frill, the choir boy who always brought their pet mouse to Vespers.

"You were surely destined for Oxford."

"Cambridge. I was halfway through my degree when I walked out of my college. Joined some alternative kids I'd met at a festival."

"Is that when you became an eco-warrior, Yew?" I asked, for Rey's benefit.

"It was a magic time, I admit. We thought we'd change the world. We were building walkways and sleeping platforms in the trees, to stop the authorities hewing them down. We led the cops a merry dance. I'm still protesting, in a quieter way. Mostly I write letters— post them or email them—pressing for a cleaner world, one hundred percent renewable. If that doesn't happen soon, I truly believe we'll be choking in the streets. The world will slowly turn become uninhabitable."

"It's the Arthurian legend, isn't?" Morgan le Fay's message never left my mind. "The wasteland of the wounded king?"

"Yeah. I guess it's always been with us, fear of drought or famine or flood or pestilence, man-made or not."

"Did you ever finish your degree?" Rey asked.

"Nah. All that felt way too privileged … something I didn't want a part of. I never went back and I never cut my hair again."

The key-worker was returning, accompanied by a man of perhaps forty, forty-five. Or younger, I thought, but badly aged. I walked towards them.

"Hi. I'm Yew's friend, Sabbie."

"Yeah."

"Good to see you looking so well."

He didn't reply. He stood with one hand pressed against the corridor wall, blocking the way of the girl who'd stopped behind him. "Go on, Anthony," I heard her say softly. "Take them into the lounge area, eh?"

Anthony walked directly through the doors without looking back, and it occurred to me that things can get so bad, once your confidence has taken a knocking, that you simply do whatever people ask of you. I followed, Rey at my heels.

The furniture was arranged around the room so that people could talk in small groups; chairs and two-seaters with wipeable covers. I eased myself down, ready for the chill against my thighs. Rey perched on the arm of my chair. Anthony settled opposite us, on the edge of a sofa.

"This is Rey," I said. "He's my boyfriend. I'm afraid I told him about you. How someone threw a stone at you. Hope you don't mind."

"Oh, right," said Anthony.

"Thing is, Anthony, I heard about the way you were attacked like that, and it worried me—"

"Why?"

"Sorry?"

"Why would you be worried about me? You don't know me."

"Well, yes, that's true, but ..."

"Yew said you were a shaman. What's that got to do with anything?"

"It's my friend. Brice."

"Oh, yeah. Yew did say."

"Brice is Alys's husband."

He nodded, taking this in. "On the Tor. The poor, poor man."

He'd hit the nail without knowing it; Brice and Alys had been a golden couple, enjoying the fruits of their golden life. The loss of his wife had brought Brice into a sort of poverty.

"Brice keeps getting frightening emails. Someone who calls themselves Morgan Le Fay."

"I've never heard of anyone called that. Not outside the telly, anyhow."

"I wasn't thinking that you know them personally. Just maybe a rumour—a whisper?"

"I can't help you, I don't think."

Rey leant forward slightly, easing himself into the conversation. "Sometimes, going through what happened on an important day like that one can shed light on things."

Anthony scratched his stubble. "'Course, but ..."

"But?"

"It wasn't me things happened to." Without knowing he'd done so, Anthony stretched his hand across the empty seat beside him until his finger and thumb gripped the edge of an orange scatter cushion. He drew it to him, right onto his lap. His hands moved over the soft, warm surface, seeking comfort.

"Have a think," said Rey. "Start at the beginning and run through, slowly. Even the most insignificant thing ... it could be essential."

"Do you think I haven't done that? This copper got it all down. A woman. PC Wynche."

"Have the police got back to you about their investigations?" asked Rey.

"What investigations? They only came here because Yew insisted. I could see her thinking ... it were only a stone someone threw."

"Someone tried to hurt you for no reason."

"You ain't here for that, though. Not really."

"No," I said. "We're here because of Brice. Who lost his Alys then started getting these poison pen emails. We're here because he's grieving and sick of it."

"I s'pose he is, but what can I do?"

I had a sudden thought. I dipped into my bag and brought out my phone, scrolling through until I had the emails. I read the first one out.

It has begun. The dancing damsel, the maiden from the well, was cut down on the hallowed hill with a dolorous blow. The wasteland is upon us; a desert of death. Those who laughed — those who pushed forward to gloat — have been punished. The

Green Knight has been taken down and others will perish like-wise if they bring opprobrium to the ancient land of Logres.

"That is sick." I could tell Anthony was holding his breath, as he visualized that day. I held mine, in sympathy. After half a minute or more, he breathed out, a long snort of air down his nose. "I weren't bloody gloating. I didn't mean to laugh."

"Of course not. We've all had that happen to us."

"She was so young. Delicate. It got me bad." He made a fist and thudded it against his breastbone. "So I went. Left."

"I guess a lot of people walked off the Tor at that point," said Rey.

"Quite a few. People were shook up."

"What were you wearing?" I asked.

"Me cords. Me shirt. And me jacket, but I was carrying that."

"What colours were they?"

"Sorta … khaki."

"Greenish khaki?"

"I suppose."

"So," said Rey. "You came down the hill and went into Glaston-bury town."

"To catch the six-thirty bus to Yeovil, yeah."

"Was it empty?"

"No, it was a working day. It was quarter full."

"Did anyone get on with you?"

Anthony shook his head. "Can't remember."

"Can you remember who got off at Yeovil?"

"It's the end of the road. Everyone on the bus got off."

"What time was that?" I asked.

"Bus gets in about quarter past seven, thereabouts."

310

"Do you happen to know what time the buses back to Glastonbury leave Yeovil?"

"They go every hour. Why?"

I had been thinking of where each of the workshoppers were after Alys had been airlifted from the Tor. Wolfs and I had started walking back to Stonedown Farm. Shell had been with Brice, and the rest—all the boys—Yew and Freaky, Juke and Ricky, and Anag—had gone into town for breakfast. Anthony's assailant could have gone to Yeovil and been in back at Stonedown Farm by around ten o'clock. None of the workshoppers had arrived before that time, but all of them were back by lunchtime.

Rey leaned forward, his hands on his knees. "Was there anything out of place, while you were on the bus?"

"He were on it too? Is that what you're saying? Him that threw the stone at me?"

"Sabbie," said Rey. "Do you have a picture of Juke on your phone?"

His words were like a slap; like opening the back door to an icy wind. I didn't move for several moments. Rey was using his detecting techniques; a process of elimination. I was using my usual instincts, which, until I'd woken from the dream in the car, had been positive; the generous feel of Juke's aura; his place in the world. I'd had to persuade Juke to come on the workshop and the celebration on the Tor. He'd started out not quite sure, although later, he'd embraced it. I didn't want my client and fellow member of the Temple of Elphame to be carted off for gross bodily harm . . . for murder.

But I had to show solidarity with Rey or Anthony would close up like a scallop.

It took me an age to scroll through the images, mostly because I'm rubbish at deleting, even a bit of floor with half a shoe at the corner. I found the photos of our night on the Tor, but held onto the phone, unable to pass it over. The best shot was a selfie; all the work-shoppers were in it, squashed close together. Wolfs, Shell and Alys next to me, Brice with Freaky, Yew and Ricky behind. Anag, waving like mad, was captured at one corner. Juke's image was right at the front, half obliterating my face, his quizzical smile sharp in the camera's lens—the natural focal point of the shot.

I didn't move, desperate to delete the photo. Rey gently lifted the phone from me and sat beside Anthony while he took the picture in.

"Oh God." He peered closer for several seconds, and as he did, he groaned, as if in pain, as if someone was grinding a stone into the back of his head.

"You see him?"

"I see them all."

"The one with the blond beard?"

"They were a nice crowd."

"Does anything stand out?" I asked, joining them, staring down at the selfie.

"*Her*. She never stopped dancing, like they never stopped drumming."

I had a sensation of internal pain. Alys's face, full of anticipation and joy, lit up the picture. She'd loved the night on the Tor, perhaps more than almost any of our party, and she glowed.

"Is there anyone there that you later saw at the bus stop in Glastonbury or on the ride home, Anthony?" Rey repeated. "Take a closer look."

"It's confusing. It's confusing, yeah? Because I did see all of these people; they were all with Alys."

"Are you sure?" It was a croak. I swallowed and tried again. "Not the one with the little beard?"

"I can't. I can't look no more."

"Try to have a think after we've gone. It might take a while to register."

"Yeah, okay."

I didn't think I'd hear from Anthony again. Why would he revisit that morning of death and pain? He'd watched Alys die. He'd been attacked for no reason. All he wanted to do was forget.

"I'll drive," said Rey, on the way back in the car. I slid into the passenger seat and sat silent as he made a whining reverse move, turned the car, and set off.

"I've been trying to work out the timing, Rey. When Anthony Bale was attacked in Yeovil, Juke was in Glastonbury with all of us. And when Gerald Evens was attacked, Juke should have been at work in Bridgwater. The only time he's in the frame is at the Angel Shopping Centre and that's only because I called him and he came to help."

Rey gave a laugh; short, unfunny. "You don't have to work out timings, Sabbie. Our search is over. We'll probably never know who threw a stone at Anthony, but it definitely was not whoever attacked Gerald Evens. And that attack isn't linked to Marty-Mac—he got himself into a dangerous mess and one of his associates took him out."

"I never did think Juke was anything to do with this." My voice came out all sulky.

"Then we're on the same wavelength—first time ever! So, to put this to rest, I'm going for a combination of number one and number two scenario."

"What?"

"Brice is sending these emails to himself; he's spotted these incidents on social media, and it's giving him perverse satisfaction roping his friends further into his grieving patterns."

I loosened my shoulders, hearing the ligaments crunch. The miles swept under our tyres.

Suddenly, Rey said, "I'm going to take you out tonight."

"What?"

"We never do that. Should get a table on a Wednesday."

"Ooo," I said. "Why not? It'd be nice."

"I need to get relaxed. Enjoy a break. I've done nothing but think of Macaskill for days. Where would you like to eat?"

I shrugged. It had been too long since I'd been to a restaurant.

"In fact, let's take a day off, shall we? A day out of our lives. You got clients booked tomorrow?"

This was so unlike Rey I could hardly think. "Not … no I haven't."

"Right. It promises fine. Let's motor down to North Devon. Exmoor. Find a nice gastro-inn and hole up for the night. Ever been to Lynton?"

"No."

"We'll pack a bag and escape for one night."

"It's the high season. There might not be any rooms."

"There's always a room if you're prepared to pay."

"What's brought this on?"

"You don't like being whirled off your feet?"

"Well, yes, as it happens, but—"

"I've got a meeting at nine on Friday morning."

"Is that to do with …"

"Yeah. They call them meetings, but they're interrogations. My Police Federation rep will be there, but so far I've emerged feeling like I've been through a car crusher."

"They have nothing on you, Rey!"

"Except an extreme dislike of any copper who doesn't play by the rules."

I shook my head. "Someone killed Marty-Mac, but instead of looking for them, they're focusing on you." He stared through the windscreen at the quiet road ahead, both hands sensibly on the steering wheel.

"We are good, aren't we Rey?"

"Christ, yes. We're solid."

"From now on, then, promise you'll tell me things?"

"I know I can be … unforthcoming. Lesley used to make the same complaint."

"I'm not Lesley," I said, keeping my voice light. "I'm not complaining at all."

All at once, he indicated into the side of the road and pulled on the handbrake. He wrapped his arms around me, squeezing so tight my breath left my lungs. His chin rested on my shoulder. I couldn't see his face properly, only that his eyes were tightly closed and his mouth was a firm, set line, like someone in the middle of making a resolution. "Let's do it, Sabbie. For twenty-four hours, let's just forget all our worries."

TWENTY-SIX

BRICE

I GOT OFF THE train at Paddington and headed straight to the crematorium. It was Friday morning, the day of the funeral. Brice and Wolfsbane were waiting for me. We couldn't go in, of course; the funerals ran in strict order, like movie showings. Ours was scheduled for two p.m., but Brice had wanted us to show up early; I couldn't blame him for that. We found the appropriate chapel, then sat on a bench in the sun to run through the ritual.

This celebration of Alys's life had to include everyone who knew her, not just her pagan friends. The family on both sides would be cautious if not downright hostile to a solely pagan affair, and we'd worked round that. Pagans like to celebrate in a circle, wearing ritual gear that focuses their intent and holding hands in a natural, open space, some sort of sacred site. The very shape of a circle suggests that no one is in charge in quite the same way as the minister who stands in front of a congregation. We hoped we'd come up with a harmonizing of both worlds.

By the time we'd finalized things I'd begun to feel less terrified. Brice took off, so that he could be in the official car that would move slowly behind the hearse bearing Alys's coffin.

"We've got two hours," said Wolfsbane. "I'm going to book in at the hotel and grab something to eat. You coming?"

"I'm not staying the night."

"What? Aren't you stopping over until the scattering of the ashes? It's all on Brice, Sabbie. Take advantage."

"Things are awful for Rey at the moment. I want to get back for him."

When Wolfsbane had left, I wandered the huge site, past row upon row of gravestones and marble monuments and beech trees in full, bright green leaf. I gazed up at chapels with gargoyles and ornate finials and walked between scented palettes of colour—gold of calendula, pink of pelargoniums, and brilliant scarlet of salvia, all in their individual beds. I sat for sometime at the edge of a lily pond, the trickle of the waterfall calming me.

Scooting off for an overnight stay had been perfect for both Rey and me. We'd found a family-run hotel in a tiny village on the north coast of Devon. We'd soaked up the sun—not brilliantly hot but not breezy either. We'd eaten great food, walked on the beach, and browsed round craft shops. Rey had bought me a bronze cast of fighting hares. We'd promised each other things … when all this is over … when Rey was reinstated … We'd talked about a life together. Rey had got close to agreeing that he might give up his bedsit. Going to Devon had felt like a crossing; like leaving one shore and reaching a better land.

This morning he'd had his "meeting"—the interview with the team investigating his status. I longed to check how things were with him, but he wasn't answering his phone. Maybe the meeting was prolonged. Protracted.

In the ladies loo behind the café, I tried smiling at myself as I stuck on a bit of makeup and tugged a wide-toothed comb through my hair. My funeral clothes were a brown skirt that hung to my calves, a black top, and a charcoal grey jacket which I'd purchased for the occasion from one of the charity shops in Bridgwater, knowing I'd never wear it again. Hanging on the wardrobe door at home, I'd been worried; every item had clashed. Brice had asked us all to wear something with strong colour; ties for men, scarves for women. I'd chosen a floaty cerise and tan scarf which had the surprising effect of pulling the mix of colours together.

I sat in the café garden, in earshot of the fountain, picking at sponge cake. The sun was weak today, with a haze that felt slightly teary. Good weather for a summer funeral.

I'd almost finished my tea when Ricky came out of the café carrying a tray of drinks and eats. Freaky and Yew followed behind. They veered towards my table, Yew picking up further bistro chairs on his way through. We made a full round of hellos, during which I stacked my dishes to give the diners more elbow room.

"You're conducting the service, aren't you?" said Yew, once I'd settled between them all.

I nodded, slightly mute. Freaky laid a hand on my shoulder. "All will be well, my dear friend." He started powering through his Danish pastry.

"Do you happen to know who else is coming?" I asked. "Juke?"

318

"No." Ricky was staring down at his hands, not touching his food or drink.

"I guess he's already pulled too many sickies."

"Stef and Esme have commitments," Freaky said. "Ahem. I saw our friend Anagarika in the George and Pilgrim. I got the feeling he knew he wasn't welcome, but he did have an excuse. Another workshop—Labyrinth Healing." Freaky moved into a passable Australian accent: "The full, advanced, practitioner training, cobber!"

"Maybe he'll drop out of sight forever," joked Yew. "Right into the Hollow Hill."

"Right down to Australia, with any luck," Freaky replied.

"We did that," said Ricky. There was a micro-pause, as we turned to him. "What my mum used to say, when we dug holes in the sand on holiday. Fall through to Australia."

The three of us chuckled. The spiky energy round him suggested he got uncomfortable at funerals and there was already an unwritten consensus between us that we needed to prevent Ricky from bursting into tears. "Anyway, you can't dig holes into the Tor. I mean, you shouldn't," he added, into the silence. "Although the upper crust is rock, quite hard, so it would be tricky."

"You'd need more than a seaside spade, then," I quipped.

"Yeah," said Yew. "Internally is the silt and clay. Plenty of chance for digging. If you could get there."

"*I walk with my companion-at-arms into the Hollow Hill.*" I looked at all three of them as I quoted from Morgan le Fay's last email. There wasn't a flicker of recognition. I wondered if Juke would have reacted—if Rey's theories about him would hold out— then remembered that Rey didn't have theories, except that the emails meant Brice was losing his mind.

My phone beeped—the alarm I'd set as reminder. I needed to get in place for the start of the funeral. "I've got to go, guys. See you outside the crematorium."

———

The chapel Brice had chosen was of ultra-modern architecture, big and white, speaking of man's accomplishments, rather than nature's beauty. Wolfsbane and I gathered everyone—the mourners, I guess they were called—together a short way off, where sun filtered through leafy trees. We encouraged them into a rough, tightly-packed circle and had them hold hands. The turnout was huge. I looked round the circle, taking in over two hundred flinted expressions, and it hit me like a fist—we were here to support them.

Wolfsbane stood directly across the circle, opposite me. Close by was Brice, flanked by his family and close friends. Yew stared ahead, well under control. Freaky had his eyes closed. Ricky's shoulders jerked constantly. Shell slipped in next to him, as if finding a space, and I saw her secret squeeze of his hand.

Wolfsbane lifted his voice, and it rang as I'd never heard before. "We will begin by bringing peace into our circle."

"For without peace," I continued, trying to let my voice carry, "we cannot accomplish the work we are here to do."

Those words set us both rolling. We brought power into the circle in the way I would do in my therapy room—we could take that core of power into the crematorium—we could even keep it going until Alys's ashes had been scattered. Yew lit incense in a heavy cauldron and placed it in the centre, where it billowed fragrant smoke. Freaky had brought spring water from Glastonbury and he walked the perimeter of our circle with it, sprinkling it in consecration. We asked everyone to take three deep breaths, while we visualized a circle of light that would keep us safe.

We explained the significance of the yew tree, which grew widely in churchyards round London. Yew had brought a basket of branches, and I'd got Shell to frantically pull them apart before we'd assembled in a circle, so there'd be enough for everyone. She took the basket around and people chose a sprig to take with them as a commemoration.

Then I handed out nightlights. Luckily, we'd brought giant Ikea bags of candles so there were plenty. I lit mine with Wolfsbane's power lighter that would burn in a force-ten storm. There was no wind, which was lucky, because our plan was that each person would light their candle from the flame of the person next to them, so allowing the little lights to grow bright one by one round the circle.

As Shell touched her burning wick against Ricky's nightlight, he finally let his emotions out. He pressed the back of his free hand to his eyes as if that would hold in the tears.

Under the protection of the tree canopy the flames grew strong on their wicks, outlining our circle shape. We'd tried to think through the practicalities; we wanted everyone to carry their tiny lights in a snaking line towards the crematorium before the wax became molten. We weren't allowed to be a fire risk, so we left them— two hundred and more flickering lights—beside the floral offerings in the courtyard.

Wolfsbane led the company in behind the coffin, which was carried by Brice, Alys's brother, and four of her workmates. Yew walked behind, the smoke rising from his cauldron of burning resins.

Freaky brought his chalice of spring water. I came last, to catch late-comers.

Inside the huge room, two of Alys's friends started with an acoustic version—guitar and vocals—of the Led Zeppelin ballad "Stairway to Heaven." They were good, but what was most affecting was the passion coming from them. They were good despite being torn to pieces.

The rest of the funeral was a celebration of Alys's life. Several people stood to read poems and Shell did her eulogy in a sweet and simple manner. There was a slideshow of pictures from Alys's birth to the day before she died—arriving at Stonedown, looking happy and expectant. Like me, Brice had captured her on his phone dancing on the Tor, but thought those too poignant to include.

Brice spoke last, without notes, a tribute that was also a love letter. Finally, the coffin began its macabre journey, accompanied by Queen's "Who Wants to Live Forever." Apparently Alys had loved '70s and '80s rock music since being introduced to it by her father. The lyrics set almost everyone off, apart from Brice, who had remained stony-faced throughout, and Ricky, who'd continue to weep steadily from the start. Alys's mother buried her face in her hand, her sobs echoing around the building. The slow disappearance of the coffin made it all too real. Ricky lurched to his feet. Tears were streaking his powdered face. His fingers chained his hands together as he reached both arms out towards the coffin.

"It never should have been," he cried out. "Surely this is against nature and reason, unless all is illusion!"

His words rang around the building, and an awful stillness settled, as if no one dared move. Finally, Shell got him back into his seat.

Brice registered his presence for the first time.

———

The wake was held in a function room just outside the crematorium gates. The congregation walked through the grounds, some pacing out the distance, eager to grab a drink, others as befitted the act of mourning. Some veered off, taking a wander through the grounds. The idea of finding a place for meditation was an attractive one, but my urgent need was to switch my phone back on. There were no missed calls. I dialed Rey's number, my mouth drying in anticipation of his answering. I didn't know what news he would give me, how he would sound after the grilling by his superiors. I didn't even get his message box. A sharp needle of concern drove through me. He'd switched the phone off. He didn't want to speak to anyone. I pushed the phone into my pocket and went into the reception.

Everyone wanted to talk to me and Wolfs. Our rite had gone down well with people—some surprised, some a little relieved at its relevance for them. Having shaken his hand on the way into the reception, I didn't manage to speak to Brice in the crush. I saw him, though, standing with various groups of people, stoic and impassive, bone-dry eyes and a firm-set mouth which opened to speak as little as possible.

A table laden with finger food and hot and cold drinks stood against a long wall. Finally I made for the queue. Yew was ahead of me. We began filling our paper plates with savouries, Yew for the second time around, I fancied.

"It's been a terrible summer," I said.

"Like a portent. Death on the Tor as the sun rose at the zenith of its powers." He dug out a piece of quiche and put it straight into his mouth. "A distressing symbol," he managed, through the pastry.

I grabbed my moment; there was something I needed to clear up. "Yew; can you remember what you did directly after Alys's body was airlifted to hospital?"

"We took the lads into Glastonbury and tried to find somewhere that was open that early in the morning. You'd've thought plenty of places would have been keen to feed the hordes coming off the Tor, but no damn place bothered. I ended up talking the manager of the Crown into cooking a hotel breakfast."

"Who was there?"

"In the end, it was just me." Yew gave me the cautious look again. "I gave Wolfsbane back the cash, if that's what you're thinking."

"No, I was wondering where the others had got to."

"Freaky went back to his caravan to crash out. Anag might have gone to his digs until it was time for retail therapy." Yew let off a crack of a laugh. "Everyone was shattered twice over. Juke and Ricky wanted to get their heads down too."

"Their beds were back at Stonedown."

"That'd be it, then, yeah?"

"Yeah. That'll be it." I fell into silence, as I cast my mind back. Ricky *had* come downstairs from the boys' bedroom, at perhaps half-ten or eleven. Juke had not arrived back until almost one with Anag, but I'd never asked either of them if they'd met on the High Street, or on the way back. It was annoying that neither of them were here so I could check that out.

I looked for somewhere to plonk with my plate. Shell was sitting against the wall, pretending not to be alone in a crowd, eyeing Wolfsbane, who was holding court with Freaky and a group of London bankers in silk ties and Italian suits. I went over to her.

"Hi. Ricky not with you?"

"No." She pushed her empty plate under her chair and brushed the crumbs from her lap. "Not sure where he is."

"Ricky is pretty full-on. A little too sensitive for his own good?"

"Everything affects him so deeply. Crying like that went down like a balloon running out of gas with Brice. Truth is, he's hugely intelligent. Lot brighter than I'll ever be. Big brain. But, emotionally, he's a mess..." She chewed at her lower lip. "I think he's in love with Alys."

"They hardly spoke in the time he knew her. He danced with her for a bit on the Tor, but..."

"I mean, he fell in love *after*—with the dead Alys. I can't help wondering if he took up with me because I knew her. That I'm his link." She looked around the room, searching for Ricky, but also keeping an eye on Wolfs. "I think being in love with a dead woman is affecting him. The stuff he says gets weirder every day. The point of philosophy is to explain the unexplainable, isn't it?"

"Well, I guess..."

"At times I can't follow Ricky at all. He goes off on long, wandering sentences. Maybe he's flunking his essays because of that."

"He's not doing well at uni?"

"What worries me is that it's happened before. This degree is his second attempt. And he's working hard. He shuts himself away to study." She gave a sharp smile. "On the other hand ... when we're together ... he's shocking fun. Risky. Intense."

I bit into a falafel and rose my eyebrows at her.

"He's up for anything. Wolfsbane wouldn't even do the labyrinth walk with me. Ricky's promised and I cannot wait." She got up from her seat. "Guess I'd better find him. We're going to take off soon, preferably without explaining ourselves to Wolfsie."

"You haven't told him yet?" I don't know why I was so surprised. It would be a difficult thing to do, and there might be element of Shell hedging her bets. Wolfsbane was a catch in a lot ways, but then, Ricky was a smooch.

Shell wandered off and I left by the rear door, where a small courtyard gave me a chance to phone Rey. I gulped the cool air in for a few moments, before dialling the number. His phone was still off. I was torturing myself. I scratched at my eyes then stopped, not wanting them to look red.

Across the paving, a figure was crouched in the shadow of some bushes, hunched almost double. Hands were busy in the soil as if they were trying to bury something. The figure looked up briefly, with a whoosh of gelled hair, and I knew who this was.

I hunkered beside him. His fingernails were rimmed with black from the digging, but he hadn't made much of a hole—the soil was baked and full of shrub roots. "What're you doing, Ricky, digging for Australia?"

He looked at me in a slanted fashion. "I truly don't understand death. I know I should, as a philosopher, but I don't ... can't."

"I think it's too early. We all need a bit of healing space, first."

"Plato says that Socrates believed death was the liberation of the soul."

"Are you worried about Alys's soul, Ricky? Is that what you were trying to say at the funeral?"

"I think Alys was intrinsically good, don't you? Like she wasn't ignorant of The Good. That's what came off her. She wasn't within the shadows of the cave."

"What cave?"

"Plato's cave. It's one of his most famous metaphors."

"I've think you told me about that." I tried a grin. "I've forgotten."

"Why should you remember?" He was wearing his usual vampiric clothes—they were perfectly funereal, after all—but now they were smeared with dirt and he ineffectively brushed at his black-clad knees. "Plato describes prisoners living in a cave and seeing only the shadows on the wall, never seeing the sun that creates them. The sun is symbolic of goodness, you see. The Good. The darkness of the cave is an analogy of lack of goodness. What Plato's trying to say is that lack of virtue is only associated with ignorance."

"Okay…" I was pricking up my ears at Ricky's story. Caves featured in my shamanic work lately.

"One day, a man escapes from the cave and sees the world, the sun. Once you've seen the sun, you could never return to evil. That's part of my dissertation. Was a part, anyway." His eyes had no shine in them.

"You're … worried about your dissertation? Your degree?"

"I've had some setbacks." He scooped up a loose handful of soil and let it run through his fingers as if from a salt cellar.

"I remember being a student. It's all setbacks. You probably need to talk to your professor."

I heard him sob, once, in the back of his throat. "It's more than that. It's … I'm in a spot of bother." He slumped down further onto the earth. His eyes weren't focusing. His face was drawn. His drooping body reminded me of a piece of beefsteak that had been bludgeoned flat. "Socrates wasn't afraid to die. He took the hemlock gladly."

"I think I know that story. He was found guilty of corrupting the minds of the young, wasn't he?" I saw him look at me and added, "Wrongly, of course. Then condemned to death."

"He was willing to die. Yet Cebes asks, if philosophers are so willing to die, why is it wrong for them to kill themselves?"

"And did that question get answered?"

"Yes. Socrates's initial answer is that the gods are our guardians, and that they will be angry if one of their possessions kills itself without permission."

"I don't believe that I'm a possession of a god or goddess," I said. "Yet, it's a lovely idea that they are guardians. I feel that, when I walk between worlds."

"Was he right?" He put his hands across his face, leaving streaks of soil on his cheeks. "If there is some lovely place to go, why stay here, where things are awful all the time?"

"Honestly, everyone goes through these stages in life." I didn't want to confess that Shell had told me about his essay marks. "How has the shamanic journeying been going? You might find your answers there."

He nodded, silent, as if he was reliving some of his journeys. "My sea eagle comes to me. He says we have a task ahead of us."

"You have years ahead of you." I encircled Ricky's hunched shoulders with my arms and rocked him for a moment. "What d'you say we go in?"

He shrank into himself again, hiding his face with his long, soiled fingers.

"Shell's worrying about you. She's in there now, Ricky, wondering where you are. Please come and talk to her."

"Everyone who loves me, leaves me." His voice was muffled against his palms.

"Babette didn't mean to leave you."

I regretted saying this the instant the words left my mouth, for he leaned forward so that his face was only centimetres from mine. "Did you locate her, Sabbie? Did you get any ideas at all?"

I couldn't look at him. I desperately wanted to shift away, but my back was lodged against a rhododendron and its branches were already poking into my spine.

"I'm so sorry, Ricky. I don't know for sure, but I think she's gone. I keep seeing her in the forest—your forest. I think she's always been there. I think her bones still are ... in some lovely glade, buried deep."

He gave a deep, almost animal, sob. He swung up from the bushes and turned on one heel of his shiny boots. He hurried towards the cemetery grounds and disappeared into the long shadows of the trees. I watched him go, feeling guilty that I'd raised the central reason for his sadness.

And in a rush, I wanted Rey so much it was a force, pushing against me, pushing me over. He'd been through something foul today. I should have been waiting outside; waiting to hug him and lead him away. Now he didn't want to speak to anyone. He'd probably bought a bottle of whisky on the way home. I ached to put my arms around him.

I went inside and wound my way to the far end of the room, where Brice was talking to Shell. "I have to go. I'm sorry not to stay longer, Brice."

"I do understand." He gave a single, controlled nod. "I'll call you a cab."

"I've just seen Ricky. He's in a bit of a state. He's gone into the cemetery woodlands for a walk on his own. I think today was the last straw."

"I'd best go and find him," said Shell. "We have plans."

I moved round the room hugging my goodbyes, Brice hovering beside me, eventually escorting me towards the door.

"Well done," I said. "This must be the hardest day of your life."

"It's not over yet. We have to come back and bury the ashes in the Memorial Garden."

"Yes. I'm sorry I'm not staying."

"You've been great, getting here. And bringing some of the others." He managed a thin, grim, smile.

"Has there been any more emails?"

"There won't be any more."

"How ... how d'you mean?"

"I have a new email address. And I'm keeping a careful note of who knows it."

TWENTY-SEVEN
PIPPA

I SLEPT MOST OF the way back home, wrung out by my early start and the doings of this day, which even on reflection felt distorted—disturbed—as if I'd dropped into a parallel universe.

I'd only ever been to one other funeral, my foster dad Philip's brother, Uncle Ted. I'd been fifteen at the time, and we'd all gone over to Jamaica. Caribbean funerals are spectacular affairs, and Port Antonio turned out to be idyllic, so I couldn't possible use that memory as a yardstick. But even so, Alys's funeral had been seeped in inconsolable gloom. Morgan le Fay had stalked the crematorium, never far from Brice's side, silent, invisible, deadly.

As I changed trains at Taunton, I was suddenly achingly hungry. I grabbed something from the station buffet and ran for the Bridgwater connection.

As I ate my egg sandwich, I kept seeing Ricky, hiding in the bushes, talking about ending it all. He'd had a raw deal; when his sister had died, he'd flunked his first degree and had to start again, and now, with Alys's death leaning heavy on his mind, the same thing was happening again. I remembered kids on my degree who gave up uni life abruptly. Their mental health suffered as they tried to keep up with deadlines and getting wasted at the same time. Ricky felt loss so deeply. Watching him scrape at the earth below the bushes, his fingernails black with soil, it had felt as if he was literally trying to dig up some answers to the questions he studied: What is death? What is goodness? Can it exist without there being a God? Big questions, impossible to answer. No wonder he got depressed.

Alys wasn't within the shadows of the cave...

The opposite of light—Plato's cave. When Ricky described it, I'd found myself picturing Laura Munroe's otherworld. Her cave had been filled with the flicker of shadows. Something stirred in my gut. I pulled my phone out and Googled *Plato's Cave*. I was confused by the choice of sites that came up. I chose one at random and read the contents, muttering beneath my breath "... *let me show in a figure how far our nature is enlightened or unenlightened: —Behold! human beings living in an underground den, which has a mouth open towards the light and reaching all along the den; here they have been from their childhood, and have their legs and necks chained so that they cannot move, and can only see before them...*" I looked up from the tiny screen to take a deep breath. The image disturbed me. What a horrible thing to do to any sentient being. I had to remind myself this was an allegory, it was there to make you think about things already in the world, such as the way some people get trapped into a mode of being without even knowing about it. Plato used the cave as a symbol for lack of virtue, but there were other darknesses of the mind. What would it be like, believing the shadows on the wall were your entire reality?

And, if this prisoner was … *compelled to look straight at the light, will he not have a pain in his eyes which will make him turn away to take refuge in the objects of vision which he can see …*

Laura's otherworld place—a cave filled with shadows. Even her guardian presented itself through the flicker of shadows on the wall. It occurred to me that if your world had always been in shadow, your reaction, when you finally set eyes on sunshine, would be one of sheer panic.

Surely that didn't mean that Laura wasn't good, or even that her lost soul-part wasn't good.

Ricky had said that Plato blamed lack of virtue on ignorance; if you only see the shadows, how are you to know about the sun? I didn't see Laura as ignorant; apart from her crippling panic attacks, she was a savvy girl with a sharp intelligence and, for her age, a real knowledge of the wider world. I was left with the puzzle of her otherworld—a shadowy cave and a hallowed guardian. The image was with me all the way home, defining and clarifying itself with each clunk and click of the wheels over the rails.

The train finally pulled into Bridgwater. It was twenty to ten at night; I'd been travelling since dawn. I emerged onto the platform with a far better understanding of what Laura was, and why she had been sent into terrible panics for seemingly no reason. I would take my resolutions to the otherworld as soon as I could. More urgent was Rey; his phone was still off. A worm of dread was growing in my stomach. It might be so simple—he'd dropped it in the Parrett or lost the charger. No, he could still have got in touch with me. Found some landline or phone box. Even when you talk to no one else, you talk to your partner, don't you?

The worm raised its head and hissed at me. *Girlfriend. Not partner. You're no more than his squeeze.*

I tried concentrating on the words we'd exchanged... *we are good, aren't we Rey?... Christ, yes. We're solid...*

Rey's flat was a less than a mile from the train station, but I was too impatient to merely walk. I got into a jogging rhythm, breathing and pounding as my bag flew out and bumped into my hip with alternate steps. By the time I reached his address, I was devoid of breath. I took the stairs, still puffing, and pressed Rey's bell. I heard it ring through the bedsit, echoing round the few corners the accommodation provided. I rang it again. I lifted the letter flap and called. "It's me, Rey. Answer the door. It's me!"

I turned my back to the wood. It was ten at night. Was he down the pub with his phone dead in his pocket? I didn't believe it. I remembered how I'd asked him to stay at mine... *for a bit.* He had my spare key. That's where he was, probably sound asleep in my bed.

I went into town and took a taxi home. By the time I got there, my hope had faded and I was almost too shattered to worry any more about Rey. The house was locked and in darkness. My bed was empty.

I fell into it and slept like the dead.

———

By morning, I was thinking clearly. I knew what I had to do. I had to report Rey missing, and I shouldn't delay. He could be anywhere. He could be lying in a lane, like Marty-Mac, his head bashed in with a brick.

Taken with a single sweep of the sword.

A keening sound came into my throat. I threw on some clothes, fed the hens, and cycled into town.

Even so, as I stood in the little lobby outside the locked doors of Bridgwater Police Station, I had to fight the desire to walk away. This place always made me feel uncertain and conspicuous. The door release buzzed and I heaved my weight against its heaviness.

The male officer on duty behind the bulletproof glass gave a grimace of acknowledgment.

"I need to speak to Detective Inspector Rey Buckley. Is he here?"

"I'm sorry, he's not available." He didn't have to check the roster.

"I think he's missing, actually. I can't get hold of him."

"And you are?"

I opened my mouth and shut it again. *His girlfriend, his squeeze.* "Can I have a few moments with his deputy, then?"

"I'm sorry?" He looked at me for the first time. "Who do you mean?"

"Pippa Chaisey." I brushed my hair away from my face. My fingers were ice cold. "Please tell DS Chaisey that it's Sabbie Dare."

The officer spoke on an internal line. I didn't hear his words. My breath whistled fast along dry nostrils. A woman in civvies arrived on my side of the desk. "If you could follow me, please, Miss Dare?"

She walked me through the corridors. We went up one level. We walked some more. I was weak with the thought of seeing Pippa—or rather, her seeing me, raw and red-eyed. I was unable to concentrate on where the woman was taking me. I hoped she'd show me the way back when the time came. The woman stopped outside a door and knocked. Pippa was sitting behind a desk she had not, in my view, yet earned, her laptop open upon it and several files piled near her elbow. I was sure Rey hadn't had his own office when he was a sergeant.

"Sabbie," she said. She sounded wary, as if she didn't know what would be thrown at her.

I stepped into the office and the civilian closed the door on us. I heard her stilettos clip along the corridor.

"Do sit down."

I eyed the chair. I didn't want to sit. I wanted to launch myself over the surface of the desk, skid the laptop out of the way, and slap Pippa hard on one cheek.

"Sit down, Sabbie."

I sat. I was trying to control my breathing, so that my voice would come out loud and confident. "Rey isn't answering his phone."

She smiled, but in my buzzing head it felt like a sneer, like she'd curled her lip at me. "I'm sorry, Sabbie."

"What?"

"Rey is in custody. He's been charged and not yet bailed. I expect he will get bail, but we're still questioning him at this moment in time."

"He's not guilty."

"You know, then, what he's charged with?"

"Let me guess. The murder of Martin Macaskill? He's not bloody guilty."

"Please restrain your language. It never helps your case."

"I don't have a 'case,' Pippa." I stopped to get oxygen into my lungs. She must have heard me pant, sitting on the other side of her hard-on desk. "You don't have a case, either. Do you know that?" It occurred to me that yes, they probably did know they didn't have a case against DI Buckley. Not a watertight, evidence-based case, anyway. There was more going on here than that. "You'll never get a conviction. So what's this about?"

"You're upset," said Pippa, with startling accuracy. Her next statement hit the bullseye too. "Rey hasn't been keeping you in the loop, has he? I expect you feel you've been sidelined."

"Rey Buckley didn't kill Marty-Mac."

"Let us be the judge of that."

"Did Rey tell you about PC Wynche?"

She paused. She moved the laptop, the better to eyeball me. "Sorry?"

"Thought not. PC Wynche is the officer looking into a case of random attack on a man in Yeovil. Anthony Bale was assaulted on the morning of June the twenty-first. Has he mentioned Gerald Evens?"

"Sabbie, does this bear any relevance?"

"Of course. I'm not here to have a girlie gossip. Gerald Evens had his head pounded in on—yeah—the twenty-fourth of June, during a bright, sunny day at Glastonbury Abbey. It was a bad attack ... I guess it could be attempted murder. I believe I've established links between both those attacks and the murder of Martin Macaskill." I had to stop speaking because I'd run out of oxygen availability. I sat and puffed for several seconds, daring her with my eyes to interrupt my flow. "Certain things stand out and I want to present them to you now, so you can make an informed decision over who committed this crime. Three men have been attacked since the summer solstice. The modus operandi are similar; the injuries becoming more serious as the attacks go on. With Macaskill, the perpetrator finished what they'd started."

"I'm sorry?" The impeccable cogs in her cop-perfect brain had stalled, and I ploughed on while I had the glimmer of an advantage.

"I need to report my concerns. My suspicions. That, I believe is the prerogative of the public-spirited citizen."

"Yes, Sabbie, but you aren't one of said citizens, are you? You are a woman trying to get her man out of the cells."

"Not at all, Pippa. I'm trying to report something."

"You've lost me. You lost me some time ago." Pippa got out of her chair and it skid away on its five casters. "There's nothing here for us. Nothing."

"You haven't heard me out."

"This is a waste of your time, I'm afraid." She remained standing. She was preparing to cut me down and send me packing. I didn't get up. She'd been the one to implore me to sit, after all.

"I want to tell you about the anonymous emails my friend has been getting. They're from someone calling themselves Morgan le Fay—" My voice broke. I was not going to cry in front of this woman. I was not. "It's hard to get it all summed up—to get the measure of it all. I don't know everything, 'course not, or how it all fits to make sense. I just know … Rey isn't guilty—" I had an image of Rey, sitting on his cell bunk, staring at the wall. "If you'd just let me explain the thinking behind my suspicions. I need to lay everything out … how a person can't perceive reality if all they see are shadows on a cave wall …"

"Okay. That'll do. You can stick the lid back on your garbage." She came round the desk and stood by me; over me, almost. "Rey has told me about you. Okay, he's fond of you, but he knows you're flaky. You deal in dreams and … suchlike. My investigations deal with data. Testimonials. Documentation. Results."

"You don't have a result," I said. "You have a whitewash."

I dashed a hand into my shoulder bag. Brice's four emails were printed onto separate sheets and sealed inside an envelope, ready to hand over. I rested it on the desk. "Examine all that comes to you. That was what I was told to do. *When you eliminate that which you no longer need, one possibility will remain.*"

"Sabbie …"

"Yeah. Go ahead, remind me. I sound flaky. I can get the answers, Pippa. I've done so in the past." I had to keep ahead of her. Find some rationale that would fit with her view of the world. "Surely if a member of the public believes they have witnessed, or understood, something suspicious, you need to take their statement?"

I watched her process my words. I felt her despair. She was not going to get me out of the station that easily. "Well. It depends on a number of variants—"

"I want to make a statement."

She exploded into a laugh. "Come on, Sabbie, you have nothing to state."

"If I can't make a statement, I will make a complaint."

There was a pause. It went on and on, like someone had begun to drill foam insulation into the room; there was an invisible and increasing mound of silence, built from her seething fury and my doggedness.

Finally, it was Pippa who backtracked. "Okay. No, that's fine. I'll arrange for you to do that now, shall I?"

"And I want to see Rey."

"That isn't possible. Surely you must recognise—"

"Of course it's possible." I wasn't gong to be pushed around any longer. "Don't tell me that a prisoner cannot have a visitor."

"You'd better come with me," she said at last.

———

I gave my statement to DS Chaisey in the presence of the other woman, who turned out to be a constable seconded to CID. They must need as many investigators as they could get to do all the leg work necessary to pin this death on Rey. I told them all I knew. It turned out to be precious little, but it made me feel better to hand it over.

When they escorted me to Rey, it looked like I was going to be taken right to the door of his cell in the bowels of the station. I was made to walk between them, as if I was the one under surveillance. They didn't speak, not to me, not to each other. Abruptly, the younger woman opened a door and stood there, waiting for me to enter the room.

I stepped in. Rey was sitting behind a table. I'd seen him in that position many times in the past, but it had always been the reverse of this; *he* had always been waiting to interview *me*.

Rey seemed the same as ever. He smiled, as if to reassure the witness. His folded hands lay before him on the table. I came closer. There was a darkness around his eyes. He hadn't been eating properly, perhaps. Or sleeping properly. Or even breathing properly.

"You're going to save me, I hear," he said.

"Who told you that?"

"I have my sources."

I glanced around. The door had been softly closed against us. We were alone.

"Compiling a case in opposition to the police investigation into a homicide is a risky business, Sabbie."

"No one here is taking me seriously." There was a chair, and I took it.

"You gave them the low-down on Morgan le Fay, in your statement?"

I eyed him, stonewalling. I was afraid that if I opened my mouth my perceptions would fly away, like thistle seeds.

"Sabbie Dare has run out of words," said Rey. "That's troubling."

Slowly, our hands had been moving across the tabletop. At the first touch of flesh, Rey grabbed onto mine, gripping so tightly he pinched my skin.

"She's not going to get your job, Rey. Is she?"

"Right now, my approach is that she's welcome to it."

"Oh, Rey …"

"It's okay, Sabbie. Nothing is going to happen to me. Once they've had their fun, tried to give me a bit of a scare, I'll be shunted off into some other position. Traffic, maybe. Missing Persons."

"That would kill you."

"Well." A sudden grin lit up his dark-rimmed eyes. "We have this time together. All alone. My last wish before I walk to the scaffold. What shall we do with it?"

The sight of him smiling filled my heart. "We're going work out the best way to get into the Hollow Hill and wake the Sleeping King," I replied.

TWENTY-EIGHT

SABRINA

OF COURSE, WE DID no such thing. Because there was no hollow inside Glastonbury Tor and the Sleeping King was a legend, a story of hope in bad times. We had precious minutes to kiss and make ourselves promises before Pippa and her henchwoman came back into the little room and hauled me out.

It started raining, cold July rain that would have been perfect for the funeral the previous day. As soon as I got home I put the central heating on, found a jumper, and heated some soup for lunch. I thought about the chain of events that had started with the decision to help Wolfsbane run a shape-shifting workshop. I'd felt such excitement at the idea of working with people at a heightened shamanic level. I'd had no presentment that it would end abruptly, disastrously, in sudden death and poison pen letters and horrific attacks.

Since Alys had died, nothing had been right in my world. Rey had been suspended, arrested and charged, all because—it seemed to me—I'd been accosted by Marty-Mac in the Angel Shopping Centre, where I'd never wanted to be in the first place. That was the day I'd met my grandmother. I'd learnt things I'd rather have never known and transformed myself into the Princess of Darkness in my cousin Lettice's eyes.

Freaky had warned me. ... *families always mean trouble. Always. Always* ... I had heard his words, but gone ahead anyhow.

Grandma Dare filled my mind for a moment as I wiped my soup bowl with a piece of bread. Her erect frame, her ripe-plum voice, her sharp eyes. The softness of her pashmina in my hands. She'd plied me with sweet biscuits and talk of baronets. She'd told me I'd been named for my great-grandmother. Sabrina fair. Then she'd hit me with her bigotry and contempt.

It had been a lovely moment, when she'd recited that poem which had inspired her mother's name. Milton, she'd said, as if I knew anything about any poet. I closed my eyes to bring the words back. Something about lilies, and amber hair, and cool waves ...

My eyes popped open. My scalp prickled. I went into the therapy room and got out my shamanic journal. I had written those words, copying down what the Lady of the River had told me the day after Alys's death ... *I am the river of cool, translucent waves.*

I typed *Milton + Sabrina* into a search engine on my laptop. Almost the first site I tried was a copy of a long and rambling poem called "Comus" which was all about Greek deities and debauched rakes after the virtue of pure virgins. It took me ages to scroll down and down, reading steadily, but when I reached the little song I'd heard my grandmother recite it jumped out of the screen, and I couldn't help but read, almost sing, it aloud.

343

Sabrina fair,

Listen where thou art sitting

Under the glassy, cool, translucent wave...

I read Milton's story of Sabrina, line by line, my eyes screwed against the tight, tiny writing on the screen. Long ago, a girl, the daughter of an ancient British king, drowned in the River Severn and so became its goddess.

The Lady of the River had tried her best to direct me, but in the end it was my grandmother who'd given me the answer. The irony made me shake my head. Lady Savile-Dare had not intended to bequeath anything to me, but unwittingly, she'd given me what I needed most: the name of my spirit guardian.

———

Honey, rich, warm, running from the comb. The drumbeat singing from my CD player, the slight tickle of the scarf over my eyes. I was walking with Trendle above the fast-flowing River Severn. With each step, the deep foliage of the lime tree came more into focus, and the smell it exuded was more powerful in my nostrils. I couldn't help but walk closer, breathing in the perfume.

I now knew that it was the tree itself that gave off the thick scent of honey. I had thought my Lady of the River had conjured it up, but I'd delved into my tree books and read how limes did this; they attracted a tiny insect to their bark and it exuded this sugar smell.

She was there, in front of the lime tree. She looked steadily into my eyes, while saying nothing. She was a frustrating enigma, often only half telling me things. I always felt I'd disappointed her, not done quite enough, not taken her advice well enough to heart.

"You don't disappoint, Sabbie," she said. "You ask more of yourself than I have ever asked of you."

"I know your true name, my lady." I dropped to my knees, desperate to tell her. "You are Sabrina of the Severn."

Sabrina placed her hand on my head. It felt like a leaf had landed there. In the silence a question fell into my mind. It hadn't been what I'd planned to ask, but I knew it was the right one. The deepest question that was in my heart. I looked up into her fluid grey eyes.

"It keeps happening, doesn't it? I keep falling into ... trouble. I keep meeting ... sorrow and disaster. Since I started my shamanic work, I have met such people that I didn't know walked in the apparent world. Evil. I've come face to face with evil." I breathed deeply, desperate for the scent of honey, clear as if I held it on a spoon. "Damned. Depraved. Corrupt. Villainous."

"It is your inheritance, Sabbie."

My thoughts slowed until there were almost none at all.

"You come from two strong lines, Sabbie. In you, they've fused to shine with a light. And the further you pursue your practice, the more blinding that light will become. It is visible to others in a way you cannot see. It will always attract those with the deepest and the most troubled questions. Sorrow and disaster. And villainy, yes."

"A strong line?" I thought of Lady Dare's proud frame and suspicious eyes.

"Most of all, your father. And his father. All your fathers in a line before you."

"I know next to nothing about my father," I whispered. "An old address. And his name." Such a name. Frivolous, mocking. Lucky

Luc Rameau, the only thing I knew for sure about him, because it was on my birth certificate.

"Those strong lines gird you to take on the world's trouble. Such people quiet the moving plates of the earth; they calm volcanoes. For you, the challenges are as you've described. The corrupt. The depraved, as well as the vulnerable. That is your path, and you will keep to it; I see that tenacity in you, Sabbie Dare."

"Will you always be here to help me?"

"As I always have." She chuffed a laugh. Its sound was the warmth and softness of a nighttime pillow, when you wake into darkness. "You have your father, also. Those roots penetrate deep. Those roots bind tight."

I was still kneeling on the path. I could feel the dampness rise through my jeans. Small stones bit into my flesh. I didn't move. "I did what you asked. I laid everything out in order—in a statement for the police—and things became ... not *clear*, but ..."

"Ah. Like river water. Even when it is at its most limpid, you will never see the bottom as it really is, for the water is in constant motion and distorts the images below."

"Yes. Like that. I've been trying to help Brice Hollingberry. I felt so sorry for his loss, and for the awful way someone was goading him."

"I understand," said the lady.

"I've ended up with shadows, a philosopher's allegory, his truth about good and evil."

Her mouth was a hard line. "Indeed. To read shadows is to read the bottom of the river."

"But you said, didn't you? It's my inheritance. I have to try."

Sabrina spoke directly to Trendle, who was waiting by my feet. "Take her then. Take her."

Trendle didn't take me to a shadowed cave, as I'd expected. Almost instantly, I was standing on cracked earth, the desert of dried soil in the Lower Realm I'd visited at Stonedown Farm. Nothing had changed in the month since I was last here. There was not a tree, not a plant, not even a weed. Only the bare, rutted, dried-out soil and the billions of worms, still writhing as if in their death throes; as if they gasped for moisture.

A hot wind moved the dusty soil. It blew into my face, into my ears and nostrils. The sun was white with heat; already it burned the back of my neck. I shaded my eyes and looked to the edge of the horizon in every direction, searching for the wattle fence and the rough timber hut of the old man.

Nothing. Just heat haze and hot, dry breeze and worms crawling over the trainers I had worn to the police station.

And then, for just a few, blissful seconds, a shadow moved over the sun. I gasped with relief. The coolness felt glorious. I looked up. Something was hovering, high up in the sky, so large it blocked out the brightness. A bird, gigantic against the sun.

It saw me. It marked me. Its dive was so fast it seemed set to crash me into the ground. It opened its hooked beak and screeched.

"*Death of beauty! Death of grace! Death of love!*"

For a second, I was mesmerized. Against the sun, the bird had seemed big, but as it soared down, it expanded, its wings stretching wider and wider. Its feet pushed out, ready for the smash and grab. I could see its talons, the razor points that would rip skin, find flesh, kill prey.

"Sabbie!"

Seconds before it hit me, Trendle's bark brought me out of my spell. I threw myself to the ground. Worms squished beneath me, slithered over me. I had to clamp my mouth shut to prevent them squirming in.

When I looked up again, the creature had lifted on the air currents and was disappearing towards the horizon. I pulled myself up. "What was that, Trendle?"

"One thing you did not lay out in order."

———

Sabrina had told me to call her by her true name. Finally I'd found it, and now everything was different. Instead of talking in ciphers, what she showed me rang as clear as a bell. I pulled the scarf from my eyes and scrabbled up. Drumbeats were still pounding from my CD player, but I'd had my vision. I understood my one possibility. A shiver went across my shoulders. I didn't want this to be true. Three berserk attacks on passers-by. I'd assumed such an offender would be true to form—wicked, a villain. It was hard to process what Sabrina had revealed.

Now I needed to get to my phone. Shell was at the heart of my mystery, and I had to talk to her before I did any other thing. I found her number in my contacts, but the call went straight to voicemail. I left a message, making it plain we urgently needed to speak, and almost as I put the phone down, it rang.

"Sabbie?" came a male voice. "Sabbie Dare? This is Eijaz."

"Eijaz?" Deep in the back of my mind I knew that name. I just couldn't bring up a picture of the face.

"Ricky's flatmate. I went to that party with you, d'you remember?"

I paused for a second. "Where is Shell? Why are you on her phone?"

"She's here, in Bristol. With Ricky. They arrived about an hour ago, yeah?"

"They've left the funeral?"

"Yeah, man, there's some things going on, I can't work out what. Shell's left her bag here and buggered off again. Her phone was ringing and I saw that you'd called her."

"In Bristol? In your house?"

"Yeah. She's..." He trailed off. "There's something wrong. Can't put my finger on it." He tried a laugh. "Can't be done on a spreadsheet, for sure, man. Sorta... weird. Like, what's happening between them....weird. You're Shell's friend, right?"

"Er—absolutely."

"She needs a friend. Right now. That's what she needs. Could you get here? Would that be possible?"

"Eijaz, you're not making much sense. Can't you just put her on, please?"

"They've gone out somewhere. To get food, I think." His voice dropped, in tone and register. "This is what I was saying at the party. This shamanism stuff, it messes with your head. Ask me they've gone mad. I don't like it, Sabbie, and I reckon you should be the one to sort it out."

I remembered how Eijaz, the full-on business student, hadn't liked Ricky's involvement with shamanism. Some people only see the stereotypes. I'd only seen detached, remorseless bankers, until I'd met Alys and Brice; Eijaz probably imagined rituals that included chicken blood and drug-maddened witch doctors.

"Let's slow down here. Can you tell me what Shell said? How she acted?"

"They were talking … not to me, but I overheard. I didn't mean to, but … I hated what they were saying. They're involved in something and just listening—just the bits I heard—they need help and I don't want to be the only one. I mean, when they get back—I don't wanna to be the only one here."

I swallowed. Eijaz's cool body language had gone down well with my brother and his friends He exuded that sense of trendy-tough. What could have scared him? Shell had talked about taking risks … *shocking fun. Intense.*

"Sabbie? There's something in Ricky's room … you have to … see."

"Eijaz? Can you please explain what you mean?"

"Please come." Eijaz's voice faltered.

He thought I'd begun it, that was the subtext. That this was my fault. I had introduced Ricky to shamanism … and to Wolfsbane's girlfriend.

I was on my feet, snatching up my shoulder bag and car keys.

"Look, keep in touch, okay? I'll be an hour getting to you and I don't want to find out that they've headed back to London or something crazy."

"It's out of my depth, that's for sure."

His voice had dropped into a growl. As I headed for the door, I realized that was because he was terror-stricken.

TWENTY-NINE
ANAGARIKA

EIJAZ LET ME INTO the flat. The hallway was dark and silent. "Everything okay?" I asked. "Only you didn't phone me en route, so I'm guessing Shell is still here."

He looked down at the ground, nudged a dust ball into a corner with the sharp point of his black leather shoe. For once, he wasn't wearing his shades. His eyes were points of deep brown in the gloom. "No sign of them. I'm sure they'll be back."

"Eijaz! I've used a lot of petrol coming here."

He lifted his hand. He was holding Shell's phone. "Why should she leave it behind?"

"Isn't Ricky answering his?"

"It's dead. Not surprising—he didn't take his charger to London, left it plugged into the kitchen socket."

"So they're both incommunicado."

"I'm wondering how accidental that is." He held my gaze for the first time. A lot of his natural cockiness was missing. "I got something I wanna show you. You better prepare yourself."

The hallway was silent, but I could hear a regular plop-plop from the kitchen. A dripping tap. My heart was thudding in sympathy behind my ribs. "Show me what, Eijaz?"

"You know." It was almost an accusation. "When I phoned you, I could tell. You *know*, don't you?"

"I don't know a thing."

It wasn't the truth; I did know something. Not in the same way that Rey would piece a case together—not like Pippa would methodically reach a conclusion. But my way, the way of the shaman. The things Ricky had told me, crouched in the shrubbery at the crematorium, and the journey Sabrina of the Severn had sent me on had become a succession of keys fitting into locks.

He walked away, taking the stairs. "Up here, Sabbie."

I didn't move. My feet were lodged in some sort of groove that held them fast.

"You gotta to confirm this," he said, "or tell me I'm completely off my rocker."

Finally, I was up the stairs. Eijaz pushed Ricky's bedroom door half open, but he didn't step inside. He was waiting for me to take my look and make my comment. "I'd prefer to be off my rocker, okay?"

The room was dim, the blinds pulled to the sill. I almost turned to ask what I was supposed to be looking for, but thought better of it. I fumbled with the light switch; it was hidden behind a long piece of black paper, pinned in place. A low-watt energy bulb flickered on overhead, taking its own sweet time to illuminate the scene, so that,

352

as my sight adjusted, the surreal nature of the room became apparent in increments.

Ricky's bedroom had once been as orderly as a pharmacy. Now it was a maelstrom. There was total chaos, yet the chaos seemed to have a purpose, almost a plan within itself. Books and files were scattered over the floor, layered one on the next, each open at a specific page, as if Ricky had so much to remember, he didn't dare lose the pages he'd read.

I closed my eyes and heard the whispers.

The last time I was here, the spirits of the room had spoken to me, but I'd failed to listen. Today, they forced me to hear their lament, which rose and fell, moving from croon to wail. Even the walls cried out. Perhaps Ricky knew they did, for there were no walls to see. They were plastered with reproductions depicting Arthurian legends, posters of sea eagles, and photographs of pagan sites he'd maybe taken himself. Long sheets of paper hung down the walls, some placed so high he would have to use a chair to check what was on them. They were filled with scribbles and diagrams and archaic runes. The picture of Glastonbury had strips of white paper pasted over them—single phrases in thick black marker, like "playing tonight" flashes on flyers.

I stepped into the room. A tight line snatched at my hair. Another dug into my cheek. I raised my hands and they were caught too. Threads stretched tight across my path. It felt like an attack; a trap laid for trespassers. As if Ricky had brought a mutant spider into his room and I was caught in a web that was taut with menace and control.

The ceiling light finally reached its full brightness. Ricky had used strands of nylon cord to join up his ideas. The lines of connection ran from the pictures to the paper strips, up and down the walls and across the room. I dragged the twine from my face and heard pins pop out from the plaster.

A desperation crept up my spine, begging me to get out—to turn and run.

I glanced back at Eijaz. He was hanging onto the doorframe as if in some house supposed haunted.

"Yeah ... like, he put his mattress on the floor and he crawls onto to it."

The stink of unwashed slumber rose from the bare pillow and duvet. His clothes still lay in knotted heaps below the bed frame, which was piled with even more open books and files and a half-eaten shop-bought cake.

I remembered the altar inside the wardrobe space that Freaky had admired last time we were here. I slithered across the carpet, trying not to get caught in the lines of twine. The ancient coffee spills felt sticky below my hands. The doors to the wardrobe were open. The interior beckoned.

"He's been burning candles here," I murmured. The nightlight holders contained nothing but their black wicks. They might still have been alight when Ricky had left for London.

I sensed the reverence Freaky had picked up; this was Ricky's place of devotion. A scent of joss stick lingered inside the wooden frame. The wind chimes tinkled slightly as my movement disturbed the air currents.

A photo of Alys's face had been pinned to the back of the wardrobe, blown-up to such a size that everything was slightly pixelated. She was laughing, her teeth glinting toothpaste-white in the flash. I could see the outline of St. Michael's Tower behind her, and the deep purple sky as the shortest night fell. This wasn't here last time, and I fancied he'd got Shell to print it out from her camera. *I think he's in love… with the dead Alys,* Shell had confessed. As he had also loved his own sister.

At the very centre of the wardrobe floor stood the framed picture Babette had sketched. Now Ricky wasn't breathing down my neck, I felt able to pick it up and look closer.

Babette had used black ink with a fine-pointed pen. Thousands of lines built the image up. The face was long, with raised cheekbones above hollowed cheeks. The raven hair was wayward, escaping from a clip at the back, perhaps. The lips held the only defining colour, blocked in with red ink. The woman had stunning eyes—Babette had cleverly created a glint within them that made them feel alive. They were looking directly at me. They were boring into my eyes. Along the bottom, Babette had scrawled her name as artist. I brought the surface closer to my face, in order to see the signature clearly.

For almost a minute, I crouched on my hands and knees, staring at the woman's image and the words Babette had written beneath it. I was seeing the likeness of someone I had longed to meet, face to face.

Eijaz coughed in his throat. "Like I said, yeah? Ricky's nutty method of revision, innit?"

His words brought me back to life. I sucked in a breath and rocked on my heels. I crawled to the door and snapped off the ceiling light, sending the room back into shadow. I had brought Babette's picture with me.

"Any chance of a cup of tea?"

Eijaz made two teas using one tea bag and broke open a packet of cheap digestives. We took our drinks to the kitchen table and I laid Babette's picture flat upon it.

"It's shocking," said Eijaz. He stared down at his mug. "When somebody changes. Like, they're another person. He's not the Ricky I knew no more." He barked a laugh. "Right—we all pretend a bit, don't we? Put on an act? Get all dressed up to make a statement an' all, but this ain't no act, man. This is like ... a *takeover*."

I nodded. "Can you remember when it started?"

"I dunno. Months, maybe. It was more under control, you get me? Like, it's escalating lately."

"Did it start when Alys died?" I asked.

There was a silence. "He told me he saw her spirit rise. I'm like, man ... you can't see no thing like that. But he couldn't shut up about this Alys. Like a trigger set something off inside his head."

"You can get obsessed with death."

"Yeah, Sabbie, but that's what I meant about this shaman shit he's been getting into. Like, what I was saying that time. You didn't want to hear, I know you didn't, but after that shaman workshop, he got weirder and weirder."

"There was no workshop. It was cancelled when Alys died."

"I only spoke true, man. It worried me, even back then. What I think is, meddle with that shit that and ... pop!" he slapped his hands together.

"Shamanism can't make you crazy," I said. "But walking in the otherworld can make you feel powerful. It's important to remember it's not *your* power. If you have mental health issues and the wrong person to guide you, I'm not disputing your emotions could go out of control."

It was easy to forgot that Eijaz knew nothing about Brice's emails, or Morgan le Fey or Marty-Mac. All he knew was that his flatmate was behaving strangely. Before we'd gone to Dennon's party, Eijaz had voiced his concerns. I'd assumed he was slamming shamanism without knowing about it. That happened a lot and it always got my hackles raised. I'd bitten back, shut him up. If only I'd waited, listened to what he was really saying.

I pushed the picture frame towards him. "There are names on this sketch. Does he ever mention them?"

Eijaz took it and read aloud. "'Morgan le Fay by Babette Johnson.' I don't know neither of them names."

It was time for some honesty. "Babette is Ricky's younger sister. Morgan le Fay is an assumed name—a writer of poison pen emails—whoever this person is, they're vile and destructive."

"There is someone he's seeing. He goes AWOL for, like, days—leaves looking good, his usual gothic image, but when he comes back—he's in a state. Not shaved, not washed. Then for days after, he don't come outta that room. Nose in a book or Googling things or doing bits to his wall. Then he bursts out, gets showered at last, gets all gothed up, and disappears again."

"Where does he go? Would he be with Shell, perhaps?"

"No. Shell's phoning up, asking where the hell he is."

"So is he with Juke Webber?"

Eijaz shrugged. "Could be."

My heart had got out of place; somehow it was up in my throat and thudding like some archaic steam engine. I'd long ago worked out that any of the workshoppers could have attacked Anthony Bale, if they'd caught his bus to Yeovil. But I'd never thought to ask them where they were the day that Gerald Evens was attacked. However, I did know who had been close to Marty-Mac the day he'd been killed.

"Look," I said to Eijaz, "can you give me a minute to make a phone call?"

I waited until he'd left the room before I called Juke's number. He replied with a brief "Yep?" His breath came down the line in fast huffs.

"You okay?"

"In the gym—hotel."

"You don't happen to know where Ricky is at the moment, do you?"

"No—frankly—past caring. Hey—wait a sec."

I hung on. The background noise echoed with piped music and loud voices. "That's better," he said at last. "I'm off the treadmill. I deserve a break."

"I won't hold you up, Juke. I just want to know if Ricky was with you when you came to the Angel Shopping Centre."

He didn't need to stop to think. "That was why I rang you that day—remember? I was going to cancel my session with you because he'd turned up, which had become a problem. Since we reconnected at the Solstice, he's become a bit of a pest."

"So he was with you that day."

"He arrived out of the blue, begging a bed for the night. When I said I had an appointment with you, his eyes lit up. He wanted to come with me. I didn't think it was appropriate; I was ringing to find out how you felt."

"I didn't see Ricky at the mall."

"We agreed he should hang back while I dealt with things. After you left, I couldn't find him. I went home; I was thoroughly pissed off with the guy. After I got back from seeing you at the pub, he turned up."

"Juke, can you tell me how he was?"

"Huh? Well, it's strange that you put it like that because he was all over the shop. And wet. Very wet. Said he'd fallen in the canal, which is hard to believe because it's nigh impossible to get out again, but his clothes were stained dark with mud so I guess he must have."

I felt my phone slipping from my grasp. "Ricky's a bit ..." The word *unhinged* came to me. "Upset. About the cremation. He's come back home with Shell, but now they've disappeared."

"Frankly, he can stay disappeared, for all I care. The guy's a liability."

"If he rings, can you find out where he is and what he's doing, then let me know?" I broke off, remembering Ricky's phone had run out of juice.

"Yeah, yeah," said Juke. He was longing to get back on the tread-mill and push his cardiovascular rate back up.

"I'll let you go, shall I?"

I stared at the sketch of Morgan le Fay. Babette Johnson must have drawn the likeness at least five years ago. Did that mean they both knew the woman back then? Was that part of the implication of Babe's disappearance? If Morgan had been some kind of sha-manic mentor to either of them, perhaps Ricky had asked me to search for Babette because I, too, was a shaman.

Ricky was a star-child—an innocent—the sort who rescues spi-ders from baths even though they're terrified of them. I sometimes meet people like Ricky in my practice. They arrive at my therapy room hoping that I will cure them of the charm or spell worked on them by some strong and beguiling necromancer. Mostly what I find is a pattern of events which had nothing to do with their previous mentor, who they're blaming for the mysterious illness that's beset them. Rather, it's an innate part of their themselves—perhaps an early trauma that's left them vulnerable. Trendle will help me retrieve the part of their soul that had been shocked away from their whole. I could guess that Ricky's soul might have been broken into pieces by the disappearance of his sister.

Star-children are vulnerable to psychic attack. If Ricky had met someone with charisma, he would be susceptible to sliding under their charms. He'd been the first person to know Alys was dead. His own subtle body would have been raw and open to attack at that moment. And there's always a predator among a crowd of love-drenched, enlightened hippie types. Someone who relishes domination over others. I visualize a silken cloak to ward off such attacks, but Ricky wouldn't know what had hit him.

My phone trilled out, making me leap up from my seat. I grabbed it, in the hope Juke was ringing with new information. It was Wolfsbane.

"Things have gone apeshit," he began.

"Well, hello to you too."

"No, honestly Sabbie, why did you have to leave London? I need some support here. It's going to be me and a load of bankers scattering the ashes at this rate."

"People aren't keen?"

"Yew and Juke are leaving tomorrow for work on Monday. Freaky's still here—he's never stayed in a hotel before and I don't think we'll ever prize him out—but Ricky disappeared right after the funeral, and Shell's gone. Sabbie … I think she's two-timing me."

"You've been two-timing her, Wolfs, so that sounds fair."

"Uh?"

"You and Esme."

There was a pause, while Wolfsbane processed this.

"Anag saw you both in the Chalice Well Gardens, didn't he? I'm afraid he has trouble keeping his mouth shut."

"Is that why Shell's done it? She's gone off with that Aussie fucker."

"Wolfsbane," I barked. "She's not with Anag."

"She is now," he said. "He's going to show her how to walk the Tor labyrinth." Wolfs's voice had deteriorated to whine. "She asked me to walk the labyrinth with her and I didn't listen. It's on her bucket list, Sabbie, I should have taken her. Now she's not even answering her phone."

"When is this walk taking place?"

"No idea. It must be soon; she's taken my staff. Said it would add resonance to the occasion, which I couldn't dispute."

"And you want your staff back."

"I want her back! Can't you speak to her? Make her see sense? Tell her I'll take her into any labyrinth she chooses."

I found Anag's number and dialled.

"Sabs!" he began familiarly. "I was gutted I wasn't at the funeral, but I wouldn't have missed my Labyrinth Workshop for a double crate of lager. It was ripper. Hey, did y'know that when you walk into the centre of the labyrinth, you're walking towards you own soul?"

"Look, Anag—"

"We had these lectures on the history of the labyrinth, we went to see this church that's got one in the yard there, then we built our own with a pile of boulders. And yesterday, we walked the Tor. It's not just a question of getting to the bloody top, y'know; it's hours and hours of bloody hard graft."

"I'll come to the point, Anag. What's this about you taking Shell up the Tor?"

"You got it. It's a full moon tonight. Not a speck of cloud. Perfect for walking the labyrinth path. How's that for a bonzo thrill?"

"I'm asking you to call it off."

"It's not dangerous. It's life enhancing, right?"

He was right; with the moon lighting the way better that torches, walking the labyrinth should be inspiring, rather than terrifying. "Not the Tor. I don't mean walking the labyrinth. I mean ..."

I worked my tongue around a reasonable explanation of things, but I couldn't put my fears into the right words. It was impossible to pass on the monstrous thoughts I was having, and Anag, his mind full of moonlight and labyrinths, would never have believed me.

"Look, Sabs old girl. I gotta go. I'll be as busy as a cat burying shit before we get going."

"When are you starting out?"

"Sun's gotta be right down, moon's gotta be right up. We're meeting at the Living Rock."

"Anag, could I come too?"

"Yeah, no worries. Make it merrier. You ever done a thing like this before?"

"Not really."

It was hard to slot the pieces of the puzzle into place, sitting in someone else's kitchen. In the living room, Eijaz had switched on the TV; canned laughter blared. Above my head was Ricky's bedroom, where long lines of twine connected images of knights rescuing damsels to pictures of the winding paths of Glastonbury Tor.

Shadows in a cave. A dried-out wasteland. A bird plunging in attack. A red hind, shyly blinking in a forest glade. Slowly keys were turning in locks.

"No, Anag," I repeated. "I have never done anything like this before."

THIRTY

THE COMPANION-AT-ARMS

A LABYRINTH IS NOT a maze. A maze is a puzzle; its paths have many branches and its exits are blocked to trap the unwary adventurer. A labyrinth has one shape only and one path leading to its core. It can be found all over the world, carved into rock as early as the Neolithic, engraved on ancient silver coins and on the floors of cathedrals.

The labyrinth winds over the hillside of the Glastonbury Tor, spiralling seven times round on seven levels, each equal in status to a chakra of the human body. It moves to its central point in a devious manner, round and back, upwards and downwards, through three dimensions—and within those three, the seeker can find the fourth dimension, the magical realm at the summit. The entrance to the Hollow Hill.

And after that, it will be easy. There will be no need for more killing.

———

The acolyte starts his labyrinth walk at the Living Rock, a smooth outcrop close to the base of the hill. Twilight is approaching and he keeps his eyes on the track hidden in long grass.

"Life from life. This is true. Morgan works entirely with apothegm. Ergo, what she says is always true. The Sleeping King should be woken if there is dire need. No—must—be woken."

"Ricky?" Shell shimmies close and speaks into his ear. "Stop muttering to yourself, Ricky. We're supposed to walk in silence."

He withdraws his hand from hers. The texture is clammy. Besides, he's trembling and he doesn't want to transmit his fear to her.

At first the labyrinth walk is not steep; it traces the latitude of the hill. Then all at once the walk is vertical, tough going. As they struggle through knapweed and hogweed, Shell falls slightly behind, her breathing no more than shallow gasps. She could do with losing a few pounds.

He stops to wait for her. Above, he can see the tower on the summit, a tall black box against the darkening sky. Is there movement up there? Is there a shadow within the shadows?

He tramps on, steadily moving towards the entrance into the Hollow Hill. Ring the bell to wake the Sleeping King. Save the wasteland. Save the living world. Crops will flourish, cattle will thrive, children will be born chuckling with delight. He tries to use a measured pace, but his mind is screaming at him.

He is companion-in-arms to the goddess Morgan, but she's not here for him. She's always arriving at the wrong time, like when she burst into his room as he was managing to study for an essay and screamed at him.

Find it! Find it now! The world is crashing and burning and you stay here, with your stupid books and pictures when you should sound the Bell of Doomsday!

He had gone to shut the door behind her, so that Eijaz would not hear, and Morgan snatched the spool of black twine and hurled it at him. It had unravelled as it sailed across his bedroom.

Connections! Correspondences! Bind and conjoin! She'd swept the plastic pot of pins over the floor then shrieked like a hawk ... *pick them up! Mind Selkie's little paws!*

The cat is her familiar. He brings the dark edge to Morgan's magic. Morgan wrapped him in her arms, her hand over his small head as if to prevent his hearing from being damaged by her shouts. *There is still one knight to find. One foolish knight to take down. This is what stands in our way!*

The acolyte had been so shocked, he'd actually dared to respond, *I am a companion-at-arms!*

"I am a companion-at-arms!" he repeats now. He's forgotten that Shell doesn't like him muttering. He forces himself back into his body, and, without warning they're at the top of the Tor.

Shell skips along the edge of the flat summit. "We're already at the centre!"

"I don't think so." He stares at the plan of the labyrinth. Anagarika sent him the plan as an attachment. They were supposed to do this together, but the acolyte doesn't want Anag anywhere near Morgan le Fey. "It's all wrong."

"What? What's wrong? We're here, aren't we?"

"This is only the fifth turn on the path. It's taken us up here, but now we have to descend, take a couple more turns."

"Look down there, Ricky. The mist on the valley. Isn't that something?" She gazes over the darkening landscape. He walks past her. He knows where he's going next; he doesn't need the plan.

———

They reach the Egg Stone as the moon pulls free of the horizon. Neither of them have seen the stone before, and for a long time they cannot utter a word or move in the least way.

An enticing vapour rises, perhaps from the two trees that grow there, one on either side of the outcrop, sentinels of the Egg Stone, its protectors, pushing aslant from the steep slope like fingerposts. The first is an elder tree, and old at that—stunted and almost bare of leaf. Its branches glimmer pale, reminiscent of the White Tree of Gondor. It is arrayed with a rainbow of ribbons, feathers, beads, and dying flowers. A postcard wrapped in polythene is rammed in the fork of two branches.

The second tree is in full health, a hawthorn of perfect shape and colour, but less bedecked, as if the elder tree is also the most noble.

"Fuu-uuck, Ricky," says Shell. "It's awesome."

She tucks her arm into his. He wishes she would not. She's wearing the perfume again, the one that makes him so nauseous. He's asked her to only wash with soap, but she seems never to hear.

Enchantment is everywhere—redolent. The moon's rays illuminate the Egg Stone, making it glow so that the surface shines out like a reflected moon caught on the hillside. Everything magnified. That surely is how magic works? In the day, the stone would be grey as ashes.

This is where he should step into the otherworld. Where could the opening be? And where—where is Morgan le Fay?

Something tips in him. This is all levels of peril. He's given everything to Morgan that she's asked for. Done every deed. When he needs her most, when he's supposed to be leading her into the middle of the Hollow Hill, she has deserted him.

He knows she's not here, because his head is clear and free from pain. She's left him to do it alone.

"We should be able to get through, Shell, open the way by magic."

"Pardon, Ricky?"

The Egg Stone is an outcrop of hard sandstone, a burr of a good size. It could be four, five metric tons. What would Morgan do? A word—a tap from a wand. "Give me your staff."

"What?"

He stamps his foot. "The way into the otherworld should open!"

"Right." She lowers her voice. "And why should you think it won't? Hmm?"

He takes Wolfsbane's staff, gripping low on the shaft. It sings with power. Whatever comes to hand. He's no longer an acolyte. *Pound and pound.* Crack and it's opened. He raps the Egg Stone hard with the staff. *Crack, crack.*

Nothing. Did he expect it to split into two?

Shell has scrabbled up the hillside, her jeans stretched over her rump as she bends to clutch at tufts of grass. Surely that's not how it should end, pulling at grass in an effort to reach the top. She shouts back at him. "What're you waiting for?"

"We should enter the otherworld here, at the Egg Stone. It's got to be dignified. *Hallowed.*"

"C'mon, Ricky." She reaches the top of the Tor, balances on its extreme edge. "I know exactly where the entrance to the otherworld is."

And then, she's gone.

———

The summit feels different in the dark. The moon is the only light. The concrete path leading through the tower gleams white. The wind moans past his ears, deafens him to other sounds he might be vigilant for—Morgan's snigger, the cat's rasped meow.

Where is she? It's crazy. She's playing games. She begged for this. *Find the way into the Hollow Hill.*

"I've done it, Morgan." The wind blows away the words.

Within the black centre of the tower, something moves. A shadow.

"Morgan?"

Shell steps out. She's pulled off her jeans and her biker's jacket and—and all her clothes. She's standing there in leather boots and black lace, knickers and bra. There's moon-sheen on her shoulders and thighs. She raises her arms and draws her fingers through her short hair. "There's no one here," she says. "A full moon and a warm night. I thought there might be loads up here, didn't you? It's a miracle. We have the place to ourselves." She reaches out a hand. "C'mon."

She wants love. She always wants love. She is demanding. All his women are demanding. Shell asks for sex, Morgan for blood.

"Too much blood," he says.

"Shush …" She's whispering, close to him, tight to him. He feels the warmth of her, and the coolness too, at the top of her arms where he lays his hands. He can hardly bear the touch of her. He's groaning. "Where's the otherworld? Where?"

"Here," she says. "Inside of me."

"I have to find the bell. Ring the bell."

"Ding dong?" She's trying to pull him through the tower. "It's perfect, Ricky. Tantric love on the Tor, in the labyrinth, in the moonlight."

She pulls so hard his feet move anyway, even against his will. He stumbles through the tower's short, dark passage. The Tor. The dark. Is this the otherworld? Is he now inside the Hollow Hill?

Shell tightens her arms round him, pushing her pelvis against him, opening his shirt, button by button. He puts his hands over hers.

"It should be hallowed."

"It will be. It's what we planned."

Had they planned this? He can't remember.

"Ricky."

She's lying on the grass now. Her legs are slightly splayed and her arms are by her side. Passive. He drops to his knees. He lays down the staff. He straddles her, hands kneading the chill of her arms.

"Make love to me, Ricky. The way will open."

Will it? If they lie together now, at the centre of this hard-won labyrinth, will he find the passage into the Hollow Hill? He lowers his face to hers. The kisses feel damp, her breasts are slippy with sweat beneath his fingers. Humidity is rising from her flesh, clouded with the scent she's sprayed on her neck. A wave of sickness grips him. He can't bear it. "I shouldn't have brought you here," he says, almost before he's thought it.

"Ricky?"

He draws in a long ragged breath and roars out his agony. "MOR-GAN! WHERE ARE YOU! MORGAAAAN!"

And instantly, she's beside him. She comes down like sudden darkness. His head yanks back on his neck, as the pain arrives. Her dagger slashes between his eyes, slicing in. The pain can't be silenced, and he cries out with it. "Yowwww!"

"Ricky! What is it?"

The pain stops all speech, all thought. He's breathless with the agony of her presence. It's like never before. Nothing functions.

Whatever comes to hand. Extemporize, acolyte. Take whatever comes to hand!

His head is overripe, a watermelon splitting open from its own internal pressure. He remembers the Black Knight's skull, bashed, oozing, red, but also pink and grey. He should not have brought Shell. It's so clear now, he cannot understand why he did so.

"Pound and pound." He tries not to mutter, but he can't help it. "Be swift, be swift. Death of beauty. Death of love." He pulls back and screams. "RUN! RUN! GET OUT OF HERE!"

Shell's face puckers. She tightens her arms round him, rocks him a little. "It's okay. It's okay."

Her features break into black and white dots. The scent and the heat coming from her are sickening, and her face is broken into pieces. His stomach contracts. "I won't do it, I *won't* do it."

"Okay," says Shell. "That's okay."

"I'm not her acolyte. I'm not. I am a companion-at-arms. She can't make me."

"Hush, Ricky it's okay…"

Bile bitters the back of his throat. He gives a small cough. The headache is massive now, preventing thought, stopping words. Like a block. A damn. A plug in the mind.

Morgan is standing at the mouth of the Tower, and even though no ray of moonlight touches her, she's clear in his sight—her ridiculous heels, balanced perfectly, Selkie leaping on his leash after some flitting moth. She yanks the leash and a bleaching yowl stuns the night air. Morgan laughs, a high burst with a cruel edge.

"Don't look," he whispers to Shell. "Don't listen."

"Ricky," Shell says. "Tell me, what's the *matter*?"

He can hardly hear her, because Morgan's voice is like thunder.

You were instructed to find the basilica where the king sleeps. You were instructed to save the wasteland. She gestures to Shell, lying below him, deliberately harsh. *Yet you waste your time on this girl.*

"I'm not your acolyte anymore."

Morgan's eyes are black pits. With one touch of her cool hand, she could lift his migraine. He feels a touch, but when he opens his eyes, it is Shell who is stroking his face.

"What is wrong, Ricky?"

He manages a gargling cry, half swallowed in his throat. "Run, run, please … run."

"I'm not going anywhere," says Shell. "We're going to work out what's wrong together."

Morgan has made herself invisible to the girl, unheard. He tries to explain this, but the words get muddled in his mouth, and he's saying *foolish, foolish, foolish,* for he realizes now that the Foolish Knight had always been Shell. Always had to be.

He uncouples Shell's hands from around his neck and pulls back from her, using Wolfsbane's staff to lever himself up.

"Go," he says. It comes out as a sob. "Get away from us. Run, Shell. Run, now."

It's hopeless. Even if Shell careered straight down the hill, Morgan could stop her tracks by raising one finger.

Shell does not move, except to reach up and grasp the hem of his long coat, tugging. "Come on, my tantric lover. You can do this. Mmm?"

Step by step, controlling Selkie's leash, Morgan le Fay walks the distance between them. She puts her hand around his hand, which is grasping the wooden staff. She lifts the rod, and, with her tremendous strength, she lifts Ricky also. He's dangling, looking down on Shell's honest face. She cannot see the danger.

Morgan's movement is so quick. A flick of her wrist. Even before he has registered the action, it is done. The staff is balanced, not in the grass of the Tor, but at the centre of Shell's neck, at the point where the flesh dips before the bones begin. Shell's eyes flash wide and her hands come up to grasp the staff.

"Ricky!" Her voice sounds odd. She's pulling at the staff, both hands tight around it, but she can't budge it, she can only make things worse by struggling, heels digging into the ground, knees thrashing from side to side. A hand slams the ground. Each time she bucks and kicks, the rod slips deeper. She makes a sound, the sound that comes from someone in trouble.

In dire need.

Morgan is driving the pain into his head as she drives the point of the staff into Shell's throat.

Your weapon is in your hand. Finish her.

He feels Morgan's grip on the back of his fist. It's like stone from the fire. He looks down the shaft, towards Shell. Her legs are stiff now, the heels hammering as the windpipe closes. Her eyes are like balls that might roll out of her head. Her mouth is open, gasping. All at once, he's begging. "I made the sacrifice! I won my spurs, I dealt the blow…"

He dealt the blow. Each blow sickened him. This blow will defeat him.

Selkie leaps on its hind legs and lashes with its claws.

Finish her. The sacrifice must be made.

Will this death save the wasteland? His hands are burning. The staff is burning. Shell's face, below him is burning. Everything is on fire.

"How will more blood get us into the Hollow Hill?"

He holds his breath and waits.

Morgan places her hand on his forehead and while it lies there, the headache lifts. The nonpresence of that throb is so intense, he gasps. She nods once. Affirmative. Yes. One more death. The Foolish Knight. That will get them in. It will.

She takes her hand away. A shaft of pain accelerates through his head. He tightens his grip on Wolfsbane's staff.

"Death of beauty!" the acolyte shrieks. "Death of grace! Death of love!"

THIRTY-ONE
THE FOOLISH KNIGHT

Anagarika was kitted out in sensible walking gear—lace-up boots, waterproof trousers with gaiters, and an insulated jacket. That was better at least than his monk's habit.

I'd hotfooted it from my car as the sun began to set, afraid they'd start without me, but Anag was alone in Wellhouse Lane, standing under the only streetlamp, eating from his hand; chips wrapped in paper. I could smell the grease and vinegar as I came up to him.

Even if I could do nothing at all to help matters, I needed to be there when Anag showed Ricky the labyrinth path.

When you eliminate that which you no longer need, one possibility will remain. I'd taken away all the things that were not needed and the answer—impossible, unimaginable—came clear. It had been late in coming, too awful to contemplate. Perhaps if I'd taken this leap of faith earlier, Marty-Mac might still be alive.

I saw her spirit rise … Alys's death had been a cosmic explosion, expanding into this night on the Tor. Once I understood that, the entire picture had formed. A trail of bloody attacks leading here—Glastonbury Tor—where it had all begun.

Eijaz made me sit down and eat a sandwich before I left the student house. He cut the mouldy rind off some dried-out cheese and grated it onto white bread. I put the kettle on again and sneakily put two separate tea bags into our empty cups. After that I'd flung my shoulder bag onto the back seat of the Vauxhall and driven south towards the action. I could not let go of this until Ricky was safe from the influence of Morgan le Fey.

I'd been hoping, as I took the ninety-minute drive from Bristol to Glastonbury, that a plan would emerge, but so far I'd come up with nothing.

A walk up the Tor in the moonlight, had Anag and I been alone, would be a lovely thing. But Morgan le Fay's savage presence would be there, hidden out of sight, around a corner, behind a tree.

Find Morgan le Fay. That was the plan.

That was the jeopardy too.

"Hi there." Anag raised his food in the palm of his hand. "These are de-lish. Want one?"

I took a chip, absentmindedly. It was greasy in my fingers. "Where are Ricky and Shell?"

"Dunno. I sincerely hope they're not letting me down."

"When did they say they'd get here?"

He checked his watched. "Sundown. And yeah, the sun's properly down."

"I thought you said you were meeting at the Living Rock?"

Anag shrugged but moved off, gravel crunching under his big boots. We reached the start of the labyrinth walk, the Living Rock. It was an outcrop of sandstone, one of two on the Tor. Ricky was nowhere to be seen. I grabbed that opportunity.

"Anag, there's things you don't know. About Ricky. When he gets here, you have to help me persuade Shell that he has to go to hospital."

Anag gawped at me. "Ricky isn't sick!"

"He is ill. He's ill in his head. He's out of his head, not responsible for his actions. He's a risk to himself and others."

"Don't be a whacker. Little Ricky! He's fine. Fiddle-fit. He might be a stick insect, but he could carry a sheep on his back."

"I don't mean that sort of ill ..." I wasn't getting through. Anag refused to pick up the unease in my voice. As always, he was drifting in the fug of his own place in the universe. He hadn't even bothered asked how the funeral had gone. I pulled my jacket tight. The wind whipped around the cone of land after dark, even in summer. "The things I've discovered ... I'm worried ... you *must* call this off, Anag!"

"Stuff that! I can't wait for this walk, Sabbie. It was pretty okay, when we did it on the workshop, but I didn't really find my soul. Reach enlightenment. Yeah, that's how they put it. Reach enlightenment. They said we would, but they were pulling a fastie. You wouldn't, not on your first time, would you?" He picked out the rest of the good chips and screwed up the paper, and finding no bin, stuffed the screw at the base of the Living Rock.

I was sure Anag had a soul. A gentle soul, a young soul. It would benefit him to walk the Tor in the moonlight, had he not chosen precarious company. Anag wanted to do this far more than he wanted to listen to me. He was going to show us all how clever he was, how he could walk the labyrinth at night.

"What d'you know? Ricky's stood me up, the crummy bastard." Anag pull printed pages out of his map pocket. "May as well bone up anyways. Might do it on my own. You game?"

"What is that?"

"A handout from the workshop. The plan of the labyrinth." Anag passed it over for me to see. "We could start out without him? Ricky'll be all right to catch us up—he's got a copy—I sent him one."

"What?" The page fluttered from my hands. Anag scrabbled for it. "Ricky has a copy of this plan?"

The first of the stars were coming out. An owl hooted, announcing that this time belonged to the creatures of the night, who would, quite soon, be sniffing out Anag's pack of chips.

High above us, St. Michael's Tower loomed, dark against the blue-black sky. That would be where Morgan le Fay would wait.

"Who are you?" I whispered. "Goddess? Demon? And where are you?"

She was here. She was watching us.

I felt her pervade the breeze that was whipping my hair. I felt her in my marrow. I felt her try to pierce my heart.

If she was here, then so was Ricky.

I began to run. Up the gradient, steep as a wall. I felt my back ache, almost immediately. You have to be Olympic fit to run up the side of the Tor.

"Hey, Sabbie!" Anag yelled. "That's the wrong path, you dingo! That's the one that goes straight up to the top! We don't take that one."

I kept going. I didn't stop to explain. I needed every breath I had for this race.

"Come back! We need to start from down here. Go round the side of the hill ..."

Anag's voice was already fading as I made progress. Choking lungs, heaving diaphragm, thudding chest. My legs were lead. I kept going, one foot after the other, up the hill. The sweat on my forehead stung in the cold air.

I had to get to the top.

Morgan le Fay was up there. Ricky was with her. And Shell was with him. Even if my legs gave way, even if my lungs collapsed, I had to keep going.

The path levelled out as it zigged and zagged round hairpin bends. I tried picking up my pace. The way was lit by the moon, but my eyes were greying over. My ears buzzed with exhaustion. Each time I breathed there were flames in my chest.

I had no oxygen left. My calves pricked with the burn of lactic acid. Minutes were passing—long, awful minutes, while, tediously slow, the tower at the top drew nearer in my sights.

I rounded the last bend. The final torturous steps leading to the summit were before me. I was almost at the top when I collapsed onto my knees, letting the rich, sweet air into my lungs. As the buzzing in my ears receded, a voice floated down. The cry of a hawk. The cry of a madman.

"Death of beauty! Death of grace! Death of love!"

The words of the great bird in my journey.

I was running again, running towards death, my heart bursting.

I charged through the tower, onto the level plain of the summit. And stopped.

Ricky stood, his lacquered hair blown by the wind. His face was chalky in the moonlight, even though his makeup had melted and run. His eyes were sucked deep into their sockets. He looked like a man who had not slept in days. He was gripping a staff with one hand, leaning on it, as if exhausted.

Avalon lay shrouded below us. Nothing was visible. A swirling mist rose from the warmer valley, its tendrils reaching ever upwards. By the early hours of the morning only the top of the Tor would be visible above the mist; an otherworldly ghost of a hill. Now I could feel it damp on my face—I could smell it—and yet, above us, the moon was a white lamp in the sky. Her shadows cast strange angles and patterns.

I was shivering from cold; I'd climbed through mist, sweating as I'd run, and my clothes were soaking inside and out. My legs trembled like a toddler's.

I could not see Shell anywhere, but I hardly looked round, for Ricky pulled at my attention.

"Ricky?" I walked quickly towards him. "It's Sabbie. I've come to take you home, Ricky."

As if returning from another world, he properly registered my presence. "We don't want you here." He looked down. I followed his gaze. I stopped in my tracks. Shell was flat on the ground, her legs and arms splayed awkwardly. The point of the staff Ricky held was resting at her throat.

No, not resting. Pushing. *Grinding* at her throat.

Shell made a single, strangled sound and took a hooping suck of a breath. I think the movement Ricky had made as he responded to me had taken some pressure off her windpipe, but she was in a dreadful condition. Even in the moonlight I could see her colour was darkening.

"What are you doing?" I kept my voice even. I didn't want to provoke him.

The silence hung, moment after moment. I trained my eyes on Ricky, waiting for him to respond to me. I didn't dare look at Shell. I didn't want him to think too much about Shell. I swallowed and felt the hollow of my throat and thought of how the point of the staff would press down, closing it over, closing it down.

"Please, Ricky, pass me the staff." It felt like a long time passed with my hands out stretched. "You're hurting her, Ricky." I held my position. Shell's breath gurgled in her constricted throat. She squirmed below him on the ground, her hands closing round the base of the staff in a hopeless gesture. "Don't hurt Shell. She wouldn't hurt you."

He muttered to himself. The tone was monotonous, as if the emotional effort had overcome him. His head was bowed low, long spikes of hair flopping into his eyes. He hadn't taken in a word I'd said. "You're not welcome here," he said.

"Who says I'm not welcome? Morgan le Fay?"

It had been a risk to utter that name. Ricky cried out, a sound that had no words to it, just the cry of desperate man. I took one step towards him, trying to be completely silent, but my heart was thudding at such a rate that each time I took a breath I had to work at controlling it, but it was worth it, for these slow breaths did steady my thinking.

I crept one further step. I began to make out his run-together words. "Too-many," he intoned. "Too-many-blows-too-many-blows. Pound-and-pound. Too-much-blood-too-much-blood. Life-from-life. But not the Foolish Knight. Not the Foolish Knight ..." There was no passion in his voice, as though Morgan le Fay had sucked the life from Ricky, leaving him a shell.

I was outside my remit here. Ricky's attacks were sudden, random, and violent because their reasoning came directly from Morgan. He had to obey the voice of Morgan, imbedded powerfully into his mind. She had taken him over. Not a psychic intrusion; those I can deal with as a shaman, with help from Trendle and my guardians. This was different. Neither my shamanic training nor my psychology degree equipped me to work with someone like Ricky. A doctor would describe him as manic. Paranoid. Schizoid.

I preferred to think of Ricky as possessed.

I knew what Wolfsbane would advise: Get out. Get professional help. But I was five hundred feet up on this Somerset hillside, where Ricky was slowly driving the point of a staff into a girl's windpipe.

The mania growing inside him had transformed him, but underneath he was unprotected and defenseless. Open to internal attack. I fancied that the voices in his head blocked things that came in from the apparent world. As if Ricky was stuck in the Middle Realm, unable to break free. Morgan had infiltrated that inner world, had captured him and was not letting go.

"Morgan le Fay has led you into terrible trouble."

His eyes flickered to both sides. "Shush. She can hear you. She's here now. She's standing right next to me now."

"She's only in your head, Ricky."

"I know you can't see her. She is a powerful magician. But she is truly human. Her heart beats, same as yours and mine."

A shudder passed through me. I wasn't only trembling from fatigue and cold. Something had shifted. The quality of the air felt different. Ricky was wrong. Morgan wasn't in the least human. And I did detect something. A presence.

I was close to him now. He shifted, observing the hand I held out, staring at it as if it was an alien thing. It took a huge effort of will to hold my hand out to him and yet not snatch at the staff and try to pull it away. I was terrified that if I made a grab he'd stop thinking and the staff would crush through Shell's neck until the skin gave way and sinew and cartilage split open.

"She has been a goddess," he half crooned. "Taught by Merlin—powerful magic—old magic from a different time—powers of invisibility. She is only seen when she wants to be seen. She is only heard when she wants to be heard. I see her. I hear her. I am her acolyte. No! I am her companion-at-arms." He began to sob.

As the tears came, Shell bent a knee and an elbow. He'd half forgotten the staff, and she saw her chance to break free. I needed to keep his mind away from what was going on at his feet.

"Yes! I can feel her, Ricky. Show me where she is. Show me Morgan le Fay."

Fingers of mist and the moon's magic charged the air. Ricky shifted. His eyes flicked from one corner of the summit to the other.

"She has possessed you. I think you know that, Ricky."

He called out shrilly, like a girl. The cry flew off the hillside. "I am a companion-at-arms! The door to the Hollow Hill should open for me!" And as he cried out, he lifted his arms, both of them, into the air. "I hate you, Morgan!"

"SHELL!" I screamed and made my grab at the staff. We both yanked at it and the stick flew up. Ricky's eyes hardened and I felt my fingers burn. The staff rushed through them leaving me holding air. He rammed it down, hard, fast.

Shell was no longer there. She had rolled with the last of her strength. She was up on her knees, retching into the grass, dry painful heaves, only a hands-breathe from where the point of the staff now juddered in hard soil.

The impact from the staff as it hit the ground was so fierce it threw Ricky like the recoil of a rifle. The staff sprang out of his hands and he keeled backwards. I flew at him, wrapping both my arms tight around him, both an embrace and a straitjacket. He half collapsed into me, and over his sunken shoulder I saw Shell get to her feet. She was coughing, hard and dry coughs, but she was up.

"*Go,*" I hissed at her. She looked at me once. Perhaps she thought I was giving myself up for her, an exchange of sacrifice. Perhaps I was—I hardly knew. She stumbled away, her choice made for her.

"Help me." Ricky's voice was still drear with lack of emotion, but he wasn't speaking to Morgan. He was asking me. "You're the one, Sabbie. You always worked things out."

We were so close I felt the warm breath from his nostrils. His wide eyes reflected the moon's rays—black mirrors, crystal lakes, chasms of despair. I stared, unblinking, and my mind toppled in, as if falling into black crystal lakes.

———

I was standing on rutted, dried out soil, the plain that stretched to infinity. Nothing had changed since Sabrina had last sent me here.

The sky above was dark, filled with low clouds—cumulonimbus, which herald thunderstorms—but there was no dampness in the air, not a stirring of wind, just the clinging scent of cordite.

Lightning flashed across the vast, black horizon. It crashed at my ears. Hair lifted from my scalp as the electrical charge passed over the land.

This was Ricky's otherworld.

The worms were still waiting for moisture. I recoiled from them but could not escape them. There was nowhere these worms did not writhe and struggle. I stumbled about, but with each step I crushed worms, their innards oozing over other worms.

"You know this place." Trendle spoke into my ear. I relaxed. Trendle only accompanied me where I was meant to go. "Now do you understand?"

I creaked a nod. Yes. I understood. The worms belonged to Morgan le Fay. They were symbols of the thoughts she'd implanted within Ricky's otherworld, intrusions of his spirit; a swirling mass that filled his head and blocked out all other thoughts with the words he muttered.

"*Too-many-blows, pound-and-pound. Death of beauty!*"

Far out towards the dusty horizon, I saw a single figure walked on her own path—a clear circle of hard, black earth lay around and under her fine shoes and opened before her. No worm came close.

She was taller than Ricky. Her face was bolder, stronger. Her eyes were blacker, with sweeping lashes and plucked brows. She had a size-zero figure and clothes to die for. She had lips of blood. She was just as Babette had drawn her, except, in her hand was a silken leash. At the end of it was the most beautiful feline creature I had ever seen.

"She's inside of you, Ricky. Like a parasite. An intrusion. A possession. I can sense them both, inside you. They're taking you over."

"Both? You see them both?"

It seemed to be confirmation for him. I was still holding him as tightly as I could, and now he wrapped his arms round me and we fell full onto the damp night grass. He didn't struggle, didn't fight free. The time for fighting was over.

"I have to wake the Sleeping King, Sabbie. It is my quest."

I was less than half a blink away from subtle realms. I trained my eyes into his eyes. "Hold onto me," I said. "I'll come with you."

THIRTY-TWO
THE SLEEPING KING

A GAPING HOLE IN the rutted desert dust. The blackness below is unremitting.

Here, at last, is the way into the Hollow Hill. A break in the dry land. An opening deep into the earth. He knew he could locate it. If only it hadn't taken so long to find.

The wasteland is all around. It stretches in all directions. It is barren and sterile. Not a blade of grass grows here; no rodent scuttles to its burrow. The only life is the thick film of seething worms. And yet, Sabbie's arms are tight around him, the protection of a friend.

Together they move to the very edge of the opening. Nothing is visible at the base of the gaping hole. Is this really the Hollow Hill?

"Take them singly," Sabbie says.

And then he sees—steps of black marble lead down. They are dizzyingly steep and built uneven, to trick unwary knights.

Take them singly, tread deep into the hill in the soft grip of a friend. This is perfect, just as Morgan said it would be. This is truth. This is truly good. This is The Good.

"Murdoch suggests that we must restore the notion of vision. She had such courage. She pushed against the crowd. If she were here, she would be the first to ring the bell."

"Not her, Ricky. You must be the one. Take the steps. Lift the first burning brand you pass. Hold it high to light the way."

Light the way. Morgan le Fay first described it to him. She who was here on that fateful day to lay Arthur to rest. Sconces of candles throwing their light on marble steps which lead to the basilica. Gothic pillars support the vaulted ceiling. Arthur's crown, hovering eternally above the Sleeping King. Knights in a perfect circle, their feet pointing towards his bier, ready to rise when the bell is rung.

The great Bell of Doomsday hangs at the bottom of the marble way. The huge bronze dome, the orate rim, the thick rope attached to the clanger. He has held this in his mind's eye for such an age and now, all he has to do is walk down and haul the rope. The bell will ring. The knights will spring up. Arthur will wake. The crown will be lifted on the tip of a spear. The wasteland will be healed. The Holy Thorn will grow again. All will be at peace.

The friend with the soft hold squeezes him a little. "I'll be with you."

He looks down into the darkness. He manages to raise a trembling hand and point. "Morgan."

She's standing there. On the marble steps. Illuminated by a candle sconce.

Blocking the way.

Morgan knew the way! Through all his efforts, through pound and pound, through forcing him to take life from life, Morgan, all along, knew the way. She is able to enter the basilica of the Sleeping King at will! She has tricked him. She tricks him still. She stands in the way.

She moves up the steps until he can see the bloodstone tied with velvet around her throat. There is that cold smile. It flickers, then dies.

A life from a life, acolyte.

What?

Your little friend, here. She is the Foolish Knight. She must be, or she would never have come so far. Life from life, my acolyte.

"You deserve better," Sabbie whispers. "She is an oppressor, Ricky. She has possessed you."

"I—" He coughs the word. The sickness rises in his belly. The pain slams against his temples. "I ..."

He knows what to do. Only he can do it. A life from a life. She's been on at him since the start. Since Babe drew the picture.

He remembers how he described Morgan le Fay and how Babe formed a likeness. She loved to hear about the goddess blood in Morgan's veins, as in the Golden Age, when demigods walked the Earth. Babe understood that Morgan le Fay was a living psychopomp. She took up her pen and got the likeness perfectly. He took Babe's lovely picture to uni and placed it beside his bed.

Her blood red lips whispered in the night.

Life from life, acolyte.

And the worms came. They burrowed into his head. They blocked the synapses and chewed through the nerve endings. They plugged his mind.

He couldn't write a single essay while Morgan hissed ... *life-from-life ... life-from-life.* He slid into the slough of worms. He walked through anguish. Through hell.

An end. He wanted an end. Wanted it to end. End a life. Miserable life.

She had whispered the words and he had believed them. *Take a life. Save your own. The worms will go away … if you make the sacrifice.*

He knew the forest so well; they all did, the brothers and the little sister. It was easy to find Babette, to call to her. She threw down her bike and ran into his arms. Easy to lead her deeper, to where great trees had become uprooted by a recent storm. They gazed down into the hole the trees had made, both marvelling.

Then Morgan began to whisper. *Take what is to hand. Pound and pound.*

A lot of blood. It seeped between the roots. He stood above and all at once he was himself—Ricky, first year uni student. Babette was lying a decade of metres below him, a cold, pale, shrunken body.

For the first time in a long time, he felt something. Fear. Dread. He could never explain this to his parents. He could never look at them and tell them. Morgan le Fay passed him the strength to lift the sapling trunks—lever them upright, let them crash down in the gaping grave. As if in some massive grinder, Babette's body was crushed. He tore the roots from the crater sides and soft soil fell in like rain, became a landslide. The body—pale, awful, small—disappeared under tons of loam, dry from the summer. He dragged the bigger trunks over the grave as best he could. Morgan gave him the strength to succeed, and the invisibility to get back to his student room, blooded and filthy as he was.

No one knew he'd been home. He lay on his bed and waited for the worms to leave him alone.

When the shriek of the awful, agonizing phone call finally came, it was a shock. His sister was missing. He should have known this, but he did not; not for one moment, as he had pounded down, had he believed he was killing his sister. He thought he was getting rid of Morgan. In fact, he was cementing himself to her. His mind was plugged and useless and the thread which leashed him to Morgan le Fay was already pulled taut.

———

Life from life.

Morgan le Fay continues to mount the marble steps. Below her is the Bell of Doomsday. Above her, the acolyte and his friend, who holds him close—who holds him *up*, for without her support he would crumple into dust and worms.

Sabbie has the nicest eyes. She has the courage of great philosophers. She does not give a fig. She grips his wrist—maybe a sign of solidarity, but no—it's a signal. She hoists his entire arm above his head. As if to call. She is calling with his raised arm. She is making his arm call as the falconers did of yore.

Sea Eagle comes in from the very horizon of the wasteland. The arcing tail is white as quartz as it catches the sun. The span of his wings stretches across the sun. At their ends are feathery fingers, and he has stroked these, as he befriended the bird. He knows they feel like silk.

The bird settles on his outstretched wrist. It is almost too heavy to support. His arm groans under the weight, longs to drop. Hold on. Hold on. Sea Eagle turns one eye, bright as a raindrop, and observes the acolyte steadily.

"Tell him," says Sabbie. "He's waiting for your instruction."

What instruction? Until that second, he had no idea, but now, he knows implicitly what Sea Eagle must do.

"TAKE THE CAT!"

Sea Eagle lifts up, flaps once, moving stale air into strong wind. He swoops and his feet, the great, sharp claws, reach for his prey.

Even Morgan le Fay does not expect it. All are rooted to the spot as Sea Eagle tightens its horny feet around Selkie.

The cat lets out a yowl. Morgan screeches and lunges at the bird. It has gone, up from the hole where the black steps plunge. Its wings stretch and pull with a deafening beat.

In its claws is Selkie, caterwauling his plight as Sea Eagle rises and soars.

Morgan le Fay pushes past them, out into the wasteland, arms reaching up, crying to the lost cat, following the flight of the eagle. For the first time—for the first time ever—she trips on her dagger heels. The worms crawl over her prostrate body.

The power in him is so great, he feels the thread between them snap and when he takes a breath, his sinuses are clear. His migraine lifts. He points the hand that held his bird and screams at the worms.

"She is soil! Eat her!"

At first, he doesn't think his cry has been heard. She's stumbled, but she's on her knees, she's getting up. She looks round at him, as if she will return, cat or no cat.

By the worms have begun.

They have begun their crawl, their slithering, squirming, skewing journey, up her legs, over the backs of her hands, into her armpits, to her neck, to her mouth, to her eyes . . .

She collapses onto the dried out land, writhing as if she were a worm herself. Her body distorts. Skin from skin, flesh from flesh, limb from limb, bone from bone.

Life from life.

She disintegrates, until there is nothing. Nothing but worm-casts.

Sabbie is still focusing on his eyes. All this time, her gaze has bored into his gaze. But now she stands to one side and looks down into the shaft that opens below.

"Go on," she says.

The acolyte drops a single steep step, turns back, holds his hand out to his friend.

"No," says Sabbic. "You alone should do this."

He take the marble steps, one by one. He lifts the first burning brand, holds it high to light the way.

Pillars bring breakneck height. They are painted gold and red to reflect the ever-burning candles in the sconces mounted on the walls. Their golden glow lights the central arena. The king sleeps on his canopied bier. He is still as young as the day he came here, skin un-lined, eyes loosely closed. A sleep light enough to wake to an alarm. Above the canopy is the crown, ready to be taken down on the tip of a spear. His knights lie stretched upon their backs in full armour, ready to spring up if the bell rings. Lancelot, Galahad, Percival, Ga-wain, Kaye … twelve in number, all chivalric knights.

The great Bell of Doomsday hangs mute, high in the vaulted ceil-ing. Its thick bell rope dangles to the floor. It is rough in his hand.

The clang is deafening. It throws him to the ground.

For a moment, as the buzzing recedes, all is silent.

Then a scrape. A shift. A creak of amour after long sleep.

The knights spring up.

They take up their arms—long swords and short.
They lift the crown on the tip of a spear.
They shout out, "Doomsday!"
And the Sleeping King awakes.

———

They climb hand in hand, Sabbie and Ricky, from inside the Hollow Hill. As they leave the deep shaft, they find the wasteland transformed. Children play in the lush grass, collecting meadow flowers. A maiden draws clear water from a well. And the Holy Thorn is in full blossom.

THIRTY-THREE

SABBIE

WE STILL HAD OUR arms around each other when I came round. We were lying like lovers, Ricky and me, at the very edge of the Tor.

I eased myself away, lifting and resting his arms. They were limp. He didn't stir. I could see his chest rise and fall and wondered if he was rousable. I went to shake him, but thought better of it. Maybe his exhausted mind had closed right down. I had no idea how he would respond to being woken.

At was midnight dark on the Tor. I stood, almost stumbling, half in and half out of the otherworld, trying to make sense of where I had been.

"S'ruth! What's been happening here?"

Shadows moved, close to the tower. Someone arriving from the footpath that led up to the top. I knew it was Anag because the voice was resonant of crocodile wrestling and barbecued steaks. I moved away from Ricky's body to meet him at the centre of the summit.

Shell was with him. She'd found her clothes and pulled them on, but I could hear how bad her breathing was. She leant heavily on Anag's arm. I reached them and she fell into me. I hugged her. She'd been brave to bring Anag back here. "Are you okay, Shell?"

"She can't talk, Sabs. Sort of hoarse. Came hobbling down the hill just as I'd got fed up waiting and started the climb. Saw her stumble, fit to faint, went to help. Couldn't make head or tail, 'cept that Ricky had done it to her and she thought you were up shit creek."

"Never mind me. I think Ricky's had a sort of seizure."

"Sure thing." He pointed through the night. "Where is he?"

I ran to where Ricky had lain. The edge sheered away precipitously. It was like looking into the shaft in my journey, where the black steps led into the Hollow Hill.

Anag arrived next to me. "Where's the bugger gone?"

"He's a danger. I told you, didn't I, when we were waiting in the lane."

"Too right. The guy's a psycho."

"Ricky needs a doctor, fast."

"Doc? The boys in blue is what we need."

Ricky could be in any state of mind. He could he lying low in the bracken on the sides of the Tor, waiting to strike. He'd used stones, bricks, and sticks, to attack his victims in the past and the three of us were standing here, unguarded, unprotected.

I heard a dry, grunting croak and swung round. In the darkness I picked out Shell's pale face against the indigo sky. She was leaning dangerously over the edge, her arm outstretched. We ran to her.

Ricky was careening down the slope, impossibly fast, his feet going from under him. He rolled, clawed the grass, picked himself up.

Shell raised her ruined voice. "Ricky!"

He didn't look up. He was too far into his own anguish to hear any of us. He began a crablike crawl around the side of the hill.

"He's heading for the Egg Stone," I said.

Shell tore herself out of my grasp and dropped over the edge in pursuit. Almost instantly, she lost her footing on the precipitous hillside and hurtled away.

"It's quicker to take the path around the Tor!" I started running. I looked behind. Anag had gone over the edge closer to the Egg Stone. "RICKY! MATE!" I heard him yell. His voice carried over the valley and single crow, disturbed from its roost, cawed and flapped once.

I let myself slide down onto the first terrace and moved around the curve of the hill.

At last, I saw Ricky. He was balanced on a tiny ledge, perhaps nothing more than clump of grass. He swayed to keep his balance. Shell was an arm's length above Ricky's head. Directly below him, bright in the moon's glow, was the Egg Stone.

Shell reached out with one hand. The hillside was so steep, it seemed she was clinging to the side of a wall. "Ricky," she said, her voice husky and breaking. "Ricky, my love…"

Her fingers swiped at the shoulder of his long black coat. She must have hoped he would clutch at her fingers, but he made no response, except to sob, once.

"We can sort it, love…"

It had been so wrong of me to take my eyes off him for even a second as we'd returned from the otherworld. I'd wanted to believe that Morgan had gone—if only temporarily—from Ricky's mind. In reality, I had no idea what I was dealing with.

I heard the sob again, and then Ricky began to speak. "Just a push. That's all." In the silence of the night, his words carried clear on the air. "A leap. That's right. That's good. That's The Good. Life from life. From life!"

Almost in slow motion, he swayed out at an impossible angle. He was clutching at weeds and air. For a second he seemed suspended—head, shoulders, hips—hanging there as if he was ready to fly. Then the roots of the weeds came bursting out of the dry soil and he did fly; he soared, out and down.

We were all pushing towards Ricky, but Anag had already dropped down onto the tiny ledge where the Egg Stone lay. He rushed at the falling body, his arms outstretched.

A sharp crack rang out; something colliding, hard and brittle.

They collapsed together on the surface of the Egg Stone, Ricky and Anag, a confusion of arms and legs. Their bodies rolled from the rounded rock and lay still. Ricky was on top of Anag, who had taken the full impact of both the men's weight as they hit the Egg.

Shell and I were held in the starburst of the crash, our mouths ridged and open. Then Shell moved, skidding towards the two men. The hawthorn tree broke her fall, but it clutched at her clothing with its thorns. She broke free. She stood over the two men. She gave a whimper.

I was scrabbling for my torch, buried deep in my pocket. I hadn't thought I'd need it, but now I was glad to feel its weight in my hand. I trained its beam downward. There was blood on the Egg Stone, a smear of maroon.

Ricky's eyes opened. He found Shell's face and screwed his eyes closed again.

"Why can't I die? Why can't *I* be the one?" His voice had lost its robotic feel. He was returning to the apparent world.

By the time I reached them, Shell had her arms around him, whispering his name, pulling at him gently. Ricky struggled upright, his hands pushing against the softness of Anag's prone body. He registered what was beneath him and froze.

"I've killed him. Oh God in heaven. Life ... from life. Oh God."

I dropped onto my knees and rolled Anag as best I could onto his side. I could see the wound at the back of his head. Blood oozed into his hair. I put my hand on his cheek. It felt chilled, but all our faces were cold from the night air.

"Anag? Anag?"

His eyes flickered. He groaned. He groaned louder.

"Anag! You're okay!" It seemed a daft thing to say, but I could think of nothing better.

"Got one hell of a headache." We eased him into a sitting position.

"You got stunned for a second there," I said. I thought how lucky he was.

Anag coughed once into his fist. He put his hands to his head and winced. He looked at his hands and jolted to see the sticky red on his fingers. "Fucking fuck me," he said. "Didn't that go off like a bucket of prawns in the sun?"

I couldn't help but grin. Good on Anag. He'd manned-up in the end.

———

After we'd got down off the Tor, the four of us drove to the police station in my car. By that time, Ricky seemed almost normal. He had walked up to the officer on duty, looked him in the eye, and told him he was guilty of murder—of two murders—his sister Babette Johnson and Martin Macaskill. He had been taken directly into custody. Shell and Anag were examined by the police surgeon and after we had all been interviewed, they were admitted overnight into West Mendip Hospital. By the time I was on my own again, taking the road to Bridgwater, the sun was well up, balanced on the top of the Tor behind me, streaking the black road with rosy light.

I parked up in front of the station and had time to get some lippy on and pull a comb through my hair before Rey came out into the lovely July sunshine. He gave a little start when he saw me leaning against the bonnet of the Vauxhall. It almost seemed too much for him, that I was here, waiting for his release. He got in the car without speaking.

"You're coming to stay with me, Rey," I said.

I'd indicated and moved off before he'd even given a nod.

There was a vat of silence as I navigated the light traffic. You can't keep chattering if someone doesn't respond. He didn't ask me what had happened to secure his release, and I didn't feel like enlightening him. The memory of Shell, a starfish splayed on a beach, flashed on and off like neon in my head.

I pulled up outside my house. He got out of the car. I locked it and walked round to where he stood.

He was wearing the things he'd worn on Friday morning—best interview suit, tie, polished shoes, newly clipped hair, the lot. Fat lot of good that had done him. He'd been arrested and charged at the end of the interview. As he'd suspected, it hadn't been an interview at all.

"D'you get time off, now?"

"Yep," said Rey. "A formality, in fact. Special leave. After that, a special sideways promotion, I imagine."

"Is that a sort of apology?"

"More like a couple of fingers in the air."

I frowned at him.

"If I retain inspector level I'll be surprised. I might be offered a post somewhere as sergeant. I'll probably have to do some retraining."

My heart rolled over and over like a child down a hill. "And Pippa?"

"Happy as a lark. Already heading up a team and moving on to a recent failed investigation. All she's got to do is come up with some goods and the job—my job—is hers."

He walked away from me without the least brush of a hand, through my gate and round to the kitchen door. I found him staring out over my vegetable plot.

"Thing is, it won't be round here."

"Sorry?"

"Whatever I'm offered. It won't be with Avon and Somerset."

"Oh, Rey!" Just when I thought we were good. When he was agreeing to move in. "How far ... how far d'you think?"

"Could be anywhere. Thames Valley, Northumbria..."

"No!"

"I will miss this," he admitted.

I swallowed. I had to stay positive. "You'll get back. From wherever. Weekends and that?"

There was a tiny pause. "Weekends are when you're at your busiest, Sabbie."

I'd picked up a bottle of Cava at a twenty-four hour petrol station. It was still in the boot. I'd thought this would be a celebration;

the charges had been dropped, Rey had been exonerated. I felt a sob work its way up and suppressed it with my fist.

The garden was shadowless and dry with the burning heat. A robin fluted on a telephone wire. I could smell the phlox I'd planted in the spring, a deep, nourishing scent of summer. I was standing right next to him, but still Rey hadn't touched me. He was hardly looking at me.

"I'll miss the hens." His voice broke a little, as if he'd got out of the habit of using it.

"Will you?"

"You didn't say you had new ones."

"I don't have new ones."

"You do," said Rey. "Babies. There!"

I followed his pointing finger. Picking their way across the back of the lawn were seven pompoms of fluffed-up yellow wool. Yellow pompoms on skinny pink legs. They walked in a neat school-time line, following a hen who marched ahead, confident of her place in the world as a mother.

"Florence!" I screeched. "Florence, Florence! I thought you were dead!"

She turned her head and observed me with bright, interested eyes. I rushed towards her. She watched my approach and didn't waste a second. She opened her beak and made a strange clucking sound I'd never heard one of my hens make before. She lifted her wings. At the call, the seven yellow pompoms ran under her wings. I was amazed that they could all disappear from sight, but they did. Florence settled down, right there on the grass, as if she didn't have a care in the world—or a chick to her name.

"How did she stay safe from harm?" Rey had come up beside me. I heard him chuckle. I looked up into his face. It was seasoned, like good wood, ready to withstand the brunt of whatever it was exposed to. His eyes were green as bottle glass, but against the sun they'd narrowed and the wrinkles around their edges told a story of all his years of pondering, cogitating, working on hunches. He would be so wasted as a detective sergeant.

I began to laugh with joy and hysterical relief. "Hens are a bloody miracle, that's all I can say."

"Life's a bit of a miracle," said Rey. His arm went around me. I warmed in his hold. I knew how Flo's chicks felt—secure. At peace.

"Don't get all philosophical on me."

"Perish the thought."

"I've had enough of philosophy." I kissed him, a peck on the cheek. It opened something in him, took away whatever had been the blockage. He kissed me and kissed me and it was a long time before I could speak again. "Miracles, though … you can never have enough of those."

THIRTY-FOUR
LAURIE

By THE FOLLOWING TUESDAY morning, when Laura Munroe arrived for her appointment, I had regained my equanimity. I was ready for her.

"How are you?" I asked as we sat down.

"Okay, ta. I've got lots to tell you about my chick—you know, my animal guide. There's been developments ... like you said there would."

She seemed relaxed, and that was just what I'd hoped for. "The first thing I want to do is to blow your soul-part back into you."

I was tingling with the things I now knew about my client, but there were threads of dread loose at the edges. I would be winging it, but I felt strong enough to fly.

"My soul-part? Thank heavens for that."

"We've learnt so much together, haven't we? You and me both."

"Yeah."

I told her about Plato's cave. I kept it simple, kept it factual. I didn't offer any fancy ideas about why anyone should be tied up in a cave and unable to see the sun. I just told the story.

"I've been thinking about the time your panic attacks started," I said. "When you were in the Royal Navy."

"Right."

"I think you were offered a glimpse of the sun and it blinded you."

She frowned, but she was staying calm. I knew she hadn't had a panic attack in the last two weeks and I wanted to keep it that way. I moved steadily forward in my argument.

"I believe you do remember what initiated the first attack. It's in your mind, Laura. It's in your hidden memories."

"No, it's not."

"Shall I tell you?"

She looked at me. Her mouth was open, to facilitate her heavy breathing. She closed it and blew took a long breath out. "Okay."

"Someone kissed you."

Her mouth clamped together and she shook her head vigorously.

"It was another rating, yes? A girl?"

"I'm not a lesbian!" The shout rang out. "I'm not, I'm not!"

"That's right. You're not." I grasped her hand and gripped firm. "You're not."

She swore, like a rating, several times under her breath. Then she looked up. "I do feel better for saying that."

"Turn your chair towards the desk, Laura, and I'll blow your soul-part into you."

As she scooched round, she did a little double-take and shot me a questioning look. The desk was cleared and centrally I'd stood a frame, covered in a black silk scarf, flanked by candles in holders on either side. Also on the desk was a little tin of makeup remover pads, a comb, a box of tissues, and a sharp pair of scissors.

"What is this?"

"I'm going to breathe your soul-part into you. After that ... once that is done ... I'm going to ask you to trust me."

She thought about this; she thought for several seconds. "I do trust you, Sabbie. I have since the moment we first met." Even so, she took a cautious moment to settle herself.

I stood behind her, my hands on her shoulders. I summoned Laura's guardian in my mind, being careful to keep a sense of Trendle's presence close to me. I stood on the bank of my little stream and saw Raichu, moving through the air, carrying the netting bundle. Within the otherworld I put up my spirit arm, to direct him to me, but in the apparent world my hands were still on Laura's shoulders. In fact, almost unknown to me, I had begun to massage her shoulders gently. I was in the exact stance I'd take up to do an Indian Head Massage, and I could hardly prevent myself from starting one.

The spirit guardian alighted at my portal. Its height and presence was filled with light. It was taller than Morgan le Fay's malevolent spirit, which I'd confronted only three nights ago.

Trendle spoke for me, spirit to spirit.

"This is Laura's soul-part?"

"Yes. It lifted from her at a young age. No one took it; it wasn't stolen away. It lifted in fear and from confusion. It has been unable to reattach itself."

"Due to continued fear and confusion?"

"Yes. So be wary. She may not be happy to have this part of her returned."

Trendle looked up at me and his otter eyes blinked once. "Are you prepared to do what is necessary?"

I jerked a nod. I held out my hands and the spirit rolled the netted bundle across to me. My stomach was knotted with the gravity of the burden.

I took several moments to capture this vision properly. As I came back into the room, I discovered I was running my hands over Laura's scalp. I took the image of the netted bundle in my mind and cupped my hands over the top of her head, where her seventh chakra, the Sahasrara or thousand-petalled lotus, was located on her subtle body. I blew the bundle through the funnel of my hands, fierce and long, so that the soul-part could not dissipate or disappear.

I stepped back, catching my breath.

"Okay. Let that settle. Don't move, Laura, or even try to think about things. Just let it be for a moment."

I switched on the player. Perhaps she was expecting drumming; she looked up, a flicker of interest on her face. I'd looped a single download onto a CD, running it over and over into a fifteen-minute track. The echo of guitar cords came through.

"It's Local Natives," she said. "'Shape Shifter.'"

"I love this group now." I lit the candles and let their flames settle. The lyrics kicked in. The singer's voice was plum rich. I began to sing as well, which probably spoilt the quality, but I couldn't stop myself.

I stood behind her and rested my hands on her scalp, then took her left ear gently between my thumb and forefinger, manipulating the earring, drawing the hoop out. She jumped a little. I'd expected this; I hadn't explained, as I normally would, what I was about to do. The song continued, and I continued singing with it. I opened the ring box and rested the earring on it. I gave her a mirror smile, adding the second earring. The candles made both our faces glow. "Close your eyes."

"What?"

"Go on. Close your eyes. It'll feel cold, but don't blink."

Again, she thought for a moment, but she did close her eyes and didn't react as I took a makeup remover pad and wiped off her lipstick. I started on her eyeliner and her lick of mascara, using a separate pad for each eye. "Okay."

She opened her eyes again, blinking fast. She began to relax into what was happening, singing with me in a low tone. I pulled the silk scarf away, revealing my bedroom mirror.

The candles' flicker made Laura's skin golden in her mirror reflection. I went behind her again and picked up her hair, using my fingers as two fat combs, pulling strands away from her face, then loosening my hold so that, in the mirror, the hair looked shorter. We sang together.

Her eyes were wide. We stood, linked by my hands in her hair, both staring into the mirror.

"What do you think, shape shifter?"

I slid a towel off the back of her chair and draped her shoulders. I held the harmless blades of my scissors in my hands. "Shall I? I don't promise to be an expert."

For a brief moment, she seemed bewildered, but now I was sure that was only on the surface. Deep down, she knew what was up. Her subtle body had known all along. It was why part of her soul had slid away.

"Your guardian told me something had juddered your soul. I can see that in your face now. Let it go."

I held thick locks with my left hand and chopped with my right, until all her hair was three or four centimetres long. I tidied the edges—behind the ears, around the nape of the neck.

Mid-blond hair lay everywhere. I brushed it from her shoulders then squirted a little mousse into my fingers and rubbed it into her scalp, combing down the result. "Short back and sides, I'm afraid, but I'm sure a barber will get it looking good for you."

I fetched the other chair and sat beside her, both of us taking in the new person in the mirror. Neither of us spoke. I felt the shift inside, and in the mirror, Laura's expression altered, fraction by fraction, from shock to wonder. From fright to expectation.

Laura had gone. Or rather, had been transformed. There was almost nothing left of the girl who had cowered, breathless, on the floor, who had run away from her home. Instead, here was the person who had been hiding inside her, all this time, all the time she had been on this earth. She had even named him, long ago; had conversations with him.

After a moment or two, I held out my hand. "Pleased to meet you, Laurie. You got control. You shifted shape. Welcome to the world."

I knew Laurie would cry. I'd expected that. I just held him until he'd done.

———

I knew, and so did Laurie, that this was only a beginning, and, if this had been difficult, with a labour as painful as before any birthing, then the following stages would be harder still.

We talked the rest of the morning. Laurie had a lot to process, but things fell into place faster than I'd imagined.

"There was a fire in me," he said, "when I saw the boy peeing under the pier. I went home and tried peeing standing up, and my mother caught me with wet pants and gave me a massive telling off."

"I think when you let your soul-part go, the memory lingered. To the extent of hating to play with dolls; cutting up your Barbie."

We could both see it was more than snipping off a finger. Barbies's little pink appendage made a great penis. "I tried to stick it in place on the doll," he said, remembering, "but it didn't work, so I hid it in my favourite Pokémon."

Laurie looked up, as if something had occurred to him. It occurred to me at the same time.

"That was why Raichu came to you at the moment. He understood everything. He was keeping your soul-part safe."

Laurie glanced at his mirror image again. "I did know that I'm a boy. A bloke! I've known it all my life. I've kept it trapped somewhere, that knowledge. It was too difficult to cope with." He pushed forward, his legs pressed wide against the chair arms, his hands on his knees. "I didn't tell you about my chick."

"He's grown up, hasn't he?"

"Yes—and how. He's this fantastic crowing cockerel."

"Raichu said it was the time for both of you to evolve. The thing about chicks is, you can't sex them. You have to be patient, wait for their feathers to grow. Eventually, that's how you find out if you've got a hen or a cock."

We grinned at each other.

"I'll need to see you a couple more times."

"I don't want to stop coming, no way. It's massive, going off into this otherworld."

I suggested that before he left my house, Laurie should ring Daniel. "Daniel's going to be your ally now. He can be there for you when you tell your parents. He'll explain what to do next. He's bound to know where to refer you, who can counsel you. You won't need him as a psychiatric nurse anymore."

"Nope." Laurie shrugged on his jacket and, as always, pulled my fee from his back pocket. "I'm cured."

"You were never ill, Laurie," I said as we hugged. "Just mispositioned."

THIRTY-FIVE
THREE WEEKS LATER

I CONTINUED SEEING LAURIE once a week. We both knew that things were going to be a tough for a long time. In those three weeks, he'd already got an appointment with a surgeon and started the long process towards a complete sex change.

In the real word, he had to convince his family and friends—everyone he knew—to change their approach. To think of him as male. Luckily, he had Daniel on his side. Mostly, now, he'd come and give me a report on how things were going, but I'd started showing him how to walk between the worlds, so that he could use this to help keep the process stable. After all, he had powerful allies in the otherworld. They would answer his questions and help him work through each problem as it arose.

That's what I hoped, anyhow. Sometimes we talked about that moment in my therapy room when, before our eyes, he transformed. That was the most amazing piece of magic I had ever witnessed, but

I'd had only the smallest hand in it; just a finger-tip push for some-one already balancing on a needlepoint. I hadn't turned Laurie into a man; he'd always been one. The difficulty was that how he felt inside was not how he looked outside.

I had some inkling of how that might feel. When I'd been tiny—four or five, perhaps—I could listen to the spirit world as others listen to a radio. I walked around in a dreamtime and no one had stopped me, or berated me for my imaginings. Like Laurie, a little bit of my soul had gone missing the day my mother had died, and it had changed me. At the point of her death I'd been thrust into a Lower Realm that was full of menace, a crazy, mirror-image fairy tale land in which I had to fight to survive. It wasn't until I met Wolfsbane and studied with him that it became clear how bad things had become inside of me; how I'd lost that person I'd first been. He was the one that retrieved my soul-part.

I will always respect Wolfsbane as a shaman. I knew he had feet of clay—what person does not? And when I saw him at Alys's inquest, I felt proud of him, that he'd turned up and shaken Brice's hand and wished him well.

Despite Wolfsbane's fears, none of us had to stand up and give evidence at Alys's inquest. There were only expert witnesses—the paramedics, hospital staff, and the pathologist. There were few documents presented to the court, the most necessary being the blood pathologies.

Even so, things were a lot more complicated than they had seemed.

The courtroom was packed. People from London, mostly—Brice's family, Alys's wider family, and a lot of their friends, including Shell, who had gone back to London after Ricky was Sectioned and taken away. I'd been hoping others from the ill-fated shape-shifing work-shop would come to the inquest, but weeks had passed since the fu-neral and people had moved on with their lives.

I'd been in touch with Anagarika over the phone—I knew his head wound was healing and I also knew that he was planning to go back to Melbourne. He'd done every workshop he could find in Glastonbury, but it wasn't until he prevented Ricky from cracking open his head on the Egg Stone that he'd finally found the centre of his soul.

That's what he'd told me, anyway.

At the inquest I sat with Wolfsbane, and as the pathologist—a silver-haired woman in a sage green trouser suit—was called to give evidence, I found myself grasping his hand for comfort.

The pathologist began by describing what she had found in Alys's samples, the most worrying of these being the DMAA.

"Tell the court about this substance," the coroner had said.

"It has similar properties to amphetamines. It boosts energy and metabolism. It also can raise heart and respiratory rates."

"It is a banned substance?" the coroner asked.

"Not as such, but it has been was withdrawn from sale in the UK. However, it's still widely available."

"And what danger does it pose?"

"In small doses, it might pose no threat at all. The reason it's been withdrawn is that, if taken in excess, along with extensive phys-ical exertion, it can attribute to cardiac failure, even cardiac arrest."

"Cardiac failure being the cause of Mrs. Hollingberry's death?"

"The amount that she had taken, during that night of extreme activity, was, I should hazard, a smallish dose. It should not have resulted in the failure of a healthy heart."

"Can you explain what you mean by *during* the night? Did she take a tablet?"

"There is a powdered form of the drug, which can be mixed into a sports water bottle. This is what we believe Mrs. Hollingberry did. As I say, not a large dose. I believe she medicated herself in this way with some personal care, at least."

"Can you tell us what did cause her heart to fail, please?"

The pathologist coughed, and the court stirred, briefly shifting and resettling in their seats. "The high potassium levels in her blood."

She began to demonstrate her findings. Firstly, Alys had lost blood, in the natural way. She had also dosed herself up on over-the-counter analgesia, ibuprofen, which, the pathologist told us, did contain a certain amount of potassium. And in her water bottle was the Jack3d in powdered form.

"She was not drinking water," said the pathologist. "She enjoyed a sports drink that was mostly coconut water. This has a high content of potassium."

"Can you explain which of these were actually the cause of her death?"

"What we have is a number of negative, but unpredictable factors. Loss of blood, increase of potassium in the blood from two external sources, plus raised heart rate from the dimethylamylamine. Added to this, was a level of activity over several hours, at what I would describe as endurance level. None of them are to blame overall. The combination of complications effectively created a unique event. Each circumstance aggravated the situation, causing a confluence that resulted in this lady's death."

"A perfect storm," suggested the coroner.

"Yes. That describes my findings exactly. A perfect storm."

415

The coroner recorded the verdict and summed things up. I don't think I'll ever forget what he said.

"Nothing that Alys Hollingberry did during her night on Glastonbury Tor was inappropriate. She was a marathon runner; she felt she could dance all night. She'd been told that her supplement was harmless in the small dose she was using. She was also under the impression that her coconut drink was healthy. She'd taken something for her period pain and she felt well enough to enjoy herself. None of these factors should have led to her death, yet events took an unexpected turn and she suffered heart failure leading to cardiac arrest. Death, then, by misadventure."

We stumbled out into the fresh air. People looked shocked, numbed, as pale as if they'd spent a year in the courtroom. They took off in small groups. Brice was swept away by what looked like his parents. I hadn't expected him to speak to me; I'd been there because I wanted to hear the outcome of the inquest for myself.

"Hi, Sabbie." It was Shell. Her voice had returned to normal, the bruising at her throat had yellowed and she was smiling. "I've brought you something."

She handed me a little package. I peeled back the flap and pulled out a pair of earrings with a swirling design in pale blue.

"Shell! Oh, these are lovely—exquisite! What are they? Not enamelling?"

"No. It's marbling under a clear resin. I do quite a lot of different jewellery techniques."

"These are beautiful enough for Aphrodite," I said, and held them to my ears. "You shouldn't have gone to the trouble, with all this going on."

"It took my mind off things."

"You okay?"

"Good. I'm running a market stall in Croyden. My jewellery is doing so well I can't make enough of it, to be honest."

"So are these something to remember you by?"

"I guess you won't see much of me around Glastonbury. I've decided that friends are more important than lovers."

I gave a rough nod. I myself had been hoping that lovers and best friends could be the same thing, but in the three weeks since Alys's funeral, Rey had already been for an interview and been offered a job, heading up a missing persons and unsolved cases department in the Staffordshire police force. Although he'd only be a few hours' drive away, I was terrified that the distance would throw a fire blanket over our relationship only moments after we'd got it flaming. Without kindling, air, and a bit of a spark, I was worried it might fizzle out.

"Did you hear about Ricky?" I asked Shell.

He was still awaiting trial in a high-security psychiatric hospital, which I suspected he would never leave, although he had already been escorted back to the New Forest, where he had shown the police the place where Babette lay. In the five years since she died, no doubt the grass had reseeded itself and new growth had emerged. No doubt her spirit, the hind, had often fed in the glade. Now it had been attacked by diggers. They had retrieved her body from its deep grave.

"So many people have been affected by Alys's death," I said. I was thinking of the Johnson family, of Ricky, and of the three knights.

"I guess we should count ourselves lucky that we're able to get on with our lives."

I let Shell run to catch her friends. I sauntered around the shops in Wells for a while, and walked beside the Bishop's Palace moat, watching the swans, not keen to start the journey back to my empty home.

Well, not *empty,* exactly. I now had seven growing chicks. Yeah— I should count myself lucky.

A cog clicked into another cog and something in my brain shifted. The sun spun in the sky.

I don't know anything about my father, I'd told Sabrina. *Only his name... Lucky Luc Rameau.*

Can I enquire, sir, for your name? I'd asked the guardian who had sat before the hut, who had showed me Babette's place of death. He'd given me a sideways glance.

I am lucky.

The swans glided past me, unaware of this tumbling, shouting, frightening, thrilling revelation.

I turned on my heel and made for home.

THE END

© Jenefer Llewellyn Ferguson

ABOUT THE AUTHOR

Nina Milton holds an MA in creative writing, works as a tutor and writer for the Open College of the Arts, is a prize-winning short story writer, and has authored several children's books, including *Sweet'n'Sour, Tough Luck,* and *Intergalactic Holiday. Beneath the Tor* is her third novel with Midnight Ink.